D1095716

THE
CONFESSION
OF
HEMINGWAY
JONES

THE
CONFESSION
OF
HEMINGWAY
JONES

KATHLEEN HANNON

CamCat
Books

CamCat Publishing, LLC
Ft. Collins, Colorado 80524
camcatpublishing.com

Hardcover ISBN 9780744302578
Paperback ISBN 9780744302585
Large-Print Paperback ISBN 9780744302592
eBook ISBN 9780744302639
Audiobook ISBN 9780744302653

Library of Congress Control Number: 2023932310

Book and cover design by Maryann Appel

5   3   1   2   4

To my mom, Liz Saxon, who taught me my love of books.

Without you, this book would not have been possible.

Thanks, from "your weird and morbid child."

TO WHOEVER FINDS THIS

This isn't a diary. So if you're reading this in hopes that I've actually written down exactly how I did what I did, you're going to be extremely disappointed. I haven't written that down anywhere and I never will.

This is a confession, pure and simple. And I'll tell you right now, before you start reading, or listening, or whatever it is you're doing: I'm the bad guy. Don't forget that.

It's weird to be the villain in your own life story, but it is what it is.

Confessions are done for the sake of forgiveness. I don't deserve forgiveness. I know that. And I could claim I don't want forgiveness, but I guess I do. So if this is you, Melissa, know that it's your forgiveness I'm asking. I don't deserve it, but I loved you then and I love you now. I'm sorry for ruining your life.

Just for the record, I was trying to save you.

Hemingway Jones

PART I

CHAPTER ONE

It's been a few months, but sour memories of the day I killed my father still burp back up, and my gut clenches every time. Todd and I were absolutely blazed, sitting on the front steps of his family's double-wide when Dad pulled up, the tires on his Ford F250 skidding to a stop about three inches from my sneakers, while the JONES CONSTRUCTION AND RESTORATION lettering was practically shoved up my nose. Dad hiked himself out the driver's-side door with a slam and I knew I had about fifteen seconds to sober up.

We hadn't planned on doing this—skipping school and getting baked. Or at least I hadn't. But Todd had found this brick of hash in his parents' barn, and well, it was the first spring day where temps were due to hit 65 degrees. We cut out fourth period, rode our bikes back to his place, and got rocked. Seemed like a good idea at the time, and we'd had fun tormenting the chickens, but now I was going to pay for it.

I wasn't the only one who was nervous either. Todd tucked his drink behind his back while my dad crunched gravel. Todd had obviously forgotten that all he had was a Yoo-hoo. He nodded and called out, "Hey there, Mr. Jones."

Dad murmured, "Todd," in his general direction, but kept his eyes focused on me.

He was just standing there, directly in front of the late-afternoon sun. I squinted, but all I could see was this ominous black silhouette of rippling muscle.

I realize I'm making him sound scary, but he's not. Everybody likes my dad, even Todd. Even me. He's this pretty cool, off-the-grid kind of guy. He can build or fix just about anything, and I'm not just talking about when you've had a kitchen fire or a burst pipe—that's just what he does for work. He's also the guy who pulls over when you've got a flat and the one who starts applying the Heimlich on some choker in Kentucky Fried. (It's happened.) He's smart too. He doesn't have a college degree or anything, but he can talk about black holes and relativity. He can take any online Mensa or IQ test and come up genius, every time. He even beats my scores, and I'm not easy to beat.

The point is stand-up guy Bill Jones can be a little scary when he's mad. And I was about to get reamed.

He turned his face profile before he spoke, so I could see just how much air he was furiously pumping through his shadowy nostrils. "Got a call from the school. And another one from Cass."

My first impulse was to cringe, make excuses, and get up, knowing I was busted. But over the last year or so I'd learned that if I waited long enough in these fights, my pangs of guilt would pass and I'd turn into a cocky asshole, someone far more capable of fighting with Bill Jones. So I waited until I saw Dad as a thunderstorm, rudely blocking out my sun. And I shrugged. I mean, big deal. So I skipped school again. I knew the real problem was the call from Cass. I'd never skipped the Tuesday/Friday afternoon internship before, and that was what he was really pissed about. He'd filled out all the paperwork for that internship himself—he'd even written the essay when I refused—all so that I would have "the future" he never did.

"Hem, I'll uh—" Todd looked around quickly, hoping some excuse for his desertion would magically appear. "I think maybe I gotta help with dinner. See ya, Mr. Jones." He practically ran inside.

"Do you have any idea what you're doing?" Dad exhorted. "You have this gift. My God, you want to end up like that?" He gestured at Todd's disappearing form.

"Dad, that's low. Leave him alone."

He didn't even pause. He just growled, "Hemingway Jones," in that low, throaty way that he always does before lecturing. And he knows I hate my name. But he rarely calls me Hem—he says it sounds like a pronoun.

"You have absolutely no idea what you're risking. NONE!" And with that crack of thunder came the rain. He blasted on, salting his sentences liberally with words like *responsibility* and *commitment*.

I rolled my eyes. The lecture was so generic I didn't taste anything close to regret. I could recite a variation of this speech as easily as I could the periodic table. Anyway, due to some really good dope, the tweaks and nuances of this particular version are lost forever.

I finally interrupted him. "I didn't even want the fucking internship!" I stared at him, waiting for a response. That fact was empirically true. But he just stuffed his hands in his pockets, so I charged on. "I don't want college, either. School bores the crap outta me. You *know* that. Why would I *pay* for more torture, when I could be a project manager at your company and earn some money? Stanton got an honors degree from Chapel Hill. He's still working at the gym full-time AND living at home, just to pay the loans. Why would I buy into all that crap?"

I tilted a little, trying to duck down and check my face in the side view mirror of the truck without him noticing. I was pretty sure I was smirking—a dead giveaway. No smirk, but the face that looked back at me was a little worrying. My black hair had gone all stringy from sweat and was stuck in clumps around my face. My eyes, normally green, were cayenne-pepper red. I looked like a stoner. If I didn't shift the conversation soon, he'd notice. I needed a move.

So I conjured up the ghost of my mother. "Mom wouldn't make me go there. Do you have any idea what I *do* in that place? Undressing dead bodies? So some quack doctor can do experiments on them? Do you think she'd want me to do that? Do you think she'd want that done to *her*?"

That worked. Dad looked as if I'd punched him. "Of course not," he finally choked out.

I knew the image was unfair. Bottom-feeding, in fact. I instantly wished I hadn't said it, but I didn't take it back, because if the situation were reversed, he wouldn't take it back. My dad sucks at apologizing.

Still. I could practically read his memories of Mom in his body language. His shoulders sagged with her diagnosis, quickly followed by a head nodding south to the ground, as she exacted promises out of him about how I was going to be raised. By the time his hands found his hips, I knew her body was being carted out of the cancer ward at Northeast into a mortician's hearse. That was two years ago.

Now, who sucks at apologizing?

Fair would be admitting Bill Jones didn't have the faintest idea what company I'd be interning for when he applied in my name. He'd just been all excited that this fabulous new biotech research center was going to take high-school students on as interns. He'd gone on and on about what an "amazing opportunity" that would be for me. That said, he'd grimaced when I got the acceptance letter. He'd guessed almost immediately what kind of company it was. But he still wanted me to do it because he thought it would lead to better scholarships for college. He rattled on that even if I didn't want to go to college right now, I should still want the option. When I finally gave in, he told me what they *did*, or at least, what he thought they did. I absolutely flipped. I'd told him there was NO WAY I was going to work there.

The curtains shifted. Todd was watching us. I glared at him, and he pulled them tight again, but his fingertips were still visible at the seams. He really could be a dumbass.

My dad saw it too and checked himself, knowing he'd lost his temper and embarrassed me in front of my friend. He suddenly tossed me the keys.

"We'll talk about this at home. You drive." He climbed into the passenger's side.

I did pause, keys in hand. That much is true. But I didn't confess. I used to think it was because I was so shocked that I'd won the round. But the truth is, I was pleased with my merit-less victory. I didn't feel like ruining it and getting another lecture.

Plus, I really wanted my license. Bad enough I was the only senior at school that didn't have one. I wanted my freedom. I wanted to be able to get up and leave—just drive away—whenever he started in like this

Truth? I don't really remember what I was thinking. I just climbed in, stuck the keys in the ignition, and pulled away.

Todd and his parents live way the hell out on Gold Hill Road, which is the kind of road your grandparents take you on for a Sunday drive in the country. While the southern half of Concord has been transformed into commuter sprawl for the city of Charlotte, this easternmost tip is the last gasp of Cabarrus County farmland. Rolling fields of corn and collard greens rise and dip in every direction, interspersed between wide pastures of native wildflowers and woods. The road rises and curves with those fields, and there's only the occasional little clapboard house visible. Most of those are recessed way back too, stuck deep in the trees so the farmers can get a break from the scorching summer sun. Other cars are rare, but when they come, they come fast.

I remember the pickup that zoomed by, headed in the opposite direction. The road was so tight and his speed so great that I felt the backdraft blast me through the open driver's-side window. I pulled my head back inside, knowing I was a mental train wreck. But too late now. If I confessed, my dad would cut up my learner's. He'd told me if I ever got caught driving under the influence, I'd have to pay for my own car and insurance, and of course any attorney fees required to defend myself in court.

I concentrated on each turn, going over it slowly, careful to lift and twist with the road. He didn't watch me. He was lost in thought, staring out the windshield. I bet he was still thinking about Mom. But we'll never know.

The dope overtook me again in the silence. I got all caught up studying the budding spring green on the trees against the impossibly blue sky. Spring in Piedmont is something to see. Everything flowers in April—dogwoods, Bradford pears, weeping cherry trees, azaleas, *Loropetalum*, and bulbs of all kinds. We were only days away from a rainbow bath.

That's when I missed the curve.

I wasn't speeding, but I didn't have to be to wreck on this road. My reactions were slow, my instincts hairy. Dad yelled and tried to grab the wheel, but for some reason, I pushed his hand away, as I used the other to try and correct the spin. But I was going against the spin, rather than with it like he'd taught me to do.

Off the road, careening down an embankment, I felt his arm slam against my chest. He grabbed the handhold above me, pinning me in place because he didn't trust the seatbelt. When we hit rocks at the base of the creek, the resulting *smack!* lifted the bed. My airbag exploded as the truck vaulted over the creek like a gymnast doing a hand flip. I felt the roof above us buckle. The second flip—the one that righted us—was much slower, more like a backbend.

You know what the first thing I did was? I giggled. I say all this to keep reminding you—I'm no hero. I was absolutely fine, nervously wondering what kind of trouble I was in for now. I was even stifling a laugh when I turned toward Dad.

His eyes were open and glassy, his mouth gaping. A punched dent in the metal roof was seemingly melded to his brain. He wasn't breathing.

"Dad? OH FUCK." I touched him, hoping to get his eyes to blink. Nothing. "Oh God, oh God! DAD! DAD!" This time I pushed him a little. Nothing. "DAD! WE HAD AN ACCIDENT! BLINK YOUR EYES! TELL ME YOU'RE OKAY!"

But he just stared. I grabbed his wrist, and then his neck, looking anywhere for the faintest hint of a pulse.

9-1-1. No signal. 9-1-1, 9-1-1. Hold the phone out the window. Slap the phone on the dashboard. Nothing.

CPR. Compressions.

That meant moving him. I contemplated the head injury for a moment. If he was still alive, and he had to still be alive, there was seriously no alternative, he could bleed out from the head wound. I ripped off my shirt. I was shaking so badly I struggled, but eventually, I used the sleeves to knot it like a tourniquet around his head. I ran around the other side of the car, splashing in the creek, and grabbed his shoulders.

"STAY WITH ME, DAD." I held on to his shoulders, letting his legs clatter down into the water, and pulled him up on the bank. He'd forced me to take every course the Red Cross had to offer before I was ever allowed behind the wheel. I proceeded to perform them all.

Thirty compressions, two breaths, pulse. "Ah, hah, hah, hah, staying alive, staying alive." I don't know whether I was singing the song in my head or out loud, but that's what they teach you to do in CPR: sing the Bee Gees, so the compressions stay nice and even. Keep oxygenating the blood. After finishing the song the second time, I paused to check the signal—still nothing.

COLD.

The word boomed in my head like it came from a divine entity that was trying out 110-decibel speakers for added effect.

HE'S GOT TO BE COLD.

My sneakers were already soaked with freezing-cold creek water. Why hadn't I put him in the creek immediately for the compressions? I slapped my head several times—stay in the moment. I tugged at his shoulders and then at his legs until his whole body was in that frigid creek. My hands were red, raw, and shaking by the time I'd arranged him, my bare chest shaking with the slightest breeze, but I paused to hit the timer on the phone—like I *knew* what had to happen. Except I didn't. Honestly, I was still waiting for him to just wake up and start yelling.

I checked the phone again. Still no signal, out here in the boonies, down an embankment, in a creek full of frigid water.

Again, with the compressions and the song. Rinse and repeat. Nothing, and my arms were giving out.

I started screaming. Then I barfed in the grass.

I tried again—pumping his heart over and over again—while getting no frigging signal. I was going to have to climb the embankment to call, and that meant leaving him. I climbed, grabbing on to the knee-deep vines of dead kudzu to pull myself up. I kept turning back to check, fully expecting him to be awake and seriously pissed.

Calculations ran through my head as if I had nothing to do with them. It'd been approximately twenty-two minutes since the accident, so I tried to hurry up, but the ground was still loose from rain, so I kept slipping. Every time I did, the calculations shifted. It was going to take another five minutes—minimum—to get to the top of the hill. Total: twenty-seven minutes. Barring an EMT out on the prowl, it would take an ambulance at least another twenty to get here from downtown. That's forty-seven minutes. How much more time to unload and power up a defibrillator?

The answer mattered—I only had thirteen minutes left to play with. If Dad was clinically dead for more than sixty minutes when the EMTs arrived, they wouldn't even try to revive him. I knew this. They'd say he'd end up a vegetable at best, pat me on the back, and let me ride next to his body on the way to the morgue.

I could lie. Tell the medics he'd been down only a few minutes. But even if they bought it and tried to revive him, they had less than a 5-percent chance of success.

And at that point, with all that company, it wasn't like I could then move on to Plan B.

I'm not really sure when Plan B materialized. I mean, I'd instantly wanted the Gaymar machine to chill him down when I dragged him into that creek water. The Gaymar is what they put people in when they've fallen through the ice, or had a heart attack and they're completely unresponsive. Keep 'em cold until you're at the hospital and ready to go to work reviving them. But I don't know when that silent wish transformed into a plan to sneak my dad's body into the Paul D. Calhoun Biotech Research Center.

It was one or the other. Call 9-1-1. Or the Gaymar Meditherm.

The ground gave way and I fell again—that cinched it. This time I let the kudzu go and slid down the hill all the way to the bottom.

Bill Jones didn't believe in God. Or heaven. Even when my mom died, he didn't pretend he'd had some sort of a religious epiphany for my sake. He just told me she was gone and that was pretty much it, as far as he was concerned. That little nugget of truth should've told me what Bill Jones would want, what was right. But it just spurred me on: if there is no God, then there is no heaven. Only Earth. And no one deserved heaven more than my dad. So, if Earth was Bill Jones's only heaven, I had to bring him back. At least, I needed to try.

I checked my dad and the road again. Nothing from him, and no one around. No one could see us. No one had come running, and there weren't any farmhouses visible nearby with some old granny in the window dialing the police and an ambulance.

No one knew he was dead. Except me.

Did the truck work? If it didn't, this plan was over. I pocketed the cell phone, popped the airbag, and stuck the keys in the ignition. I silently vowed if the truck didn't start—or didn't run—I'd climb the hill again and call the cops no matter what.

I turned the key gently and the car responded. I stuck it in gear and lurched a few tentative feet before switching it off again: I was going to have to load up my dad. In the bed. The idea of putting him there made me nauseous, but there really wasn't any other option.

But it was more than that. He was so heavy. I'm tall, but I only weigh about 150 pounds. I tested moving him—I could drag him—barely. Lifting him by myself was a no go. I couldn't fail for this stupid reason. My hands were still shaking, and my eyes were bleeding tears, but I glanced around— Dad's dolly and incline were still trussed to the bed. He always secures them. Now I knew why. I grabbed them and set up.

I heard a car go by on the road. Then another. Every time one roared past I ducked, but they were going too fast, too high above me to notice. I guess we'd have been pretty hard to see, even if someone was looking. The embankment was high, and we were veiled in thick gray vines of kudzu that draped from all the trees like hair extensions.

Once he was inside the bed, I kissed him on the forehead and covered him with a tarp.

My next thought was ice. The cold from the water wouldn't last long enough. I needed ice right away. Lots and lots of it. Which meant I needed money, which meant I already had to go back to the bed and rifle for Dad's wallet. Took me a couple of goes to work up the nerve to do it, but I finally got his card.

Too Much Ice is at the corner of 601 and 73. I could back the bed of the truck right up under the machine and just start paying for load after load. Nothing unusual in that—Todd and I did it all the time when we had keggers.

Then I'd drive to Kannapolis. To the research center. I'd go in under the pretense of apologizing to Cass. If she was there, I'd have to wait until she left. But I needed that Gaymar.

"Warm and dead is dead. Cold and dead means hope still exists." That's what Cass had told me on the first day of my ghoulish internship as she explained to me how to strip a body, get them into the Gaymar, and artificially induce hypothermia.

If I could keep Dad cold in a Gaymar, hope still existed for us both.

The motherlode would be getting him inside, because even if Cass wasn't around, there'd still be reams of scientists wandering the halls until well past midnight. I knew this because I'd hung out there one night with Stephens and Tan, chomping on pizza while I ignored my dad's calls because I was pissed at him. Guys in lab coats kept dropping by to chat. They were all geeks, losers, toads who had Domino's delivered every night of the week. They immersed themselves in their work because they didn't have wives and families to go home to. They were nothing.

"Why'd you want me to be like them, huh?" I shouted at Dad through the back windshield. I was crying like a baby. "That was the only reason you showed up, instead of calling. Because I missed the fucking internship. If you hadn't . . ." I didn't finish, because at that point the tears won out.

I wracked my memory for Cass's schedule, but I couldn't remember. If she wasn't there, I'd wait until dark, snag a dewar, and wheel it out to the parking lot. At least the security guards never stopped me with a dewar. They just wrinkled their noses as I rolled past.

Dewars. Like the whiskey. That's what they're called. Huge, cylindrical freezers-on-wheels that cost more than your house. They fit a grown man perfectly, because that's what they're designed for: to haul and store dead bodies at Cass's mad lair, Lifebank.

Lots of medical researchers use dead bodies. I knew that even before I was offered the internship. And while I wasn't looking to get involved in that, I probably could've handled it if it was some normal research, just testing new surgical methods. Most doctors aren't trying to bring corpses back from the dead.

But Lifebank was. My dad had guessed the name Lifebank meant cryogenic storage. That's why we'd argued about whether or not I'd do the internship. But like everything else at the biotech research center, it turned out Lifebank wasn't just cryogenic storage. That would be too generic for this state-of-the-art facility. Dr. Elaine Cass was leading a research team in a quest to reanimate the dead, using a hybrid twist of cryogenics, stem-cell research, and therapeutic hypothermia.

This was the loser lot I'd drawn in the internship lottery. Most of the kids I knew were working in agricultural engineering, making genetically altered super bananas. Meanwhile, I was transporting bodies in the dewar —rodents, dogs, people. I told you I protested. I seriously did not want to do this internship, especially when I had to sign all those "nondisclosure" agreements that no one else did. But Bill Jones wasn't a quitter, which meant I couldn't be one either, at least not until I was eighteen. Plus he bribed me: if I did my stint, I'd be off the hook for Governor's School this summer. I could stay home, work with him on the Richardses' house, and hang out with my friends at the pool. No more "academically gifted" camps at Duke, no more geeks. At that point though, if I could've turned back the clock, I'd have picked Governor's School. Trotted my ass off to Raleigh and been the biggest geek on campus all summer. Then my dad would've been safe at home. He wouldn't have driven to Todd's house. I wouldn't have cost him his life and technically be an orphan right now. I'd just get chewed out for skipping school.

Frigging Gold Hill Road. The name is literal, you know. Way back when, some guy named John Reed found a seventeen-pound chunk of gold in his creek bed. He didn't know what it was—just used it as a doorstop. A visiting silversmith spotted it and ripped him off for it. Reed located more gold on his property and eventually opened a mine, and Cabarrus County, North Carolina became the site of the first Gold Rush in the United States. For real. Gold Hill Road was the dusty track that took people from the mines into Concord, where they could weigh in and bank their fortune. There are all kinds of legends about the bandits that ambushed miners along that road, people who were willing to kill for what John Reed had found. That's what a little gold will do.

I didn't know it at the time, but I was about to revive Gold Hill's legacy of priceless discovery, thieves, ambush, and death. Trouble with using that analogy is that I'm dumbass John Reed, using his chunk of gold to hold the kitchen door open.

I turned right at 73 and punched the gas.

CHAPTER TWO

The station attendant at Too Much Ice didn't say anything when I pulled up. He made me nervous though, circumnavigating the truck, examining the damage. I was all ready to say, "Yeah, I'm in for it now, so I figured I might as well have a party," but the guy just shook his head finally, took my dad's card, and swiped it. Maybe my face said enough. Somewhere in between loads I felt a breeze and suddenly remembered I was shirtless, plus my Nikes were still soaking wet from the creek. That probably looked weird, considering it was March. I reached around in the cab—Dad always kept a couple shirts there. It was a couple sizes too big, but I threw it on, feeling like a little kid playing dress-up.

Once the bed was full, I spun out and hit Highway 3, eyeballing the speedometer, using turn signals, everything. I was pretty sure I couldn't pull off talking to a police officer right now.

Let's be real here. I wasn't thinking about the history of the research center right then. I was watching minutes tick away on my cell phone and absolutely freaking out. I'm not gonna give you some phony explanation for the information I'm going to stick in right here. Fact is, you'll need it—all of it—if you want to keep up.

Twenty years ago, a young guy by the name of Paul Calhoun inherited a cotton mill in downtown Kannapolis—a mill that used to sit where the research center is now. He promptly sold the mill to another company. He claimed he didn't know they'd immediately shut it down, causing the highest localized unemployment since the Great Depression and totally ruining the lives of thousands of people. He said sorry, but he kept the money.

Calhoun invested the money elsewhere and became a billionaire. About fifteen years later, when he was in his late thirties or early forties, he had a heart attack. Bad karma? No such thing, I promise you. Anyway, he survived and got real obsessed with his health. For most guys, this would mean eating some organic spinach and taking an occasional jog around the block. But billionaires don't do things in half measures. Calhoun interviewed the most cutting-edge researchers in biotech and offered himself up as their guinea pig, intent on becoming the healthiest guy on the planet.

He bought the empty mill back—at a rock-bottom price of course—and razed it so he could build the biotech research center. He claimed he felt bad about what had happened to Kannapolis. And Concord. Basically, the whole county. He said he wanted to revive what he'd destroyed, give everyone new jobs. And maybe that's true. Uneducated mill workers always become biotech scientists and engineers, don't they?

Duke, Chapel Hill, the military, pretty much everybody started leasing space at the biotech, after they got a tour of the state-of-the-art equipment. The place has everything from the most expensive medical equipment in the world to the latest in agricultural engineering. Name any brand of health science, and I promise you, the top researcher in the field is either already in Kannapolis or in the process of moving there. The local papers cover every new scientist who signs on, while they simultaneously hail Calhoun as a hero. Weird how they seem to have forgotten he was the guy who bankrupted us in the first place. Calhoun read about Cass in some medical journal. She was a pioneer in something called therapeutic hypothermia. It's a method for reviving heart-attack victims by chilling them. The patients can be brought back hours after they've been declared legally dead, without the brain damage that usually occurs. The article detailed how she'd brought like sixteen people back from the dead at that point, using her method. And her patients left the hospital days later, absolutely fine.

When I started working for her, Cass said to me, "Death is a process, rather than a singular event. And a process can be interrupted." I just stared at her like she was nuts. Calhoun probably gave her a standing ovation.

He wooed her away from UPenn with the most insane goal of all time: for Cass to fuse her work with the latest in cryogenics and stem-cell research, on a quest to conquer death. He agreed to fund the whole thing himself. Cass probably could've had Calhoun locked up in a mental ward just for suggesting it. But she agreed, provided she was in charge. And Life-bank was born.

So that's where I was going. I was going to get my dad on the Gaymar, the machine Cass helped design to induce hypothermia. I was going to chill him properly, use the paddles, and see if I could restore a heartbeat. Then I'd call 9-1-1.

I suddenly thought of another problem: security cameras.

I hit the steering wheel in frustration. How the hell did I think I could get my dad from the bed of the truck and into a dewar in broad daylight, with security cameras scanning the entire parking lot? Dad couldn't wait for dark—every minute mattered.

I made an abrupt U-turn, heading back up Highway 3 for the funeral home, praying Charlie would still be at work. Charlie's our next-door neighbor. He's also a mortician.

I pulled into Blackwelder Funeral Home and spotted him just getting out of the hearse, his blond comb-over lifting in the wind, flashing his bald spot. His brow wrinkled when he saw the truck. "Hem? Everything all right?"

I wanted to tell him everything. Just give up and tell, before I even tried. I needed somebody so bad, and I knew he'd do anything for me. Charlie's halfway between my dad's age and mine. He's divorced and kind of lonely, so when he's home, he's often hanging out with us, watching basketball and baseball games. He's gone to bat for me a few times.

Mentally I was halfway through confessing everything when I remembered he was waiting for an answer. I choked out, "I wrecked the truck. On Gold Hill."

Charlie's eyes widened. "You were in it when that happened? Have you called your dad? Hem, you should be at the hospital, getting checked out—"

"I'm fine. I'm not going to the hospital."

Charlie let out a low whistle. "We've all done it," he reassured me. "Your dad will be grateful you're okay." He pulled out his cell phone and started dialing. My eyes bugged. I knew who he was calling, and the phone was still in my dad's pocket. I'd forgotten it. It would ring . . .

I shouted, "No!" and batted his cell phone away before he could finish dialing. Charlie stared at me in disbelief, but I blurted out, "Can I borrow your pass to the depot?"

There's a depot underneath the research center for deliveries. Mostly it's used for multimillion-dollar equipment, but Charlie delivers bodies—bodies that are going to be cryogenically stored at Lifebank—and since no one wants those coming through the front door, he's got a pass.

I thought fast. "Uh, Todd's bringing some tools. We're gonna try and fix up the truck a little before my dad sees it."

He shook his head. "There's no way you're gonna—" He saw my face and paused, feeling bad for me. He changed tactics. "Why wouldn't you just take it to a garage?"

I begged. "Please, Charlie. I don't have time to explain. I've never asked before and I never will again. I've got to try." My voice cracked as I said it.

It is still absolutely amazing to me that he believed I was this panicked about wrecking a truck. But he did.

He pulled a pass card from his shirt pocket with a sigh. "I could lose my privileges at the biotech and my license if you're caught. So if you are, you stole this and I'll have to press charges. The code is 0321. Just drop the card back through my door when you get home tonight. And when you GET home," he cautioned, "be aware I'll have had a talk with your dad." I started to protest, not wanting him to call my dad's cell anymore. But Charlie held up a hand. "I have to. He'd never speak to me again if I didn't. I'll try and soften the blow, but—"

I didn't even let him finish. "Thanks. Anyone watching stuff come in?"

Charlie tilted his head from side to side, evaluating, and checked his watch. "You should be all right after seven. But don't take too long. I don't know what it is you hope to do, but good luck." He waved and headed inside.

I stuck the keys back in the ignition and peeled out as I dialed Todd on my cell. Meanwhile, I heard my dad's cell ringing in the bed. Goddammit, Charlie. I kept driving.

You know you've hit Kannapolis when everything starts looking like the edge of town—low-slung mill houses with peeling paint have all been converted into low-rent hairdressers, tattoo parlors, and consignment shops. Blip past the dilapidated sixties shopping plaza that is our massive Department of Social Services and Unemployment Office (thanks, Calhoun), a few convenience stores, and about a million fast-food restaurants, and suddenly Calhoun's chic new downtown and the aluminum dome of the Core Lab appears in the distance. A tale of two towns: one for the residents Calhoun bankrupted, another for his invited guests.

All of it is so new it glitters. There's a new minor-league baseball stadium smack-dab in the center of town, as well as craft breweries, Asian fusion restaurants, and twinkle lights on every young tree he's had planted. Something to appeal to spouses forced to leave glamorous Swiss cities for a rinky-dink town twenty miles outside of Charlotte, and just enough gentrification to lure renovation-oriented hipsters and higher real-estate values. As you get closer to the biotech, Buildings One and Two appear, flanking the Core Lab with their massive Roman columns and burgundy brick. Lush lawns and fountains further enhance the extraterrestrial feel of the place.

I swung in past bulldozers that were still grading Carolina red clay around the foundations for additional buildings and parked in proximity to the other Ford F250s in the dirt. I tucked the keys, pass, and code under the seat for Todd and called him.

"Code Red." I just stuck to the story I'd told Charlie, told him what I needed him to do, and headed inside, reminding myself not to run.

Inside the grand foyer of Building Two, my footsteps echoed loudly on the marble tiles of the winding staircase. So much for not running—anyone listening would've thought I was winning the Boston Marathon. Lifebank's on the second floor at the end of the hall, as close to the Core Lab as you can get.

I pushed the door open and spotted Cass. "Dr. Ass" was still at work.

I'll pause here, in case you're taking offense. I didn't make up that nickname—all the guys at the biotech called her that. But they called her that because they think she's a cougar: forty or so, long, curly red hair, and a fit-as-fuck triathlete. But I called her Dr. Ass because she's a hardnosed bitch. Personally, I loathed her so much I'd come to loathe the whole hard-bodied style. Plus, she was bent over a body in a dewar, which just made her more repulsive.

She looked over her shoulder at me with those ice-blue eyes of hers. "Good. You're alive. Your father is looking for you." Her voice was brusque to the point of scathing. "So was I. Rough day?" She went back to examining the body.

Cass talks that way to everybody, so I couldn't have cared less. I was too focused on the body in the dewar. There was a body. Another complication. "Is that an A or a B?" I asked, trying to suppress my panic.

"An A. Stephens and Tan had already left when the call came in. They're halfway to Raleigh. I need you to suit up and prep the lab for vitrification. You ought to thank him," she smirked, pointing to the dewar. "If I didn't need an assistant tonight, you'd be on your way out the door. Permanently."

I gave a nod to the stiff and said, "Thanks for dying." Cass looked like she wanted to kick me in the nuts.

"Guess I'll get going then, shall I?" My heart was flip-flopping as I hurried away. Cass was going to be here all weekend unless I could get rid of her. (An "A" is some millionaire or billionaire who signed on for cryogenic storage before they died. Prepping the body takes two days.) The extant information was this: I wouldn't be able to use the lab. And Todd was going to be here in twenty minutes.

"Where the hell have you been?" Cass called after me.

"I had a car accident," I shouted back, knowing this would buy me time. The best lies, after all, are the ones closest to the truth. A car wreck is a plausible reason for anyone to miss work.

But I've also learned when you're a teenager and score high enough on all those dumbass IQ tests—the Hoeflin, the Mega, the Titan—people will bend over backward to give you a break, under the presumption you're a well-meaning and promising kid.

Which just goes to show you.

I switched on the showers—so Cass would assume I was in there—and ducked into her office.

Pulling the fire alarm wouldn't work. I needed more time. With Cass bent on staying in the office, there was only one way to get it. I rifled through her papers—the desk was absolutely stacked with details about the A—but I knew I'd find the number. Lisa Hobbs called like every other day.

She picked up right away, positively oozing. "Dr. Cass! How great to finally hear from you!"

"Uh, hey, this is actually her intern, but she wanted me to call you back. You wanted to hear more about the cryogenic storage here at Lifebank?"

The excitement in her voice was unmistakable. "Are you saying there are cryogenic storage facilities at Lifebank?"

Remembering the NDA, I backed off. "I uh, I'm not at liberty to say, but Dr. Cass said she's happy to talk about it, but not here. Can we maybe set something up? How does Tuesday work? And she wanted to know if you guys could meet somewhere kinda outta the way?"

"Sure we can do that. I know just the place . . ."

I waited, utterly impatient to hang up as she prattled on about a coffee shop she knew.

"You sound really young to be in a place like that," Lisa finally commented. "You don't find it a little eerie?"

Now she was just fishing and it was irritating. "I'm uh, not at liberty to talk about anything that goes on here at the lab. Might interfere with my scholarship to Harvard." I bolstered my voice with false pride to really sell it.

"Oh wow! You're going to Harvard? You must be some smart cookie. What did you say your name was?"

I held the phone without covering the mouthpiece. "I'll be right there Dr. Cass! I set the appointment with Lisa Hobbs for Tuesday!" I pulled the phone back to my ear. "I'm sorry I have to go. Dr. Cass says she'll see you then, okay?"

"Just one more question!"

"Bye now."

I hung up and hit the showers. The office phone rang again, and Cass started braying for me to answer it. I ignored her, hoping it wasn't Lisa again. After a few insistent rings, she finally stomped over to the extension.

I started scrubbing up. On her way out, Cass slammed the door so loudly the water rippled.

Remember those nondisclosure papers I had to sign to even work at Lifebank? *Nondisclosure* means you can't tell anyone what you're doing. No one. The contract was as thick as a textbook. My dad had to sign one too, because I was a minor and couldn't sign on my own. The deal was this: they could take my dad's business if I ever told anyone what the company did. My dad and I weren't the only ones who had to sign one, either. Cass, Tan, Stephens—they all had to sign their lives away to work here. If you so much as answered a phone call from a journalist, security would trace it—instantly. Lisa Hobbs had called on my first day. Dr. Tan had stopped me just as I was about to pick up and showed me a taped-up list he and Stephens kept of all the journalists' phone numbers they could identify. So when I dialed this Lisa chick from Cass's office, I knew she'd be summoned. And since I'd set an appointment with Lisa on her behalf, she'd be questioned. Given the topic was cryogenic storage, safe to say she'd be gone for hours.

I'd feel bad if I'd done it to Dr. Tan or Dr. Stephens, but don't get me wrong—I would've done it, even if it meant they lost their jobs. I couldn't care less about Dr. Ass. Or the A. His body would wait in the dewar in the front room, rotting past the point of salvaging. I'd be working on my dad.

I fired up another dewar and checked the time—ten minutes till Todd got here.

Cass would know it was me who made the call. But she couldn't prove to security that she hadn't asked me to call since we're the only office without cameras. (The billionaire doesn't trust the security guards to see what goes on at Lifebank.) But she'd know. This was probably the last time I would ever be in this office. And that was just fine by me.

I went to the farthest lab and switched on everything I might need: defibrillator, EKG, heart-lung bypass, xenon tank, IVs of epinephrine and saline, and the Gaymar Meditherm. Same stuff you'd see on *ER*, except for the xenon and the Gaymar. The Gaymar is just a small machine—but the wraps for the patient make them look like they've broken every bone in their body.

My cell phone chirped. "Okay, I'm down here." Todd's voice sounded a little strangled.

"I'll be right there. Don't get out of the truck yet," I ordered. I started pushing an empty dewar toward the service elevator.

The depot was dark—I had to hit several light switches just to see Todd inside the truck—he was sitting behind the wheel, his eyes huge. Scared. He knew.

How he knew was answered a moment later—when my dad's cell phone rang again in the bed. Fucking Charlie. Fucking me. I'd forgotten about the phone again when I got to Lifebank. Todd must've heard it and looked through the ice in the bed.

I don't know how long we stared at each other. Lies swirled around my head like gnats to a sweaty face. I couldn't believe I'd screwed up so badly, so early—with a frigging cell phone. Stoner Todd was going to be my dad's undoing.

I squared my shoulders. "It's not what you think. Not yet anyway."

Todd exploded. "What the f—"

Leaning over the driver's-side door, I slapped a hand over his mouth before I even knew what I was doing. I pinched his mouth tight, jerking my head toward the high corners of the depot. "There are cameras up there," I spat through gritted teeth. "I didn't intend to involve you any more than just bringing the truck around. I forgot about the phone. I'm sorry."

Todd batted at my hand and I finally let go. He pleaded quietly, "Hem, you are in some serious shit. He's dead. I saw him. We should just call—"

"He's not dead. I swear it. He's just suspended. Look, I can't explain it to you, I don't have time. There's stuff here that can save his life. But I'm begging you—don't call the cops. Not yet. If you call them right now, he will die. They'll take him to a regular hospital and put him in the morgue."

"He's under ice! He's already dead!" he hissed back.

I lost it. "Please. I'm begging you. He's all I've got. If I don't call you from the hospital in the next twenty-four hours, you can call the police and tell them everything. Please."

Todd pounded his fists on the steering wheel and stared out the wind-shield at the concrete walls. He finally sighed. "What do you need?"

I pointed to the dewar and handed him Charlie's pass. "Help me get him in the dewar. Then just take the truck and drop this in Charlie's mailbox on your way home. If you have to rat me out, please don't mention the part about the pass."

Todd thought for a moment and said, "Turn the lights low first."

He was in. I dashed for the lights—it was actually a good idea. No one would be able to tell it was him in the truck or my dad in the bed.

We moved Dad in silence. I don't think we could've had a conversation right then even if we needed to—we wouldn't know what verb tense to use to talk about my dad.

Closing the dewar, Todd pulled the keys but stared at the walls. "You have to lose the truck, man. You want me to do it?"

Floored. He's been my best friend since kindergarten, but I'd already resigned myself to the fact that our friendship was probably history. I tried to say something, but the rasp in my throat sounded like a punctured tire. So I nodded and started wheeling my dad for the elevator. I finally croaked, "Todd?" He turned. "I won't forget this."

"Doubt I will either." He started up the truck as the elevator door closed.

I was alone. And I wasn't. At least I hoped I wasn't. I looked at the dewar. "Let's get you upstairs and conscious. And just this once? Please don't argue with me."

CHAPTER THREE

In the elevator, halfway up, I ordered myself to stop thinking about Todd.
Or Cass. Or the police. They were all tomorrow's problems, and tomorrow
was a hazy proposition for me, one contingent on success or failure reviving
Dad at Lifebank.

Maybe you're calling bullshit right now. But that's what I was thinking
about—the exact cabinet cocktail it would take to finish me off if I failed. I
knew Cass had a wide variety of juices that would do the job.

And let's not overdramatize my reasoning here. I could live without my
dad. I mean, I love him and need him around, but people live without their
parents, right? Kids much younger than me. They may not like it, but they
get by.

What I couldn't live with was that I'd killed him. That would never be
untrue. I'd have to wake up every day and remember it. Maybe I'd learn to
live with it, but who wants to be that guy? Plus, there's telling other people. It's inevitable. I mean, say I was even capable of forgiving myself. Does
that mean anyone else would? If I told someone, wouldn't they just say

something polite and shuffle quickly away to talk to someone else? Someone *normal*? Even say I did find someone—eventually—who forgave me and loved me, what would *that* person look like—the one who thinks it's okay I killed my dad?

I killed my dad. The words jammed in my throat like a chicken bone. I was either going to regurgitate his life—reverse the natural order—or choke to death on self-loathing.

I opened the dewar. His unseeing eyes stared at me while I grabbed his shoulders and worked him slowly out of that high-tech refrigerated casket and onto the machine that could restore him. I hit the switch and the white surround of the Gaymar inflated like a cocoon. Dad was the chrysalis, the grub, sleeping through his transformation. That's how I needed to think about it, in order to do what I was going to do next.

I had to bring his heartbeat back. I couldn't do anything about his head injury except cool it down.

I had to strip him naked. While in theory this should've been no big deal—I'd done this before on Cass's subjects—it was harder than I thought. But he had to be naked before I could get the cooling blanket on him. I sucked in a breath and decided to go quick, get it over with. I yanked at his shirt and heard a small pop. One of the fingers in his left hand had caught on his sleeve. I'd broken a bone in his middle finger. He didn't even twitch.

I gagged and sucked back tears, desperate to stop. But another part of me was already cussing myself out for being such a baby. I reminded myself that EMTs often break a patient's ribs while trying to resuscitate them, and if it saves the patient's life, a few broken bones hardly matter. And if the EMT fails, a few broken bones don't matter at all, do they? That's what I told myself as I started yanking on his pants. I wasn't stripping away *Dad's* humanity. Just mine.

And yes, of course I started with parameters of what I was going to do and how long I was going to give this project. What project do you start where you don't have parameters? I wasn't going to just wing it in the lab, throw down whatever meds happened to be in the cabinet. I was just going to perform the treatments you'd find in the best trauma centers in the world. We didn't have that equipment at Northeast Hospital. But I had everything at Lifebank.

I was performing therapeutic hypothermia on the Gaymar. Nothing revolutionary. You can google it if you don't believe me. Getting his body properly chilled would help his organs and the cells in his brain to hunker down and wait while I tried to figure out what the hell I was going to do to get his heart started.

I turned on the tanks, hooked up the saline and epinephrine IVs, and hooked him up to the EKG. This was most of my job at Lifebank—firing up all this heavy machinery—while Cass shocked and killed some rodent. Then I'd watch her try to revive it. I'd watched enough times to know what I had to do. I needed the EKG to find at least some electrical activity in his body. And epinephrine's a shot of adrenaline—textbook stuff in cardiac-arrest cases. I waited a full minute, hoping the adrenaline boost would create a blip on the EKG. Nothing. So, I hit him with the paddles.

His body jolted, and the EKG registered it, but he flopped back to nothingness. No heartbeat, no electrical activity whatsoever. He hadn't drawn a breath in two and a half hours and his blood hadn't circulated in almost as long. The blood on his head wound had crystallized.

I don't know how many minutes passed as I repeated this protocol over and over. It felt like hours, but was probably only twenty or thirty minutes. The only sounds were the echoing punches from the defibrillator and the hum of the cryonic fridges. Mostly white noise, but when the sun set, I imagined the bodies inside those morgue-like drawers peering out through keyholes with keen personal interest, watching Dad and me. As if they were saying, "Hey, if this works, can I be next?"

Maybe I'd just lost it.

To be honest, I don't remember how long it was before I moved on to human trials stuff. Like dosing him up with hydrogen sulfide. Cass made us all watch that TED Talk—this guy Dr. Elks talking about hibernation. How a bear's heartbeat and breath diminish to unnaturally low levels in that state.

He was postulating that if humans could hibernate, we could get wounded soldiers to a hospital—they wouldn't bleed out on the way. So, he was trying to see if you could teach animals to hibernate, and he'd succeeded with a mouse and even some dogs by using hydrogen sulfide. Get them cold, dose them up and they appear dead—but if you push them out into the sun, after about twenty minutes they revive naturally. He'd been so successful he was moving on to human trials. But it didn't work on my dad.

From there I went on to the more radical stuff, like the chemical cocktail Yale University is using to successfully revive pig organs. That definitely didn't work. The more I failed, the more I tried, each time with fewer clinical facts to support what I was doing. I still couldn't find any electrical activity in his body. Like turning the ignition in the car and getting nothing.

I should've given up. But every little step of the way—every line I crossed—was so close in theory to what I'd just tried that it didn't seem to be a major, invasive stretch. I mean, the fact is, these days there are so many protocols in "clinical treatment of the dead" (their term, not mine) that the only true uncertainty is when you're supposed to give up and plan the funeral.

You can say you'd have gone all religious, or accepted "fate," maybe said a prayer if it was your dad, and called the cops. But I doubt it. Everyone sets parameters—even for the stupidest, most pain-in-the-ass projects—and then violates them. Every time. Because when you're in it, it's easier to move the mental goalposts than to quit.

A few weeks ago, I cleaned my fish tank. I vowed I'd be done by seven, eat dinner, and start on homework. But there were complications. The fish started fighting in the Tupperware, so I had to get another container to separate them. Then I found mold underneath the gravel in the tank. I could've ignored it, but that meant I'd just have to do this again in a few weeks. And I wasn't hungry for dinner anyway, so I kept going. Only then I was pissed off. I scrubbed the glass so hard I cracked it. I had to go buy a new tank and fill it. Suddenly, it was midnight; I hadn't eaten or written my history paper. And the only thing that mattered was getting the goddamn fish back in that tank.

That's about how it went—except I never had any reason to feel I was getting close. In all this time, my father's heart never beat in response to epinephrine, or the defibrillator, or any of the six thousand things I tried. Not even once.

My dad wasn't "dead" in the sense of Cass's patients at her resuscitation clinics. Or even "clinically dead" like the arrest and trauma patients. Because in all those cases, doctors always managed to get the victim's heart beating, even if just for a few seconds. With just a few beats, a doctor can hook them up to a heart-lung bypass, let the machine do the work, and buy time while they come up with a new idea.

A new sound penetrated the tomb-like silence: my cell phone. I checked the caller ID, in case it was Charlie or Todd. But it wasn't. It was Cass. So she was able to make calls. That meant I was just about out of time. I switched it off and wracked my brain.

All this time I'd been operating under the assumption that my dad was still a living human being, capable of being revived. That he still had brain activity, like the drowning victims Cass had revived.

The death of the brain and the organs are, to some extent, separate processes. Usually, an organ gives out first, which causes failure in the other organs, specifically heart and lungs, and when that happens, the brain is deprived of oxygen and dies. It's only once your brain dies that whatever makes you you is well and truly gone.

But Bill Jones had finished that process. He had no brain activity or organ function. He was dead like the A—the one I'd left lying in a dewar in the main room—the one I was ignoring. If I wanted to have any chance of saving my dad, I was going to have to treat him like the A. Dial things back even further—take him to cryogenic status—and do what Cass had so far failed to do: bring him back from heaven, or wherever the hell he'd gone. That's when I got the idea.

I started raiding the lab for products I wasn't even allowed to handle. But I'd seen Dr. Stephens work with them, so I knew they were there. I flipped on the lights and started opening cabinets until I found them. I loaded a syringe, pushed the proceeds into my dad, and started vitrification. That's the first step in the cryopreservation process.

Human beings are 98 percent water. If someone wants to be cryogenically stored when they die, you can't just stick them in the freezer, because the water molecules in their body turn to ice and destroy everything else. Vitrification works like antifreeze on a car engine. It's a fluid that slows the water molecules down until the body is so cold the cells become solid. The process has been around since the sixties.

But the thing is, no one's ever brought a vitrified human body *back to life*. All those people you hear about being cryogenically frozen—Walt Disney, Ted Williams—some are just rumors, but others are real, and still around, stored in a giant freezer like ziplocked sides of beef, waiting for someone like Cass to figure out how to revive them. That's what I was up against. But what choice did I have? If Cass came back, game over. I had to do what no one's ever done—vitrify him and bring him back. And I was winging it.

So I got to work. And if you think I'm going to share what I did at this stage, sorry. This is a confession, not a "How To."

The office phone rang—a lot. I ignored it as long as I could. I needed time. I waited until the spacing between calls was reduced to every five minutes. She'd show up soon. Cass went to med school via the Army. She served in the Second Gulf War. Trust me. If I didn't answer, she'd be back, barking in my face like a drill sergeant.

I picked up the handset. "Yeah."

"Core Lab. Now."

She knew about the reporter. More? Possibly. Just because there aren't *supposed* to be security cameras inside Lifebank doesn't mean there aren't any. But unlikely. I weighed my options: Stall? Or just go? If I went to the Core Lab, chances were good I wouldn't be back. My dad's death would be discovered and irreversible. And this thing needed more time to work. I checked the hallway. My eyes landed on the A. I kept my voice indifferent. "Where the hell are you? I thought you wanted the A done."

"Now, Jones."

I hadn't expected that to work, but if I hadn't asked, she'd know something else was up. I let out a big sigh, milking my annoyance. "I need like fifteen minutes. Vitrification's taking a while." And held my breath.

"That's fine. Fifteen minutes then." She hung up.

I dropped the handset and ran, knowing security was already on the way.

Some people are absolutes. "Yes" and "no," once spoken aloud, are unchangeable. That's Cass. When she said "now," she never budged. Or at least, not with me. I'd talked about the A simply because I didn't know what else to do. I'd hoped I'd get an idea while I played along. But Cass's "That's fine" meant she was stalling *me*. She wanted to keep me on the phone while they came in.

I shorted the electrics on the security doors and heard the generator come to life. The A in the dewar kept getting in my way, so I used him as a barricade. Why not? His fault everything wasn't going to plan—if he hadn't died, Cass would've left and the lab would've been empty. I'd have had the entire weekend to work.

Someone tried the doors a few times, followed by pounding fists. Voices started calling my name.

"Hemingway Jones? Can you open the door please? C'mon, son. Law enforcement is on their way."

"Okay, I'll be out in a minute!" I was of course lying, but who cared? They'd stop trying to force their way in for a while if I said I was going to open it.

Eventually, they started knocking and cajoling me to open up: first sweet-talking me and then threatening me. Then they started hurling themselves at it, two, maybe three guys, I didn't really know. But the door held. I did tell you everything here was state-of-the-art.

Apparently, that included the doors.

"He's got something in the way! SOMEONE GET A DRILL! We're going to have to take the hinges off!"

Okay, that could be a problem.

Someone else said, "How're they making out at the back?" Their radios squawked and a debate ensued about my battlements. I was now the biggest security threat the research center had confronted, and their training hadn't covered insurrection. Obviously.

I sat on the floor, my back against the dewar, wondering what I was go-ing to do when they took the door off, when a little dust fell on me. My eyes rolled toward the ceiling.

As I watched, the tile above me moved a bit, pushing into the room, sending another flurry of dust. I swore, realizing it was a hand testing whether the tile could support human weight. The rent-a-guards were trying to come in through the ceiling.

Then I heard a drill fire up on the other side of the door. Once they got the door off, they'd only have to climb over the dewar. The whole lab was as permeable as a sponge, and everything I was doing was absolutely useless.

There was only one way to get them to stop. And that was to make them stop *wanting* to come in. I dragged myself up to the reception desk and scaled the redial screen for her number. When it rang, I hit conference and pressed the volume as loud as it would go, so the security guys in the hall would hear.

A sleepy voice at the other end shrieked through the lab. "Dr. Cass?"

"Ms. Hobbs? This is Hemingway Jones. The intern that called you earlier? I'm only seventeen. And I'm locked inside the lab—"

The annoyance in her voice was obvious. "What time is it?"

Jesus. Primal screaming was going to come easily. "I'M SEVENTEEN. MY NAME IS HEMINGWAY JONES. I'VE LOCKED MYSELF IN THE RESEARCH CENTER. I'VE GOT A WHOLE BUNCH OF OXYGEN TANKS HERE AND IF THEY KEEP TRYING TO COME IN, I'M GON-NA BLOW THEM ALL."

Somewhere, a radio squawked. The drill stopped. Hissing conversations. A petulant voice protested: "But we're almost in. They've hit the override on the elevator." Their voices died away.

Pink eventually peered through the blinds—dawn. Or maybe it was just all the flashing lights—every emergency vehicle in the county was outside and had been for hours. Even a chopper. I didn't even know Cabarrus County had one. In any case, I was so wiped and such a failure that I really didn't care.

"Hemingway? You still with me?"

Oh yeah. The reporter. What's-her-name. She'd kept me talking all through the night, but I was now so tired I'd lost the plot.

"Hemingway?" Her voice had taken on that sickly sweet quality, the kind of voice you reserve for a chance encounter with the violently insane.

I sat on the floor, my back against the Gaymar. My dad was still inside it, absolutely lifeless. I was loading up the cabinet cocktail. The one for me. "Yeah, Lisa. I'm here."

"So what happened?"

I debated whether to finish. We'd been talking on the hands-free, excepting the times the offended hostage negotiator insisted on barging in on the conversation. I didn't have any hostages, so I just went mute when he came on the line, until Lisa eventually came back. I knew the police were listening too, but who cared? Not me at that point. We'd started with my story of what had happened.

I really intended to tell Lisa the truth about the accident, but I'd had second thoughts. I'd already involved Charlie and Todd against their wills. Wasn't exactly fair if I then ratted them out. So, I wove a story, as close to the truth as I could make it: that my dad had driven me to the research center so I could apologize to Cass. He'd stayed outside in the truck initially, but Cass had work for me to do. Shortly after she left, he got bored and came inside, and he'd had a heart attack. I told her that he'd hit his head on the dewar when he collapsed. (I had to account for the head injury.) I explained there was a Gaymar here, what it did, and that I knew Cass wouldn't let me use it, so I'd barricaded myself in here and done it anyway.

Sounded good. To me, at least.

Lisa bought it. In fact, she ate it up. Since then, I'd kept her interested with stories about my dad—how he'd cared for my mom—and for me since her death. You see, I was still banking on Dad coming back. And if he did, that nondisclosure contract meant that the research center could take his business. So, I figured if I made him look great, Calhoun would look like an asshole if he came after him.

But now it looked like Dad wouldn't need his business after all. No signs of life, and the cops were going to come in soon. No way they'd leave me here as daytime employees arrived and lined the perimeter.

I looked at the syringe. Why not finish the story? I'd either be dead or in jail when it came time for my dad's memorial, so at least they'd have this on tape. One last tribute. I took a breath and continued.

"I wanted to do the stand-up thing. I wanted to trust Max. He'd been my friend for years. I knew Dad didn't approve, but he just shook his head and said, 'Then go with it.' So, a day later I met with the principal and stuck to Max's cover story. But when it's his turn, he doesn't cover for me. In fact, he lays the whole prank on me, and I'm suspended for a week. Still, I figured it wouldn't be that bad, right? Big deal, I miss school for a week. Dad knows I didn't do it, so so what? Be like a mini vacation. At lunchtime, I loaded up my bike to ride to Whataburger. Dad found me and was like, 'Where do you think you're going?' He put his hands on the bike and said, 'You're suspended. In this house, that means you're grounded. Weekends included.' I couldn't believe it. I mean he *knew* I was innocent. But he shrugged and said, 'You gambled on your friend telling the truth. I understand why you did it, and I am proud of you for it. But you bet wrong. You've got to know what it feels like to pay the penalty, so next time you'll understand exactly what you're risking. You'll serve the suspension as if you'd done it.' He confiscated my bike, my computer, and the TV. Total house arrest for ten days."

"Wow, that's harsh." Lisa admitted, "But I guess he did have a point."

My throat constricted. "Yeah, he usually does."

"How's your dad doing?"

"Not too good. Not too good at all."

"I'm sorry to hear that. You think maybe you should let the ambulance guys in now, so they can look at him?"

I sighed. "We'll be opening our doors in just a few minutes here, Lisa. I know everyone's excited and all, but if you can just get them to hold on, I'll be ready and waiting for the cuffs."

Hushed whispers on the other end of the line. Lisa finally came back. "Hem, the EMTs want to know what the EKG reads. Just so they can be ready, have the equipment they need to treat your Dad?"

I rolled my eyes. "I'm, uh, fairly certain it doesn't read anything at this time, Lisa."

More harsh whispers. "Aren't you checking?" And more. Lisa finally came back. "Hem, one of the EMT guys is kinda listening in. He says he hears activity on the EKG. He thinks your dad is showing signs of electrical activity."

I didn't want to look. I had a syringe poised and ready. Checking meant I'd have to put that down. Checking meant getting my hopes up one last futile time. Checking meant sinking back to the floor and working up the nerve to pick up that syringe again and plunge.

Personally, I couldn't hear anything but the loud buzzing in my head and Lisa's voice. The buzzing had surfaced around 2:00 a.m. The police weren't the only ones doling out ultimatums here—my body was too. My brain wanted sleep and was preparing to take me hostage. Talking with Lisa had helped stave that off for a while, but as I set the syringe on the floor and stood up, the blood rushed to my head much too fast. I had to get this one last check done and use the syringe, or I'd be trying to find another way to kill myself in jail, which might not be as easy.

I tilted and swayed, but as I grabbed the Gaymar for support, I spotted the blood.

My dad's head was bleeding. If he was bleeding, he was alive. I looked over at the EKG, just as it emitted a half-hearted beep.

Thoughts were like butterflies at this point—hard to predict which way they were moving and therefore almost impossible to catch. Only one stood out: My dad was alive. "Oh my God. Oh my God. Dad? Dad! DAD!" I leaned over to shake him, but when you're sleep-deprived, equilibrium is a precarious thing—I started swooning.

Lisa's voice was panicky. "Hem? What's the matter?"

The matter was I was going to faint, and I didn't know how long I was going to be out. My dad was alive! ALIVE! And needing a doctor! A real one. I staunched the blood on his wound and wobbled again, a quick reminder that I had seconds to deal with details. "Yeah. I guess you better tell those guys to get their asses in here, right now. Cass should probably come too, because they don't know the Gaymar. Do NOT let those guys touch my dad without Cass!"

"I'll tell them, but bear in mind, I'm not in charge here. You're sure? We can come in? You won't blow anything up?"

"No way." My vision suddenly dimmed to the size of a pinpoint, then spanned back out like a zoom lens. I heard footsteps above me in the ceiling tiles. "And hey, Lisa? I hope you don't mind my asking, but I really don't have anyone else to ask. Do you think maybe you can call a lawyer for me?"

I didn't even hear her answer before I passed out cold on the marble floor.

CHAPTER FOUR

I don't remember being revived by the EMTs. I do remember getting arrested, though. I was still lying on the floor, getting the "follow-the-light" test from a medic while a Kannapolis cop read me my Miranda rights, rolled me over and snapped on the cuffs. He talked into his shirt. "Yeah, we got him." He started to haul me up.

"Wait. Can you just wait until they take my dad away?"

The cop looked at me, glanced over at Cass and finally at the EMTs working on my dad. He sighed one of those long, parental heaves that predicates "No" as he continued trying to get me up.

I hooked my foot on the desk so he couldn't haul me away. A beefy, dark-haired guy in his thirties wearing a sheriff's uniform came over to help. I yelled at both of them, "Okay, I'm arrested, I get it! Look, can you just leave me here a minute? Just till my dad's taken out." I nodded my head over at my dad. I begged. "Please. They're taking him out in a minute," I added.

The sheriff shrugged at the Kannapolis cop. "I don't have a problem with it. But it's your call."

"I don't have time for this crap," the Kannapolis cop sneered. He nodded at two guys from his squad, who both came lumbering over. "Kick his foot out from there, you get his other arm." He looked at the sheriff with distaste. "We got this one."

The sheriff held up both palms. "Hey, I'm only here to help out."

They dragged me. I was still screaming, "Hey! Wait!" But they didn't so much as pause. Outside I was stuffed into a squad car, while reporters were calling out to me from behind a taped-off area.

"Hemingway." Fingers pinched my earlobe. "Hey, kid."

I'd fallen asleep. In cuffs and in the back of a squad car. The guilty man sleeps, right? I blinked, waiting for the world to come into focus. I was at the Kannapolis police station.

"Let's go." They guided me firmly—but to be fair, not roughly—into the station, past all the desks. Is that a perp walk? I don't know, just asking. The whole thing was pretty strange. We got to one of those interrogation rooms and I hadn't so much as sat down in a chair before I used the only line I knew to use. "I want a lawyer."

I expected them to argue with me, the way they do on TV. Instead, they just rolled their eyes. One of them handed me a form, some kind of waiver. I signed it.

"Let's go then. Up you git," the cop ordered, in that twangy homegrown North Carolina way.

"Where're we going?"

He shrugged. "Detention center in Concord."

I think he expected me to be upset. But all I could feel was relief. Finally. I was going home. Okay, not "home home," but the jail was only three blocks away from my house. More cuffs, back through the station, back in a squad car to the brand-spanking-new jail in downtown Concord. We pulled up behind the detention center and the deputy sheriff who'd been at the research center was waiting. He took custody of me without saying any-thing. I wondered if the guy had ever said an unnecessary word in his life, because he acted like every word he said somehow threatened his health.

I didn't ask what would happen next and he didn't offer anything. He stared straight ahead while I spotted reporters on the sidewalk fifty yards away—loads of them, TV cameras and all. I nodded at them. "Those for me?" He shrugged and swung around back, past a sign that read "Intake Area."

I looked at the jail and giggled. The sheriff's deputy, who I later learned was named Burkhardt, swiveled to look at me. "Something funny?"

I was pretty delirious at this point. Other than the ride in the car, I hadn't slept in twenty-four hours. And given what had happened, I felt like I'd aged about a hundred years. So I found it frigging hilarious that I'd been dragged from one gleaming new brick structure—the research center—to the only other new brick structure in the region—the jail. One's supposed to represent futuristic progress, while the other's a repository for failure. And yet weirdly enough, from the outside they looked pretty much the same. What's that tell you?

"Architecture," I answered him. "Architecture's pretty funny." He wrin-kled his nose and opened the back door. He didn't have the slightest idea what I was talking about and I suppose he couldn't have cared less if he did.

I was so tired I was tripping over my own feet, and utterly incapable of righting myself, thanks to the handcuffs. He grabbed me, but I shrugged him off. "What happens now?"

He shrugged back. "Now you're processed," he said, and two sets of doors magically slid open. The natural light disappeared when the first set of doors closed. The entire jail is built on a hillside. What you see from the higher street level are the sheriff's offices. Scum like me are led in through the back, into the basement hole designated "Pre-Booking."

We arrived at a small glass window, through which Burkhardt read off, "Felony Larceny of Secret Technical Processes. Willful and Wanton Injury to Real Property. Resisting, Delaying, or Obstructing an Officer. Practice of Medicine Without a License. No priors. Accused has requested an attorney."

Inside the window, a fat bureaucrat sat at a desk. He typed the charges into a computer while Burkhardt turned to me. "That's just the sampler plate when it comes to charges," he said. "Dinner—as in, attempted murder—might or might not be served up later, depending on the results of the Kannapolis investigation."

Whatever. One of my charges was already a felony. Weirdly enough, practicing medicine without a license is only a misdemeanor.

The bureaucrat came to the window. "Twenty-five thousand dollars for the felony, one thousand dollars on each misdemeanor. Fifteen percent." He peered at me. "Should you make bail, you are instructed by law to appear at court Monday morning promptly at nine thirty. At which time you will be appointed an attorney." His eyes moved swiftly past Burkhardt and me to the next cop in line. I thought he was going to say, "Next!" but he didn't.

Burkhardt's hand was back on my shoulder, trying to guide me out, but I planted my feet. "Wait. What does that mean?"

Again, this guy's effort to speak registered on the Richter scale. His voice was low but not hostile. "Means you need someone to spend a refundable thirty thousand dollars on the spot, or get someone to pay a bail bondsman a nonrefundable five thousand dollars to get you out. Or you sit in jail. At least until Monday."

"I could get *out*? As in, *today*?" The thought had never even occurred to me. I'd hijacked the research center. I'd threatened to blow people up. I just assumed they were going to hermetically seal the cell behind me.

"There is one more alternative. You could state that you've changed your mind and start talking."

"About what?"

"Start with why your dad's wound is on the *top* of his head. Inconsistent with a fall. He's all bruised up, and so are you." He stared me in the eyes. "Medical report's going to come back stating he's suffered blunt-force trauma. I can guarantee you that. And the longer you wait to tell me what really happened, the harder it's going to be."

I smirked. "Let's try jail. See my taxpayer dollars at work."

He shrugged for about the millionth time and another set of doors opened to a room that looked a bit like the *Starship Enterprise*: a huge semi-circular desk sat on a platform, where three booking officers' heads barely peered over the top. In the swath of gray floor space below were stainless-steel benches where inmates in orange jumpsuits sat, paperwork in hand.

"Then welcome home," Burkhardt said, as he passed me over to the warden and left.

I handed over my personal effects and traded my clothes for an orange jumpsuit.

Burkhardt flagged the medic over. I got searched and, after a quick head check, was declared louse free. The booking officer looked skeptically at the many bruises from the accident—they were just about to flower on my arms and legs. He asked if I needed anything before he finished the health screen. I shook my head.

"Need your signature on this," Burkhardt said, and passed me a consent form for a tox screen.

I tried to hand it back to him. "I'm not signing that."

Burkhardt refused to take it and answered indifferently, "Up to you. You heard what you're charged with. Tox screen comes back positive, your lawyer can claim you were under the influence and that'll work in your favor."

"I don't care."

"Kid, as I said, it's up to you. In the state of North Carolina, I don't really need your permission to get a tox screen. But if you refuse, I have to press further charges and that means another court appearance, another lawyer, the works."

"I really don't have a choice?"

"Nope."

"All right, whatever. I'll sign. Provided one thing."

"What's that?"

"You call the hospital until I'm out. Give me updates on my dad." I could tell he was considering the deal, so I added, "Please?"

Burkhardt sighed. "You got it."

I signed.

You wanna know what jail's like on the inside? I doubt this place is representative of most people's experiences, but here goes. Cost overruns on our shiny new jail had caused the county commissioners to nickname it the "Bentley" and the name suited. The place looked like the public restrooms at some swanky hotel—dark, quiet, and immaculately clean. Even smelled like a restroom too—right down to the nasty licorice deodorizer.

Nobody threw toilet paper at me. No one was screaming. No one stuck their lips through the bars, muttering threats about my imminent deflowering. These guys were too languid, their movements incremental, almost painful—they barely lifted their heads as I walked by. And the digs were so cushy and clean I frankly kept expecting one of them to hand me warm towels.

I got a cell to myself. That was unexpected, but apparently, I couldn't be housed with any adults. Never mind they intended to *try* me as one.

My "single" was in a cramped and crummy old part of the jail that stank like urine, but who cared. I was here for the good of society. Not to write a review for Zagat's.

Don't get me wrong—I *was* freaked out. Only I wasn't freaked out about jail. I could've slept anywhere at that point—like the asphalt shoulder of the freeway. But the word *bail* kept me awake for a while. I hadn't expected that was even possible. If I could get out, I could ride my bike to the hospital. I could be with my dad. But where was I going to come up with $5,000?

I sank onto the cot, wondering whether my dad was even alive. I'd only brought him back from "clinical" death. That's just your bodily functions—blood circulation, heartbeat, lungs—but he still had that head injury. Despite all I'd done, it was more likely than not that he'd be brain dead. He hadn't answered me when I called to him. He didn't so much as twitch a finger when all the SWAT team guys came pouring in. Then there were the odds—bad odds, like twenty to one—that he'd go into congestive heart failure at the hospital. I'd learned all these happy statistics during my quality time with Dr. Ass.

On the other hand, you should never take lessons from someone you call Dr. Ass. And with that, I finally drifted off to sleep.

"Kid," Burkhardt nudged me.

I woke instantly. "Have you heard something? From the hospital?"

"I did. Your dad's still in surgery—"

I cut him off. "Has he woken up at all?"

"No."

My stomach flip-flopped. He handed me more forms. "They need you to sign some paperwork. I'll take it back over there for you."

I rifled through the papers—they were medical consent forms. "I don't get it. Why am I signing these?" I asked him.

"Your dad signed a living will. He named you as his guardian in the event he was incapacitated."

My heart swelled until it stuck in my throat.

I slept. In the jail.

I feel like I'm supposed to describe these elaborate nightmares I had—the ones where you see all the people you know, only they've got tails, forked tongues, and bat wings. They magically lift off into a purple sky, while you're still in the hole, rain pouring down on you, mud caving in, and you can't get out.

Yeah, not so much. My nightmares are reserved purely for waking hours.

The lights were on, so I guessed it was still daytime. The cell door was open, a different warden was there, waiting for me to get up. "You made bail," he informed me.

"Really?" My head swiveled, looking for someone I knew. Who would pay my bail? I hadn't even called anyone. Heads lifted as I was escorted back to the *Enterprise* to be released. They glanced at me but just as quickly looked away. I figured when I went outside, I'd see Todd, or maybe one of my mom's relatives.

I went to the desk and interrupted the clerk playing solitaire on her phone. I handed over my release papers. While she shuffled around and retrieved my clothes, I asked, "Hey, who paid my bail?"

She plonked my clothes on the desk and punched up my name. "Lars Mueller."

"Who?" I'd never heard of the guy. In fact, I'd never even met anyone named Lars in my life.

I glanced at the date on her phone—it was Sunday. I'd slept at least twelve hours, it was a new day, and my dad had to be out of surgery.

The doors slid wide, and I hit the street. No one waiting for me, so I ran home at a sprint.

A tall, dark-haired woman in her mid-twenties, sporting jeans and a button-down shirt, squinted at me from my front porch. "Hemingway?"

"Yeah?" I answered hesitantly.

She held out a hand. "I'm Lisa Hobbs. We meet at last."

I shook it reluctantly. "Yeah, thanks. Hey, listen, I don't really have time to talk right now, I got to get to the hospital."

"This'll only take a few minutes. Seriously. I can even give you a ride over there. We'll talk on the way."

"No thanks. Look, I appreciate what you did for me, but I really have to go."

"How's your dad doing, by the way?" she asked, ignoring my protest.

"That's an interview question, and I honestly have no idea. I've been in jail." I put my hands on my hips and said, "Look, how about I give you a call, after I'm at the hospital? I'll probably have loads of time to kill." Lie.

"You promise you won't talk to any other reporters?"

I shook my head. "You got the exclusive. Just let me go for right now, okay?"

"You sure you don't want a lift?"

"Nah, my aunt is on her way to pick me up, thanks." Another lie.

She scribbled something on a piece of paper and handed it to me. "Here's my number, in case you lost it."

I grabbed it and practically ran inside. I chucked her number on the floor and headed for my room.

The house was a mess, presumably because the police had been searching it, but all I cared about was finding a clean shirt. When I finally laid hands on one, I checked outside for Lisa: she was gone.

I picked up my bike and started riding to the hospital.

I was still so dead tired that even with the drizzly spring rain to keep me cool, I was absolutely heaving for breath before I'd done a mile. But as the lead story in the newspaper, I can assure you getting a ride from an eager reporter, the neighbors, or even an Uber would've required answering questions I didn't want asked.

On the outside, CMC Northeast Hospital looks more like a community college than a hospital: one impressive main building with lots of Corinthian columns, while all the add-ons are long, low, and made of cheaper materials, spread over several acres of parking lot.

Inside, it looks and smells like a Best Western, teal-and-purple decor, combined with cotton-candy air freshener so noxiously strong it has to be pumped through the HVAC.

Dad had to be in the ICU, so I hit the stairs. When I twisted around the corner to the nurse's station, I heard the squawk of a radio—cops. Kannapolis's finest were here. Deputy Fuckhead must've called them and told them I was getting released. I thought about his claims of blunt trauma. The guy actually thought I'd killed my dad on purpose—hit him over the head with a rock. They probably all did.

But I *had* killed him. I had to keep reminding myself of that. It was me. I did it. I deserved everything they would charge me with if they found out. Trouble is, my dad didn't deserve to be alone. He'd already lost my mom. If he survived, he didn't need to be spending what little money he had, and all his time, trying to get me free.

It wasn't Todd who had called the cops. I was sure of that. True, I hadn't called him back on Saturday night like I said I would. But if he'd called and told them what he knew, no way they would've released me.

I followed the squawking radio to Room 609. The cop spotted me, stood, and picked up his walkie-talkie. "He's here." He moved toward me. "I can't let you in there, I'm afraid."

I spluttered. "But I—" And stopped myself by pinching my brow. If I acted like a protesting kid, I wasn't going to get anywhere. I sucked in a breath and said calmly, "I have a legal right to be here. I'm his guardian when he's incapacitated."

The cop was shaking his head. "Hospital only allows one visitor at a time. As you are under suspicion for causing him bodily harm, you would need someone to accompany you in. That's two people. So, you're out of luck."

A familiar voice of authority called from down the hall. "Let him through."

The cop and I both turned to see Dr. Cass walking toward us. Her ice-blue eyes cast a glittering stare at the cop. She repeated, "I said let him through."

The cop made the mistake of guffawing. "Ma'am, you can't—"

She cut him off. "I am this man's doctor," she stated, gesturing to my dad inside the door on the Gaymar. "Not a visitor. He can go in with me. I also speak on behalf of the research center, the one currently pressing charges against this kid. So, I'm pretty sure I can override whatever authority you think you have."

She lifted her eyebrows and gave a quick flick of her curly red mane, indicating he should move out of the way. The cop mouthed a few words, but finally stepped aside, shuffling off down the hall, radio in hand.

Cass held the door open and flicked her head again, indicating I should go in.

I had to digest the fact Dr. Cass had access to my father. I know I'd asked for her at the scene, but I'd just assumed she'd surrender control once he was at the hospital. Presumably she was here because it was her machine that was keeping my father alive. Dr. Frankenstein Cass, whose lab I'd hijacked and probably ruined. She was caring for my dad. And she was helping me get in to see him. I had no idea why.

Suspicion bled through my pores like sweat. I had an irrational impulse to run, come back when she wasn't there. But that was stupid—the knee-jerk reaction of a kid who'd broken a window. What could I possibly be afraid of? That she'd chew me out? After all I'd been through—killing my dad, reviving him, SWAT teams, jail—big fucking deal. Bring it. Anyway, she wasn't chewing me out. So why was it bugging me? Was I worried she'd unplug my dad from her machine? Pick up her toys and go home?

I made a move to open the door and she suddenly blocked it with her arm. "You so much as touch one dial on the Gaymar, or shift an IV tube, I'll call that cop back and have you arrested." I resented the hell out of her setting parameters between my dad and me, but I was pretty unnerved just being around her. I nodded and she lifted her arm.

The room was alive with monitors of all kinds, beeping and whirring. Dad was in the Gaymar, surrounded by IVs. Most of his head was wrapped in bandages—only his nose and chin were visible, and they were an unnatural ashen gray. I caught sight of a splint on his hand—the finger I'd broken taking off his clothes—and nearly threw up. I'd done that. Hell, I'd done all of it.

Cass moved across the room, checking paperwork and dials. I didn't want to talk to him with her there, but what choice did I have? Cupping the splint, I whispered to him so Cass couldn't hear. All the things you could guess I might say—that I was sorry, that I loved him, and to please, please, please wake up and not leave me all alone in this shitty town, in this shitty life.

I finally sank to the floor. His refusal to wake up felt personal. I'd arrogantly expected that he'd hear my voice and open his eyes. Now I just felt like I didn't belong here. I was the one who put him here, on machines, in this suffocating piece-of-crap hospital. Why would he want me to stay? What did I deserve? Nothing.

The lump in my throat swelled again. I thought about turning around, heading out the door, out of the hospital and Concord, away from anyone that knew me. Make sure I never hurt anyone like that again. But I sensed my dad like an electrical current. Whether I deserved it or not, I was part of his circuitry, and he was part of mine. I had to stay.

Cass said nothing. When she was done with the monitors, she opened a laptop and started typing.

Finally, I mumbled, "How is he?"

She took a long pause before answering me coolly. "He's in a coma. His labs are all over the place. I've never seen anything like them. And I've revived hundreds of heart-attack victims on this machine."

"His color . . ." I started.

She shook her head, but kept her eyes on her laptop. "I don't have any medical explanation for that. I've never seen it. Ever."

Dreading the answer, I croaked, "And his head?"

"You'll have to wait until the neurologist gets here for that assessment." She looked at the ceiling and sucked in a long breath. "Hemingway, I need to know what you did. Exactly. As in, order, dosage, amps—everything. I can't help him until you tell me."

Like a kid, the words started pouring out of my mouth. "I got him on the Gaymar. Per protocol. But I couldn't find any electrical activity, so I hit him with the epinephrine and then the paddles. But he didn't respond."

"And when exactly did this all take place? And don't lie to me. I already know he was injured before you sent me to security. That's why you did it."

My head almost snapped back. There it was. Impatient, exacting, and annoyingly brilliant Dr. Ass. We both listened to the beeping of the EKG for a few minutes, while the nagging feeling chewed at my stomach. I finally mumbled an indifferent "Yeah." Cass folded her arms and stared me down, waiting.

What the hell was wrong with me? I intended to spill everything to the doctor who was looking after my dad. In fact, I intended to inundate that doctor with info. But the doctor was Dr. Ass.

She finally threw her hands off those bony hips and hissed, "Then what? Why? Why didn't you come to me? I'm the only one who could've helped him and instead you sent me to security. And the A . . ." She trailed off for a moment, absolutely furious. "His family is burying him today, thanks to you. They're probably suing." Her hiss was growing louder. "You trashed the lab and jeopardized everyone working on this project. Hell, you jeopardized the entire research park by going to the press. Why?" Her voice was surprisingly pleading.

I stared at the floor a full minute. It felt like an hour. In the end, all I could do was shrug. She let out a long—I mean LONG—exasperated sigh. She shook her head and picked up her clipboard. "Have you got any paper? Never mind, here." She yanked some sheets from the back of her clipboard and shoved them at me. "Write down what you did, as best you can remember. Every last detail, what his responses were, and when, and I'll see what I can do."

I didn't touch the paper. I refused to even look at her.

She read my inaction and got in my face. "Hemingway, you have to do this. Your father's not likely to live through the night. If we're lucky, and your memory's good enough then just maybe—I mean MAYBE—I can save him." She stood up again and opened the door.

I finally mumbled "Sorry," without directly addressing her. I meant the lab. The phone call. All of it.

She sagged momentarily and softened her tone. "I'm sorry about your dad. I will do everything in my power to save him. But this is bigger than just your dad, Hemingway. This is . . ." She trailed off for a moment. "I mean, it's just a start. Maybe. Potentially. Maybe it's nothing but something to rule out."

Snap. There it was. Her eyes gave it away—they were bright and feverish; the same look evangelicals have when they talk about heaven. She didn't want to save my dad so much as she wanted the information for her work. I shifted, uncomfortable.

She read my body language like I read her eyes.

Drawing herself up to her full height with a sniff, her voice grew cold. "You honestly think your father is the only person in the world entitled to that?"

I just stared at her. Same as I do when those evangelicals stand on my doorstep, trying to hand me some fiction reading.

Her tight mouth twitched with impatience. "I have to make a phone call, which means you need to leave this room." And just like that, she was back to barking orders. "Get out in the hall and get writing." She opened the door and stomped out.

The Kannapolis city cop returned to his post and flagged me from the doorway—I had to leave.

I moved to the lobby and flopped down on the sofa, spreading the papers over the generic oak coffee table. I wrote out the therapeutic hypothermia treatments I'd given him, the xenon, and tried to remember the order in which I'd attempted other things I'd only read about. But my memories of that night were as sour and slushy as a day-old milkshake.

My father's skin haunted me—he was absolutely ashen. So unnatural that it was hard to believe he'd ever return to a healthy pink. I looked at the notes. I thought of the A, and then all the A's. And all the B's. And then I thought of the dog.

It wasn't a big deal when I watched Cass zap rodent after rodent with an electrical prod, intent on killing them just so she could revive them. They were just lab rats, after all. I'm no PETA advocate. Please. You have to try this stuff out on *something* before you try it on humans.

But then Cass brought in the dog. Some sort of Australian shepherd mix with hardly any teeth, so I nicknamed her Flossie as I fed her in her cage, never really registering why she was there. I guess I knew, but there was only one way for me to work in that lab—with blinkers on my eyes and a blanket over my brain.

Don't get me wrong, it's not like I wanted to take this dog home. Flossie bit, every chance she got. Cleaning her cage required giving her sedatives. That's why she wasn't adopted from the pound. But she wasn't old, and she wasn't sick. She was just some nasty, mangy dog no one wanted. One day Cass brought her into the lab and handed me the electrical prod. She wanted me to kill the fucking dog, so she could try and revive it. I walked out without saying a word. Cass killed her anyway, while I was gone, and—big surprise—failed to bring her back. I know this because when Cass left for dinner, she told me to arrange biohazard disposal.

This was my shitty, shitty internship at the biotech research center. And I was gonna give her the keys to my DAD? You know what? The decision was surprisingly easy to make.

I looked at my notes and ripped 'em, again and again, until they were snow.

CHAPTER FIVE

I wandered down the hall of the ICU, headed for the elevator. I didn't even have to check the signs. My feet wandered these halls as knowingly as they did Concord High. Northeast Hospital was home when my mom was sick—nurses brought me supplies to do school projects and sent me to the lab techs for chemistry and math. Orderlies encouraged me to throw my laundry in with their rounds and, at a doctor's prompt, invited me to dinner in the cafeteria. (The docs always wanted me out of the room before they talked to my dad.)

My last day at the hospital was in June, two years ago—the day my mother died. The shift in my status was abrupt; they hugged and kissed me good-bye, assuring me I was on my way to great things, and then turned their backs on me to strip the bed. They weren't there for me anymore. They were there for the next kid whose mom or dad was dying rather than dead. None of them came to the funeral.

I'd been there so long that our house felt like a motel—just somewhere to sleep. Some cousins I barely knew came for the funeral and stayed a few days—that part was okay. But sitting down for dinner with just my dad a few days later felt like I'd lost more than just my mom. More like I'd lost my entire family in a plane crash. The adjustment was that sudden and catastrophic.

And now here I was again. For my dad.

It only occurred to me now that no one had so much as said hello to me since I walked into the hospital. Not that I'd said hello to anyone either, but c'mon, somebody had to know who I was. Or did they even recognize me? I'd grown, sure, but had I changed that much? And if I had, was the change in the last two years or in the last thirty-six hours?

Chanting interrupted my thoughts. Chanting and clapping.

Two girls were singing out. "CONCENTRATION," clap, clap, clap. "SIXTY-FOUR," clap, clap, clap. A jump-rope rhyme.

"NO REPEATS," clap, clap, clap. "OR HESITATION," clap, clap, clap.

I really don't know why I poked my head inside that room. I guess it was the song. Maybe I just felt like hearing a jump-rope rhyme.

Melissa was sitting on the edge of the hospital bed, clapping and singing with a kid that I guessed was her little sister. Her hair was hiding her face at first, but I recognized her instantly from school.

She'd been in my year. We'd had chorus together at school, but we'd only spoken a few times, just for group projects and stuff. Our lone encounter was when her car wouldn't start in the school parking lot. I tried to help her out, making a few adjustments until her dented little orange Element rumbled to life. Her voice caught while she was trying to thank me—this cute, tiny gulping sound. She'd rolled her eyes at herself, mumbled thanks, and taken off.

I heard she'd dropped out weeks later when some obsequious cheerleader stuck a sympathy card in my face and demanded I sign it. She mentioned that someone in the family was ill—terminally ill—but she didn't know any details and I didn't follow up. I didn't know it was her little sister.

I'd never really noticed Melissa at school. Maybe because so many of the girls at school were louder and flashier? Constantly drawing attention to themselves by flipping their hair, and wearing clothes that would occasionally expose a shoulder or a thigh? I can't really account for why I was so obtuse when she was so obviously beautiful, so I have no way of accounting for why she thunderstruck me the way she did that afternoon. Her wavy brown hair was down, her big hazel eyes tired but smiling at her little sister, her jeans and T-shirt loose, as if to say they were just clothes, functional and uninteresting. No knotting of the T-shirt in back, or colored bra strap teasing through an off-kilter shoulder, and no makeup. She had absolutely no affectation; so I'm sorry, there's no way to refute how beautiful she looked.

Her sister called out, "Barry!" Clap, clap, clap—I think you get the picture. They went back and forth a few more times—Kaitlyn, Lila, Patrick, and Punchy. I remember thinking that only in the South do you get credit for a name like Punchy.

Melissa watched her sister, and I watched her. There was this stormy gloom in the lines around her mouth and she held herself incredibly rigid on the edge of that bed.

Have you ever seen a tree after an ice storm? One that's been crystallized from top to trunk? They're so intractable in their frozen beauty that when you look at them, you sometimes forget there's something warm, wonderful, and vibrantly alive underneath. But when the sun comes out, the ice melts and those trees radiate giant sparkling prisms in every direction. That's the closest I can come to describing what she was doing to me at that particular moment.

I stood there staring at her so long that I forgot I wasn't supposed to be there. My cell beeped with a text message. That's when she looked over and saw me gawking in the doorway like a tool. She just said, "Can I help you?" She wasn't accusing or anything, but I felt like a dick, so I just mumbled, "Sorry, wrong room," and ran out.

The phone rang—Cass. "Get back here. Something's happening."

I took the stairs two at a time. I heard the sound of my dad's roaring as soon as I got to the ICU. I raced toward it, screaming, "What's happening? What's happening?"

The guard rose to get in my way, but his face was pale and his hands were shaky. He tried to formulate words, but they just wouldn't come. Through the door, I saw why.

The bandages around Dad's face had been removed. In the time I'd been gone, his skin had morphed from gray to black. Coal black. He looked like a piece of fruit that had been rotting in the sun for a week. I had no idea whether he was conscious of his screaming or not. His eyes were closed, and his arms and legs were immobile inside the Gaymar. Only his mouth moved, pain etched in the muscles. One of the techs went to adjust a dial and accidentally brushed against his hand. He leaped back like my dad's hand had some sort of deadly contagion.

Cass saw it too and barked at him, "Oh, get over it! And take it down! Take it down now!" Her words jolted the guy into action.

"Dad!" I shouted from the hallway. "I'm here. I'm right here!"

He screamed again.

Cass smacked her fist on the bedside table in frustration. She didn't even turn as she said, "Hemingway, SHUT UP. Sit your ass down in the hallway. Do not move." She finally turned and looked at the guard. "Make sure he stays there, all right? No trips to the bathroom, no cafeteria visits, NOTHING." She turned back to the nurses. "Now someone shut that goddamn door."

The door slammed in my face three seconds later.

I turned around, only noticing Charlie there for the first time. He was sitting on the floor, his face bleached, hands fluttering nervously. He reminded me of a moth on the wrong side of a window. I wasn't even sure he saw me. I sank to the floor next to him.

He struggled to find words. "What's wrong—"

"I don't know, but thanks for coming."

What had I done? I briefly wondered if Dad's body was dead, only his brain didn't know it yet.

He screamed again and we both rattled like marbles in a bag, sinking lower to the floor. For half an hour, we flinched and shook with every one, until they slowly faded to the pitiful wails of a gull. That was way worse because I didn't even recognize the sound as belonging to my dad.

I let them rip right into me. Gut me. I wanted to hurt. You want to know why? Because in all the movies, and in the newspaper stories you read, the families that love the sick person eventually pray for them to die, be released from all that pain. Not me. Not once. I didn't so much as telepath an idle thought encouraging him to let go. If anything, I was sending him screams of my own like a coach on a football field—to fight his way through it. To stay here, with me, no matter how much pain he was in. I was willing to share the pain, not absorb it all.

Cass finally came out, spotted me, and charged over. "Are you satisfied? Do you have something for me now?"

Took me a minute to register what she was asking. She wanted my report, my summary of what I'd done, to my dad. I looked up at her. And you know, at that moment, if I had written down what she asked earlier, I would've handed it to her. But I'd ripped that up, and—for once—my voice was gone. My mouth moved, but no sound came out.

Cass took my response as further stonewalling and stomped off down the hall.

He started up again a short while later. Cass ran in again, followed by a crew of doctors, nurses, and techs. I sat on my ass. And that's how it went. For hours. An otherworldly roar, followed by screams and finally wails. And then silence.

I still hear them sometimes.

The whole thing was so terrifying it started drawing staff from other floors. Around eleven o'clock, some nurse poked her head around the corner to ask her ICU friend in a loud whisper, "Is it true?" The ICU nurse yanked her arm to go another six feet down the hall. She tossed her head in the direction of Charlie and me as justification for the detour. Flushed whispers and widened eyes constantly floated back to me. As if I couldn't hear what they were saying. If Dad was a demon like they were saying, then hell's made of ice, not fire. Because Cass kept trying to warm him back up to normal temperature, and that's when the screaming would start. Even the room couldn't be more than fifty-five degrees.

Another voice rang out in the hall, interrupting them. The nurses slunk off as someone slid to the floor next to me. I glanced over—Melissa. I was too stunned to say anything.

"Hey, sorry about when you came into my sister's room. Just didn't expect you there, that's all. I asked around after you left. They said your dad's here. I can't stay long, but I thought maybe you could use some company. All right if I stay?"

I think I fell in love with her, right then and there.

Charlie shot a hand out across me to Melissa. "I'm Charlie."

Melissa shook it. "Melissa."

"Are you and Hemingway—"

I cut him off. "What did you say to those nurses?"

She shrugged. "I mentioned how some of the nurses on my floor were complaining about a surprise review. Made it sound like I was tipping them off. I've used it before." Her eyes lowered. "I am incredibly grateful for everything the doctors and nurses in this hospital do for my sister. Most of the time, they're wonderful. But I really hate when they forget we're here and talk about the patients like we're all deaf."

At midnight Dad started again. Melissa jolted with the sound, righted herself, and bowed her head, her eyes closed, her mouth moving. I finally realized she was praying. For Dad. Awkward—I mean, I appreciated the hell out of her intention, and I hoped it would help. But I'm an unbeliever, like Dad, so I wasn't sure if I should join in. Would that make that big Santa in the sky—happy? Or mad? I wanted whatever was best for Dad. (And by the way, to this day, I don't have an answer on this issue, so ping me if you know.)

I finally just decided to bow my head out of respect for her religion, but not pray.

The neurologist came out an hour later. He looked at us hesitantly, as if he was uncertain whether or not it was his job to fill us in. I rolled my eyes, knowing Cass had massively upended the natural order.

"We've induced a coma, so he won't feel the hypothermia. He's stable for now; I'll be back in the morning for a consultation. She said you could go in. One at a time."

I leaped to my feet. Melissa stood up and said, "I should go. Get back to Lila's room. But I'll stop by tomorrow, okay?"

I nodded, not really wanting her to leave. I finally choked out, "Thanks for coming. Means a lot." She nodded and walked off down the hall. Meanwhile, Charlie was taking his time getting up. I looked at him expectantly, wondering what the hell was wrong. We'd waited here for hours. We could finally go in and he was shuffling around like he was trying to come up with an excuse not to.

The realization slapped me in the face. That was it, wasn't it? He was scared. Even a mortician was scared to look at my dad.

I looked at the neurologist for relief. "His color. Is it—?"

"I'm afraid there's no change. We won't know more till the morning." He hustled away.

Charlie refused to meet my eyes. He just said, "Uh, look, Hem. This is really a family thing, and technically, I'm not family. I'll just wait for you in the car, 'kay? Give you a lift home."

I planted my eyes on the ceiling, furious with him. And me. Because the truth was, I didn't want to go in either.

I pushed the door open. The lights had been dimmed to an after-hours emergency glow, while the noticeable chill stung any exposed inch of my skin.

I eyeballed the ravaged form of my dad. You know, something cancerous had formed in my stomach the first time I saw him discolored to an ashen gray. Now that feeling swelled to the size of a grapefruit. I'd been so focused on hating myself for the accident, that I hadn't given much thought to what I'd done in the lab. I only thought I'd made some kind of medical discovery, one I had to keep secret from Cass. But the thing in my stomach oozed a different truth: that wasn't a medical discovery. It was an aberration.

He looked otherworldly—a Halloween exhibit in a haunted house. His skin suggested meat long forgotten on a grill and reduced to carbon. The gray was so uniform it was difficult to recognize where his eyebrows left off and his forehead began. The only contrast in color was his fingernails, which were now the gelatinous yellow of an eighty-year-old. He groaned, low and throaty, the skin on his throat reverberating with the effort.

Cass stared at me and said, "I want to show you something." With a touch more delicate than I'd imagined she had, she peeled back my father's eyelid to show me the whites of his eyes—they'd yellowed as well, viscous and glowing in their sockets. I gagged.

"They're both that way," she said coolly, as she released his eyelid and adjusted the monitors. "He can't take either fluids or food, even on an IV. He's produced no urine since he got here. His blood samples continue to defy medical science. He can't tolerate temperatures higher than fifty-five degrees without going into a painful frenzy, as you heard." She folded her arms and stared me down. "Hemingway. I know you love your father and you would never deliberately hurt him. I haven't told the police anything except that. But I think it's time to tell me exactly what you've done."

And what had I done? I had no idea. It wasn't medical science; I knew that much. Not even close. Because medical science is reserved for human beings, and my father wasn't human. Not anymore. I hadn't saved his life, as I'd originally thought. He'd died, and I'd refused to let him go. I'd taken him to a lab. Conducted experiments. Or were they spells? I didn't know anything about witchcraft but based on the way my dad looked, I was pretty sure what I'd done was more akin to necromancy than medicine. But if that was true—if what'd I done wasn't medical science—did I owe a doctor an explanation?

I wanted to tell her. Well, not her, because I didn't think she could bring him back to the man he'd been. I wasn't even sure she'd want to, and that was the biggest problem. But I wanted to tell someone. Some adult. Let them handle it rather than me. But the unnamable thing in my stomach rumbled in protest and the words, "*He's not human, he's not human,*" just kept drumming in my head. But he was my dad. And he was in horrible pain that I potentially had the power to stop. I met her gaze. "Try hydrogen sulfide instead of oxygen. And let's see what happens in the morning."

Charlie and I didn't say a word, even as we loaded my bike into the back, or in the car, even as we pulled into the gravel driveway we shared. Just in case you're wondering, my house is nothing impressive. While it's a modest 1940s airplane bungalow, the white paint is dirty gray and peeling off the columns, the porch sags from wood rot, and there are even a few gaps in the floorboards that look like an old man's missing front teeth. While it's true my dad can fix anything, that doesn't mean he always does. Cobbler's son has no shoes, right? The only thing Dad takes care of is my mom's roses, which line the driveway all the way to the curb.

And no, the place didn't provide me a moment's relief, even as Charlie followed me up to the kitchen door and I fumbled for the keys. Because I wasn't sure I knew the people who lived here anymore.

I pushed the door open, flipped on the light and stared in shock.

Now, I knew the house had been searched—I'd seen that much when I'd stopped off to change my clothes. But they'd obviously been back—the whole house looked like it'd thrown up.

Dad and I aren't exactly tidy. You'll always find a sweatshirt or towel tossed over the ratty sofa in the living room, maybe an abandoned cereal bowl on the coffee table. And paperwork in stacks on the floor—one mine and one his—maybe a few coffee mugs and wrappers strewn across the desk. But we aren't hamsters in a cage, either.

And that's what the house looked like now. Every cabinet in the kitchen had been emptied, all the pots and plates dumped on the kitchen table and left. In the living room, every drawer of the desk and sideboard was open and disheveled, papers streaming out. The computer was gone, while the closet under the stairs was burping up jackets and tools. Crossing to check out his bedroom, my feet kicked what used to be our junk drawer—unopened bills my dad couldn't pay, newspapers, notes from school that still needed my dad's signature. They all had dirty footprints across them. The worst part was when I kicked the glass and saw they'd broken my mom's crystal display in the front window. There'd be hell to pay if and when my dad caught up with them.

"Holy shit," Charlie muttered. "Forget about it for now. Go to bed," he urged.

I climbed the stairs to my gabled bedroom, the lone room upstairs in our tiny house. This one was the worst, as they'd taken apart the bed, the closet, pretty much everything.

Charlie shouted up the stairs after me. "You've got court in the morning. Hey, you want me to stay over? I can sleep on the couch."

I went back downstairs, flopped into the armchair, and put my head in my hands. Was there any part of my dad's life I hadn't ruined in a single weekend? The saddest part of it was that despite all I'd done, I knew he'd forgive me. Instantly. He'd still want me around. He'd still need me. And I needed him too.

I shook my head at Charlie. "Afraid I'm going to need the couch myself. They ripped up my mattress."

Charlie nodded quietly and headed toward the door.

The cell rang just as I got comfortable on the sofa. He didn't even wait for me to say hello. "You tested positive for THC," Burkhardt informed me. "As in, pot."

"We're already up to pillow talk? I must be a cheap date. You haven't even bought me dinner."

He paused. "Kannapolis cops can't find your dad's truck." He let the words hang in the air while I sifted through my foggy brain, attempting to process what that meant. He reminded me, "You told us your dad came to pick you up at the research center and that he had a heart attack once he was inside. They're trying to verify your story, only they can't, because your dad's truck isn't anywhere in the parking lot."

Got it. No truck meant that my story about my dad's collapse was a lie. If they found the truck, they could match my dad's injury to the dent in the passenger's-side roof. They would know my dad had been injured before I'd brought him to the research center. And they'd know he was in the passenger seat, which meant I'd been driving. Under the influence. The charges would escalate to homicide.

Burkhardt interrupted my train of thought like he'd been listening to it rumble past. "They find a wrecked truck, there won't be any bail, which means no sitting by a hospital bed." My hand started shaking, but I didn't say anything. He sighed and continued: "I can still help you. This isn't my investigation—it's Kannapolis's. But if you happen to tell me—as an officer of the law—what really happened, I can probably make sure they see it in the right light. The accident, I mean. I'm pretty sure it was an accident. Was it?"

I was tempted to tell him, right up to the point where he pulled that crap. *Was it*? Please. Like he's Perry Mason and I'm the dumb asshole that'll just slip up. I summoned my nerve. "Listen, I don't know where my dad parked the frigging truck. I wasn't *in* the truck, remember? Maybe he parked on the street. Or maybe it got stolen. You're a cop. You find it."

"Stolen, huh?" He paused. "Guess I should start a case file then."

"Guess you should." I heard him shuffle some paper around. I continued: "Thanks for redecorating the house, by the way. Very thoughtful. I particularly liked the way you guys wiped out my mom's crystal collection."

"Kid, I wasn't there. You know the license plate number?"

"I'm guessing you already have it." I hung up on him, furious and scared.

Sleep was now just about impossible. I flipped the pillow about a thousand times, reminding myself I needed to be clearheaded the next day. No-go.

In desperation, I granted myself one little extravagance: I thought of Melissa. I didn't have any right to think about her because I barely knew her. I mean, she was just being nice showing up that night because we'd gone to school together. But I was still in awe that she'd come—and stayed—when anyone else would've run away at Dad's first roar.

Despite everything I had going on, I could still see her sitting on the bed with her little sister, like a favorite photograph taped to the dashboard of my brain. I experimented with a waking dream that everything would turn out fine, that one day she'd be standing in my front yard, pruning my mom's roses while Dad and I worked on the porch. I got absolutely punch drunk just thinking about it and finally slept the blank nothingness that only drunks sleep.

CHAPTER SIX

It was still dark when I woke up, so the flickering candles that illuminated the flowers and cards outside caught my attention from the window. People had been by to pay their respects to my dad. That was the best that Concord had to offer: a community of people always eager to ooze all over you when your family suffered a catastrophe, while they quietly celebrated the fact it had happened to you and not them. Still, my dad might want to know that people cared. I dug around on the floor of my room and found a pair of jeans.

I opened the front door and was startled when I heard something tear. Two halves of a newspaper article, taped to either side of the door, dangled and flapped in the brisk spring breeze. I yanked both ends off the doorway and pieced them back together.

My picture was once again on the front page, only this time they'd used a long shot; I was being physically hauled from the research center in cuffs. My hair was matted, and my clothes were filthy. Lisa's headline read HERO OR HOMICIDE? Not difficult to guess what the paper thought—I looked absolutely mental. Guess Lisa didn't appreciate me lying to her and skipping out on the interview. I scanned it.

Yesterday, I'd been a hero trying to save his father's life. In today's paper, I was potentially a deranged murderer. Burkhardt had been telling the truth—the missing truck was grounds for Kannapolis Police to doubt my story. The police chief suggested I'd deliberately hurt my father. They also cited the neurologist's preliminary report, which stated my father's head injury was inconsistent with a fall.

The predawn breeze slapped my bare chest like a wet towel. Someone had taped this to the door so I'd see it. I'd no idea why. I crumpled up the article and tossed it to the ground. Folding my arms, I headed to the curb to read the cards.

One insipid Hallmark sentiment after another: "He is with you," and "In your time of need." Inside were sentiments to me—some called me a hero, some encouraged me to consult my savior for guidance, others offered the names of lawyers. They weren't a totally delusional bunch—there were a few sentient individuals who told me I should be locked up for the rest of my life. Those were from my dad's contractor friends. They never liked me anyway—all the more reason to appreciate them.

I tossed the cards back in a heap and headed inside to shower and dress for court.

When I came downstairs, Charlie had already walked through the door and was eating a bowl of cereal. "Morning. You might want to eat something before we go to court."

I started to protest. "I don't need anyone at court with me."

"You. Need. Someone. At. Court." Something flashed across his face. "I'll take you to court and ask the questions I need answered. Make sure you lawyer up. Isn't that what they say?" I shrugged and he continued: "Then I'll drop you by the hospital on my way to work." He dumped his bowl in the sink and declared, "We gotta get moving."

He wouldn't meet my eyes. It was a subtle change from the night before, but last night everything had been about Dad. Today was about me. And the law. The laws I'd broken, with his help. I'd used him, jeopardized his whole career. And he knew it.

I pushed my chair away from the table. "I'm coming."

Charlie turned to head out and tripped on some CDs. "This place looks like a street in Kherson."

"Yeah, watch where you're going. As you can see, I just cleaned."

We fought our way to the door, Charlie muttering, "I made sure they were being careful. The cops, I mean. I didn't have any say about whether they came in, they had a subpoena, and it's not my house. But I did stay as long as I could. And they were careful until I left for work." He was still muttering about the wreckage as we climbed in his hearse.

When we pulled out of the driveway, Charlie finally broached the subject. "They asked me if I knew where your dad's truck is." He glanced over at me, but I kept my eyes on the road. "You know, it's weird. Friday, you told me you'd wrecked the truck and you were headed to the research center, and you were going to try and fix it. All of sudden, your dad's in the hospital, you're in jail, and the truck is nowhere to be found." He waited a long minute, but I still wouldn't even look at him. "Hem. I haven't told them anything. But you need to be honest with me about what happened."

My mouth tightened. "You're better off not knowing."

Charlie spluttered, "Better off? How?" He yanked the car to the curb and started yelling. "And who the hell do you think you are? Huh? You did what you did, you involved me, and you want to decide what it's safe for me to know? Now, where's the goddamn truck?"

I took a deep breath and answered him truthfully. "I don't know." Which was true. I didn't know what Todd had done with the truck. But I made a mental note to ask.

Charlie slapped his hands on the steering wheel in frustration and started the car again. "Fine. That's just great. Don't expect me to cover your ass."

I interrupted him coldly: "If it's just your precious hide you're so worried about, relax. I'll say I stole your pass. In fact, I'll plead guilty to that one right off the bat."

Now he exploded. "OH JUST SHUT IT." He slammed the car into a space by the courthouse and climbed out without looking at me again.

Court was surprisingly no big deal. I was assigned a lawyer—some skinny dude with too little hair wearing a suit about three sizes too big—and that was about it. More dates were set, but the lawyer told me not to worry, he planned to ask for as many continuances as he could get.

One little nugget he had to say stood out—about the tox screen.

"Why'd you consent to that?"

"Deputy told me I didn't have any choice. He said something about implied consent."

"Implied consent is purely for cases where the defendant was driving a vehicle. You weren't, were you?"

I leaned forward, my words slicing the air. "No. I wasn't."

He flipped through some papers and squinted at something. "Well," he drawled, "he's listed it as suspicion of driving under the influence. Means he thinks you were driving, but he doesn't have any proof. It's a gray area, but as long as they can't find that truck, there's nothing to argue. I might get that tox screen thrown out. Seeing as you're a minor."

I had half a mind to walk across the street to the sheriff's office and punch Burkhardt in the nose. He was right and all—I had been driving—but all that nice-guy-just-doing-a-job stuff was crap. He'd lied to me.

"Let's just direct all the deputy's calls to me from now on, shall we? And no talking to the papers either."

I just nodded a lot, wanting all this over so I could get to the hospital. Charlie was frustrated. He tried to ask a few questions, but the lawyer-guy just said he had to be back in court, and we should set an appointment with his secretary.

Heading to the car to get to the hospital, two things happened: first, I saw Todd being led into the sheriff's office across the street. He wasn't cuffed, but he didn't look like he was taking a school field trip either. Burkhardt spotted me and waved, while Todd gave me a look of utter panic. At the same time, the phone rang. Cass.

"Your father's awake," she told me curtly. And hung up.

I hung up and looked at Charlie in utter amazement. "He's awake."

Charlie shouted, "Get in the car!"

As we rode to the hospital, my own thoughts whizzed around noisily, talking over each other so much that they were hard to hear. Bill Jones was awake. Talking? Sentient? I had no idea. In any case, he wasn't a vegetable on a machine.

The next thought wiped the smile right off my face—if he's talking, what's he saying? What would I say to him? How much should I tell him about what I'd done? I didn't mean about the accident—I was going to tell him exactly how I killed him. But what should I say about the lab? How would he feel about that? Dad didn't believe in heaven, but even death was—in some sense at least—a way to be with my mom. Which is where he wanted to be. And I'd selfishly dragged him back.

What did he look like? Had his skin lightened in recovery? Had his eyes whitened? Would he look more like his old self? If he looked as sinister as he did yesterday, what would he say about that? What would I say?

A final thought made my entire body shudder—what if he'd changed? Mentally, I mean, as well as physically? What if the person in Bill Jones's body wasn't my dad?

I finally decided to embrace my happiness: I had a dad again. I wasn't alone. He was the adult, which meant I got to be the kid again. He could make whatever decisions needed to be made.

Charlie dropped me by the cafeteria, and I hit the stairs two at a time, zigzagging around the doctors, nurses, gurneys, and wheelchairs in my path. When I got to Room 609, the guard rose, his hand up in protest. I'd forgotten about him.

"Oh come on!" I shouted, knowing I would interrupt the murmuring voices of doctors inside the room. "He's my dad! Get the hell out of the way!"

It worked. Cass popped her head out the door and waggled a finger at me. "He's asking for you."

I dashed in. Everybody turned to stare at me. Everyone except Dad. I could see his open eye in profile—still yellow—and I wondered why he didn't turn his head. I ran up to the bedside. "Oh thank God. Thank God! You're here! Hah! You're here!"

He was a pale shade of gray as I approached the bed, but that was an improvement from the day before. His face was contorted with effort—he'd obviously been trying to turn his head but couldn't. His eyes were full of confusion, while his mouth was moving uncontrollably—opening, shutting, and shaking. Took me a full minute to remember he was still on the Gaymar and therefore suffering from hypothermia. He finally stuttered out, "Hemmay."

I'd never been so glad to hear my name in all my life. It's the name my mother gave me, after her favorite writer. Growing up, teachers always oohed and aahed over it, which ensured I was going to get beaten up after school. I always insisted on Hem, but today, Hemingway sounded awesome. I'd have taken a beating from every bully in the county, just to hear it again. Because it meant that my dad was still my dad—his brain was intact.

I interrupted Cass's whispered discussions with the neurologist. "He's cold! He's absolutely freezing. Can we start to dial this thing up?"

She scorched a look at me. "Hemingway, I realize you've been playing doctor for a while now, but please try to remember that you aren't one. You're not here for a consultation. You're here to visit with your dad."

All I could think was *Welcome back, Dr. Ass.* I'm sorry, but I wanted to deck her. All her fancy degrees and what the hell did she know? I'd done what she couldn't, even if, to be fair, she didn't know the full extent of what I'd done. Still, I had to prove myself. I asked calmly, "Can't he at least get the meperidine now? Might help with the shivering."

The neurologist's eyebrows lifted in surprise. Cass's frown absorbed her whole face. She turned to the technician. "What's the status of his NMBs?" The tech handed her a chart. She reviewed it and said quietly, "Twelve and a half milligrams of meperidine every four to six hours."

I was doing my best to hide it, but I bet she read the smug satisfaction on my face.

My dad was still looking at me expectantly and I wondered what to say with all these doctors around. I leaned over him and whispered, "We had an accident. I brought you here. I'll tell you everything later. Right now, you need all your strength just to get well. So go back to sleep."

I could tell he was trying to shake his immobilized head and I almost laughed out loud. He was protesting—pure, unadulterated Bill Jones. He was himself.

Cass tapped me on the shoulder. "Visiting hours are over for now. We have to run some tests. Please just go wait for me in the lobby."

I leaned over my dad and kissed his forehead. "I'll be back as soon as I can."

I paced around the lobby until Dad's phone rang. I checked the number: Concord High School. I answered, "Yeah."

"Mr. Jones? This is Quincy Blackwelder from the front office at Concord High. We spoke on Friday?" I said nothing, and she finally continued: "Yes, well, we have Hemingway down as an unexcused absence again. Is he home ill?"

"No, his grandmother died again."

She started to say "I'm sorry for your—" but paused, finally registering what I'd said.

I hung up. This was exactly why school was a waste of time. I mean, school's supposed to be about reading, right? And here's someone from administration, basically admitting she hasn't so much as glanced at the front page of a newspaper in three days.

Still. Only dawned on me right then that I wasn't going back. Either I was going to be home, caring for my dad, or getting my GED in jail. The realization freaked me out. I'd never liked school, but I never saw myself becoming a "high-school dropout" either.

My dad—the version of him that lives in my head—chimed in instantly, "Maybe you don't like school now, but you might like to have the option of college later." Smart man. I finally understood what he'd meant. Now that it was too late.

I felt a set of claws pinching my arm. Cass pulled me into a corner and said, "The next time you question my authority in that room will be your last. You're only there because I got you past that guard. So, if I stop, the next time you'll see him is once he's released. Do I make myself clear?"

"I was just—" I stared at the carpeting. She had a point. She'd helped me, and I'd paid her back by embarrassing her. I sighed and said, "Crystal."

"Good. Now. Tell me about the hydrogen sulfide."

"You used it?"

"In a word, yes. And he woke up an hour later. How did you know that would work?"

"I didn't. But I'd given him some in the lab. To stop him from bleeding out." I gestured to my head.

Her voice was leading, probing. "Okaaay, then what did you do?"

I opened my mouth and closed it again several times. She threw up her hands in exasperation. "You're not going to start this shit again now, are you? Really?"

I folded my arms across my chest and met her eyes. "Well, why do you want to know?"

Irritation spread across her face like a rash. "Legally, I could recuse myself from your father's treatment, Hemingway. But I won't because I'm his best chance in this redneck hospital. I have no such allegiance to you. I don't care if you're here while he's healing or not, but I'm guessing you care. And I'm guessing your dad does too." She waited, but I said nothing. "A detective from the sheriff's office was asking me about your missing truck. I seem to recall you telling me you'd had a car accident on Friday. Wonder what he'd say to that."

This time I froze.

"Wise up, and start being honest with me. And me only." She stalked off.

Cass didn't give a rat's ass if I'd killed my dad or not. The only extant information, as far as she was concerned, was that he'd died and I'd brought him back and I wouldn't tell her how. She was willing to threaten me for the information. The worst part was she *could* threaten me. My dad needed her equipment, supplies, and care. I needed my freedom to be with him, and she had that in her possession too.

She could basically manipulate both of us any way she wanted.

But I couldn't help myself. I shouted after her down the hall. "You want honesty? Fine. I think the military is for morons that don't have money. I think Ironman competitions are for morons that do have money. And you should probably give up on flat ironing your hair, because you never get the back."

CHAPTER SEVEN

The hydrogen sulfide worked. I—not Cass—had revived my dad.

Hydrogen sulfide's a gas that has the potential to achieve suspended animation in humans. A dose of the gas, chill 'em down, and it'll bind to all the places oxygen does in the human body. And for a time, that person will look dead, not requiring oxygen, water, or food. But they're not dead— they're more like a hibernating bear. I'd given my dad some at the lab because of his head injury. I didn't want him to bleed out on the table or en route to the hospital.

Anyway, the stuff metabolizes incredibly quickly. At least it usually does. That's why I hadn't thought of it when he first got to the hospital: I'd assumed it was gone from his system. But what if the stuff had modified his chemical makeup in some way? And what if I couldn't modify it back?

I stumbled off to the cafeteria, trying to put a finger on why I wouldn't just tell Cass everything. I had no idea why I was still balking. I really didn't. She was my dad's doctor; he was in pain. Why didn't I just spill and tell her everything?

The answer fell into my head: because something was off at Lifebank. Way off. Something bigger than just killing feral dogs. I knew that before the accident. And whatever it was, I didn't want to be involved. And I certainly didn't want my dad involved either.

I mentioned the A's and the B's. Here's what I knew. Lifebank has a limited number of cryogenic vaults, and those were for the A's. The A's are wealthy old guys, friends of Calhoun, the billionaire who owned Lifebank and the research center. They'd booked their crypts years ago, so when they died, they'd be prepped and stored at Lifebank until the company had the capacity to bring them back to life. I saw their bodies come in, I saw them prepped and placed in the fridge. Part of my job was even returning their Armani suits to their families.

The B's were more mysterious. Unlike the white and wealthy A's, who'd lived plump, full lives, the B's were every color, creed, and age. The only thing they had in common was the fact they all looked like five miles of bad road. The protocols were completely different too—dosages, treatments, everything. I never saw where their bodies were stored, and unlike the A's, I was allowed to put a B's cheap personal possessions in the incinerator.

That's why I wouldn't tell Cass anything. She had secrets of her own. I didn't want any part of it—not before the accident, and certainly not now. That might obligate me to *do* something, and frankly, I had enough to do. But even if I told Cass how I'd treated my dad, I sensed that I'd somehow enable her in a way I shouldn't. A way that would come back and bite me in the ass.

On the other hand, without her and Lifebank, I'd be an orphan right now. Dad would be gone. I'd done this, not her. Both of us understood that much. The difference was that I didn't want to repeat the experiment, and I could tell she did. She didn't—couldn't—know the emotional price I'd paid for reviving my dad already. What it felt like to wonder, what if he never looks any different than he does now? How will people treat him? How will he live? I would be responsible for his care, sure, but I'd be in pain for every rejection he felt too. Right now, she was fixated on the fact that I'd gotten a positive result in the experiment. She wasn't seeing what I was seeing. The revival itself—in her eyes—was the end of the story. And even then, I knew it wasn't. And for a moment, I wished I'd never gotten her involved. I didn't need any of her problems, and she didn't need any of mine.

Charlie called while I was in line buying coffee. "How's your dad?"

I deliberated what to say, remembering the shock on his face the night before. "He's awake and he's conscious. We still got a long way to go, but I'm hopeful."

"That's great, wish him my best, would you? Hey, I'm over at your house. Thought I'd help you guys out and give this place a cleanup."

He'd opted to clean our house, rather than visit his best friend—my dad—in the hospital. I decided not to comment on it.

"Thanks," I fumbled, handing the cashier a couple of bucks.

"Yeah, well don't get too excited. Power's out. They uh, cut you guys off. I guess the bill was overdue?"

I swore under my breath. "How much do they want?"

"Like four hundred bucks. Hem, I've got like a hundred bucks until next Wednesday, when I get my next paycheck. Is there anywhere you can think of where I might find some money?"

"Nothing that's going to solve the problem today," I answered. "I can cash in my college fund, but that'll take like a week, at least. You think there's any chance they'll cut us a break?" He laughed, and I scowled. "Yeah, I know, dumb question."

I held the coffee in one hand while I used my head to pin the phone to my shoulder. My eyes scoured the cafeteria for a place to sit. I repeated myself, just to let him know I was still there. "Let's see, where can we get four hundred bucks to get the lights switched back on?"

"Campus Christian Ministries." I spun around, sloshing hot coffee all over my hand.

"Hey." Melissa was looking at me with this irritatingly friendly expression that let me know I had absolutely no effect on her whatsoever. At least, nothing akin to the cataclysmic effect she'd had on me the day before.

I shook coffee off my hand. "Hi."

"Sorry I didn't make it your way this morning. Lila's had all kinds of tests."

"That's okay," I fumbled.

Charlie was confused. "Who're you talking to?" I ignored him.

Melissa scribbled the name and a phone number on the back of an envelope and held it up. "Campus Christian Ministries. It's a charity."

My back arched and my stomach roiled at the word "charity." Beyond my visceral reaction to the word, there was a secondary panic she'd think I was some kind of freeloading loser. Not exactly the kind of guy that a girl will eagerly say "yes" to when he asks her out on a date. I waved off the piece of paper. "Oh, ah, thanks, but no. I think I've got this one."

She shrugged and continued holding up the piece of paper. "They helped me when the gas company cut us off." She gestured to the cafeteria table as evidence, where she'd mounded a pile of windowed envelopes with red FINAL NOTICE stamps on them. "I've been doing this for my parents for the last six months. Anyway, whoever you're talking to on the phone might appreciate it. Didn't they just lose power?"

I reluctantly took the piece of paper just as Charlie shouted a final, "'Kay, you obviously have that cute girl's attention. I can hear her, so I'm gonna go. Let me know if you hook up." I hung up, hoping Melissa hadn't heard his parting line.

I looked again at the mound of bills. "What're you doing—ranking those?"

She nodded without looking up, so I just decided to carry on the conversation by myself. "By due date or priority?"

A somber smile escaped her frustrated mouth. "Oh, it's so much more complicated than that. This pile's gone to debt collection," she said, gently patting them. She pointed to a smaller pile and said, "These keep my sister's medical insurance going." She looked up at me and shrugged again. "I'm well past worrying about what people think of me for using charities. If I can't use them when I need them, what good are they?"

I grimaced. "Okay, okay. I admit it. It's my house and they've cut off the power." I stuck my hands in my pockets. "I'm new at this. My dad . . ." I shut my mouth, unwilling to blame him for the power bill.

She started gathering up her stuff. "So was I. Does he have disability insurance?"

I shook my head, feeling like a kid. What the hell is disability insurance, anyway?

Melissa continued, "How about power of attorney?"

I admitted, "I know absolutely nothing about anything practical or useful."

Melissa grabbed another discarded envelope and wrote on it. "Here. My parents spend all their time either working or looking after my little sister, so I've had to take over a bunch of this stuff. She's getting moved to a hospital in Raleigh tomorrow, so I won't be back till the weekend. But if you need help with something, just give me a call."

She was leaving. Panic set in—I wanted her to stay. "Thanks. How is your sister?" I couldn't remember her name.

Melissa filled in the word. "Lila."

"I'm sorry."

"Me too. Thanks, though." Her voice grew soft and apologetic. "I really have to go." She wrapped the bills in rubber bands and stuffed them into a huge black backpack.

I called after her. "Melissa? Thanks. For hanging out last night, I mean. Meant a lot." Weak, but I couldn't come up with anything else.

Nevertheless, the barest hint of a smile showed on her face. "It's okay."

When I got back to Room 609, I spotted a wreath of lilies leaning against my dad's door. Funeral flowers. Someone had left a wreath of funeral flowers for my dad. Useless the Guard was nowhere to be found. I grabbed the wreath and barged through the door.

Dad was asleep. Cass's mouth opened—probably to tell me to go away—but I held up the wreath. "You know anything about this?" Her brow wrinkled in confusion, so I tossed the card at her. Inside was a lone line of scripture: "A stone of stumbling, and a rock of offense. They stumble because they disobey the word, as they were destined to do."

For once, we actually shared a reaction—fury. She glanced toward the door. "Guard's gone," I informed her, but my tone implied blame.

"Stay here," she ordered and marched down the hall.

I sucked in my lips and glanced at Dad. He just lay there, grayed and diminished in the Gaymar, utterly helpless. Any deranged Bible thumper could walk right in and hurt him. And what the hell could I do about it? I felt like a hamster some kid had shoved in a microwave—pressure was mounting, I was about to be blood and furry guts, and there wasn't a dammed thing I could do about any of it. I couldn't so much as take Dad home and crank up the air-conditioning—we didn't have any power. We had no money. I didn't even have a job.

I heard Cass's officious voice thundering down the hall, the guard mumbling some pathetic response. She yanked open the door and met my eyes. "Guard's back. I'm sorry that happened. It won't happen again. Now you need to leave. Unless you have something to contribute?" She planted her cold, airy eyes on me and waited. Her message was clear: unless I started talking about how I'd revived my dad, I served no purpose. I thought about arguing, but I finally shook my head and waved good-bye, knowing she had no intention of letting me back in the room the rest of the day.

My phone beeped with a text: *COME OVR*.

Todd. Considering all he'd done on Friday night, and where he'd been today, I wasn't exactly in a position to refuse.

Riding out Gold Hill, I got to the top and forced myself to look back at the gulch where I'd wrecked. Muddy tire prints, diluted by rain, were barely visible. The knee-deep, seaweed-like vines of kudzu were just starting to leaf—once they bloomed they'd canopy the spot. The rain and creek bed would take care of the rest.

High stratus clouds drifted overhead, wafting occasional and other-worldly sunbeams on the wild azaleas that I suddenly realized were in full bloom. When had that happened? I glanced across the fields. Daffodils were nodding their silly yellow heads, dogwoods were pregnant with blooms, and the air was fragrant with wisteria. Spring was already here. First time in my life I'd missed its arrival.

Todd was sitting on the wooden deck outside his parents' trailer when I rode up. At the sight of me he stood up and paced, only to sit down again like he couldn't find a way to get comfortable.

I prompted him as I rode up. "Hey. Saw you with Detective Burkhardt."

"He found me." He looked away. "How's your dad?"

"Don't ask."

He nodded again and said, "My mom's praying for him."

That was the South. Everybody has prayers for you. Even trailer dwellers like Todd's emotionally devoid parents. His mom was probably going to make a casserole. For some reason, Southerners think they're a cure-all.

An opossum's tail disappeared into the astilbe, and Todd started again. "Look man, I . . ."

I held up a hand to gently cut him off. "Do what you have to do. Show them the truck. Tell them I lied to you, or say that I dumped it. Tell them whatever you want to tell them. I'll back you up. My dad won't lie when they get around to asking him, so I don't expect you to either."

He snorted. "Is that why you think I called? Dude!" He exploded. "My parents have been pot farmers my whole life. You think they taught me to talk to cops?"

"Todd, be serious. They think I killed him on purpose. That's attempted murder. At some point, they're going to find the truck. If you lie now, you'll be on the hook as an accomplice, and for obstruction, and a whole lot of other stuff."

He laughed. "I already lied. And they ain't ever gonna find the truck, man."

"Where is it?"

"It's . . . in a safe place." He grinned, which only made me worry. Todd's the best friend I've ever had, but not because he's bright. He continued, "I can handle the cops. And just so you know, I told them your dad came by on Friday, but you'd already left for the research center. Nah, I'm not worried about that."

"So what are you worried about?"

Todd's eyes bugged. "You really don't know?" I shook my head and he exploded again, this time in agony. "Your dad! I'm . . ." He sucked in a breath. "He was dead, man. I touched him. He was ice cold. That's dead. Then all that crap at the research center, and suddenly he's alive again. I mean, what the fuck, Hem? What did you do? There are all these rumors floating around. You know Julie at school? Yeah, well, her mom, she works at the hospital and she's told everybody that he's like, like . . ."

I interrupted, doing my best to suppress the cold fury that swept over me. "Like what, Todd? Say it." I moved in closer. "Say it."

He exhaled the words. "Like the undead."

My stomach sank. The funeral flowers weren't a one-off. The narrative of Bill Jones had been drafted and was currently circulating this Bible Belt Podunk for editorial enhancements. Even if I found a way to improve how Dad looked, it wouldn't matter. It wouldn't matter if he cycled the Tour de France. He was now a leper in his hometown.

Dad's phone rang—Charlie. I answered, relieved to have a moment's pause in this insane conversation. "Yeah."

"Lights are back on," he announced. "What'd you do?"

"I didn't do anything."

"Well, then I guess there's a short somewhere. You want me to check it out?"

"I'll check the wiring when I get home. I'll be a few minutes. Have to stop at the store." I stared at Todd. "Food Lion's got brains on special and I'm sure Dad'll be hungry."

Todd threw up his hands in frustration.

Charlie had no idea what was going on. "Conversations with you are getting weirder all the time, you know that?"

I hung up.

Todd was instantly embarrassed. "Dude, don't. Those were her words, not mine."

"And you were worried enough about them to ask me over. Do you have any idea how moronic that sounds? Hang on a sec." I plunged into the weeds next to the trailer. "There's always some wild garlic growing around here someplace. I mean, you just never know—"

He stood up and shouted, "I'm sorry! It's just—"

I folded my arms. "Just what? My dad's been nothing but good to you. Remember eighth-grade math? Who tutored you? And when your dad refused to come to Scouts. Who came in his place?"

"I know all that! He was a great guy!"

"IS! He *is* a great guy. He's still alive. He had an accident, that's all. And he's . . ." I fumbled for words, not really sure what to say. I decided to skip it. "You know what? I appreciate the hell out of what you did Friday night. I'll never forget it. But I don't need this crap, and my dad really doesn't. He's Bill Jones. I have to go. His coffin's open, it's daytime and that can get kinda messy. I'll see ya around."

Todd looked at me pleadingly, but he didn't say anything. I grabbed my bike and rode home.

The wiring was fine. It was too late to call the city to ask if they'd cut us off. Charlie ordered some pizza and flipped on March Madness while I scoured Dad's financial records to see if we had any money lying around. (We didn't.) I made a mental note to apply for a job at Walmart the next day.

I called the hospital and got a nurse at the desk. My dad had been awake that afternoon, but was now resting. No change.

CHAPTER EIGHT

In the morning, another article was taped to my front door: HEALER OR HELLRAISER? My dad's rumored condition had made the front page. I ripped it to shreds as Burkhardt pulled up and climbed out. I scowled. "You find my dad's truck yet?"

"No, but I can pretty much promise you'll be the first to know when I do." He scratched his nose. "Kannapolis police are dropping the attempted-murder investigation. For now."

"Really? Why?" I couldn't figure out why Burkhardt was here. Cops don't usually stop by to announce they're done investigating you.

He shrugged. "No truck, no witnesses, and it's an election year. You're still on the hook for your little stunt at the research center, though."

I nodded. "Kids will be kids."

Burkhardt stuffed his hands in his pockets with a sigh. "The fallout is there won't be a cop on your dad's room at the hospital anymore."

I squinted at him narrowly. "You know my dad's been getting death threats, right? You heard about the funeral flowers? Then there are these little love letters on my door." I showed him the tattered remains of Lisa's articles. "My dad has no motor skills. If someone came in—"

Burkhardt interrupted, "I know, I know. That's why I'm here. But here's the situation: the guard was to protect him from you. If they're dropping the attempted-murder investigation, no need for a guard. That's the thinking in Kannapolis. Meanwhile, I don't—the sheriff's department, that is—have any charges against you—yet. I talked to my boss. He said no-go on protection. Election year and all."

Frustration pulsed through my circulatory system. There was no end to this—solving one problem meant the beginning of another. I asked him: "When are they pulling the cop?"

"Happened about an hour ago."

"Christ." I grabbed my jacket and started for my bike.

Burkhardt called after me. "I'm off duty. I can give you a lift."

It goes against the grain to accept a ride from a cop who's trying to put you in jail for the rest of your life. But these were strange days, you know? I wheeled around and nodded.

"Thanks."

It was definitely nicer to sit in the passenger seat rather than the cage in the back. On the other hand, riding in any kind of cop car is a little annoying, because everyone around you inevitably drives slower than the speed limit. No wonder cops are always hitting their sirens and zipping off. Must drive 'em crazy.

I started punching imaginary pedals—my dad had been alone for an hour unless Cass happened to be there when the guard left. No Walmart today. I was going to have to guard his door. And when I needed a break, I only had Charlie to relieve me. And that was only *if* he was off work and willing to do it. How was this going to work?

Burkhardt seemed to be reading my thoughts. "I can take a shift or two. When I'm off duty."

I scoffed. "You'd be wasting your time. You know my dad's not going to tell you anything."

He nodded. "I know."

I challenged him. "So why would you—?"

"You're the little shit that hurt him in the first place." Not loud, not accusing, not emotional. Just a statement of fact.

He swung the car to the curb, right in front of Danny's on Church Street. It's a greasy cesspool of a place that also happens to have the best fried chicken in town. I think the secret is all the cigarette ash, thanks to the chain-smoking cooks. You kinda have to open your mind to try it, but when you do, it's damn good.

He kept the engine running as he pointed at me. "And before you start running your mouth, which you do, incessantly, I'll admit I don't have any proof. But I *believe* it was an accident, based on your reaction. You wear your dad's injuries like snot on your sleeve. But you committed a crime, and your dad's the victim. And now there seem to be an awful lot of people who want a piece of him, and all he's got is you. Yeah, I think maybe I can make some time in my schedule to help him out. Not you. Him. It's the right thing to do."

He kept staring at me, and I didn't know whether to punch him or kiss him, because he saw what I was and hated me almost as much as I hated myself. He was waiting for me to talk, and I didn't know what to say. I couldn't admit to what I'd done, because then we'd be on our way back to jail, when I had to get to the hospital. But I didn't feel like convincing him he was wrong about me either.

Just then a kid ran out of Danny's—just some kid, maybe about ten years old, in a formerly white T-shirt about ten sizes too big, ripped-up jeans, and no shoes—his arms crossed over his chest like he was protecting something. He saw Burkhardt's car, opened his arms, and ran. A load of candy bars fell to the ground.

Burkhardt was still staring at me, so he missed the kid. Slowly I said, "How do you know what's the right thing to do?"

It was an honest question. You know, right up till the accident I'd used that phrase—the right thing to do—like hundreds of times. And I'd been pretty smug in my confidence that I knew what that was. Now? The right thing to do seemed like a slippery eel I had to catch, and I was fishing in the ocean. If Detective Burkhardt knew somewhere I could look this stuff up, I wanted him to bring it because I was out of my depth.

He grunted and turned the steering wheel, waiting to pull the car into traffic again. "You just do."

Graying, stooped old Danny came out the door, pushing up his glasses with one hand, a bat in the other. A frigging bat. For a ten-year-old who maybe didn't get fed at home. Danny huffed and gestured at the car, as if to ask why the cop hadn't helped him out, but Burkhardt was still focused on me.

Still. I know what Burkhardt would've done if he'd seen the kid—he'd have gone after him. Arrested him. Never mind the kid's not in school, that he didn't have shoes or even clothes of his own. The right thing to do, in Burkhardt's tiny little world, was to send the kid off to juvy.

I finally peeled my eyes away from Danny, met his eyes, and sneered, "Yeah, well that's a load of crap. Wonder how your precious morals justify lying to a kid. Just so you can get a tox screen out of him."

Not surprisingly, that was the end of our conversation. He dropped me off at the doors without so much as a good-bye.

At the hospital, I made my way to Room 609, but it was empty. I flagged down a nurse.

"My dad? Bill Jones?"

Her expression was momentarily helpful, but when she recognized my dad's name, her features shrank. "He's um, been moved. Your dad . . ." She searched for words. "I'm not really sure where he is now. You'll need to check at the front desk. Excuse me." She hustled away so fast you'd have thought they were bringing in burn victims.

I pulled out my cell phone and called Cass. "Hey. I'm in the ICU. Where are you guys?"

Her answer floored me.

I took the elevator to the basement and headed into the cafeteria. Cooks and janitors paused in their breakfast cleanup to stare at me and whisper. I kept my eyes forward and my expression neutral. I wasn't exactly sure where I was going, but it had to be back here. I barged past the cash register, the ovens, and the steel countertops on my way to the walk-in freezers.

The farthest meat locker on the left was my dad's new room.

I twisted and yanked on the handle, pulling it wide as the cold beat an apparitional exit past the thick, stainless-steel doors and into the steamy kitchen. I paused, trying to comprehend what I was seeing until Cass ordered, "Shut the door."

I did. The cacophonic sounds of pots, pans, and running water abruptly disappeared. Cass was in a parka. A frigging parka. She sat in a chair next to a regular hospital bed that contained my dad.

I absorbed the surreal space. The walls of the fridge were scrubbed sterile and reeked of polish. The dim and greenish fluorescence from the ceiling light had been amplified and brightened by lab lamps that cast other-worldly shadows on the walls with every step I took. The heart-lung bypass, the Gaymar, and a litany of supplies still had that rumpled look that comes with transporting anything.

I snarked at Cass: "I take it the insurance company rejected our claim?"

Her eyes flared, but she kept the rest of her face relatively neutral. "Hemingway. Your father's been unable to tolerate normal room temperatures, while the other patients in the ICU were jeopardized by the extreme cold. This is the interim solution. As he recovers, we will attempt to slowly adjust the temperature in here, but meanwhile, he has what he needs."

I exploded, "HE'S IN A FRIGGIN' MEAT LOCKER—"

"HEMINGWAY."

I froze, recognizing my dad's commanding tone. I'd just assumed he was unconscious when I came in. A shiver of guilt passed through me. He was awake and sentient, and it was time to tell him what I'd done. My eyes landed on him. No IVs, but plenty of wires connecting him to computers that churned out all kinds of graphs. The bandages on his head were gone. His hair was gone too, leaving a seamless gray dome. He looked even less human than he had when he was coal black. Hues of ash, battleship, and slate played in the creases of his face. His eyes were still yellowed, almost glowing, like headlights in a thunderstorm. He shifted them, aware that my first reaction wasn't positive.

I sucked in a breath and tried to say something, but all that came out was a choked, "Dad."

He answered me firmly. "Come here." The clarity of his voice threw me. Had to be the only physical characteristic that hadn't changed about him. I shuffled toward him, horrific questions written all over my face.

"You're awake. Talking, I mean. When did . . ." On autopilot, I reviewed his physical state, checking the stitches on his head—there weren't any. I looked at Cass, baffled. "His head? What about—?"

Cass interrupted. "I'll get to the head wound. Your father's been cognizant for several hours now. We've had a nice chat, actually." Implication was written in her brows.

"I assume that's supposed to worry me, but it doesn't." I turned my focus back to Dad and hesitantly asked, "How are you feeling?"

Dad finally said, "Dr. Cass, would you mind if I had a few minutes alone with my son?"

Cass tilted her red curls back and forth to suggest she was weighing whether or not this was a good idea, and finally said, "No, I think you two should talk. I'll be right outside." She lifted the handle and pulled hard, the sounds of the kitchen momentarily returning and then gone. Nothing left but the hum of the fridge and medical equipment.

I went to open my mouth, but nothing came out. I was finally alone with my father, and I had no idea what to say. I'd spent so much time arguing to see him I'd given hardly any thought to what I'd say. I tried again, but my dad spoke first.

"I suspect we're not as alone as we might think." He met eyes with me, and I nodded silently in agreement. He absorbed this and asked, "I don't know what's going on here. I don't know what happened, why I'm in the hospital, let alone here. I don't know why I can't move. Why my skin is this color, why Dr. Cass is suddenly my personal physician, or why I think someone might be listening. I don't know why the cops wanted to talk to me. Can you tell me what has happened, or might that jeopardize you in some way?"

I shrugged. "Probably. I don't care."

"I do. You're my son, and I—"

I cut him off. "I don't deserve to be," I whispered as heat rushed to my face. I felt the tears coming. I didn't want to cry—not because it was unmanly, but because tears naturally evoked pity, and I didn't want or deserve my father's pity, while I was staring at his broken, hideously discolored body lying on a bed in a fucking meat locker.

"It's my fault," I hissed at him. "I did this to you." His eyes grew wide with shock. "Not like they think. Not on purpose. I didn't do anything to deliberately hurt you. I was—"

He mouthed, "Show me."

"Remember Todd's house on Friday?" Dad tried to nod—I could see the strain on his face—but he couldn't. "I was . . ." I flailed for a moment and finally gestured toking a joint. "With Todd," I explained. "Then you came and told me to—" I held up my hands to mime a steering wheel. Dad's lips tightened in cold fury. "It was an accident, and you weren't breathing. You were . . ." I didn't want to finish that sentence. "So I . . ." I gasped for breath. "I took you to Lifebank. I did some things. I brought you back. I didn't think this"—I gestured at him—"would happen. It's not supposed to—oh God, I'm sorry. I didn't want you to die. I didn't want to be alone. That's seriously weak, isn't it? But that's all I got. And now Cass wants to know what I did. And she wants you. I can't . . ." I gestured uselessly and finally crumpled on the edge of the bed next to him.

Pathetic. He couldn't even reach out to touch me and *I* was the one who was crying? *I* was the one who needed comforting? I folded my arms and pinched between my eyebrows to make it stop. If I wasn't absolutely positive Cass was listening in, I would have said more. I wasn't going to hide anything from him.

Dad was stonily silent for a long while, and finally said, "I want a mirror." I shook my head, but he said again, "Something. Something that would work as a mirror. Now."

I wasn't in a position to refuse him. I climbed off the bed, wiping tears and snot on my sleeve as I glanced at all the medical equipment. A stainless-steel bedpan was on the third shelf. I brought it over and said, "You sure you want to do this?"

He mouthed, "Yes," and I held up the bottom side where he could see his reflection. His eyes widened in amazement. I started to say something, but he cut me off before I spoke. "I need a minute here."

"You want me to go?"

"Just—shut it for a minute, would you?"

So I did, while he continued staring at his new reflection in the bedpan. I could imagine him wondering whether there was a God, and if so, what he'd done to piss him off so much. He'd already lost the wife he loved, and now his own life as he knew it. Now he was some sort of monster. Not to mention dependent on the insane and worthless son who'd put him in that situation.

I balked at the word *son*, suddenly questioning—was he even my dad anymore? I wondered. I mean, technically my dad had died. And I'd gone into Frankenstein's lair and, in a manner of speaking, given birth to this new version of him. That was true whether I liked what I'd made or not, and whether he—as my progeny—could stand it, either.

I thought about the reactions that were now starting to pour in—Todd, the neurologist, and even our mysterious florist. People who refused to help him or even look at him. People who thought he might be the spawn of Satan.

No matter what they thought—hell, even if they were right—I was responsible. I created him, so I was responsible for him. The realization was cataclysmic. All along I'd been waiting for Bill Jones to wake up and be the adult. I mean, I'd known I'd have to take care of him physically for a time, possibly for the rest of his life. But Bill Jones was still going to be in charge, make all the decisions. I'd figured I could eventually go back to being a snarky kid, grousing about being told what to do. Even if I was in jail, I was still going to be shitty-assed me. (It's weird to think that I'd wanted to go back to being that kid, seeing as that kid killed his father, but it was all I knew.)

But I couldn't go back. Neither of us could.

I studied my dad, trying to absorb how somebody like Todd—or the workers in the cafeteria who must've had a glimpse of him in transit—might look at him. His grayness overwhelmed, even in the tone-on-tone gray of that meat locker. The creases and folds in his skin created hungry shadows, while his now-hairless dome and yellowed eyes only aggravated his dehumanization. He did look like a monster. A zombie. The undead. Pick your nightmare.

But, the truth? I loved him like I loved no one else in the world. Maybe more than the Bill Jones I'd destroyed on Friday. That's the thing about kids, isn't it? Doesn't matter what they look like, or what they do. To you, they're the most beautiful things in the world and you'll do anything for them. At least that's what Bill Jones used to tell me. And now I felt it.

"We have to get you out of here, as soon as possible," I whispered.

He sighed. "Yeah."

"I have to figure out how to do that. I mean, even if you refused any further treatment from here on in, I doubt they'd release you. Plus, I'm not sure yet what it will take to keep you at home. But I'll find out, and I'll get it. And I'll—"

"Hemingway. That's not what I mean. Can you put that fucking thing down now, please?" His swearing shook me. He rarely swears. I've seen him shoot a nail straight through his hand and say nothing. I set the bedpan on top of the EKG monitor and sat again.

My dad's voice was far away. "What the hell am I?"

I choked, knowing how inadequate my answer was, but I said it anyway. "You're my dad. You're Bill Jones."

"No, I'm not. I don't even feel like me."

"Dad, you were in a major accident. You're gonna get better."

"Hemingway, look at me!" His face contorted in fury. "I am NOT going to get better!"

Just then, the computers went nuts—alarms ringing. Cass rushed in and scanned the screens.

I just about blew a gasket. "We're just talking! What's going on?"

She didn't even look at me as she adjusted various instruments and checked Dad's pulse. "Anger makes him hot. Heat drives up his core temperature. Now I've got to bring it down. You. Outside. Now. And don't go anywhere. I need to talk to you once I'm finished."

Really sucks that you can't slam a fridge door. Even on a meat locker. No matter how hard you push, they have all these rubber seals that just suction gently back into place. I know this because I tried.

Outside I found a bouncer gone to seed sitting in a chair by the door. Not a Kannapolis cop—different uniform. I studied his "First Alert" badge —a rent-a-cop. Somebody had hired a rent-a-cop to watch my dad.

Clearly, I'd lost the plot. I asked the only question I could think of. "Who the hell are you?"

He glanced at me and replied, "Who the hell are you?"

"I don't have time for this, and you can't be here without my permission. So start talking or leave. Who hired you?"

A heavily accented, gravelly voice echoed down the tiled hallway. "I hired him." I turned and spotted a guy who looked like Albert Einstein, dressed in an expensive wool cardigan and cream-colored linen pants. He walked slowly down the hall, briefcase in hand, and held out the other for me to shake. "You are Hemingway. I am Lars Mueller."

All the hair on my body bristled at his name—like when you hear rodents rustling in the walls of your house. "You're the guy who paid my bail," I said finally.

He nodded. "I did. I'm an attorney and I did so at the request of my client, Mr. Calhoun. He—"

"I'm sorry, I have to interrupt you just now. Calhoun paid my bail? He's the guy that had me arrested in the first place. Why the hell would he pay my bail? Why not just drop the charges?"

Mueller sighed, stuck his briefcase on an abandoned dish cart and opened it. "Mr. Calhoun requested I hire security for your father. They will be here twenty-four hours a day." He gestured proudly at the rent-a-cop. Seeing I was unmoved, Mueller sighed. "I must be early. Dr. Cass was supposed to speak with you first." He pulled out a stack of papers and looked around. "Is there somewhere we could talk?"

"Sure, we can talk in my office." I started for the cafeteria. He followed.

The cafeteria was empty except for the guy mopping the floor. Nurses hustled in and out to buy coffee. Mueller pointed to a table by the window and without waiting on me sat, the papers still in his hand.

"Okay, now we're here, so answer the question. Why?"

"Shut up." His words were so clipped, tight, and nasty that I shut up. Mueller nodded with satisfaction and continued: "Mr. Calhoun would like you to come work for him. Under Dr. Cass's supervision. At Lifebank." He held out the papers, which I could now see were a thick contract. "He didn't think you'd accept."

I scoffed, "Too fucking right . . ."

"So he decided to manipulate you." My eyebrows lifted and the Eurotrash lawyer continued: "He had you arrested. Then he found out what you'd achieved and bailed you out. He did that so you could continue to provide input on your father's care. He didn't drop the charges, because as long as those charges exist, you must stay here."

I was so angry I was shaking. "He can blow me."

Mueller interrupted with, "The power to your house was cut yesterday. Then it was back on. That's because I paid the bill on Mr. Calhoun's behalf." He lifted his head again and smirked. "Are you starting to see now?"

I froze.

He nodded again. "Good. You don't have any money to pay this hospital or care for your father. You don't have your freedom either. As long as the charges exist, you can't run without the police chasing you. And your father can't go anywhere in his current condition. If you don't sign this contract, Mr. Calhoun will prosecute you. Immediately." He paused, I assume for effect. "Your options, as best I can lay them out, are as follows. You can run if you abandon your father. Or you can sit in jail for years, and abandon your father. The last option is by far the best: you can come work for Mr. Calhoun at Lifebank. You can detail all that you've done for Dr. Cass, and provide input to further your discovery. Lifebank will retain all rights to the project. For this you will receive a salary of one hundred and fifty thousand dollars a year. In addition, all your father's medical bills, needs, and care will be provided for."

I swear to God, he could see the wheels turning in my head as he continued: "There is the issue of what happens once your father is stable. To ensure your continued participation and enthusiasm, the charges will continue to exist. I will personally file your continuances for a period of one year. If at the end of that year you are making progress, the charges will be dropped. If you do not make progress, you will be prosecuted." He shrugged. "At least if you do this, you will bank some money for a criminal attorney. I can assure you, you'll need it."

He finished with, "Finally, I should specify that if at any time your father dies, this contract is null and void. Your job will be terminated, and you will be prosecuted. I'll leave the forms with Dr. Cass. You have until the end of the day tomorrow to sign. Good-bye."

He snapped his briefcase shut and sauntered back toward the fridge that held my dad.

I put my head in my hands on the linoleum table. My elbows slid out from under me, due to the grime, but I really didn't care. Too busy wondering just how many pieces I was going to be carved into before this was over.

Cass came and joined me a few minutes later. "Contrary to what you may think, you coming to work at Lifebank was not my idea. Any more than I thought putting the screws to you was right or necessary."

I nodded and said scathingly, "Your moral fiber goes without saying."

She laughed abrasively. "You know I had to fight Calhoun to get an intern? He didn't want me to have one, thought it was too risky. Why? Because of perceptions like yours—that what I'm doing is somehow wrong. I'm a doctor, just trying to save lives. When we argued about it, I told him we could never hope for success if we catered to that perception—hide what we're doing. He caved and I got you."

She leveled her eyes at me while I changed the subject. "My dad?"

"Stabilized. For now. You can see him in a minute. I just thought you and I should talk." She sank onto the bench seat of the cafeteria table, her voice suddenly and uncharacteristically tired. "Hemingway, when it comes to your dad, none of us knows for certain what we're doing."

"And here I thought you were the expert. You seem so confident about what's right for Dad."

Cass talked right over me. "Hemingway, we have to accept the fact that your father's not entirely human. Not anymore."

Not entirely human. A doctor was saying this. An empiricist. I was instantly dizzy. "Not you too." My head flopped into my hands. I couldn't even look at her as I asked, "So what's next? Séances?"

"Oh Hemingway, come on, you don't seriously think . . . oh for God's sake." She snorted. "You and I may not get along, but I'm pretty sure we're in agreement on religion and the paranormal. Aren't we?"

Despite myself, I nodded. She continued: "That doesn't alter the fact that I'm looking at hard evidence that he's genetically altered into something unknown." She waited for a reaction, but I didn't say anything. "Hemingway, the head wound alone should've killed him. Now even the stitches have disappeared without a trace. His blood circulation and heartbeat are well below the margins for human life. Then there's the hydrogen sulfide, which he's digesting like food."

This news surprised me. "Come again?"

"I traced the hydrogen sulfide in his system. He's digesting the gas instead of food. At my best guess, he'll need another dose in a few hours or he'll start to discolor again. Beyond that, he can't tolerate temperatures more than fifty-five degrees, and based on the minute shifts upward that I've already attempted, I sense that will not change. His motor skills may recover to some degree, but I don't know."

I struggled, trying to figure out the safest way to respond. Laugh in her face? Argue with her? Insist on another doctor? I could do any of them, but I'd be faking. I guessed what she was saying was true. I didn't like her, but I couldn't argue with her skills as a doctor and scientist. And for once I had to agree with her—I didn't know what my father was at this point, but he wasn't entirely human.

I finally asked, "What is it you want?"

She made her big pitch. "I want to get him discharged from this hospital and take him back to Lifebank." I was already shaking my head furiously. Seeing my reaction, she changed her wording. "To the research center. I need your consent to do that."

"No. No way."

I was trying to scramble off the bench and leave, but she caught my hand. "Hemingway let's forget—just for a moment—Mueller's offer. And the fact that you and I don't care for one another. Let's just focus on your dad, shall we? He's in a refrigerator, in the cafeteria of this backward hospital. And that's the best they have to offer him. Half of the staff has refused to treat him; the other half are about to start conducting exorcisms. Doctors included, by the way. His neurologist has already put in a formal request to be removed from the case."

"No way. Absolutely not. If he has to leave, he's coming home with me."

"To what? Die again? Hemingway, I'm guessing you don't have a walk-in fridge or hydrogen sulfide lying around. And even if you did, he needs around-the-clock care—"

"That is none of your business."

"He'll have the best care—"

I exploded. "Of any animal in the lab! I know!" We stared each other down. "Look, you and that Mueller guy can keep pulling your little extortion games, but—"

"I told you I didn't have anything to do with that."

"I have *every* confidence you *did*. You know why? Because I know you. You're a bully. At the lab. And here. You think I haven't noticed your little games about how, when, and why I get to see my dad? Not exactly what you expect from a doctor and a soldier, but I don't have time to deal with your personality disorder right now. You know what? Putting aside how I feel about you is impossible because it's not about like or dislike. It's about trust and I wouldn't let you so much as give me a flu shot. My dad's not going to be your lab rat at the research center. Ever. Sorry."

As I yanked my jacket off the back of the chair, I caught sight of her face. I was surprised to see that her pale skin had become practically translucent, highlighting blue veins and faint freckles that must've dogged her self-confidence horribly until she was old enough to wear makeup. Her normally ice-blue eyes were watery and surprised. It was a look of genuine shock.

I ignored the rent-a-cop at the door as I yanked open the fridge and was surprised to see a book collapsed on Dad's lap.

"You're reading?" I pointed at the book. "You can hold the book? Turn the pages? That's good, I mean that's great—"

He hesitated. "Yes and no. Let's get to that in a minute. I take it you've met Mueller?"

I nodded. "You met him?"

"Cass introduced us." He exhaled loudly.

I was livid. Cass had invited her pit bull in to meet Dad while she kept me busy in the cafeteria. Frigging figured. I wondered what Mueller had said to him, what he'd threatened, what they'd told him about the offer.

We both listened to the hum of the fridge for a minute, until I finally said, "They want you."

"I know. I'll sign whatever they want and live wherever they want. If they leave you alone. That's what I told him."

I protested: "You know I won't agree to that."

We started talking over each other. "Hemingway, you have no idea—"

"YOU have no idea what goes on there—"

"And you don't EITHER! So stop being a smart ass!" He growled in frustration. The computer monitors beeped in warning. He'd be in agony all over again if we carried on this way.

He started again. "Look. You want to know how I'm able to read the book? I'll show you." He set his eyes on the broken spine of the book and stared at it. The book lifted and flopped again, like he'd just shuffled in the bed and bounced it. "Hold on a sec, I only just learned how to do this." Then slowly the book rose up again, while Dad's hands remained at his sides. Once it reached a standing position, he focused on the corner of the page, which turned as if by magic.

My dad had become telekinetic.

I stared at him, jaw dropped in amazement, as he said, "They don't know—yet. Or if they do, they're not letting on."

"How did you know you could do that?!" I asked, incredulous.

"I didn't. There was a book on that little table, where Cass was sitting. I was wishing I could grab it and read it, just for something to do. And when I did, something rustled. I thought there had to be a phone buzzing underneath or something. But that just made me focus on it more . . . and then it did . . . that. Please don't ask anything more specific in case we have an audience." His gaze darted to the corner of the room and then back to me.

I was so thrilled to know he could obtain things for himself that I refused to acknowledge the risk. "Unbelievable. Have you tried anything heavier? Like . . . that?" I pointed at the door.

His gaze landed on the door, and for just a second, I could hear the rubber seals start to separate and then gently suction back into place.

I laughed out loud. "You're like, like—"

"I don't know what I am. What I do know is that whatever I am, it's something they want. Calhoun wants," he corrected himself. He met my eyes. "So we don't need him to know anything that might make my . . ." he searched for a term—"situation even more alluring to him than it is right now, understand? No one can know about that, except you and me."

I nodded reluctantly.

He continued: "That said, it's not like he'll give up based on what he already knows. I can promise you that, without even meeting the guy. I've built million-dollar homes for guys who look like paupers next to him. If Calhoun wants me, he'll find a way to get me. It's not like I'm hard to find. The only thing I can do—maybe—is save you."

I shook my head. "I don't need saving. I did this to you. I'm fine. I can go to work for them. You can . . ." I scrounged for words. After all, what could he do? I decided to take a different tack. "I have to pay the price, remember? That's what you taught me."

"No. Not this time." He paused, obviously framing his words before continuing, "Look. Hemingway, I know I was angry before. I also know what lengths you went to, to save my life."

So Mueller had told him about the charges.

Dad went on. "You're a brilliant kid, with your whole life ahead of you. And I'm . . . whatever this is. I'm still your dad. It's my job to protect you. These guys want both of us, but they might be willing to settle for just one. They might be happy with just me."

"And what am I supposed to do? You play lab rat while I—what? Finish school? Go to college?" I snorted in contempt.

"*YOU'RE SUPPOSED TO RUN LIKE HELL*." The words boomed inside my head. I shook my head furiously after it happened, wondering what the hell was wrong with me, because it was my dad's voice. In my head.

"*Hemingway, look at me.*"

I met his yellowed eyes, feeling like a deer in the headlights.

"*Nod if you hear me.*" I did.

His lips did not move as I heard him say, "*This is the other thing I thought I could do. I didn't know for sure, until I tried just now.*"

My eyes bugged. My dad wasn't just telekinetic—he was telepathic too. He couldn't move his arms or his legs, but he could flex his brain as powerfully as he used to flex his bicep.

He carried on talking, inside my head. "*Don't say anything. Just listen. You've tripped on something, Hem. Something people have been looking for a very long time. A way to cheat death. And more. You can't possibly imagine, at your age, what that's worth. But I promise you, there are plenty of people with a lot of money who will be willing to do whatever they have to, to get it out of you. My job is to protect you. If I can get Calhoun to take just me, you run. Cash in your college fund and go. As fast and as far as you can, and do not contact me. Start again somewhere else."*

I simply whispered, "No." I thought about handing Dad the contract to show him I couldn't run, but I didn't, because frankly that wasn't the reason I wouldn't go.

I needed air. And heat—my fingers were absolutely numb as I pulled on the latched door. I turned to him and said, "You're all I've got. So, what happens to you happens to me. Who knows? Maybe I can improve on what I've done to you." I checked the time. "I'll be back later. I've gotta make some calls."

At the curb by my house, I grabbed all the cards left by my dad's contractor friends at the end of the driveway and started making calls. They came as soon as their workday was over, reviewing the house, discussing exactly what it would take to convert the downstairs into an eighteen-hundred-square-foot fridge. Their expressions were chilly with suspicion and loathing, but I didn't care. I just described exactly what Bill Jones would need and played secretary while they priced it out.

I called Mueller that night. As soon as I heard his crusty voice on the phone I started talking. "Here's the deal. I will work for your psycho boss, and you can keep the charges over my head for as long as you want. Whatever. But my dad stays with me. At home. Nonnegotiable. You supply him with what he needs, and you pay for the remodel on our house."

I hung up without waiting for an answer.

Hours later, I was still awake, lying on top of the covers, staring into space, unable to so much as play a game on my phone. I'd written Melissa about a dozen texts, only to erase them, telling myself she had enough problems, but I couldn't let it go. I finally texted, *YOU AROUND?*

She responded right away. *I AM. JUST SITTING HERE WATCHING LILA SLEEP.*

HOW IS SHE?

WE HAVE TO ADJUST HER MEDS AGAIN. TRIAL AND ERROR NIGHTMARE.

I GET IT. TRUST ME.

WHAT'S UP?

I wrote and erased, and wrote and erased.

WHAT ISN'T? I finally responded lamely. I couldn't dump my problems on her. *NEVER MIND I GOT THIS. YOU LOOK AFTER LILA.*

You know what an event horizon is, Mel? It's the surface area around every black hole in space, and it marks the point of no return. Everything that meets the event horizon is sucked into the black hole. No exceptions. A black hole is called a black hole because it absorbs everything—whole suns, whole solar systems, all life, all mass, and most noticeably all light—compacting everything into an ever-growing black body that has no reflection.

I didn't know it yet, but I'd just traveled through space and inadvertently landed on one. I was about to get sucked in. We all were—me, my dad, Cass, even Charlie and Todd. And you, Melissa. Because you were all tied to me.

My dad, Todd, Charlie—they had no choice but to follow me down. It was like I was a sun and they were my planets. The gravitational pull of their orbits was going to drag them with me, whether I wanted that or not. Saving them was impossible.

You were a different story, Mel. You were more like another sun, just outside the vortex. I could see your light and feel your warmth from where I was standing, but I should have looked away. I wish I had, because I forgot that, as another sun, you were responsible for a solar system of your own.

Oh, and if you're just some stranger who found this and started reading? You gotta help me out. Find Melissa. Please tell her what you read. She deserves to know none of this was her fault.

PART II

CHAPTER NINE

The nighttime air was syrupy-thick as Charlie pulled the Blackwelder Funeral Home hearse up to our house. We'd waited until well after midnight, hoping the thunderstorm due from Greenville would arrive and momentarily cool everything down. Concord always hits a hundred-plus degrees in July, but rarely in June. This June we were already at nine straight days and still going. It wasn't even officially summer.

This was my new reality: heat was an enemy.

The thunderstorm just missed us, delivering relief to neighboring Rowan County, while all we got was a hot breeze that baked the ground like a clay pot until it cracked.

I hopped out at the curb, checking for nosy neighbors, the roar of a passing car, or the footfalls of a jogger. But the street was dark. No surprise, as I'd shot out the streetlamp with a BB gun a few days ago in prep. Quiet too. All I could hear was the ground wrinkling and cracking like ancient leather from the heat.

Charlie rolled down the driver's-side window, awaiting instructions.

"Straight up on the lawn—don't worry about it. Close as you can to the ramp. I'll get the alarm and open the door, because we need to be quick."

He nodded, but his eyes shifted nervously. I just turned and walked up the drive.

Sucked my dad wouldn't get more than a glimpse of Mom's roses. I'd hoped it'd be cool enough that he could spend at least a minute outside, even if it was too dark for him to see the colors. While most of the roses were papery remnants, the climbers were still pretty spectacular; they'd knotted their way along the fence like a feather boa. I'd sprayed and deadheaded them during his two-month stay at the hospital and I'd really wanted him to see that. I knew he'd appreciate it.

The hearse humped the curb and shifted a neat three-point turn over the lawn. Charlie stuck it in park and went around the back while I punched the code on our new, state-of the-art alarm system. A minute later, I was wheeling out the $65,000 quadriplegic wheelchair Mueller had purchased; it rattled down the ramp like a homemade go-kart.

I propped the front door open, sweat freezing on the back of my neck as it met the refrigerated air wafting out. Charlie waited for me behind the hearse, his hand on the latch. I walked back down the ramp.

"Ready?" I nodded and he opened the back.

While it's fortunate to have a mortician's hearse at our disposal to transport Dad, unfortunately there's only one way for him to travel in it: flat packed, like a body. Charlie pulled him out on the roller tray. Dad's eyes glowed in the darkness, widening as the heat hit him.

Charlie peered into his face. "You okay, Bill?"

"Hot," was all he said.

"Let's get him inside." Charlie and I put our arms underneath Dad on either side. "Ready? On three. One, two, three . . ." and we hoisted him into the chair.

From the street a bulb flashed.

My dad roared, "Son of a bitch!" as I whipped around to see a shadow, standing under the busted lamppost. A woman, I guessed, judging by size and movement. But I couldn't be sure. I pulled the hood on Dad's sweatsuit up—an automatic reaction at this point—but I knew I was too late.

Dad roared, "LEAVE ME THE HELL ALONE!"

Charlie broke into a run. The photographer took off, disappearing into the woods just past our house. She'd obviously mapped an escape route in advance.

"Charlie! Nothing we can do about it," I said with resignation. I turned my attention to Dad, asking, "You okay?"

Dad groaned in response. Heat and fury emulsified, attacking him. We'd already been out here too long. I wanted to kick something. I'd planned this transfer so carefully, and now it had all gone to shit.

Charlie came back as I pushed on the chair, guiding my dad up the ramp. "Get the door and check the temp."

He was muttering furiously as he peered at the temperature gauge and dashed back. "Fifty-five."

The magic number. If the room went up another degree, Dad's roaring pain would be heard all over the neighborhood. "Take it down ten degrees," I ordered. "And plug in the standing units too. They're in the corner. In fact, bring one right over here, next to him. Use it like a fan. We need to cool him down."

Charlie handed me the hydrogen sulfide and syringe kit from the medical bag slung over his shoulder. "You know what you're doing with that, or you need some help?" Charlie asked anxiously.

"I got it," I responded, ripping the bag open. I set up a dose and injected it into Dad's abdomen. I'd trained at this for weeks in the hospital. Dad's yellow eyes rolled with confusion, and he went catatonic for a few minutes. We waited.

"Is this what happens?" Charlie asked.

I nodded, my irritation obvious. I had to remind myself that tonight was the first time Charlie had seen Dad since that night at the hospital, when he was roaring with pain. Dad had refused all visitors except me. I had tried to insist, but not surprisingly, Cass and crew sided with Dad. Come to think of it, Charlie didn't make so much as a squeak of protest either. To be fair, Charlie had absorbed his shock at seeing Dad surprisingly well. His back had arched slightly, and he'd been a bit speechless, but within minutes he was able to chat baseball. And why not? I mean, the guy *is* a mortician.

"This is what happens," I assured him. "It'll pass. Give him a few minutes."

Dad's eyes slowly resumed focus, and he was able to take in his house. His contractor buddies had delivered on every specification I asked for, in record time. The bay windows, dentil crown moldings, and sage-green cracked plaster of our historic home were gone. We now lived in a petroleum-insulated, windowless, and sterile cube. Canned lights poked through the ceiling every foot or so. The wooden floors had been tiled over to help retain the cold. The built-in bookcases were the only modification he might appreciate. He'd always meant to build some, and I'd dressed them with his favorite books, which had previously sat in cardboard boxes on the floor. On the wall to the far right was a giant plasma-screen TV, complete with a computer system and multiple monitors.

Most of our furniture was gone too. Dad needed to be able to navigate the space in a wheelchair, plus we needed room for the voluminous medical equipment he required: a hospital bed, a rolling medical table, a defibrillator, a heart-lung bypass, a standing freezer and fridge for supplies, two generators for emergencies, and a medical bathtub. We'd left the Barca lounger, as something he'd recognize and that I could sit on while I was with him. Looked more like the hospital than home sweet home, but it is what it is.

"What do you think?" I asked hesitantly.

He didn't respond. He just turned his attention to the wheelchair, intent on learning how to operate it. I shuffled my feet, wondering when Krakatoa would erupt. Dad was a contractor by trade, and he'd reworked the interior of this house with his own hands for the wife he'd loved and lost. I'd eradicated his museum, converting it into a fridge that would accommodate him in the incapacitated state I'd caused. Son of the Year.

"Bill? You okay?" Charlie asked, worry etched on his face.

"Huh? Oh hey, Charlie. Yeah." Dad's voice was soft, almost wistful. Missing the home he'd always known and been expecting, I guessed. He called out, "Hemingway?"

"Yeah," I answered as I walked around to face him.

"You're grounded," Dad said. "For the rest of your life. Or mine. Whichever comes first."

I grinned. "I know, right?"

He was back. We were back. We were home. Finally.

Charlie shuffled his feet, obviously ready to go. "You need help getting him in there?" He pointed to the hospital bed.

I shook my head as Dad answered, "I think I've had enough of one of those for right now. Rather spend the night in this."

Charlie nodded and patted Dad's shoulder. "I'll see you guys tomorrow. You take care."

Dad responded. "Will do. Thanks, Charlie, I mean that."

Charlie waved as he shut the door. Dad turned his attention to me. "I'm guessing it's a little cold in here for you. Where're you supposed to sleep?"

I gestured to the new door blocking off the now-enclosed stairwell. "Upstairs is pretty much unchanged."

"Then go to bed. It's late."

I opened my mouth to protest. Having been up at all hours for months, it seemed a little late in the day to be sent to bed. On the other hand, the barest hint of a smile was cracking on my face, a reaction so unfamiliar at this point that it took me a minute to register what it was. I'd craved this. And now I had it.

I turned to check on him as I got to the stairwell and saw he was smiling too.

I tiptoed downstairs and grabbed the morning paper from the yard, figuring if there was a picture of Dad on the front page, I wanted lead time before Dad saw it. But there was nothing. Lisa and her photographer must've missed the deadline.

As I walked back inside, the wheelchair suddenly whizzed to life, as if unseen hands were navigating the controls. Dad steered it toward the medical bathtub. I used the opportunity to drop the paper on the kitchen countertop. "You're getting good at that. How fast can that thing go?"

"Thirty-five."

"The velociraptor."

The faucet handle rotated on its own and water started pouring in. "Don't change the subject. Where's the picture?"

I sighed. "Not in there," I admitted. "Here, have a look." I grabbed the paper and held it up.

Dad seemed as surprised as I was. "You sure it was Lisa? Check the temp, would you?"

I reached over and tested the water—too warm. "Let me get some ice." I went to the freezer and scooped as I answered, "No, I'm not sure. But how do you even know that?" A realization dawned on me. "It's not just that you can send me messages. You can read my thoughts too, can't you?"

"Yeah. I can. I haven't figured out how to switch it off either. So, sorry about that. Help me get these things off."

Our conversation paused during the awkward violation of privacy that comes with undressing a parent. The nurses had always done this at the hospital—I'd studiously avoided it, even as I'd told myself I'd have to do this once we got home.

It was seriously awkward for both of us. Especially once he was naked, waiting for me to lift and lower him into the tub. The humiliation was written all over his face.

I hated it as much as he did. But a singular thought permeated my brain as I scooped him up and placed him in the tub as gently as I could. "That is just wrong on soooo many levels." His eyes flashed. Realizing he thought I was talking about the tub, I hurried to add, "The mind-reading thing. I meant the mind reading."

Dad relaxed and asked, "Why? Because now you're a teen who can't get away with anything?"

I scrubbed him as I answered, "No, because I was a teen who couldn't get away with anything *before*."

My thoughts were as naked to him as he was to me in that tub. I was violating his privacy, and he was violating mine, in completely different ways. We both paused on this mutual realization, knowing nothing would be quite the same between us, ever again. Dad finally asked, "So what time do you have to be there?"

I glanced at the clock and shrugged. "About five minutes ago. Traffic was a bitch."

"Let's get me out of here, then."

Lifting him out and dressing him suddenly seemed okay, for both of us. "Blue shirt," he insisted. I grabbed it and started dressing him as he switched subjects. "Planning on riding the bike?"

More awkwardness. I said, "Yeah," and stopped there. I hadn't driven since the day of the accident. At first, it was a simple case of not having a car and still being on my learner's permit. But even when Charlie offered his assistance in going to the DMV, I surprised myself by refusing. I didn't want to drive, quite possibly ever again. Despite my protests, Mueller was having a company car delivered today; he insisted I'd need one for work and emergencies.

But I had no intention of using it. My bike could get me anywhere I needed to go. And that way I couldn't hurt anyone but myself.

I picked up my backpack. "Research center said you could have an attending nurse. I just have to call Calhoun's office. You want me to call?"

"After six weeks in a hospital, I finally have no nurses. You want me to give that up? So soon?"

"What're you going to do?"

By way of an answer, he stared at the remote for a moment and the plasma screen flipped on. The famous overture to *The Great Escape* began. Dad loves Steve McQueen.

"The Cooler King. Funny." I threw the backpack over my shoulder. "Be back as soon as I can." I started for the door and paused, realizing I'd heard him say the same thing on like a million different Saturdays while I was doing . . . exactly what he was doing right now.

I opened my mouth, but he shut me up with, "Don't say it."

That mind-reading thing was definitely going to be a problem.

I climbed on my bike and headed down 29, over the railroad tracks and toward Kannapolis. I was returning to the one place I never thought I'd be allowed into again—the biotech research center.

How was I going to get through eight-hour days, five days a week there? My eyes used to roll back in my head just going there for an afternoon twice a week. What would it be like? Would I even have anyone to talk to, about something normal? And if I did, should I? People tend to talk too much when they get comfortable.

Remember Prometheus? The guy in Greek mythology who stole fire from Zeus and gave it to humans? Yeah, Zeus never really forgave Prometheus for doing that. He sent Pandora in revenge, and her evil fucking box, unleashing all the miseries of the world. I was kinda like Prometheus, only I'd stolen immortality itself, which was worse. And if a billionaire like Calhoun was Zeus, then Cass was Pandora. And the whole thing a cautionary tale in what could happen if I ever talked.

CHAPTER TEN

I arrived in downtown Kannapolis soppy with sweat and dusty with the film of car exhaust. I was at least an hour late. I idly wondered what kind of car Mueller was going to deliver, and just how committed I was to not driving.

I heard cheers and someone talking on a megaphone as I rode into the research center parking lot. A protest was being staged outside Building Two. Had to be at least a hundred people there. Not exactly the March on Washington, I know, but big by local standards.

I didn't focus on *why* they were there, just that they were, and they were in my way. I pushed through, shoving my baseball cap a little lower when I saw the reporters and TV crews. After the last two months, I fully expected them to spot me, but as it turns out, the bike distracted them. They were so intent on protecting their legs from getting scraped by pedals and spokes that they didn't even glance at my face.

Normally, protestors outside the research center looked a lot crunchier: aging vegans in Birkenstocks who were protesting animal testing. These protestors looked like an aisle in Walmart: a mixture of morbidly obese older people with bad dye jobs and comb-overs, with a dash of clean-cut preppy teens who wore sad, meaningful expressions. I recognized some of them from the many times they'd eagerly urged me to join their youth groups.

Signage was everywhere. A banner on the steps proclaimed, BLESSED ARE THE DEAD THAT DIE IN THE LORD. Mitt-like hands held handmade signs that said things like "No Lords of Death" and "Only God Should Choose When We Die."

A zit-faced skinny kid met my eyes and held up a sign, offering it to me. I glanced at it out of pure curiosity. On caution-yellow cardboard was a circle with a slash through a single word: "Deathbank." As in, No Death-bank. It finally hit me this was a protest of Lifebank. I'd done this. I'd exposed Lifebank's existence and purpose to the papers. Now the god-fear-ing locals wanted Cass and company *out*. I grinned. Maybe I didn't agree with what the protestors were doing, but I was grateful and entertained, nonethe-less. I grabbed at the sign, tucking the post in my backpack, so the wording was prominently displayed. I couldn't wait to see Cass's face when I carried it inside.

At the front of the protest was a small podium on which a beatific-faced preacher was reading from Revelations. "I am the Alpha and the Omega, the first and the last, the Beginning and the End. This is God's word! He alone will choose when we come to greet him in his Kingdom!"

Most of the audience clapped and cheered, "AMEN!" Some of the women crossed themselves and wailed like they were being burned. All of their faces were drippy with sweat. They looked ready to cut out of here soon and head to the revival tent for some snake-handling good times.

As I got to the bike rack, the preacher was working the crowd up to an orgasmic climax of Revelations horror. "I'm Brother Frank and I'm here to tell you God has spoken on this company's mission! He KNOWS they have attempted his purpose, and He has sent them straight to the Devil! The Dev-il transforms their skins and their souls and reveals his work to us in the form of a monster! A monster is in our midst! They have unleashed this monster! This is not Lifebank! This is DEATHBANK!"

My enthusiasm for the protest evaporated as quickly as the sweat on my shirt. These people weren't just protesting Lifebank. They were protesting Dad. That was why they were here today: he'd been released from the hospital, and they thought he was here. I finished locking up my bike and moved into the shadows of the portico.

Brother Frank insisted, "Don't believe me! Listen to this lady! She can tell you!" A thin, nervous-looking woman approached the podium. I recognized her. She was one of the ICU nurses at Northeast. She took the mic and said, "I don't normally protest medical research," she told the crowd. "I'm a nurse. I believe in life. But as a nurse, I have to believe in the sanctity of death too."

She was surprisingly well-spoken for a cretin.

"We are born to die. It is part of God's plan. What this company is doing defies that plan. I cared for that poor man and I pity what he's become. I worry about his everlasting soul. Lifebank isn't about life. It's about breeding a race of the living dead."

The audience started chanting, "NO MORE DEATHBANK. NO MORE DEATHBANK."

I took the sign from my pack and broke it in two, heaving the splintered bits in a nearby trash can. I was busy shredding the poster itself when a voice interrupted me.

"Hemingway?"

Melissa squinted into the sun, a hand cupped over her eyes to look at me from the other side of the trash can. Seeing the sign in her hand, my eyes popped wide with incredulity.

She lowered it until it was resting on the ground. "I didn't know. I didn't . . ." Embarrassed, she walked over. "How's your dad doing?"

I wasn't having any of it. I couldn't put a finger on why I was so angry at her, but I was. I pointed at her sign. "You too?"

Her brow wrinkled. "Um, I believe you had one too?"

"Only to piss somebody off. Changed my mind, though. You know that's my dad they're talking about, up there. Bill Jones, the monster."

"Yeah, that's why I was taking the sign to the trash. I came here to protest what Lifebank is doing, not to protest your dad's existence." She sighed, and leaned her sign against the trash can.

"You know he's had multiple death threats? So, if these people get all worked up and head to my house with pitchforks, you're going to . . . what? Feel just fine because your intentions were good? Or are you going to stand in their way? Or will you just be relieved he's . . ." I waggled my fingers for quotation marks. "Finally at peace?"

Now she was angry. "Again, I'm sorry. I didn't know they'd be ranting about your dad, calling him a monster! And for the record, I'd get in the way of anybody who was trying to harm him."

"But *that's* what they're saying, and that's what they want to do. The whole reason this protest is today is because he was released from the hospital last night."

"Again, I'm sorry. I didn't think about why it was today." The gold crucifix dangled like a pendulum on her chest, reminding me of her prayers in the hospital.

I wrinkled my nose. "Oh, I forgot. You're a Bible thumper."

Her eyes fluttered at the insult. "I take it you don't believe in God."

"There isn't a term for people who don't believe in Santa Claus. Let me ask you something. What is my dad to you, huh?"

She hesitated, thinking, and finally said, "A mistake. An innocent mistake, okay? Let me finish. You were trying to save him, right? He had a heart attack and you tried to bring him back?"

"I'm sorry, I did ask, but I really can't have this conversation right now."

Melissa talked over me. "From what I understand, these people"—she gestured at Building Two—"see your dad as a discovery. They want to do it again."

My fingers tightened into knots, and I wondered if there was ever a time I wasn't going to feel angry, ashamed, and frustrated all at once. "You just don't get it," I told her finally. "You think you do, but you don't."

"Then help me understand."

"You shouldn't be here."

"But you should?" Her brown eyes penetrated me. "I saw you heading into the building. You're going in there? After everything that's happened?"

I met her gaze and said icily, "I work here now. And I'm late." Her eyes grew wide when I said that, but I didn't care. I turned and headed into Building Two.

You know, on the one hand, she was echoing what I thought about Lifebank. I had first-hand knowledge that they wanted to repeat what I'd done to my dad, and I didn't want to. I was relieved someone finally got that. Nobody else around here did. In their eyes, I was either a necromancer or a visionary, depending on whom you talked to and filtered that through what you believed.

Only Melissa had asked me what I thought of what I'd done—whether I was proud of my work or horrified. I doubted most of them even cared. In everyone else's eyes, teams had been picked: Team Lifebank or Team God. As ill-fitting as our uniforms were, the Jones family had been placed on the Lifebank team. Melissa was with the Jesus freaks. I wondered what victory looked like for either side.

Still. I resented the hell out of Melissa being there. Everything I felt for her diminished as I walked up those steps. I could feel it wrinkling into something smaller, messier. And it smelled like disappointment.

"Mmmm, the prodigal son returns," a voice purred from across the lobby. Dr. Belinda Stephens was seated in the window, watching the protest like it was daytime television—mindless, bizarre, and therefore thoroughly entertaining.

She was eating yogurt. I use the term "eating" rather loosely because the way she handled the spoon suggested something else. You know, I'd never wanted to be a spoon before, but I did now. Badly. I never really understood why the other interns had coined Cass "Dr. Ass," when Stephens inhabited the same space. Cass had a great body and all, but she was otherwise extremely normal-looking. Stephens was the real deal in my book. Think hot librarian—about thirty-five and willowy, with jet-black hair done up in a bun, and high cheekbones hidden behind a pair of birth-control-sized reading glasses. (She also had a medical degree from Harvard and a post-doctorate from Duke.)

"Hey," I answered. I was still kind of flipping out, just walking through the door.

"Welcome back." She flashed a smile of brilliantly white teeth as she stood up and gestured for a hug. I moved like an arson-induced fire across the room.

"Miss me?" she asked teasingly.

"Mm-hmm. Don't let go," I pleaded.

She laughed and released me as Cass's voice interrupted my fantasies. "Belinda, he works here now, which means all the come-ons are strictly off-limits, even in play."

"Who's playing?" Stephens responded, keeping her smiling eyes on me. "I'm just waiting for him to be legal." She wiggled surreptitiously in my direction. I grinned appreciatively.

"I *meant* what I said," Cass interjected.

Exasperated, Stephens responded, "Jesus, Ellie, you remember I'm gay, right?"

My face fell. "You are?"

Belinda shrugged. "Of course. I thought everyone knew that."

Cass wasn't waiting. "Everyone in the conference room, *now*. We've already lost enough time. You're late, Hemingway." She stalked out of the lobby, proof that no matter how many times you say the glass is half full, there's some buzzkill around to tell you it's poisoned.

Dr. Tan lifted a hand and waved at me as I slouched in. I waved back, relieved my relationships with him and Stephens were still intact, despite what I'd done. I genuinely liked Dr. Linus Tan, just as much as I liked Dr. Belinda Stephens. (Well, okay, maybe not *quite* as much.) As someone to work with, he was pretty cool. Accepted to MIT at age sixteen, Tan had doctorates in medicine, cognitive psychology, and genetic engineering by the time he was thirty. He'd worked at NIH before accepting Cass's offer. Definitely one of those Domino's-every-night geeks—but he's a damn good point guard in a game of hoops. And if any of us ever got under his skin at the lab, he never showed it. Ever. Which was handy, considering our boss.

Cass pulled out a notepad. "Before we begin, I want to address what's going on outside. I wish to remind all of you of the confidentiality clauses in your contracts . . ."

Stephens and Tan mirrored my bored expression as Cass droned on.

"Now that we've covered that, let's focus on the agenda. For the time being, the board has asked us to suspend our work in clinical resuscitation in favor of determining the causes, makeup, and characteristics of the Gray. Linus, I take it you had a chance to review the bloodwork?"

Before Tan could answer, I interrupted, "Um, the Gray?"

Cass answered coolly, "Yes, Hemingway, that is the term we're using to represent your father's condition. Not very scientific, I know, but apropos of his physical state." She focused again on Tan. "Linus? What have you found out?"

Tan pushed a report in front of Cass. "You were right. The Gray's genetic code no longer matches that of Bill Jones. And while it is similar to a human code, it can't be mistaken for one either."

I shuddered visibly, unsure what disturbed me more: referencing my father by some stupid brand name, or the fact that he needed one.

"Hemingway?" Cass peered into my face, affecting concern. "Your reaction is understandable."

"I'm fine," I insisted and slouched lower in my chair.

Cass nodded and continued. "Having already made that assumption, I've broken down our fields of study. Dr. Tan and I will conduct further studies to determine whether this is a sustainable or temporary mutation. I will be testing for viability and longevity. Linus, I want you to focus on physical attributes. Organ study first, to see what in his system has suffered lasting damage and may need replacing in the near future. Additionally, ambulation is a primary concern—"

My interest was suddenly piqued and I turned eagerly to Tan. "Ambulation? As in, you think there's some chance my dad could move again?"

Tan thought for a moment. "I honestly don't know, Hem. I don't know whether the quadriplegia is a fault in his system or a characteristic of what he's become. Even if his condition doesn't prohibit movement, the longer he goes without moving, the more his muscles atrophy and the harder it gets. But I'd like to try."

I nodded. "I'll help. Anything to get Dad mobile again."

Cass cut me off with, "You won't have time."

"I'll work with Tan in the evenings," I insisted.

"Working evenings goes without saying. But you're only here to help us understand how your father became a Gray. You will be assisting Belinda, working to identify what methodologies were used, in what order, and isolate which one, or what sequence, resulted in a Gray."

"How are we supposed to do that?"

Stephens and Tan shuffled, uncomfortable with the fact I was so obtuse. Cass simply stated, "We will have to recreate the experiment, multiple times."

I shook my head furiously. "No. No fucking way."

Cass paused, folding her hands neatly on the table. "I'm sorry, but I need to speak to Hemingway alone for a few minutes. Please excuse us."

"Need coffee anyway," Stephens responded pleasantly as she climbed out of her seat. Tan simply flipped his folder shut with a sigh and headed out.

Once the door closed, Cass waited a full minute more before starting. "Okay, number one, you are my employee, not my equal."

"How about warden? Works just as well."

She slapped her hand on the table in frustration and paused for an entire minute before she spoke. "I can't go on like this. I've got too much riding on this to put up with your crap." She stopped herself and started again: "What did you think we were doing?"

Her cell phone rang. Emitting a sigh of exasperation, she checked the number and moved to the corner of the room to answer it. "Yes," she said in a hushed tone. The caller said something, and Cass answered, her voice barely above a whisper. I couldn't make it out. "All right, I see." She flipped it shut and looked at me, fury written all over her face. She folded her arms and said, "Hemingway, what are you planning to give your father for dinner tonight?"

My interest in her phone call died away and my lips pinched. My dad needed a liquid injection of hydrogen sulfide gas to live. That's what he ate instead of food, ever since the accident, and you can't exactly buy the necessary quantity on eBay. Not unless you want Homeland Security to descend on your house. But the research center had it. In fact, it was the only place in the world I could get what my dad needed to stay alive. He'd live or die at Cass's discretion, and she was willing to point that out.

"So I play ball, or Dad dies? I see your bedside manner hasn't improved any."

Cass ignored the jab. "That was the deal. Your complicity in this project in exchange for your dad's supplies."

"You don't seriously expect me to believe—"

"I don't care what you believe. I care about this project. I also care what happens to your dad. So, I'm working here. I'm giving it everything I've got. I'm just wondering if you've given it the same amount of thought. Have you?"

I stared at my hands and realized they were knotted into fists. No, I hadn't really thought about where and how to get hydrogen sulfide, if I didn't get it from Lifebank. But I didn't want to admit that to her.

I finally mumbled, "We're using humans?"

"Go talk to Belinda. There will be no more mouthing off, or I will give the board of this company a choice—you or me. Who do you think they will pick?" She opened the door and left.

I stared at the ceiling, trying to gather my thoughts.

I had to get out of here. I had to get my dad out of here.

Leaving town was always my plan, but honestly, I hadn't put too much thought into it. Getting Dad well enough to come home from the hospital, and the house ready to accommodate him, had occupied my every waking thought the last two months. I was only on Step Two—banking some coin. I'd come here figuring I'd play saboteur of my own experiment, making sure they came close to recreating what I'd done, without ever actually succeeding—just long enough so I could put some money together. Step Three was finding someplace where I could house my Dad—somewhere they wouldn't know about. And I was miles off from handling that one, seeing as I didn't have any money.

So, sorry and all, but I hadn't gotten to Step Four, which was where I'd get the hydrogen sulfide after we took off.

The idea of recreating the experiment on dead bodies made me want to puke. I wondered: If I gave them what they wanted, just told them everything I remembered, right now, would they let me go?

Truth? I didn't remember exactly what I did that night in the lab, in what specific order. Hello, I was a little stressed out at the time? I hadn't exactly taken any notes.

I wondered what would happen if I couldn't remember. Would she seriously cut Dad off if she decided I was absolutely useless? And what would happen if I *did* remember? Would they still supply my dad with what he needed, once they had what they wanted?

This was impossible. Dr. Cass didn't want me here; she knew I didn't want any part of this. And my success or failure came with the exact same risks for Dad.

Still roiling at having been threatened, and having absolutely no solutions, I decided to just get on with faking it. I walked over to Dr. Stephens's office and flopped down in a chair across from her desk. She gave me one of those slow, alluring smiles as she peeled her eyes away from the computer screen and focused on me.

"Ready to talk?" she murmured.

I answered, "Quid pro quo, Agent Starling."

She looked confused. I shrugged. "Didn't you ever see *Silence of the Lambs*?"

"Is that a movie? I don't watch movies."

"Well, there's this serial killer, Hannibal Lecter. That's me. And he's got the hots for an FBI agent, Starling. That's you. And he tells her 'quid pro quo'—details about what he did in exchange for details about her. So, even though she's not into him, because serial killer isn't really her thing, she plays along. Thought we'd do a little role-playing."

She grinned flirtatiously. "I love role-playing."

"Yeah, I figured you probably did. So here's the deal. I tell you about what I did in the lab. In exchange, you tell me about what you'd do to me if I were twenty-one and not working here. And if you weren't gay, of course, which, by the way, is really shitty information."

Slanting late-afternoon light poured through the windows by the time we were done. As freshly full of illicit fantasies as I was, I still had to ask her, "So when do we start? Trying this, I mean."

"What?" Stephens looked at me blankly and finally shrugged. "As soon as a new B comes in. Keep your phone by you at all times."

CHAPTER ELEVEN

"So how was your first day of work?" Dad asked.

The physical therapist lifted and flexed Dad's left knee. Mueller had sent the guy over, despite Dad's simple request to be left alone for a single day. Dad grunted, and the therapist twitched involuntarily.

Irritated by the therapist's reaction, my "Fine," was a little sharper than I intended. I headed to the fridge for some orange juice and gulped it like a fish, straight from the carton.

The heat was merciless on the ride home. By the time I got there, I'd been ready to stand under the backyard hose. And I would've too if Concord didn't already have drought restrictions on water usage.

I finally managed to stop long enough to ask, "How was your day, honey?"

The therapist got up, keeping his eyes on the floor. "Well, I guess that's about it for today. I'll be back tomorrow, if that's all right."

He couldn't bear to look at Dad. I rolled my eyes.

Dad's voice was quiet. "That's fine. See you then."

When the door swung shut I asked, "You all right?"

The velociraptor zoomed across the room, and he stared at the bookshelves. "I'm fine."

"'Kay, 'cause you look a little off."

"I'm fine," he repeated with emphasis. He continued to stare.

He was hiding something. I pressed. "How long was that guy here?"

"Huh? Only about an hour."

"So what else did you do?"

"Look, Hemingway, what is this? What do you want? A nurse's log? I watched a movie. Took a nap. I had no pisses, no craps. And lunch was a juicy dose of hydrogen sulfide. Then the therapist showed up and was so invasive that by the time he was done, I felt like asking him for a cigarette. Does that answer your questions?"

"All right, all right! Geez. I was just asking." A deafening silence lasted a little too long for comfort. We were talking about something, but I wasn't sure what it was, and he wasn't about to tell me. I tossed the empty carton in the trash and changed the subject. "What're you looking for?" I demanded.

Dad concentrated on the shelves for a minute.

"Your yearbook. Where is it? I paid eighty bucks for that thing, and I can't find it anywhere."

"S'in my room. What do you want it for?"

A slow smile emerged on his face. "Thought I'd get a look at that girl that's got you in such a twist."

I groaned. "Stop looking so frigging pleased! And new rules. You can't just break into my head that way. I have to invite you there. We need a code. Maybe I'll say something like, 'I'm thinking,' and then you can look."

"Stalling," he accused, grinning wider.

"And I already knew her! And yes, I was interested in her, for like, five seconds. But that's all done now." I started for the stairs before he could read any more.

He called after me. "I saw the protest on TV, if that's what you're worried about."

My sweat-soaked clothes felt positively icy when he said that. But I turned and asked, "If you know everything I've been doing today, how the hell could my meeting a girl be the only thing you're interested in?"

"Because the girl's new information. I already knew what Cass would do. I knew there would be protests too. I told you all that back at the hospital." His face darkened. "Son, Cass is not the enemy. I know you think she is, but she's a good person."

"Everybody thinks they're a good person. I'm sure Jeffrey Dahmer thought he was a great guy."

"Don't be hyperbolic."

"Hang on a sec, I'm thinking." I conjured up Cass's face while she was threatening his life. "Still think she's not the enemy?"

Dad argued. "There was a phone call—"

"Oh, c'mon!" I exploded. "Look, if you're gonna get inside Cass's head, what I need are facts. What she's up to, what she's worried about, and why. Not analysis of her morality and ethics."

He sighed. "That's not a bad idea, actually. I'll work on it, but I can't just tune in any old time I like. Only works from so far away or over the phone. Probably something to do with frequency. As for you, tell me more about Melissa and I'll stay out of your head, I promise."

"That's just so wrong! Do you hear yourself?" I stared at him, but he simply waited. "You want to know? Fine. She went to my high school until she dropped out, because her little sister's sick with some rare disease. I saw her again at the hospital and she helped me with some stuff—bills—and I thought she was kinda cool. Then I saw her today, doing something I really didn't like. So yes, she's beautiful, but she's not for me. Can I go now?"

"Sure." But his voice caught me on the steps. "You didn't let her finish. About why she was there. She had a point."

I sagged. "I don't recall saying, 'I'm thinking.'"

"I'm sorry, I'm working on it. But Hemingway, seriously. Plenty of people are going to have an issue with what I am. Hell, even I have an issue with it. You can't block everyone out, son."

"Showering now!" I shouted as I shut the door. "Can't hear you!"

Melissa was on my doorstep early the next morning.

I opened the door and managed to choke out, "What're you doing here?"

"I thought this was probably a mistake." She sighed. "You sent me a text?"

"I didn't text you."

Melissa looked confused but pulled out her phone. Scrolling through, she finally held it up. Message from me: HEY, THINGS GOT A LITTLE OUT OF CONTROL. CAN WE TALK IN THE MORNING?

The TV suddenly blared dramatic music in the background. "Hang on for a sec." I shut the door firmly and let my eyes adjust to the dark.

Dad's eyes gleamed in front of the TV. McQueen was mid high jinks in *The Honeymoon Machine*.

"Funny," I said scathingly, gesturing to the TV.

"I thought you'd appreciate it."

"You can manipulate my phone too? And you told her to come over? Why?"

"Because you wouldn't." He concentrated for a moment and the wheelchair started to move. He got right up under me before saying, "Go. Talk to her. You're only seventeen once. Steve and I will be fine here."

"You have no idea." I gave up and went to head out the door again.

"She needs something from you," he cautioned. "But that's not why she's here. She's here because of you. But what she needs is important, so make sure you ask." He swiveled the wheelchair around to go back to his movie.

"You know that because she told you?"

In lieu of an answer, the volume on the plasma screen suddenly blared.

I threw up my hands in frustration and stepped out. Melissa jolted a bit.

"I should just go," she said finally. "This was a mistake. I'm sorry." She hopped off the ramp and started hustling for the curb.

Now I felt like crap. I called out to her, "I could use a walk. You?"

She shook her head, but I walked over anyway. Her eyes were watery. *Nice move, Hem.* "Look, I'm sorry," I told her. "I was pissed about the protest, but I didn't know any more about it than you did, so it's not fair to judge. Guess I'm a bit sensitive about my dad. That doesn't give me the right to take it out on you, though." She nodded but said nothing. "Come with me?" I asked. "Please?"

She sighed. "Where do you want to go?"

"Greenway's just down the hill. Let's head there."

We banked down the switchbacks behind the post office. The greenway's a cycling and tree-lined footpath that bends away from downtown, following the creek and Highway 3 for a mile and a half. Place is usually crawling with joggers and geriatrics, but this morning the blacktop was already gooey from heat, so only a few diehards panted past us.

Small rivulets of sweat began dripping down the back of Melissa's tank top. I resisted the urge to lick them off. I have no idea how.

Without saying a word our pace picked up as we spotted the shade just past the wooden footbridge. The cat was waiting for us on the other side. He switched his tail expectantly and I scratched his head.

"He yours?" Melissa asked.

"Nah. I'm not sure he belongs to anybody. He's always here, right by this bridge. He seems to like it that way, and so do I."

An opossum wobbled across the path, headed into the dense shrubbery. The cat took off.

The canopy absorbed us. I tried to think of something to say, but the sound of our feet was all the conversation we had. I finally tried: "My dad said you had something you wanted to ask me?"

Her brow wrinkled in confusion. "I didn't say that. I mean, I do, but how did he know?"

If Dad was going to use my phone, we were definitely going to need to distinguish between what he'd heard out loud and what he'd hacked from someone's brain.

I answered, "He's uh, pretty perceptive." I changed the subject. "Tell me about Lila."

She halted in the path for the briefest second, swallowed, and kept her focus on the trees. "Okay, what do you want to know?"

"What's wrong with her?"

Melissa's answer held a hint of irritation. "There's nothing wrong with her. She's perfect. She's just dying."

"Oh. Sorry. Maybe I phrased that wrong." I looked away, embarrassed.

"No, you're fine, I'm sorry. Guess you're not the only one who is sensitive about a family member. I get that question all the time and it's a stupid pet peeve. She has mitochondrial disease. Have you ever heard of it?"

I shook my head. Not wanting to sound like a douche, I carried on: "I mean, I know what mitochondria are."

"Okay, well, so everyone's got mitochondria. You can't live without them, and hers are self-destructing. It's a genetic disorder and it's terminal. No cure." Melissa's hazel eyes met mine, full of pain. "She started going deaf about two years ago—no one knew why. About six months ago, she started having problems with her legs too. Went to Duke and they diagnosed her. She was near complete heart failure. According to them, she's got maybe two months."

I had no idea what to say.

Melissa started walking again. "My parents blame themselves for what's happening to her. Because it's genetic, you know? Like they should have known, should've done something." Melissa scoffed.

"What's wrong with that? If I was in their shoes, I'd be thinking the same thing."

The angry tweak was back again. "Because it sounds like they wished she'd never been born. That's prioritizing their pain over letting Lila know how grateful we are she's been here at all. What if she picks up on that? How's that going to make her feel?"

I'd never really thought about it that way. "Crap," was all I said.

"What?"

"I'm standing here, trying to calculate how many times I wished—throughout middle school—that my mom had died before I could remember her. Because if she had, it wouldn't have hurt so much." I shrugged. "You've got me wondering if she knew I thought that way."

Melissa's eyes fell to the ground. "Now I'm sorry, I didn't realize."

"No, it's fine. I'm just saying don't be too hard on your parents. You say things; you do things. To protect yourself from that kind of pain. Sometimes you're so obsessed with it you forget to think about the pain you might be causing someone else."

"Are we still talking about your mom?" she asked quietly.

"Not sure."

This time Melissa hesitated. "Your dad seems really nice. I haven't met him yet, obviously, but he sounds really nice."

"Best guy I know," I said. The words almost sounded like an accusation.

She stopped in her tracks. "Maybe we oughta clear the air on this protest thing. I keep wondering. If you had to do it all over again—to your dad, I mean—and you knew this was how it would turn out, would you still do it?"

I balked and finally whispered, "I've asked myself the same question about a thousand times since April. And you know what I come up with? Yes. Every time."

I'd never admitted that to anyone. Not even Dad.

"And what about what you're doing at the research center now?"

"I can't talk about that, but no."

She nodded. "I still have to say sorry. About the protest. I didn't know they were going to attack your dad. I should've known, but I didn't—"

"Forget about that right now. You said you have issues with it, but your sister's arguably the reason why it's worth researching. I mean my dad's fifty-three. He's lived more than half a natural lifetime. Your sister's what, ten? If you could give her more time, even if she was something else, wouldn't you want to give her that time?"

Melissa shook her head.

Her reaction was freaking me out. Here I was, with absolutely no desire to repeat what I'd done, but I was still suggesting she do the same to her sister. It didn't make any sense, but for some reason it did. I was defending the value of what I'd achieved.

"Really? I mean, you don't even know what my dad's become. Is that it? Are you afraid?"

"No, it's not that."

"Then what is it? Why wouldn't you do what I did?"

Melissa plopped herself down on a boulder by the creek before continuing, "Because I have my faith. And so does she. Anyway, you don't want to do it again. You said so yourself."

"Do I just want to bring back random people? No. Save a kid, that's something else."

"Yeah, I know that makes it sound better, but it's really not. Because where does it end? If we start bringing back the dead?"

"Environmentalist too, are you?" I cut in. "Worried about the population problem?" I chucked a rock into the creek.

"God, you're so defensive." She clasped her hands against her face for a moment in order to calm herself and started again. "Hemingway, say you perfected—whatever it is you did. People would suddenly have to start deciding whose life is worth saving, and whose isn't. And who gets to decide that—you? Me? The guy who owns the research center? How many would get to live? Can't be that many, because we do have a population problem."

I was still trying to extrapolate knowledge from her argument when she started on a new tack. "And do you honestly think Lila would get to live, just because she's a kid? What about a single mother of two small kids? And who's to say Lila's, or that single's mom's life, is more important than some eighty-year-old Albert Einstein? And what if none of the parameters I just named are even factors? What if it's only available if you're insanely rich? What if that turns out to be the criteria? Don't you see?"

I folded my arms. "It needs some serious ethical parameters; I'll give you that. That doesn't mean we should abandon this. Because you're arguing perception. I mean, say you had a time machine and a defibrillator. If you went back to the thirteenth century and revived some guy dying of a heart attack, they'd think you'd performed witchcraft. They'd say the guy you revived was a card-carrying member of the Undead. And all you did was use what's medically available and completely acceptable today. Who's to say in fifty—or even fifteen—years' time this won't be medically acceptable? How's this any different?"

Melissa thought for a moment and started awkwardly: "Well, I don't know for sure, because I don't know what's going on with your dad, and please don't take this the wrong way, but I'm guessing the difference is the guy in the thirteenth century comes back human."

Now I balked.

"I'm sorry, I'm just using the terminology you used."

"I know," but my voice was snippy. In frustration, I finally changed the subject. "You said you had something to ask me. What was it?"

She inhaled deeply and admitted, "There's a new clinical trial at the research center. Some vitamin therapy. It won't save Lila, but it might extend her life. I wondered if you had any pull there." She looked at me, her eyes now frank with honesty. "I have absolutely no right to ask . . ." Her voice faded away at my nonreaction. She threw up her hands. "Remember when our biggest worry was a D on a chem test?"

I nodded, momentarily haunted by good times. I'd been in school until a couple of months ago, and I already felt like I'd been gone for fifty years. "And who to sit with in the cafeteria," I reminded her softly.

"And whether you were going to be grounded and miss the party," she echoed.

"And whether that girl in the Honda Element with the loose distributor cap would go to the movies with you on Friday night."

I suddenly felt something on my hand. I looked down to see Melissa's hand, gently snaking its way into mine. She smiled softly before admitting, "Why do you think she loosened the distributor cap?"

I lifted my brows in surprise, but I was smiling, nevertheless. "For real?"

She nodded. "I can change the oil too."

"I don't know anything about vitamin therapy. But I'll ask around. It's just . . ." I sucked in another breath, trying to figure out what to say. I finally gasped: "I don't know how you stand it. Knowing she's dying."

"Because I don't think like you do. I believe in God, and heaven. I know you think it's akin to Santa Claus, which, frankly, is a little insulting."

"Sorry." But we both chuckled. I was stroking her hand, enjoying the smoothness of her skin.

"It's okay. I can see your point of view. I'm asking you to see mine: that there's a time to live and a time to die. Lila's time here is almost up. That sucks for me, and for my parents. But not for her. She's going someplace great. Someplace where she'll feel great. I would never stand between her and that place, just because I want her with me. Can you understand that?"

"Not really," I mumbled. "I dunno. I wish I did believe," I said finally and honestly. "That would be a whole heck of a lot easier than accepting what I believe."

She shook her head. "You're wrong. It's easy to have faith when things are going well. Much harder when things look . . . like they do now." She smiled sadly at me. "It's the age-old question, isn't it? If there really is a God, how does he let someone like Lila die? The nonbeliever says because God doesn't exist." Her eyes grew watery. "Harder for the believer, who has to admit, 'I have no idea and still believe.'"

"I get it." I hesitated again. "I still gotta ask you one more awkward question."

She nodded. "That's fair. I've asked you some pretty tough ones."

I was still marveling at the softness of her fingers, despite the fact that they'd gone all sweaty from being in mine. "What does Lila want?"

"I do know the answer to that question, but just to make sure, why don't you come meet her? Ask her yourself?" she challenged. "She'll be home in another week." Her brow wrinkled. "Although it's only fair to warn you my house is pretty weird right now."

I laughed. "You have *no* idea how weird home can be."

"No, you'll see," she assured me. "My parents—"

I didn't let her finish the sentence. I just smothered her mouth with my own and tasted what was left of her salty tears. Her lips responded, moving gently over mine.

I'm not sure how long we stayed like that, kissing on that rock. It wasn't long enough; I know that much. Everything I'd done, and all I'd talked about for the last two months, was death and dying. This was the first time in a very long time that I remembered why it was so vitally important to be alive.

CHAPTER TWELVE

The media coverage of Dad started to die a slow death from lack of oxygen. The photo taken of him the night he came home never surfaced. Not in the Wednesday edition of the *Tribune*, or the Friday one. Lisa's byline disappeared too. I started wondering if she'd taken another job somewhere else.

Over the next couple of weeks, Stephens and I tried to piece together some version of what I'd done to Dad. I say "version" because that's what it was. I still held some details back. I was pretty sure the vitrification protocols were the key here, so I got deliberately inaccurate.

Meanwhile, we waited on a fresh "B" to conduct our initial experiment. But none came in. Plenty of people were dropping dead in the heat wave, but the reasons for their deaths ruled them out as subjects: warm and dead is just dead. No chance of revival.

Days at Lifebank mirrored the shimmering summer heat wave: close, oppressive, and unwavering. I spent so much time looking forward to the weekend that I didn't really give much thought to what I'd do when I got there. Except when Melissa hinted around that she'd like to come over and meet Dad. I shifted uncomfortably at the idea that Friday night, switching the phone from one hand to the other, trying to envision how she might react when she saw him.

Would she be cool with it, or would she dump me? And if she did dump me, how would Dad handle it? How would I? She was the only positive thing I had going in my life.

"We're not doing anything but watching old movies," I argued.

Melissa pressed. "Sounds great. I'll bring popcorn."

I fumbled for another excuse, incredibly nervous. "You know, I've been cooped up all week at that lab and I'll be stuck inside some more on Saturday—"

She interrupted calmly. "Hemingway."

"What?"

"I'm coming over."

"Awesome." I hung up.

Dad stared at his computer, but I knew without looking he had a shit-eating grin on his face. "You should probably do the dishes in the sink. Maybe run a vacuum."

"Shut it!" But I picked up the sponge and turned on the water, hiding the fact I was grinning too.

Melissa arrived in long pants and a sweater, despite the heat. In her arms was a blanket and a grocery bag full of snacks. I met her at the stoop. "You sure you're ready for this?"

"He's your dad," she said simply.

"Yeah, it's just, he's, y'know—"

"Hemingway, I was there at the hospital, remember? Let me in, I'm roasting out here."

I pushed the door wide in surrender and she stepped into the cool. Her eyes scanned the room and landed on Dad.

"Hi, Mr. Jones, I'm Melissa." She set down the blanket and grocery bag on the table and crossed the room. There was a pregnant pause as she absorbed the color of his skin and the yellow of his eyes. Even having been prepared, there was still a ripple of shock. She shook herself out of it and extended her hand. "Nice to meet you."

Dad's mouth opened and closed without a word.

"Melissa, he can't—"

Her eyes widened as she realized her mistake and took her hand back. "Oh my God, I'm so sorry! I'm so stupid." Her cheeks burned red.

"Not at all," Dad responded warmly and softly. "Still takes me a minute sometimes to remember myself. Please have a seat." She glanced around, clearly still nervous after her faux pas and sank into the Barca lounger. Dad's eyes focused on me. "Hemingway, can you get our guest a glass of water?"

"Sure." I went to the kitchen, listening to them talk to each other in soft tones. I knew he wanted time to chat with her, get to know her. And who could blame him? He'd only had me to talk to for months. So I puttered around, handing Melissa some water, retrieving the bag of groceries, and putting the popcorn in the microwave.

"So how did you two meet? I mean, I know you went to school together."

Melissa smiled in embarrassment and planted her fingers on the furrow in her brow. "I, uh, faked a problem with my car."

She continued with the story, and suddenly I heard Dad laugh. I froze, and it took me a moment to figure out why the sound of his laughter was such a shock. I realized it was the first time I'd heard him laugh since before the accident. Tears immediately welled in my eyes.

I stumbled back into the kitchen to wipe them away, berating myself. How could I have possibly thought about denying him her company? How could I have been so fixated on myself? I threw some water on my face to cover up any trace of tears, grabbed the popcorn and threw it into a bowl before returning to them nattering away.

They looked at me expectantly.

"Everything okay?" Melissa asked.

Guess the water didn't work. I grabbed the remote. "I'm fine. We're doing a Steve McQueen retrospective, so the choices are *Bullitt* or *The Sand Pebbles*."

Dad objected, "Hemingway, we don't have to watch that old stuff. Let Melissa pick something—"

Melissa interrupted. "I pick *Bullitt*!" She shrugged at Dad. "I've never seen a Steve McQueen movie. Let's see what all the fuss is about."

We ended up watching both movies, Melissa listening in amusement as Dad and I recited lines from each film. Mel and I devoured the popcorn and the chocolate as she snuggled closer to me in the Barca lounger for warmth. Dad smiled throughout the whole evening. It all seemed so normal, despite the "at a glance" fact that none of it was, and that the situation couldn't possibly last. I decided just this once I'd let myself off the hook—for both their sakes—and enjoy myself.

When it was over, she went over and hugged Dad good-bye. He was so touched he couldn't do more than mumble.

I walked her out to her car, barely able to restrain myself for the moment she turned to say good night. I kissed her like my life depended on it. And for reasons known only to her, she kissed me back with the same energy.

When we finally came up for air, I whispered, "You are the most amazing girl I've ever met in my life."

There was that cute little gulp in response.

The next day, Charlie and Dad were yelling at the Braves game on TV when the doorbell rang. I raced downstairs, worried some nosey lookie-loo had brought a casserole in the hope of getting a glimpse of Dad. I checked the security monitors and saw Detective Burkhardt shifting from foot to foot on the porch. I turned to Dad and Charlie and lied, "Just some kids selling stuff." Dad would know who it was, but I didn't want Charlie to know. He still got squirrelly every time the charges against me were mentioned. Hearing Burkhardt was at the door might just send him running.

I punched the security code and squeezed through the door onto our porch-turned-wheelchair-ramp. Burkhardt tried to glimpse inside, but I shut the door as I asked, "You find our truck yet?"

Burkhardt rolled his eyes. "I see you've given up on Most Popular."

"Yeah, well I got my GED in the mail the other day. I didn't think they'd remember me at yearbook time. You have to let some dreams go."

He looked surprised. "You took the GED? When? Why?"

"Weeks ago. I had some time to kill at the hospital."

"Aren't you like some brainiac? That's not what you're . . . ah, never mind. Done now." Burkhardt changed subjects. "How's your dad?"

"Busy," I informed him.

"Still getting harassed? I try and swing by here when I'm on duty."

I sighed, knowing this was true. I'd seen him several times on the security cameras. I knew he did so out of genuine concern for my dad, and I appreciated it. Weird too, considering he was trying to put me in jail, but I did. I admitted: "That seems to have died off a bit in the last week or so. No one's taped any articles to the door and no more floral arrangements. Maybe it's because you keep cruising past. I dunno."

He nodded and continued standing there. I shoved my hands in my pockets and finally asked, "Do you have something you need to talk about, or is this just a checkup? Because I still haven't changed my mind."

"Yeah, I got something to talk to you about, I'm afraid."

"Well, let's walk around to the backyard. I got enough rumors floating around." I nudged past him and down the ramp, heading around the house. He followed.

June was everywhere—the din from the cicadas was almost deafening. If you've never heard a cicada, you've never spent a summer in the South. They're like this raucous percussive band that plays every evening. The mimosa trees were just about to get going too, their frond-like branches pregnant with blooms—a few pink pompons were even peeking out, as if to check whether blooming was okay. I'd have to find a way to get my dad out here to see them, especially seeing as he'd already missed the roses. Mimosa trees were another of my mom's favorites; she used to tell me the Seussian flowers reminded her of the Whos down in Whoville.

"Christ, it's hot out here," Burkhardt said. "You sure we can't go inside to talk?"

"I'm sure," I told him firmly, as I grabbed a folding chair from the shed. "Here. If you're hot, put this over there," and I pointed to the mimosas. I grabbed another chair and followed him, and we set up our impromptu patio.

"So, what's going on?" I asked him finally as I leaned back in the chair, my face skyward, looking up at the canopy of the mimosas.

Burkhardt scrunched up his face. "What're you doing?"

"Just wait for it. Say what you gotta say, ask what you gotta ask."

He shrugged. "Whatever. The reporter? The one you talked to on the phone at the lab?"

"Lisa? Yeah? What about her?"

"She's dead." He paused, waiting for a reaction from me, so I kept staring at the canopy, careful not to so much as scratch my nose.

"Sorry to hear that, wow," I said finally. "What happened?"

"Accident." His voice was tense with frustration. "From the looks of things, she fell, split her head open, and died." He waited for a reaction. I kept looking up, and he finally said, "Look, do you mind making eye contact when we're talking? This is kinda weird."

I sighed and let the two front legs of the chair plop back to the ground. "Fine. I'm looking. I barely knew the woman, and you said it was an accident. And it sounds like an accident. I don't know why you're here or what this has to do with me."

"I'm just checking around. See, there's something strange about the whole thing. She had a cell phone and even a landline. The cell was right next to her body. Thing is, she didn't dial 9-1-1. Last call she made was to this house."

"What? I didn't talk to her. And Dad can't even pick up a phone."

"She also had a note in her phone: the time your dad was scheduled to come home from the hospital." He looked at me intently. "Did you or your dad happen to see her that night?"

A flutter in my gut. Two more droplets landed on my head. I shrugged. "We saw someone—a photographer. Snapped a few photos as we took my dad out of the van. But it was dark. Whoever it was, they ran off."

Burkhardt's cell phone vibrated. He checked it before continuing, "Hmm. I don't recall seeing any photos of your dad in the paper."

"I know. Never ran. We kept waiting for it. Dad was dreading it."

He responded, "Really." It wasn't a question. He stood up. "Trib reporters usually take their own shots—it's a pretty low-budget operation. I'll have another look around her apartment, see if I can find a camera." He checked his watch. "I've got to get going, but by way of recap, let's see. First, your dad has an accident with you around, and you claim you're innocent. Then the reporter at the scene has an accident. Last place she was going was to see you and your dad. Possibly to take a picture you didn't want taken. Last place she called was here."

"I know, looks bad."

"And meanwhile you're working for the people who have charges against you that could land you in prison until you're your dad's age."

"I didn't have a choice about that."

"Everybody has a choice." He slapped at the back of his neck and said, "I keep feeling water. Is that rain? Are we about to get a storm?"

I pointed to the canopy. "It's the trees. Mimosas close their blooms at dusk, which causes them to squeeze all their dew out. Like nature's little misting machine." I shrugged. "You said you were hot."

"What? Never mind. GED my ass." He folded up the chair and stuffed it back in the shed. "I'll see you around."

He left, and I sat in the yard for a while longer, hoping the knot in my stomach would untie itself. Lisa Hobbs was dead. I pictured her again, standing on my front porch—just doing her job. And now she was dead.

Like Burkhardt, I thought the whole thing was awfully convenient for me too. That was what was causing the knot. I mean, wasn't like I'd made her fall, but what if her death was somehow related to the articles she wrote about Dad and me?

"There you are," Charlie called as he walked around the side of the house. "I texted you like five times."

"Who won the game?" I asked. Of course I'd heard the pings, but I frankly couldn't have cared less. I just needed something to say. Something normal. Normal seemed to evaporate so quickly these days. I'd do just about anything to keep it around a little longer.

"Game's still on. Top of the seventh. I was just coming to find you, let you know I got called out. Thought you might want to sit with your dad." He pulled out a tin of Altoids and took two. "Shouldn't have had that beer," he admitted. "You coming in?"

I sighed and climbed out of the chair, but my cell started screeching. Dr. Stephens. I answered, but she didn't even wait for me to say hello.

"First B will be here in about an hour." She hung up.

I grimaced at Charlie. "You're not the only one getting called into work."

Normal was definitely over. It was time to try and raise the dead.

CHAPTER THIRTEEN

I had to take Dad's mountain bike to ride at night—it was the only one equipped with lights.

Dad wanted to talk about Burkhardt's visit—he'd obviously tuned in at some point to our conversation. I didn't want to talk about it, for reasons I couldn't quite put my finger on, so I changed the subject and called Calhoun's office to get a nurse. That got Dad pissed. He started arguing he didn't need a babysitter, while some soothing-voiced secretary answered on the first ring and assured me the nurse would be right over. Dad angrily flipped on *The Magnificent Seven*.

The B was in a Gaymar in the foyer when I got there. Alone. No sign of Stephens or Cass or anybody. I called out, but no one answered.

The guy tucked neatly in the Gaymar wrap offered a haunting déjà vu. My breath got shallow as I moved closer to get a better look.

His huge dark eyes were wide open, his mouth gaped slightly, the barest hint of a gold front tooth visible. He was young—I guessed not much more than twenty—skinny, and seriously tall. I wondered if he was one of the guys I always saw playing hoops at the rec center. His broad hands and feet poked at the perimeters of the cooling blanket.

I felt positively light-headed as I wondered what had killed him.

Stephens answered like I'd asked the question aloud. "Heart attack. During a break-in." She sauntered into the room in full scrubs. "Sorry, I was in the shower, getting ready. Dr. Cass will be out in a minute or two. You need to go do the same—quickly."

"I had to wait until the nurse got to our house." I excluded the word *sorry*, seeing as I was there under protest. I kept staring at the B. "Some guy tried to break into his house, and he had a heart attack?"

"Noooo," she answered. "He was the one breaking in." She checked various readings and continued, "He's almost cooled. We'll start protocols in ten minutes."

I didn't move. I finally croaked, "What was his name?"

Stephens scoffed and said, "Hem, he died trying to steal money from his own mother. For crack, apparently. So, let's limit the tears, shall we?"

I stared after Stephens like I'd never seen her before. She just got behind the Gaymar and started pushing him into the lab.

"Let's get another dose of epinephrine in the subject and try it again," Cass ordered. Stephens raised her eyebrows defiantly before inserting the syringe, while I readied the paddles.

There had been some heated debate between them in terms of how to proceed: go in the order of what I'd tried that appeared to fail, or move immediately to the more revolutionary stuff. Cass insisted on following exactly what I'd done. (At least, what I *said* I'd done.) So, we'd started with the therapeutic hypothermia protocols, despite Stephens's repeated insistence that this couldn't possibly be the solution. They'd been rather snippy with each other for the last three hours.

I zapped him again with the paddles. Nothing. I decided to try and break the chilly silence. "So. Do people get paid for donating their loved one's remains? Or are they just interested in furthering medical science?"

"Fifty grand," Stephens answered. "Better than paying for a casket, right?" Cass gave Stephens a withering look before nodding at me. I zapped him again.

Stephens shrugged. "He's going to find out anyway from his friend." Now Cass's eyes burned with fury.

I perked up. "Charlie? Charlie picked this guy up?"

"Belinda," Cass said, a chastising tone in her voice. She stopped, though, and suddenly squinted at the EKG. "That's impossible." Her voice grew sharp. "I'm getting a reading over here."

Now Stephens was genuinely surprised. "What?" We both glanced at the screen. She moaned, "Oh for God's sake, he's alive. Stupid hick EMTs. They assured me—"

"BELINDA," Cass barked. "Task at hand."

Stephens took his pulse as she carried on muttering in annoyance about the inadequacies of our local rescue teams.

Cass turned to me, her face dark with concern. "Get the heart-lung bypass on and ready. We might need it in a minute." She bent over the B. "Gerald? Gerald! Wake up!" She climbed onto the Gaymar and started performing CPR.

Stephens and Cass snapped at one another as I shouted over them, utterly confused. "What's wrong? I thought this was what we were trying to do?" My stomach lurched as I switched on the bypass. What if I'd given away too much? What if I'd made another Gray?

Stephens turned with a syringe in hand. "Uh, no. The guy was never dead in the first place. If this stupid hick town bought a Gaymar, they could've brought him back on their own. But now we must pretend we're an ER." She rolled her eyes and injected another syringe.

Gerald's eyes suddenly opened in terror. "He's awake!" Cass focused on him. "Gerald, can you hear me?" Gerald gave the slightest of nods, his eyes searching the room, trying to comprehend where he was. A split second later, his body started to shake uncontrollably, and his eyes rolled back in his head.

"He's cold! Start the meperidine!" Cass ordered. "Belinda! Take him down, now! Hemingway, get that bypass over here!"

But I just stared. My mouth moved, but no sound came out.

"Hemingway! Goddammit." Cass climbed off the Gaymar and headed straight for me, grabbing at the connections as she demanded, "What the hell's wrong with you?"

I pointed at Gerald, still having trouble finding my voice. "Black spots."

"What black spots? Where?" Cass whipped around, following my finger to Gerald's chest, where blackness pooled like spilled ink on his chest. "Oh, goddammit, he's ischemic!" She dropped the bypass connections and started calling to him. "Gerald! Stay with me! Gerald!"

Gerald suddenly fish-flopped on the table. A moment later he did it again, crunching his legs to meet his rising chest. Just as abruptly his legs went ramrod straight, and then he crunched again. His entire body moved as though it was manipulated by invisible Pilates, alternately coiling and springing. He groaned in agony.

"What's happening?" I was totally freaked. No one answered me. Stephens barged past en route to whatever it was she needed.

"Help me hold him down!" Cass barked. I did as she asked, reluctantly grabbing at his spastic arms and legs. Blood was leaching into his chest in a black pool. I caught an arm, but he slithered right through my grip.

Cass yelled at me, "GRAB HIM AND HOLD ON!"

I caught him and held, bracing my elbow against the Gaymar so he wouldn't slip away. The EKG sped up. Cass went to work again. I caught a whiff of methane. "What is—" I stopped, feeling something wet at my elbow. I lifted it slightly to look and realized he'd lost control of his bowels and bladder.

Stephens called to me. "Hem, it happens."

But I wasn't listening. I was too busy gagging.

Shit pooled inside the Gaymar. That was the damp I felt on my elbow—Gerald's bowels had exploded. Barf forced its way up my throat. Sending it back down involved inhaling deeply, which just started the vicious cycle all over again. I struggled as the EKG slowed. I finally registered what it meant. "He's dying?" Cass nodded and her efforts went slack.

The EKG flatlined about a minute later. Cass let go.

I whispered hoarsely, "What're you doing? Isn't this what you do? Why don't you keep going? You can still bring him back."

Cass shook her head.

Stephens explained, "There's nothing to do. His organs went ischemic, and the resulting diarrhea warmed up his bowels. You know what that means. He's dead. No hope of bringing him back."

I let go of Gerald like he was poison and ran out into the hall, barely managing to tear off my filthy scrub shirt before barfing in a trash can. I sank to the floor and started shaking, utterly confused by my own response.

I'd wanted this project to fail. So in a sense, I'd gotten what I wanted, right? So why was I demanding Cass keep trying?

Because we'd brought him back. And I'd watched him suffer, dying all over again, bathed in his own shit. That's why. We'd tortured him, for nothing.

Stephens found me about twenty minutes later. She sniffed the air. "Ugh . . . was that you?" I nodded. "C'mon, get up." I ignored her, but she tsked. "I can't deal with two of you like this. Good God, he was pronounced dead before he got here."

I reluctantly stood up and demanded, "What the hell was that?"

"A snafu," Stephens answered coolly. "And not ours. He should never have been brought here in the first place. This is what happens when you don't properly screen candidates. I told him this wouldn't work."

"You have to be picked for clinical trials even when you're dead?"

Stephens shrugged. "Of course. It's still testing."

"And who? You told who it wouldn't work?"

"Oh, never mind. Point is, he wasn't really dead. And it turns out his mother lied to us. Gerald had been taking clotting medication for his heart condition. She wanted the money. She thought disclosing his medication meant we would reject him, which we would have. We'd have known he was high risk." Stephens blinked at me matter-of-factly, utterly convinced this information would appease any queasiness I had.

"And the black spots? The mess? Did we—?" I couldn't even finish the question.

She smiled and shook her head. "Clotting medication thins the blood. So when he suddenly revived, his circulation went nuts—induced intestinal ischemia. This was in no way your fault. Not to worry. A real subject will come along soon, I'm sure." She glanced out the window. "Sun's up? What time is it?"

"Eight o'clock." I stared at her again, flabbergasted by her shifts in conversation. Did she honestly think I was holding my breath to do this again? The ethics of the situation didn't trouble her. We'd revived Gerald from the dead—purely for the sake of an experiment—and we'd caused him to die all over again in absolute agony. Stephens couldn't care less.

I'd always thought Dr. Stephens was insanely cool, because she laughed at all the jokes I made at Lifebank's expense. I thought she was laughing because she agreed with me, that she saw the hypocrisy of Cass's alchemic quest. But she wasn't laughing at the hypocrisy. She was laughing because she found ethics funny.

She abruptly announced, "I'm going home to sleep. You should do the same."

"What about—" I gestured at the lab.

"What? Oh." She waved a hand. "Cass already called Calhoun's office for a private crew. They'll clean it up." She turned and headed out the door.

I suppose it's needless to mention, but I really wasn't bothered about getting some 409 on the lab. I'd meant, What about Cass? but I decided not to press the point.

I'd left my regular clothes on the floor of the bathroom. As desperate as I was to get out of there and go home, I wanted my own clothes. No way was I walking out of this place with shit all over me.

As I passed the lab, I saw Cass inside and paused. She was staring at Gerald's body, her hands steepled together, covering her mouth. Tears slid down her cheeks.

I suddenly remembered Stephens saying, "I can't handle two of you like this." Hadn't even registered at the time that Cass was crying too. I'd never regarded it as scientifically possible.

She couldn't possibly be crying for the guy. Had to be for the failure of this experiment. Had to be. Something told me I was wrong, but I didn't care. As far as I was concerned, the only tears a crocodile cries are of the crocodile kind. And if I was wrong? Good. If ever there was ever a time where Cass should reevaluate just what the hell she was doing, it was right now.

I hit the showers, to cleanse myself of Gerald and Lifebank. By the time I came out, she was gone.

The sun was already up and blazing when I climbed on the bike. I got nauseous again about halfway home. I kept seeing Gerald, turning black on the table, groaning in pain as his organs disintegrated.

I focused on the task at hand: I had to get out of Lifebank. No way could I sit around, attempting to raise Geralds for another year. But I needed a bargaining tool to do that. What did that look like? Everyone knew what Lifebank was doing—to some extent at least—but there wasn't anything illegal about any of it. Or was there?

I idly wondered if there was something illegal in how Lifebank obtained the bodies. There's a ton of paperwork to be done when someone dies, and it takes time: the coroner has to arrive, check the body, fill out paperwork, and there has to be a witness. There's a major amount of bureaucratic time slippage just to get a death certificate. Cass needed subjects who had been cooled within minutes of dying. Even if Lifebank was right there—Gaymar ready—when the subject died, which, in and of itself is impossible, there'd be a formidable time gap before they could legally begin the cooling process. I'd bypassed all that with Dad, simply by breaking the law. Was Lifebank breaking the law too?

I needed to go home and start searching again in earnest for Dr. David Elks, the guy who gave the TED Talk about hydrogen sulfide. The guy whose idea had saved Dad. He'd proudly announced at the talk that he was starting human trials, but when I'd tried to look him up, there was simply a notice that those trials were over. I'd called the University of Pittsburgh, but they said he no longer worked there and they didn't know where he'd gone. I'd searched online too, but found nothing—no social media, no new address, no new articles.

He was just gone.

The question was, Why?

Tuesday was a long post-mortem on Gerald. And no, that's not a pun. At least it's not mine. That's what Cass called the four-hour inquisition into what had gone wrong with the revival.

She read off the notes, checking me repeatedly, hoping I'd correct some protocol or dosage we'd performed, but I didn't. Luckily, Stephens interrupted multiple times. Cass got pissed off with her and stopped focusing on me.

My phone beeped.

GUESS WHERE I AM.

WHERE?

FIRST FLOOR. BUILDING TWO. JUST SIGNED THE PAPERWORK. LILA'S A VITAMIN THERAPY SUBJECT.

THAT'S AWESOME! SO GLAD THEY CAME THRU. HOW'S SHE DOING?

TODAY'S A GOOD DAY. WANT 2 GET SOME LUNCH WITH US?

CAN'T. WISH I COULD. STUCK IN

"Hemingway." Cass's voice was arctic. "This would be the third time I've asked you."

I looked at her blankly and plonked my phone on the conference table. "Sorry. Answering a text. What was the question?"

Cass pinched her forehead. "Could you be wrong about the xenon? You said"—she shuffled through her notes—"one gram, ninety minutes."

I pretended to weigh the estimate. "Might've been two."

Stephens and Tan sighed. I reached again for my phone, but a hand slapped over mine. I looked up at Cass in surprise. She turned the notes around and showed them to me. "I lied," she informed me. "You didn't use xenon. And you know it." Busted.

Tan interrupted. "Why are we even doing this? The guy was ischemic. That's not Hemingway's fault."

"Because a man . . ." Cass faltered for a moment, her lips moving but no sound coming out. She took a breath and tried again, but ended up pinching her forehead just between her eyebrows.

The phone rang, interrupting the debate. Cass disappeared from the office for the rest of the afternoon.

I fully expected to get fired. I was surprised how much I was dreading it. Not because I wanted to stay, obviously, but Dad needed the hydrogen sulfide. I sat at my desk, silently trying to count just how many doses I'd seen in the fridge. I was frankly amazed to discover I was still employed at five o'clock.

The hammer fell hours later, once I was home. Mueller called at eight. "A van will come for you at midnight—when it's coolest. You both need to be ready. I would recommend a sweatsuit—something with a hood—that will keep prying eyes off. The van will be refrigerated to balance out the extra clothing he'll have to wear. Someone will help you get him inside."

Took me a while to register the fact he was talking about Dad. "What? No. You want to see Dad, you can come here."

"This meeting is neither optional nor negotiable. It's with Mr. Calhoun. We will see you shortly after midnight." He hung up.

I turned to Dad. "That was Calhoun."

Dad just said, "I'm frankly surprised he waited so long."

Dad telepathed me as a tinted black van pulled up. *"We have to go manual on everything, remember that. You have to push me in the chair."*

"I know."

Two research center security guards rang the bell. They were perfectly polite in their clone-like efficiency. They didn't react to Dad, just introduced themselves and asked whether he was ready. Then they picked up the wheelchair on either side and took him to the van. I followed, half fearing they'd take off with Dad and leave me.

Once inside, Dad kept staring at the back of the security guards' heads. I opened my mind as best I could, inviting Dad in with the thought, *"You okay?"*

"They've seen me before. The one on the left thought I'd be heavier."

The lights of the Core Lab were dark, except for the glow of the dome that was Paul Calhoun's personal office. The van segued around back, utilizing the depot to extract Dad and plonk him in an elevator that required a key. They hit the button for the top floor and left.

Despite the summer heat outside, inside was as chilly as home.

Mueller was waiting for us in a North Face jacket. "Mr. Jones, good to see you again. I apologize for the inconvenience this trip has caused you, but as you can see, we've done our best to accommodate you in every way." He nodded indifferently at me. "Hemingway."

Dad stared hungrily at the panoramic 180-degree view out the windows. He hadn't had so much as a glimpse outside since he'd come home. Kannapolis didn't make much of a splash—the lights of the little town were few and far between at midnight. But the nighttime sky was luminescent with stars. A telescope made of aged copper was cordoned off with velvet ropes close by, like a museum exhibit.

Mueller followed Dad's eyes and gestured at the telescope. "Galileo's. The other two are in museums, but Mr. Calhoun purchased this one from a private collector."

A voice boomed from across the foyer. "The owner made the mistake of showing it to me. He wanted one of my companies. I made that telescope part of the deal."

Using a cane, Paul Calhoun carefully picked his way across the marble floors toward us. My mouth loosened a little in surprise at the sight of him. There are pictures of him all over the research center—shaking hands with presidents, playing polo with Prince Charles. In all the photos, he's this tall, robust guy. I expected him to be older in person, but given his obsession with health, I'd also expected him to be fit. But this Paul Calhoun, wearing no jacket himself, was gaunt. His biceps sagged like flags left out in the rain.

His eyes were fervent with excitement, though. He smiled at Dad like he was Michael Jordan. He bent forward and touched Dad's hand. "Bill Jones, I'm Paul Calhoun and I can't tell you how pleased I am to meet you."

Dad was pleasant. "Nice to meet you as well, Mr. Calhoun."

"Would you care for a look?" He gestured at the telescope.

Dad's eyes lit up. "I most definitely would." I pushed him toward the telescope as Mueller moved the velvet ropes surrounding it. Calhoun adjusted the eyepiece to Dad's level, and he peered through.

"Incredible, isn't it? Earth's practically unrecognizable to Galileo, yet look through his telescope and it's all pretty much the same as what he saw five hundred years ago. I'm a big fan of his. Of any man who sacrifices his faith for the chaos of science." He paused, waiting for Dad to be impressed by his musings, but Dad said nothing.

Calhoun finally continued: "Please call me Paul, by the way, as I'm planning on us being great friends." Still no answer from Dad. Calhoun finally turned his attention to me. "You must be Hemingway." He patted my shoulder like a proud uncle. "Quite a son you've got here, Bill."

Dad finally answered him. "Mr. Calhoun, I appreciate your hospitality. And I apologize for my confusion, but why am I here?"

Calhoun nodded. "Very direct. Like me. My office." He turned carefully with his cane and headed for the hall without a second glance. But when I went to push Dad's chair, he called out, "I already know about the telekinesis. No need for showmanship."

Dad's face wrinkled with irritation. The velociraptor gears suddenly shifted, and he whizzed after Calhoun.

Calhoun's private office was reluctantly decorated like a Texas ranch: knotty log sofas, a bolted leather armchair, an ottoman, and some Navajo paintings and rugs.

It didn't suit him, but he apparently didn't care enough to start over. He'd simply shoved a museum's worth of Indigenous artifacts into a corner to make room for messy miniature hydroponic gardens, microscopes, maps, medical equipment, and reams of paper. He was a science enthusiast, not an aesthete.

He sat, unnaturally erect on the edge of an ottoman, despite the instant and obvious strain it was causing his sagging frame. Mueller gently gestured for him to take the chair, but Calhoun waved him off with an irritated frown. I briefly wondered which of Calhoun's parents had taught him good posture, and at what cost.

Calhoun finally answered my dad's question. "You're here because we need to talk about Hemingway. He's made the greatest discovery since Galileo postulated the Earth revolved around the sun."

I actually liked the guy when he said that.

"And he made it under my roof, without my permission. He made a deal with me to repeat what he did to you, in exchange for staying out of jail." He lowered his eyes in my direction. "He's been deliberately defying the terms of that deal."

Yeah, maybe not so much.

Dad was reasonable, but frank. "My son has my ethics. You made him attempt to revive someone who hadn't signed off to become what I am."

"Nor did you."

"True, but emotion outweighed reason in my case. I'm his dad."

"Also true, but irrelevant. There are no clauses in the contract for his ethics. Either he honors what he signed, or you both face the consequences." He paused, anticipating immediate surrender.

Dad didn't budge. "I'm familiar with the terms of the contract. And yes, I also knew what he was doing and why. I also happen to agree with him. I'm guessing you already knew that. Which again, brings me back to the question, why am I here?"

Calhoun's eyebrows flared momentarily, but he caught himself and laughed. "I tried to muscle you, Bill. That was clumsy. I've got my hands full, as you can imagine, so when I see what needs to happen, I'm in a hurry to get there. And I admit, I'm a little too accustomed to getting my way without a fight. I should have given you more credit."

Dad was generous. "No offense taken."

"Let's get on with it, then. I was hoping I could change your mind about the ethics. And in changing your mind, change his too. I'm a humanist, Mr. Jones. I built this center to save lives. And your son can save more lives than I ever imagined possible."

Dad spoke delicately. "I'm willing to hear your arguments, Mr. Calhoun, and I consider myself a humanist, but not in the same way as you, I'm guessing. In any case, I'll be equally frank. You'd have Hemingway repeat the experiment—improve and expand upon it because—and you'll forgive me for noticing—you're dying. You'd like to become what I am. That's why you're in a hurry. That's why you'd like us to be friends. You'll want company."

My eyes bugged with realization—Dad had called it. That was why Calhoun was so gaunt—he was close to kicking it.

Calhoun turned to Mueller. "Can you beat that? His cognitive MRIs were through the roof. His brain is firing on all cylinders." He turned back to Dad. "No human in history has been able to do what you're doing, right now. Do you have any idea what we'll change, once we give that to more people? No more idiots running countries into the ground. No more religious nuts holding up logical and humane research. How can you possibly dilute the argument down to just me?"

"Because it's first and foremost what you're after. You're not without bias. And it's okay, neither am I. Second, Hemingway's right, that man . . ."

"With everything you can do, you're worried about a few test subjects? Really? I thought you weren't a member of the Flat Earth Society."

Dad was calm but emphatic. "I assume by Flat Earth Society you mean anti-science. I'm neither anti-science nor religious, although I think the latter is not without its purpose in this debate. I've only just learned that. And yes, I am worried. If you believe I have the talents I do, you should listen too. There aren't enough resources to sustain this. You're talking about a species superior to humans, one that can live—potentially indefinitely."

Dad had hoped this would make Calhoun pause. But the guy just leaned forward, fascinated.

"You know this how?"

Dad was instantly uncomfortable. "I'll tell you, provided two things. First, you listen and promise to think about it. Second, Hemingway leaves the room."

My eyes bugged. "Are you kidding me? No. I'm good right here."

Calhoun ordered, "Done. Lars, take Hemingway back to the lobby."

I leaped up and got in Dad's face. "You're shitting me, right?"

Mueller stood and gestured to me. "Hemingway. After me, please." He opened the door and gestured to me. I looked at Dad, incredulous.

"It's all right, son. It's about bias, not intelligence. I'll fill you in later."

"Yes, I know the drill. Let the grown-ups talk."

"Hemingway!" Dad snapped.

I raised my hands in surrender and headed for the door, but I couldn't resist throwing out a parting shot. I looked at Calhoun. "Not all advances in science are good, you know. Einstein said that after we made the atomic bomb."

"True," Calhoun admitted. "Some science is bad."

"So how do we know—?"

"We don't," he admitted. "We have no chance of knowing unless we study it. Study the miracle you've made of your dad. That's science."

Is it possible to be pissed and flattered at the same time?

Mueller didn't try to entertain me or even talk to me in the twenty minutes I spent in the lobby. And yes, I played with Galileo's telescope, just to piss him off. He just tapped away on his laptop.

When I finally stopped acting like a kid, I obsessed about what Dad had said. About how he could potentially live indefinitely. I wondered why he'd say that. How he'd *know*.

There was only one way. Dad had tried to kill himself.

The back of my neck suddenly burned with rejection. He'd tried to leave me. After all I'd done. *How? When?*

The security guys had barely shut the door to our house when I turned to Dad. I was so angry I was shaking. "Let's start with the part where you tried to kick it."

He sighed. "I'm really tired, this could wait."

"Oh, you can sleep, can you? That's good. For you, I mean. Personally, I doubt I'd get much after hearing that my dad tried to commit suicide." I folded my arms and looked at him. "When? When did you do this?"

"The first day you started at Lifebank. It was stupid. I swallowed a bunch of pills, figured that the therapist would find me."

I kicked the chair. The first day I went to work at Lifebank. In short, his first opportunity.

I remembered asking why he was acting so weird. Even though I dreaded the answer, I choked out, "Why?"

"Is it really any great mystery? Because I didn't want to live like this." He cast his eyes at the chair. "Anyway, it was stupid, and I'm sorry. You've no idea. And if it's any comfort to you, I didn't so much as take a nap. Hemingway, I love you, son. I was wrong. It was just a knee-jerk reaction to what I've become. I'm not leaving you—"

"And I'm supposed to believe that why?"

"Because as I explained, I don't know if I can die. Everything on me heals, except the quadriplegia. I'm not even sure I can get sick. The only things so far that I'm susceptible to are heat and lack of hydrogen sulfide."

We paused, neither of us knowing what to say.

"Is it really all bad?" I finally choked out, dreading the answer.

Dad paused long and hard before saying, "No. Quite the opposite. And that's the biggest point I'm trying to make to you here. It's been a couple of weeks, and I've had a chance to come to terms with what I am. I've learned things I never would have as Bill Jones. Stuff that maybe no one's ever thought of before. It's an incredible gift."

I shook my head furiously, unable to speak.

He saw my refusal and argued, "I'm not telling you this because I want you to forgive yourself. Or me. I'm telling you because it's true."

Damn that mind-reading thing.

Dad continued. "I might be stuck in this room, but I don't feel that way. I go away—in my head—and I can picture solutions to problems no one's been able to solve. And you know what? It's absolutely intoxicating. I imagine it's a little like being on drugs, because sometimes I have to really work to bring myself back to the here and now. In my head, there's no strife, or war, or catastrophe, because I have potential solutions, you know? Think about that. You gave me that. What a gift. So, thank you."

"I didn't give that to you. It just happened," I said hoarsely.

He grunted. "Fair enough, but I'm grateful anyway, just so you know. Now. Tonight, and Paul Calhoun."

I interrupted. "He wants to sell Gray technology?"

"That much was obvious from the beginning. No. I have thought about this on loads of levels, but I'll reduce it to the two that matter most. First, the big picture. As a Gray, I'm seeing some things that aren't such a good idea. Ideas, that, if I was a greedy or amoral guy, I'd jump on. So, I'm worried about what would happen if you gave this gift to Paul Calhoun. Hemingway, I read that man's mind. And while he's incredibly bright, he has a limited capacity for empathy. So, I started thinking, what happens if you give unlimited intelligence and powers to a guy of unlimited resources and limited empathy?"

"I get what you're saying, but don't you think becoming a Gray would make him more humane?"

"If that were true, why would I even be coming up with bad ideas? Becoming a Gray doesn't make you an archangel, son. I'd like to say I'm better than Calhoun, but I'm not. You know the biggest thing holding me back? It's not morality."

"Me?" I guessed.

"Nope, you're the reason I'm thinking about doing all this stuff."

"Thanks?"

He glowered at me.

I thought. "It's money, isn't it?"

"That's the one. I'd need operating capital and it takes a while to build that up. Now. Calhoun's already got money. Think of what he could do as a Gray. He could solve any problem in his own favor . . . And who could stop him?"

"Because as a Gray he could read their minds and know what they're planning."

"Yes. So, the only conclusion I keep coming back to is that Paul Calhoun must never become a Gray. He's got to die. Like every other person on this planet."

"Well, forgive me if I'm a little confused here, but didn't you just tell him I'd help him out? Make him a Gray? I mean, you guys were pretty buddy-buddy when you came out of that office."

"What else was I supposed to say? As long as he thinks he's in control, you're safe." He paused. "How close are you? To remembering what you did?"

"Close, I think."

"Work slow. And maybe nature will take its course. Calhoun hasn't got that long."

"Yeah? And what're you gonna do?"

"I'm gonna start working with Tan. On ambulation. Calhoun wants to be able to move."

"We're carpooling?"

"No. I've got a work-from-home situation. If I can solve it, it'll really help."

I froze, reminded again of how I'd incapacitated him.

He spotted it. "Not like that. Look. We're hoping Calhoun dies and this whole project goes away. But that might not happen before we need to get out of here. If Calhoun doesn't die and they go full-court press, we need a backup plan to escape. Being able to move would help make that possible."

"Let's talk about that. We need money, a place to go, a way to get you there, and oh, of course, an unlimited supply of hydrogen sulfide."

"That one's the stickler. I haven't solved that," Dad admitted.

"Work faster."

"Agreed." His yellow eyes looked up at me hopefully. "We good?"

"No, not really, but I'll work on it." I headed for the stairs when I remembered. "What was the other level?"

"What?"

"You said you'd thought about this on loads of levels and then you said, 'first, big picture.' That implies there's at least one more issue."

"Oh." He paused in thought. "You know, I'd rather wait on that one. That's a long conversation. And I might want to talk to that detective first."

The hairs on my arm bristled. "You want to talk to Burkhardt? Do you really think that's a good idea?"

"No," he answered simply. "But stop being so paranoid. It's not about you. I want to talk to him about that reporter."

My eyes bugged. "You think Calhoun had something to do with that?"

Dad weighed the question before answering, "Like I said, I might just want to talk to the guy."

CHAPTER FOURTEEN

I wasn't included in any more meetings at Lifebank. That was the punish-ment for my attempted sabotage. They'd go into the conference room and shut the door while I idled around. When they came out, Cass would snap off whatever questions they'd compiled, and I'd answer, then she'd turn on her heels and head back to her office.

It was a little lonely, but Melissa kept me going. She and Lila had gone back to Duke Medical Center in Durham, but she texted whenever Lila was asleep. Those conversations were about nothing and everything.

FAVORITE KIDS' BOOK?

She fired back without hesitation. GREEN EGGS AND HAM.

My mother would've loved her. I responded, *BETTER THAN* THE CAT IN THE HAT? HERESY. I DO NOT LIKE IT, SAM I AM.

YOU MAY NOT LIKE IT, SO YOU SAY, BUT TRY IT, TRY IT AND YOU MAY.

THAT WHAT YOU'RE MAKING FOR DINNER FRI—DAY?

A one-word answer to that one. *COLD.*

NOT AT ALL, LOOK HERE! LOOK, LOOK! YOU DID SAY YOU ARE A LOUSY COOK. ☺

Friday night did eventually roll around, with the long-promised visit to meet Lila and her parents. I stood on the front porch of Melissa's turn-of-the-century house on Union Street, absolutely itching to see her. I rang the bell and waited, listening to the minor eruption it caused: voices calling to one another, a dog barking, feet pounding on the stairs. There was something fragrant about the whole thing—a whiff of family I hadn't experienced since my mom died.

I shifted my feet waiting, noting how the house told the story of her sister's illness: evidence was everywhere of how her family lived prior to Lila's diagnosis and how they lived now.

It would've taken the whole family's best efforts to achieve this kind of restoration. There wasn't a smidgen of rot—the wood siding and porch boards were fresh and firm. Even the paint was relatively new—a sunny yellow on the siding accented with Charleston-style black trim. The garden was full of glossy red cannas and papery crepe myrtles situated in homemade beds that a dad had dug and a mom had planted. No evidence of a landscaper's designer mulching. This family had done all the work themselves. And they'd put a lot of love into it too.

But the fans and white wicker furniture on the porch were draped in cobwebs that had been brushed out of the way but never cleared because no one had time. The local newspapers rotted on the sidewalk and lawn where they'd been thrown, the roses needed deadheading and the lawn was covered in land mines. Dog owners had obviously decided no one at this house would care whether they cleaned up after their animal or not.

The door finally swung open, and a one-hundred-pound coonhound barreled at my crotch. At the last moment, he jumped up and lapped at my face.

"Dobro, down! DOWN!" Melissa shouted at the dog. The dog ignored her and bounced around my feet. "Sorry," she pleaded to me. "He's friendly. He just thinks he's a lot smaller than he is."

"S'okay!" Dobro finally settled for a pat on the head. "Umm . . . Dobro?"

"It's Czech. My family's Czech originally. Means good."

I smiled. "Good, the dog? You validate the dog?"

She grinned and pulled the door wide. "Every chance I get. C'mon in."

I stepped inside and finally registered her chestnut hair—down, lush, and swishing with every tilt of her head. She wore a fitted white blouse and a pair of red shorts. No makeup, no earrings, and absolutely gorgeous.

We stood there awkwardly for a minute, suddenly and mutually aware that I was a foreign substance in her house. Her parents broke the silence. Her mom, a diminutive blonde with a world-weary smile, came down the hallway and offered a hand. "Hello, you must be Hemingway. I'm Mary and this is my husband, Kevin." She gestured to Melissa's dad, who'd trailed in behind her—a big guy with chestnut hair and a twitching frown as he offered a hand but said nothing.

"It's Hem, mostly," I told them, as I shook Kevin's hand.

"Well, come in, come in! Sit down!" Mary waved at me to follow her down the hall.

We all turned to follow—me, Mel, Kevin, and Dobro—and bumped into one another, generating an awkward round of "After you."

Melissa whispered agitatedly as we walked, "This is going to be seriously weird, isn't it? I didn't really think this through. I just wanted you to meet Lila and we only got home today. I didn't plan all this."

"It's a little weird," I acknowledged. "But it's fine."

We bypassed the front parlors, stiffly decked in period glory, and headed back to a large modern kitchen and a glowing, comfortable sunroom that served as a family room. Both were warm with late-afternoon light and littered with further evidence of the family's refuge: jars of medicines, vitamins, and small medical devices that covered every end table and the coffee table. Curled on the sofa was a tiny figure, watching TV.

"Lila, meet Hemingway," Mary urged.

Lila turned to me, and I met her eyes. I hadn't really paid attention to what she looked like at the hospital. I'd been too focused on the variety of disabilities she had—the leg brace and the hearing aid. I now realized she didn't look anything like Melissa, beyond being tiny. She was a virtual replica of Mary—white-blonde hair, pale skin, and alert blue eyes.

She gave me the first happy smile I'd gotten all week as she pointed an accusing ten-year-old finger. "You're the boyfriend."

"Lila!" Melissa protested.

Lila turned a full-wattage grin on Mel and argued, "YOU kissed him. You told me!" She turned to me with a sly smile. "You kissed my sister."

I pointed right back at her. "You're the annoying little sister. The one who's faking being sick."

"Am not!"

"Are too!"

"Am not! I'm sick and I'm going to die," she announced, triumphantly. I froze and glanced over at Mel. She lifted her empty hands, a gesture that said, "Told you."

Kevin visibly paled and abruptly declared, "I'm just gonna run to the store. Be right back." He grabbed his keys off the counter and hustled out of the room.

I'd already screwed it up.

A look passed between Melissa and her mom at her dad's sudden disappearance, but I decided not to ask questions. Not knowing what to do, I flopped onto the sofa next to Lila. "What're we watching?" I asked.

"*The Baby-Sitters Club.*"

I wrinkled my nose. "Sounds girly."

She giggled. "I like it." She switched the TV off and peered into my face. "Why are you sad?"

"I'm sad?"

She nodded gravely. "Why? 'Cause your dad is sick? Melissa said he's really sick and can't leave the house."

"Kind of." I nodded. "It's kind of about that."

"Are you sad because he's sad? Because he can't go outside? I know all about not being able to go outside," she assured me.

"Sucks, doesn't it?" I agreed. "If you could go outside right now and do anything you wanted, what would you do?"

She thought for a moment. "I'd fly."

Having expected her to say something ordinary, something doable, like biking, swimming, or running, I liked her answer. I had said *anything*, so why should she settle for ordinary? Which begged another question: Where had my own imagination gone? Lila was only seven years younger than me. Technically, I was still a kid. And a few months ago, I'd have expected an answer like that. Now I just felt tired. Tired in that grown-up kind of way, where nothing is new, nothing excites you anymore, and you only get up in the morning because that's what you did the day before.

I leaned back on the corner sofa and got comfortable. "Sounds cool. I'm in."

She snuggled in closer. "Where should we fly to?"

I thought for a moment. "North Pole. See what Santa's up to."

Lila laughed. "I know there's no Santa, Hemingway."

"Is too!"

"Is not."

"Well, then you're going to have to get me a bike light for Christmas, because that's what I wrote to him and said I wanted, and I fully expect to get one."

She giggled. "I don't have any money."

"Well, then you better write to him too. Maybe apologize for questioning whether he exists."

We went on in this vein for a while, but Melissa's dad didn't come back. She and her mom stalled as best they could. Mary kept smiling, but dipped out into the hallway with her phone multiple times. Lila and I played Mario Kart. (I'd like to say I let her win, but the fact is, I sucked.)

By the time they gave up on Kevin, Melissa was apologizing for dinner, now old and gooey beef stroganoff.

"This is the first homemade dinner I've had since—" Realizing the answer was "before the accident," I decided I didn't want to go there. I changed tacks. "It's fabulous, seriously, and I'm starving." I lifted my loaded fork to prove it.

"We have to say grace first!" Lila said chidingly.

Religious people. Right. I was hitting it right out of the park in terms of first impressions. Lila suddenly offered me her hand, and I took it, confused, as Melissa took my hand on the other side. I glanced across the table to see Mary was holding both her daughters' hands too, her head bowed. Once again, awkward. I hate faking, so bowing my head like I'm joining a prayer just goes against the grain. In general, I prefer to err on the side of disrespect, but that's because most people are shitty. Mary was not only caring for a terminally ill daughter but she was also being nice and gracious to an accused and decidedly guilty felon that was macking on her daughter. I decided I'd make an exception in her case and bowed my head. I still felt like a fraud, though.

"Dear Heavenly Father, we thank thee for the food that has been provided and the hands that have prepared the food. We ask thee to bless it that it may nourish and strengthen our bodies."

"Amen!" Lila proclaimed, and Mary leaned over and kissed her daughter's hand.

This time I waited until everyone else started to eat before even lifting my fork. Despite the awkwardness of Kevin's disappearance, Mary kept up table conversation all by herself too, asking questions about me and Dad without so much as hinting whether she knew anything about us.

Lila suddenly interrupted, "I want to talk to him." She met her mom's eyes. "Can I? Can we call him?" Then her eyes trailed over to me. "Please?"

I was a blank. "I'm sorry, who do you want to talk to?"

"Your dad."

I hesitated. Melissa's sentiments about Lifebank were born from a devout religious faith she'd clearly been taught by her parents. Chances were good her mom already knew about my dad and did not approve.

Mary was thoughtful for a moment and then nodded. "That's a lovely thought. It's okay with me if it's okay with Hemingway." She turned to me, "Is it? Is he okay to come to the phone?"

I hesitated. "He's, ummm—"

Melissa read my thoughts. "Hem. It's fine. I told her what a great guy he is."

Mary chimed in. "Would probably be good for both of them." I pushed emotion away and looked over at Lila. "I bet he'd love to talk to you."

Once we'd cleared the dishes, I pulled out my cell and dialed. Dad answered on the first ring and I explained who was really calling.

"No. I don't think that's a good idea, son—"

I didn't hear the rest of his protest because Lila grabbed the phone out of my hand. "Hello, I'm Lila! I heard you were sad because you're sick. I'm sick too, and I hardly ever get to see my friends. So, I thought we could be friends, since we're both sick." He said something and she laughed. "I'm ten, how old are you?" Quickly followed by, "How old is Hemingway?" They chatted for a few minutes and Lila's eyes landed on me, a grin on her face. "No, he hasn't. Ewww! Okay, I'll tell him." She held the phone down and looked at me, her button nose wrinkling. "He says you need to kiss Melissa again."

Melissa laughed, I colored. "Tell him he needs to mind his own business."

Mary interrupted: "I hate to break this up, but Lila, I have to get you in the bath, sweetie."

Lila nodded, held up a finger, and talked into the phone. "I have to go. But we can talk tomorrow, okay?" He said something and she nodded, forgetting he couldn't see that. "Okay, bye friend." She handed me the phone. "He sounds nice. I don't know why people are so scared of him."

Melissa and Mary turned bright red.

"Bath, I think," Mary said.

Noting their discomfort, I waived it off. "It's okay. I don't mind. She didn't say anything that isn't true." To prove my mettle, I got up and offered, "Here. Why don't you let me carry her upstairs?" Mary nodded.

"C'mon you," was all I said as I gathered her in my arms and held her close.

Once Lila was upstairs, Mel and I stepped out onto the patio and watched the fireflies float in the air just above the grass. I trapped one in my hand and watched it glow. "I love these guys," I admitted to her. "Every summer I have to repress my urge to get a jelly jar and catch some. Did you know the adult ones don't eat? They're literally one-hundred-percent cold energy—emitting light, but no heat."

Was I just rambling on about bugs? For real? I opened my hand again and we both watched him take off.

"How do you know so much about bugs? And plants?" Melissa asked.

"My mom. She was a biology teacher at the community college. Until she got breast cancer. You know the rest of that story."

"Seems like every conversation we have seems to circle back to death." Mel sank onto the brick retaining wall that surrounded her family's patio and exhaled. "I'm sorry."

I sat down on the wall next to her. "For what?"

She groaned. "Where do I start? My dad?"

I shrugged. "I didn't come here for dinner with Kevin." To punctuate my point, I smiled and took her hand. It was a sweaty night, but I didn't care.

She smiled softly. "He can't stand it when Lila talks that way. He's still holding out hope. So, when she responds that way, he just gets up and leaves. I have no idea where he goes."

"Bar?"

She shook her head. "He doesn't drink. I think he just drives around— he goes through a lot of gas. He doesn't even work anymore, or help with Lila—I care for her while my mom works two jobs, just so we can keep the lights on." She sighed and continued: "And I have to apologize for what Lila said about your dad."

I looked away. "Far as I'm concerned, nobody has to apologize for Lila."

"I'm apologizing for me. I'm the one who told her . . ."

"Seriously, it's okay. Please stop apologizing for the best dinner I've had since this mess started. And arguably even years before that? Your mom, your sister . . . they're amazing. You're so—" I stopped myself before saying "lucky," realizing just how moronic that would sound.

"Lucky," she finished. "It's okay to say it, I am. And so are you—you realize that, right?"

"Yeah, I don't really feel like either of us are lucky right now."

"And yet, if you got hit by a bus tomorrow, seeing as you insist on riding that bike everywhere, wouldn't you want today back?" She looked at me expectantly.

"What I'd want is to punch whoever hit me, but I see your point. Is it okay if I just wish I was free of Lifebank?"

Melissa laughed and then hesitated.

"Will you tell me about the accident? And how you ended up there? I just want to hear it from you."

Moment broken. I retracted my hand and sucked in a breath. "I can't. I seriously can't. I would tell you, because you deserve to know, but it's not up to me. I will tell you flat out, I'm not innocent."

She absorbed her disappointment for a moment and nodded. "Yeah, I kinda guessed that."

"I am trying to get out of it, though. The Lifebank thing. I'm only there because of what Dad needs."

"Well, how about I help?" she proposed.

"With what?"

"With whatever it is you're up to." Melissa squeezed my hand. "I'm perfectly aware you didn't do any of this as a career move. You're in a lot of trouble, you keep all of it from me—"

"Yeah, well, that's because that could land you in trouble. And, you have enough going on."

"Let me finish." She waited until I met her eyes. "I know you hate that place, and I can guess why they want you working there. And there's no way you're just letting them run all over you without formulating some kind of plan. And pardon me for noticing, but you don't seem to have many friends right now to help. I can't do much—"

"You shouldn't do any of it. You have Lila to take care of. Plus, it could be dangerous."

She scoffed at that one.

"I'm not exaggerating. Look, I've stopped myself from simply unloading on you more times than I can count. That would be absolutely amazing. Not so great for you, though. I did what I did, and I have to fix it. I don't even deserve help."

"So, skip the stuff that incriminates me, and the self-loathing. Just give me . . . something? Anything. I want to help. Not just because I care about you and your dad, but because I think what Lifebank is doing is wrong."

"Mel—"

"I let you into my life; please let me into yours, just in some small way? Or this"—she pointed at both of us—"isn't going anywhere. It's not a threat, it's just a reality. You can't have a relationship with someone who hides everything from you."

I started to protest, but the back door opened. Kevin spotted us and said, "Oh, sorry, didn't realize." He started to close the door, had another thought, and opened it again. "Is your mom upstairs?"

Melissa nodded and turned back to me. "You don't even have to tell me what it's about."

I thought long and hard. I genuinely didn't want her involved. I ultimately decided on the most innocuous task I could think of. "There's a guy I need to find. He's a professor—Dr. David Elks. He did a TED Talk about putting injured people into a hibernation state using cooling and hydrogen sulfide. Just until they can get to the hospital. Cass made me watch it when I started as an intern. That's what gave me the idea to try the stuff on my dad. After this all happened, I tried to look him up—he had a clinic at the University of Pittsburgh studying this stuff—but when I called the school, they just said he's gone. I can't find him online; guy seems to have disappeared. Maybe he just retired, or he may be as depraved as Cass. But there's a small chance he could help."

She smiled. "Elks. I'm on it."

"You can't tell anyone. ESPECIALLY not your family."

"Goes without saying."

I spotted Burkhardt's car at the curb by my house. I jumped off the bike, hustled for the door, and was reaching for the knob when the door opened from the inside and Burkhardt walked out.

He nodded in my direction. "Evening."

He'd been in my house. He'd seen my dad. "He let you in?"

Burkhardt shrugged. "I didn't break in, if that's what you're asking. He invited me over. See you around." He nudged past me and headed down the driveway.

I digested that. My dad had tried to refuse to talk to Lila, but he'd opened the door wide for the guy who was trying to arrest me for murder.

I ran after him. "Wait a minute. When did he invite you over?"

Burkhardt turned around. "Why don't you ask him?"

"'Cause I'm asking you. "

"You're awfully jumpy about me coming over," he observed.

"I'm nervous about anyone seeing Dad."

And for the first time since I'd met him, Burkhardt crumpled a bit. He finally muttered, "Yeah, I can understand that." He sighed and explained. "He had some questions about the reporter. I told him over the phone the case was closed, but he still wanted to talk about it. He said you'd be out tonight, and he thought it was a good time to talk." He met my eyes. "He specified he wouldn't answer any questions about you. That if I even brought you up, I'd immediately be asked to leave."

I rippled with irritation, rather than relief. I was being completely open with Dad, and he wasn't reciprocating. But I wasn't going to share that thought with the detective. "What do you mean, the case is closed?"

Burkhardt shrugged. "Medical report came back. Woman had some sort of a stroke. Probably what caused the fall. Also explains why she didn't pick up the phone. Probably couldn't talk. Just one of those freak things. I told him as much over the phone, but he still wanted to talk."

He headed down the steps but abruptly turned. "He's a good guy, Hemingway. He really cares about you. He deserves the best."

I whispered, "I know."

Burkhardt nodded. "You take care. 'Night."

I went inside and found Dad staring at something in his lap. He didn't even look up. I was all set to go off, but something in his face made me hesitate. "Dad? You all right? Need a dose? When was the last time you had one?" I leaned over to check his stats on the computer.

"I'm fine," he said quietly. The page flipped in his lap.

"You don't look all right," I argued. My nerves tensed. "Did he say something?"

"Who?"

"Burkhardt."

"Oh. No." The page flipped again.

"Okaaay... what are you looking at?"

"What? Oh. Medical report on Lisa."

So now she was Lisa, not "the reporter." I decided to invite a fight. "Yeah, Burkhardt said she had a stroke. Just out of curiosity, why was..." He wasn't listening and he was starting to piss me off. "Look, we have plenty of things to worry about, and this isn't one of them. You're weirding me out. What's going on?"

"Nothing," he insisted. The pages of the medical report shuffled in the air and once restored to original order, rested on his lap.

"Nothing? Really? Then you want to tell me why you called Burkhardt?"

"I told you I might call him," he grumbled.

"Yeah, but you left out the part that I wasn't going to be included in the meeting. You're doing a lot of that, lately. Care to tell me why?"

He pursed his lips. "Hemingway, I'm begging you. Just this once, for the love of God, leave it alone, would you? I need to think."

I was about to unload, but my cell rang—Lifebank. "Yeah?"

"We're on again," Stephens said. "Accidental death this time, more akin to your dad's injuries. Listen, the body isn't even here yet. I know you have to make arrangements for your dad, so I wanted to call as soon as I got the news. You've got some time." She hung up.

"Another one?" Dad asked.

"Don't change the subject. They said I have some time."

"Not if you want to follow Charlie," he advised.

"Shit." I'd forgotten. I wanted to follow Charlie, find out what his relationship was with Lifebank. He almost certainly knew something that would be of use. If I didn't do it now, who knew when I'd get another chance?

I ran up to my room, flipped open the shade, and peered at Charlie's house. The lights in the living room were on and I could see his shadow through the blinds, bustling around inside, probably looking for his keys. I had a couple of minutes—tops

I changed from "dinner with the parents" clothes to a dark T-shirt and shorts, idly wondering why Dad didn't just use his magic powers to follow Charlie. But he was as self-absorbed as a gamer right now. If I wanted truths, I was just going to have to go find them.

CHAPTER FIFTEEN

The toughest decision about following Charlie was whether or not to try and take the car. If I took the bike and he hit country roads, he'd be gone. On the other hand, if I sacrificed my refusal to drive a car and he stayed close to downtown, he'd probably spot me. This late at night, cars downtown are few and far between. If I was on the bike, he couldn't see me or hear me.

Plus, I really hated the idea of driving. The bike won.

As it turned out, he was only going about a mile. Simultaneously, it was nowhere you wanted to be at midnight.

The Bottoms is a literal and figurative turn of phrase for this part of Concord. Bank west downtown and you can roll to the Bottoms. The grade is that steep. The population contrast is just as stark; the neighborhood is as poor and Black as Union Street is white and wealthy.

Houses here are old, like those on Union Street, but if you were asked to describe one, you'd reference "rundown" rather than "historic." And that's only if you're being generous. Most of them have boards on the windows, if they have windows at all. Fences are makeshift contraptions involving chicken wire, and the dogs that police the yards are definitely not pets. Basically, I stuck out like a sore thumb. And I had absolutely no justification for being here if I was spotted. Streets that dead end at the train tracks aren't usually cycling paths, even in the daytime.

Charlie pulled onto the gravel driveway of a sixties-style brick ranch with a glowing neon sign that read, "Smythe Funeral Home." Everything about the place was bizarre. First off, it was the only commercial venture I'd ever seen in the Bottoms. Plus, hello, why the neon sign? As if somebody might wake up in the middle of the night, realize they forgot to bury their loved one, and troll the neighborhood for a funeral-home sign that says, "Open 24 Hours."

The weirdest thing of all was the name—Smythe Funeral Home. Charlie worked for Blackwelder. Why was he picking up a body from another funeral home? Not exactly the kind of business where you have to worry about customer complaints. I braked about twenty yards shy of the house, laid my bike against a row of garbage cans, and looked around for a place to hide. I felt like a dork standing behind a tree, but I didn't have many options.

The front door cracked open at Charlie's approach, only to shut again and reopen a minute later, when two guys made their way out. Charlie was busy reversing multiple times on the gravel.

A kid's voice startled me. "This your bike? Or don't you need it no more?"

I turned to see a ten-year-old kid straddling the seat, ready to take off. I answered him in a hushed tone. "Yes, it's my bike and I still need it. Put it back."

His voice rang out in protest, "Then how come you're throwing it in the garbage?"

"Shhh . . ." I hissed. "I'm just resting it there. Don't you have school or something in the morning?"

He shrugged and held on to the bike. "That's my dad," he nodded in the general direction of the two guys, who were now chatting with Charlie quietly as he opened the back of the van. "I have to go with him when he goes."

"That sucks," I volunteered, as I kept my eyes on Charlie. They were now loading a body into Charlie's hearse. "You must get tired and all."

The kid nodded and I asked casually, "He work here?" I pointed at Charlie.

The kid rolled his eyes. "No. But he works for the guy who owns this place."

"And who's that?"

"Some rich guy. He's got like lots of people who work for him. He calls and we got to go. Sometimes here, sometimes other places." The kid continued, "My dad says I gotta stay out of the way, because they don't like me being here." He added proudly, "He makes good money working for them."

"Then he makes enough to buy you a bike," I argued. "A new one."

"Yeah, he's gonna buy me a real bike. A dirt bike."

"What's your name?"

Just then another voice rang out in the darkness. A grown-up voice. An angry one. "JOHN CHARLES!"

The kid and I both turned in the direction of the yelling. Charlie was now making his way up the steep grade of the Bottoms—and the two big guys were following him.

The taller one looked from John Charles to me, and back to his son. "What're you doing, talking to this guy? And whose bike is that?"

"It's mine," I answered, cutting the kid off. "He was telling me all about the dirt bike you're going to buy for him." I turned to John Charles for confirmation. "Right?"

John Charles nodded, keeping his eyes on the pavement.

The shorter one turned to me and said, "Oh yeah? You always come out middle of the night to talk about cycling? 'Cause you don't look like you belong here."

I thought fast. "No, I came for Charlie. He's my next-door neighbor. I got called in to work, and I needed a lift. But he left, so I was trying to catch up. I only have a learner's permit." I made sure to make eye contact as I said the last part.

John Charles's dad turned to Charlie. "You know this kid?"

Charlie nodded nervously. "Yeah. He's my neighbor."

"Yeah? He don't look like no janitor."

"Well . . . he is. At Food Lion." Charlie was trying hard to make it sound like no big deal. "C'mon guys, his mom's sick. I said I'd help him out with a lift when I could." Charlie looked me dead in the eye, silently urging me to play along. "Pete, you really shouldn't . . . follow me when I'm working. Next time just call, okay? Get in the hearse. I'll be there in a minute."

I nodded and turned to get my bike, but John Charles was still sitting on it. I was deliberating what to say when Charlie interrupted. "Pete, why don't you just leave the bike? I don't have room for it anyway. I'm sure John Charles will look after it for you. Won't you?" He turned to the kid.

John Charles's eyes glowed. "Awesome!"

I mumbled, "Yeah, have fun."

We climbed the hill out of the Bottoms and were headed down Union Street before Charlie exploded. "What the fuck, Hem? What were you doing following me?"

"You owe Pete a bike," I argued. "I just put Shimano brakes on that."

"What? Jesus, come off it! Buy another one. You got the salary for it. Now answer me. What were you doing following me?" He turned to me, the muscles in his face taut and his eyes wide with panic.

"I wanted to see where the B's come from," I responded airily. "See if they were legal. At just a guess, I'd have to say that's a no."

Charlie slammed his fist against the steering wheel.

"What the fuck are the B's? And you stupid fucking kid. You have no idea—"

I shouted right back at him.

"What're you doing anyway? I'm guessing this isn't on your to-do list for Blackwelder. They know about this?"

"Mind your own goddamn business. I just saved your ass."

"And why the hell does my ass need saving? Why am I Pete with the sick mom and a cleanup on aisle seven?"

"Cause if they mention to anybody that they saw you . . ." He trailed off and exhaled loudly. "Look. No, this isn't for Blackwelder. I do this occasionally for extra cash."

"Ewww. Can't you just bartend or something? Anyway, why do you need extra cash? You got a good job."

"Most of which is spent on alimony." Charlie paused before admitting, "I don't just watch the ball games, Hem. Sometimes I make a little bet on them."

"Oh Christ."

Charlie pleaded, "You mention this to anyone and it's my ass, okay? My job, my license, everything. Hell, you won't be the only one looking at jail time."

I gritted my teeth. "Tell me what you know. Where do these subjects come from?"

"I don't know. And I don't ask. You shouldn't either. Those guys aren't exactly funeral directors, in case you haven't figured that out."

"Who calls you? Cass?"

"No! God no! Look, just leave it alone, would you?"

I folded my arms.

Charlie sighed. "I just ship 'em, Hem. And I get paid. I get paid really well." He abruptly swung the car to the curb in front of the Gem Theater, five hundred yards from the research center. "Here's where you get out. I don't think it's a good idea, you showing up with me."

I was surprised at him dumping me out and briefly wondered whether Charlie was just paranoid. But I got out of the car, and he sped off.

So much for this line of inquiry. The B's were illegal, but telling Burkhardt would cost Charlie everything. And how much was everything? Jail? Or worse? I was starting to regret involving Mel in any way and secretly hoped it would take her a long while to find the professor.

Images of the whole thing haunted my head. Charlie was hauling bodies, in the middle of the night, on behalf of my employers. And he was scared shitless.

He wasn't just afraid of the guys in the Bottoms, he was afraid of being seen with me at the research center. What was he afraid they'd do?

I shook my head. I needed to get a grip. Cass and company were MDs and PhDs—not exactly central casting for ruthless villains.

Still. Charlie was scared. And if he was scared, I knew I should probably be scared too. Because I was a WAY bigger problem for the research center than Charlie.

CHAPTER SIXTEEN

"Core temperature's at thirty-four and holding," Stephens announced as she leaned over the B's immobile body. "We're ready."

I contemplated the B's bloated form and florid face. Death by misadventure—isn't that what they call it when you're a Darwin Award candidate? White guy, around forty, he'd fallen off a roof earlier in the evening, chasing a squirrel with a rifle. The rifle snagged on a tree limb and he slipped. His head injury had them all excited because the protocols would better match what I'd done to my dad.

Stephens wrinkled her nose as she pulled the blanket down. "Ugh, he's just so fat. I tried to tell them. I'll bet his arteries are denser than most metals." We'd already been here two hours, and she'd done nothing but insult the corpse.

"Tried to tell who what?" I asked her casually.

Cass ignored me and spoke to Belinda. "MRI didn't flag anything too unusual, so let's just get on with this." She turned to me. "Prep for vitrification."

I jolted in surprise. "Wait, what? I thought we were going to—"

"We're doing it my way," Stephens explained.

Cass cut us both off. "It is not your job to question why, Hemingway. Just do it. Cryoprotectants, now."

"We need 50 cc's," Stephens said as she adjusted the bag. She smiled at me. "You tired?"

I nodded. "Any chance we'll be done by noon? Like to get some sleep before tomorrow night."

"You got a date? You're not cheating on me, are you, Hem?" Stephens grinned and checked the computer readings.

You know, since Gerald, I'd kinda lost interest in flirting with Dr. Stephens. But seeing as I already had plenty of enemies, I kept up the banter. "Not cheating, per se . . . call it training. For the big day."

She laughed, but Cass didn't. "We've talked about this, Belinda. I'll be back in a few. I have to return a call." And she left.

Stephens inserted another IV. "Got to be her husband. Doubt Calhoun would call at this hour. What time is it, by the way?"

The B's blood slowly filled the bag. "About five," I told her, absolutely flabbergasted by Stephens's revelation. "Cass is married?"

Stephens nodded. "And a mommy. Adopted a son last year."

"Get out. No way." Somehow, I just couldn't picture Dr. Ass changing diapers.

"So . . ." I tried to make my voice casual and chatty. "What you were saying earlier. Who decides whether it's worthwhile? To use these guys as test subjects?"

"What? Oh. Calhoun's office." Stephens tied the bag and got another one. "I tried to tell them he wasn't a good subject before we even brought him here." She rolled her eyes. "They were just so excited he was a head injury."

"How did you even know?"

"I volunteer at a clinic a few hours a month. I'm still a licensed physician."

This was new information. "Okay, but I don't get it. How did you know the guy wasn't a good subject?"

"Because I saw him. I took care of his wife at the clinic. His wife knew he was dead when he fell. She had no money to waste on a DOA. So, she called me."

"Yeah, but why did she have your phone number?"

Stephens shrugged. "A lot of patients at the clinic have my number."

She rambled on about making some house calls, but I was lost in thought, remembering how she'd known so much about Gerald too. So that was how they found subjects—Stephens harvested the free clinic like it was a vegetable garden. It made sense that someone who had no issue hitting on a minor as a form of interrogation would volunteer for this.

I suddenly realized she'd stopped talking. "I had no idea you were so altruistic."

She smiled coyly. "I'm not."

So she wasn't volunteering. Calhoun was paying her to be there, exactly for this purpose.

At 8:00 a.m. Cass ordered, "Hit him again, but this time at lower levels."

I punched his chest with the defibrillator, my confidence buoyed by Cass's failure. Stephens was performing eye rolls in the corner. Her last mention of how overweight the guy was had generated another serious snit between them.

We'd been at it for another three hours now. Everything Cass called set off alarm bells in my head, reminding me, *Yeah, that's what I did.* Or damn close. Enough to make me worried, although mind you, there was no response from the B. I was waiting for her to call it. I could be home by nine and get some solid sleep, without having to worry that Lard Ass would join my stable of ghosts. I suddenly remembered I'd have to find a ride. I didn't have my bike. Or a car. And I somehow doubted Charlie would pick me up. I was so busy wondering how I was going to get home that it took me a minute to process Stephens's "Oh my God."

I turned and saw the EKG monitor bleep again. Lard Ass had a heartbeat.

Cass's eyes lit up, but her voice remained tense. "Cut the hydrogen sulfide. We need to steady that heartbeat." She started compressions. For the next ten minutes, she and Stephens worked, dosing Lard Ass with epinephrine in the hopes of bolstering the beat. But the EKG bleeped only occasionally, like a cell phone about to run out of juice.

"He's too cold," Stephens insisted. "Let's dial him up, get his blood circulating."

Cass turned to me. "Hemingway? What do you think?"

I was blank. I didn't want the guy to come back as a Gray, but I didn't want to be responsible for killing him either.

"HEMINGWAY!" Cass barked. "ANSWER ME NOW!"

"I, uh, didn't do that." That was a true statement. I hadn't done that to my Dad, which made it the safest thing to say.

Cass barked, "Take him up two degrees and let's see if that does anything. If we don't try something, we'll definitely lose him."

Stephens adjusted the Gaymar and the EKG started pumping out a steadier beat.

"I think you've got it, Elaine!" Stephens proclaimed proudly.

Cass's laugh was positively musical. "We've got it. It was your idea. Let's add a little CO_2 into the mix, shall we?" Stephens adjusted the dials again and they chattered back and forth excitedly about their doubts and expectations.

A few minutes later, the B coughed and we all jolted. Stephens and Cass burst into laughter at each other's nervous reactions, but Cass's laugh died quickly when she saw me. "What's on your scrubs? Did you spill blood using the centrifuge?"

"No, why?" I asked as I glanced down and saw what she was talking about. Tiny red dots were dabbled all over my scrubs. I looked like a Jackson Pollock.

Cass glanced at her own scrubs and at the floor.

"Um, Elaine?" Stephens called out nervously.

The B coughed again emitting a small stream of blood from his nose and mouth. A third cough produced a river of red that splashed out onto the floor.

"Oh my God, he's bleeding out. Belinda, take him back down to thirty-four and cut the CO_2. NOW. Hemingway! Help me roll him on his side."

"What? I can't," I said, as the B projectile-barfed blood. I felt it land on my shoes and went light-headed.

"HELP ME OR HE'LL CHOKE ON IT!" Cass barked. "Get his head!" I moved in beside her, my hands fluttering as I tried to get hold of some part of him that wasn't covered in blood.

"On three. One, two, THREE!" And we pushed him sideways. A steady stream of blood poured out his eyes, nose, and mouth, and he slithered on the table.

The EKG bleeped sadly. Cass cleared his mouth and readied a tube, but Stephens shook her head. "The varices have ulcerated. Look." She pointed to the blackness blooming on the B's neck. "Not your fault. Bet he's an alcoholic. Would explain why he fell off the roof. There's nothing to do. He's already hypoxic."

Cass's hands shook, but she finally let go. We all listened to the B as he gagged and choked, and the blood pooled. Stephens grabbed towels to sop up what she could.

I didn't protest this time; I just listened to the EKG's slow fade. He turned the lab into a wading pool before he was done.

Tan was in the foyer when we walked out. Fresh-faced from sleep, he was just starting a regular day, coffee in hand. He glanced up at us brightly and his expression changed. "Whoa," was all he said.

I glanced at my clothes and nearly hurled. We all looked like medics straight from the front.

"Exsanguination," Stephens explained. "Alcoholic."

Tan nodded and asked, "Esophagus?"

Stephens filled him in, and I caught the gist. Exsanguination is the term for someone's blood just pouring out of them. Apparently, it happens occasionally when you apply therapeutic hypothermia to an alcoholic. They cool down just fine. The struggle is in warming them back up because their blood doesn't clot properly. Add in the electric jolt of a defibrillator, and the tiny veins in their throat can burst. Once that happens, there's nothing to do but watch them bleed out from every orifice until they die.

The phone rang and Tan picked it up. He said a quick, "Okay, I'll tell her." And hung up. He glanced at Cass. "That was Calhoun's office. He wants to see you."

She whispered, "I've got to clean up first. Guess I'd better go do that." She turned down the hall to head for the showers.

Stephens called after her, "What're you going to tell him?"

Cass paused in the doorway, her fists clenched. "That we need better subjects." She turned and I was surprised to see tears streaming down her face. "We can't just keep trying this on . . ." she trailed off, upset.

Stephens finished her thought: ". . . on the dregs of society. I know. We're so limited in our capacity to test this . . ."

Cass cut her off harshly. "Belinda, those weren't the words I was going to use."

Stephens challenged: "But it's true, isn't it? This is supposed to be a serious medical inquiry and instead of appropriately screened subjects, we're all sitting around here, waiting on society's leftovers . . ."

Tan moved toward her. "Belinda, let's just . . ."

Stephens continued angrily: "Alcoholics who fall off roofs and crack addicts with heart conditions," she scoffed. "Guys who are so worthless their families would rather sell them than bury them. How can he"—she pointed at the Core Lab—"expect an accurate or positive outcome with these kinds of raw materials? Please explain that to him. From me. Because I'm fed up." She ripped off her gloves, marched past Cass, and headed for the showers.

Cass's back arched, but she didn't say anything. A first. Tan turned to me. "Uh, Hem? You need something?"

"I need a ride home."

I stared out the passenger window the whole way. When I opened the car door, Tan fumbled: "I'm guessing you want some time with your dad, so I'll come back later."

I whirled on him. "Do they even know? The people, I mean. The ones that sell you the bodies. Do they even know what you're doing with them?"

Tan shifted uncomfortably. "Fuck, I don't know. This is all new to me too—"

"Don't bullshit me!" My voice came out a little louder than I expected.

"All right! God! No! How could they know? We tell them? We can't even tell our own families."

"So, what happens if we revive one? We keep him prisoner at Lifebank? Or just send him home in a cab? And hope he has really good air-conditioning?"

Tan's hands tightened on the wheel.

"Please don't make me do this anymore," I said. "I'm serious. You're making me part of this, even though I don't agree with it. And I have to live with that. But I don't want to be in the operating room. I'll talk to you guys on the phone. Just don't make me watch. I don't want to—" I heaved. "I don't want to watch."

"Get some sleep."

My voice got louder. "I'm serious. I'm not going to watch that again."

Tan gave me a curt nod. "I'll talk to Cass."

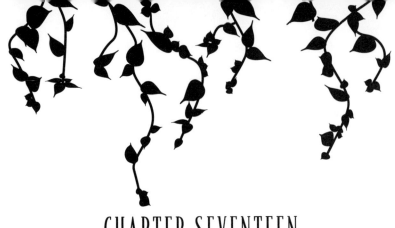

CHAPTER SEVENTEEN

Even though I'd been awake for more than twenty-four hours, I still had to take sleeping pills.

The sun was going down when I woke up, and the phone was ringing. Tan.

"Look, another one's coming in. I talked to Cass and told her you're fried. You're off the hook for now, but keep your phone with you, okay? We might need to reach you. If we don't call tonight, check in around midday tomorrow. We should know something by then."

I barely managed the words, "Got it," before he clicked off.

I put the phone down and heard a car grind to life outside. I peeked through the window of my room and saw Charlie starting up the van. I don't know whether he sensed me, or if he was checking on me in the first place, but he waggled a finger that I knew meant, *Don't follow me.*

I yanked on a sweater and headed downstairs. Dad was talking, his voice loud but gentle. "Listen to me. You have to take the vitamins."

Who the heck was here?

A kid's voice rang out: "They're huge! And they taste gross. Like fish. I don't like fish."

Lila. Dad was talking to Lila on the speakerphone. He carried on. "Fish is good for you. Eat them for me. Then we can play some more Minecraft."

Since when did Dad know about Minecraft?

"Will you come see me if I take them?" she demanded.

Dad hesitated. "I can't."

Lila argued the point. "How come? Is it because of how you look?"

"Partly. I'm kinda scary-looking."

Lila thought about it. "You shouldn't be shy because of how you look, you know. My mom says God made you."

Dad smiled sadly and said, "God made you, Lila."

Lila interrupted. "God makes everything! You know how God has angels? Well, nobody knows what angels look like. I mean, we draw them in white robes with golden halos and all, but we don't really *know*. But they're magical, and they help people. So, I think maybe that's wrong. I think angels look like you."

Dad was positively beaming. "You want to know what I think? I think you're the angel. Hemingway just walked in, so I gotta go, Lila. You promise to take the vitamins?"

Lila dodged the question, and burbled some good-byes as the phone clicked off. Dad swirled the velociraptor around toward me. "You going out with Melissa?"

"Can't. The necromancers have me on call."

"Take your cell."

"I keep seeing her and acting like I'm boyfriend material, and I'm not. Because Calhoun's too evil to die. And that leaves us with one option: running away."

"Doesn't always work out like you anticipate, Hemingway."

My radar went up at that one.

He met my eyes. "Look. We have some vague plan to escape, but that may not work out. I don't want you turning this girl away because of what might happen tomorrow. Go see her. Stop trying to calculate how little happiness you're entitled to. Just be with her as though now is all you've got. And take my bike if you want."

Mel's house was dark in the front when I rode up. I wondered if they'd gone to the hospital. Dobro barked from the side gate, and I walked over to pet his head, calling out, "Hello?"

I heard a shriek—a girl's shriek—from the back of the house.

"Mel?" I opened the gate and ran through.

The French doors to the patio were open and I bolted inside to find her swatting the wall with a book. "You all right?"

"Fine," she answered. "Lila's back at the hospital. Sorry I forgot to call, tell you I wouldn't be around."

"S'all right. I wasn't supposed to be around either. So, if she's there, what're you doing here? And why the screaming?"

She eyeballed a spot on the wall and swatted again. "I figured somebody had to let Dobro out. I came home, but Dad must've been here and left the back doors open for him." Another thwack. She waved the book ominously. "He left a bunch of lights on too. Now the whole house is full of mosquitoes." She nodded at me. "You've got one right at the top of your forehead."

I took a hand to my face and smushed it.

Melissa nodded vehemently. "My mom does NOT need to come home to this. But I have no idea how I'm going to kill them all." She gestured. "There's a magazine right over there if you want to help."

I took off my shoe instead and swatted at the walls—got one, missed one, then another one.

"On your left arm," I told her.

"Your nose."

We swatted each other's vampires. I slapped at one on her cheek.

A hand flew to her face. "Ow!"

I paused. "D'I hurt you?"

"No." But she hit me with the book.

"Cheap shot!" I eyeballed the wall. "Remember 'Seven at One Blow'?"

She nodded. "The tailor killed seven flies."

"Amateur. Watch." I took my shoe to the wall, just above the glow of the lamp.

"Not bad," she admitted. "But you're going to have to answer to my mom about the wall." She pointed to where I'd committed genocide.

"Shit."

She laughed. "I'm teasing, she won't care. Wait. Here's an idea. What if we just freeze 'em out?" She moved to the thermostat and dialed the place down to sixty degrees.

"Works for me. Meanwhile, I'm going to take you someplace. You can't stay here." I took her hand and led her out the back door. "It'll be fun."

Melissa wasn't wild about the idea of riding on the handlebars of the bike, especially at night. She tried to convince me to take her car, but I just shook my head. This was my thing, and I wanted to share it with her.

She folded her arms, suspicious. "You got lights on this thing?"

For once, I was glad I had the mountain bike. I grinned and flipped a switch. "We can ride on the sidewalks if you prefer." I stood the bike up and patted the handlebars. "C'mon. Just try."

She placed her hands over mine and lifted herself onto the handlebars. I pushed off and started gently down the sidewalk, the ridges in each square of concrete reverberating and bouncing the bike until she urged, "Gooo ontoooo the roadddd."

I veered onto the smooth blacktop, and for a few minutes, I forgot all about Lifebank and being Hemingway Jones and just enjoyed pressing my head and shoulders into Melissa's neck and back, both of us feeling the cool cross draft.

She screeched wildly as we sailed down the hill at Eastcliff. "Ohmygodohmygod, I'm gonna fall off!" But she was laughing.

"No, you're not. Hang on, almost there." We careened into the parking lot and I slowly put on the brakes as she hopped off.

The pool was closed and dark, as expected.

I hadn't been here all summer, even once. Last three years, I'd wished to just be home, so I could hang at this crappy old pool with my friends, listening to old Boston tunes blaring over tinny old speakers while eyeing the girls sunbathing on the deck. This summer, I'd finally been home, and I hadn't been here once. And summer was half over.

Melissa looked through the chain-link fence at the pool. "You're not thinking of going swimming, are you? I didn't bring my suit!"

"I'm hot, you're hot, and we could both use a break." With that, I grabbed at the chain link and started to climb. Melissa smiled, disbelief etched on her face, but she started climbing after me. The fence was high, and the ridges in the chain link were sharper than I expected at the top—I gouged a long, deep cut along the edge of my palm. Blood pumped steadily from the wound as I called to her, "Hey, wait before you go over. Let me get something."

I dropped down the other side, ran into the office, and grabbed a Band-aid. Inadequate—I probably needed stitches—but it would have to do for now. I moved over to the lost and found and grabbed a couple of wet towels, throwing them to the top of the fence. "Use those when you climb over."

"Such a gentleman." She picked her way over the spokes and leaped down.

I lifted my eyebrows. "I'm impressed."

She shrugged. "Used to do track at school. High jump."

During the day, this pool's the beach of Concord—teeming with fat housewives, sunbathing teens, and splashing kids. The music is distorted, the concrete is sticky with Sour Patch Kids, and the pool is kid soup. You never really notice the woods behind, since all the trees are too far away to provide any shade.

But at night, the woods reclaim this place. Moths and dragonflies dart above the water, raccoons and snakes breach the fence, while the swampy land outside the gates absolutely thrums with a chorus of frogs. It's like the wilderness has waited patiently in the heat of the day, and now it's taking the water by storm.

I waded into the shallow end in my shorts and wrinkled my nose—warm like bathwater.

Melissa stood on the steps, testing the surface. "You going in?"

I shrugged. "I'll do whatever it takes to cool off."

She pointed to the deep end. "Cold water's over there. By the pump." She raised her eyebrows, daring me.

I grinned, ripped off my T-shirt and threw it at her. "Fine." I swam—not prettily, mind you—I never got to stay home in the summers and learn strokes. But I dug like I was in the Olympics until I reached the pump, which was churning out Niagara-cold well water. The guys that ran this place must've left it on to make up for the evaporation from the drought. I surfaced under the pump and shook my hair in the blast. I pointed at Melissa and called out, "Your turn."

She pouted, casting an eye down on her T-shirt and shorts. "You think the mosquitoes are dead yet?"

"Stalling!"

"Fine." She grudgingly took off her T-shirt and shorts, leaving them in a heap on the concrete and dove. Her stroke was perfect as she sliced through the water toward me in only her bra and underwear.

This is it, I thought. I hadn't really planned on doing this, but on the other hand, WTF was I doing, if I wasn't doing that? I'd ridden with her on my handlebars, brought her here, no suit. I mean, what exactly did I want?

She surfaced right in front of me, her face so close I felt her warm breath. *This*, I thought, *I wanted this. Just once.* I hung onto the side with one hand and pulled her tight with the other, kissing her right under that pump, the cold water rushing over us, the chill limiting our kisses as we pulled away multiple times to gasp from cold.

My hands were moving all over her, first brushing and then cupping the taut softness of her breasts through the bra. I finally slipped a hand inside, and another one around the back, tugging at her bra, springing the hook. I reached lower. She gasped in surprise and I paused, totally expecting—and dreading—that she'd tell me to stop. But she wrapped her legs around my waist and said, "I've never done this."

"Me neither," I admitted, planting another kiss, not wanting to break the moment.

But she gently pulled back her face, her hand resting on my chest and said, "Tell me how you feel."

I dodged the question with, "Isn't it obvious?" and tried to return to kissing her.

Her legs unwound and she pushed away. "You know what I mean."

I did. And you know what? I loved her. I knew it the moment I saw her killing those mosquitoes for her mom. The reaction had been absolutely chemical—my heart started pumping, my stomach twisted in knots, and I was sweating like a pig. I wanted to be with her, no matter what she was doing, for as long as she'd let me stay.

I was fumbling for the words when I suddenly noticed a smear of blood on her face. I moved to wipe it away, and ended up smearing more. I looked at my hand in confusion, in the underwater light of the pool.

The blood on her face wasn't hers—it was mine.

The Band-aid on my cut hand was gone, and the wound pumped tiny little rivulets of red into the water. They reminded me where I'd been and what I'd done the night before.

If I was going to tell her the truth about how I felt, she deserved to know the truth about who was saying it.

"I'm crazy about you. I've never felt this way about anyone. But remember that stuff I can't tell you? Because it would incriminate you? That might change your feelings about ME. Because I did something awful—"

She put a hand over my mouth. "Then just shut up and don't tell me. Whatever awful truths you want to tell me . . . that won't change by tomorrow, will it?"

I started to protest and then shook my head.

"Everyone our age gets to be our age for a whole year. We may only have one night. Why do you want to waste it?"

"I don't." Within moments, where she ended and I began became a wonderful blur.

CHAPTER EIGHTEEN

Lifebank didn't call.

I was munching on a bagel, and Dad had his face stuck in the computer monitors when we heard a truck roar up in the driveway. I checked the surveillance—Todd. The garbage needed emptying anyway, so I grabbed it and headed out, because he was definitely not coming in.

If you're tired of hearing me say it was hot, sucks for you, it was.

Todd gave me a weak smile as he shuffled in the gravel. I ignored him, opened the lid to the garbage can and threw the bag down with force. It hit the lip and split open. Awesome. Coffee grounds in a wadded-up filter landed on his shoe. I couldn't care less.

"Dude! Watch what you're doing with that," he said loudly. "Look, I'm sorry."

I cut him off as I scooped and chucked stuff in the bin. "What do you want, Todd? Help with an exam? Isn't school over? Or are you pulling summer session . . . again?"

I chucked a half-eaten sandwich at him.

He twisted out of the way, shouting, "Quit it!" as I picked up more garbage, ready to throw. But throwing stuff felt inadequate, considering how angry I felt. I'd never needed my best friend more, and he'd completely dumped me—not over what I'd done, but over Dad. I dropped the stuff and flew at him, punching him in the shoulder. He teetered and I pushed him to make sure he went over. He grabbed at my shirt as he fell, pulling me with him. We ended up rolling on the ground, pounding each other like we'd done when we were ten.

I was more pissed than I'd realized at Todd for disappearing on me for the worst five months of my life. Mostly pissed at myself. But I felt like punching somebody, and since hitting yourself is just plain weird, Todd was a convenient and justifiable target.

I got on top of him, wailing. He made the mistake of trying to ward me off, grabbing at my arms rather than blocking. He missed and I caught him on the chin.

"All right! That's it! That's all you get!" He shouted as he pushed me off and leaped on top of me. This time he pinned me. "Say give."

I spat dirt up at his face. "What're you, like five? Get offa me."

He pressed harder, locking my arms to the ground. "SAY GIVE."

"All right! All right, give. There. Get off!"

He let go and we both spent a minute, rolling up to sitting positions there on the ground, uselessly trying to dust ourselves off. My yard has little to no grass, so all the dry dust merged with sweat and turned muddy. I spat grit through my teeth. When I finally looked over at Todd, he was examining his cracked iPhone.

"That sucks."

"Got insurance?" I asked, already knowing the answer.

"Hell no!"

We both laughed. Todd's parents were more likely to buy a llama than cell phone insurance.

"Damn, we need some rain," he said suddenly. "'Cause that ground is hard. Luckily, you still punch like a girl."

I stood up and offered him a hand. He took it and stood up too. We both stuck our hands in our pockets and looked around, not knowing what to say. Todd finally coughed and said, "So look, man. I'm sorry I weirded out like I did. That was way out of line. I've swung by a few times, but you're never around."

"Yeah, well, I'm working now."

He interrupted quickly. "Yeah, I heard that." And he apparently didn't want to hear any more. Anything related to Lifebank or my dad was clearly still off-limits. "Look, I wanted to invite you to a party I'm having."

I tried to interrupt him, "Look, I don't think—"

But Todd didn't even pause. "On your birthday. I checked and Mr. Martini's gonna be out of town that night. Figured I could round up some of the guys and we'd have a field party. Like we used to. It's your eighteenth! Please, man? What do you say?"

I exhaled long and loud while I thought. All of me longed for the familiarity of the life I used to know. I had no interest in parties, alcohol, or weed, but I admit I was absolutely starving to see smiling, carefree faces. I'd missed the hell out of Todd and my other friends the last few months. I just wanted to hang out with the guys for a while and talk smack. And those field parties had always been absolute gold. We usually had like three or four of them a year between late spring and Indian summer, in between my stints at geek camp. We'd always wait for Todd's next-door neighbor Mr. Martini to go out of town so we could use the rope swing over the pond they shared. Everybody would suit up, cool off, then we'd crank up the music, start a bonfire, and get loaded, occasionally tossing his parents' crops on the blaze.

I finally answered him with, "Don't say the party is for me." He opened his mouth and I held up a hand. "No one will come. I can promise you that. I don't even know if *I* can come. I'm not in charge of my own schedule these days, and I won't know till the day. But if I can make it, I will stop by. How's that?"

He nodded and shoved his iPhone into his pocket as I added, "And I'll buy you a new one of those too."

My own phone started ringing. I checked the ID—Lifebank. "I gotta take this, and I'm willing to bet they're gonna say I have to come in."

Todd nodded, slapped me on the shoulder, and said, "Okay, man, your birthday. Seriously. I expect you there. And pray for some RAIN!" He pointed up at the sky with both index fingers before heading back to his truck.

What was it with Todd and the rain? The pot plants were in a greenhouse. I shrugged it off. Maybe he was toked up. I just waved as my phone buzzed angrily. I finally picked up. "Yeah."

Tan's voice was tired, but I could still hear the hesitation. "Hemingway? Uh, we're going to need you to come in later, take over this evening. Make arrangements for your dad, because it will probably be all night. Maybe say, about four?"

"Whah? What do you mean 'take over'?"

I heard him exhale before admitting, "I mean we did it. Anyway, we've all been here for like thirty-six hours straight. We need you to come in tonight, keep watch."

I dropped the phone and yelled after Todd. "Hey! Wait a sec! I need a ride."

They'd done it. They'd made a Gray. I had no intention of waiting till later to go in. I needed to go in now.

The fact drummed through my head repeatedly, churning up a million worries. The primary one was survival: how long did we have before they decided they didn't need Dad and me anymore? It would happen; even if we skip the fact that Cass doesn't like me, once they'd made a few more Grays, they'd need all the hydrogen sulfide they had. They could ill afford to waste it on the prototype. I arrived at the lab and realized I should've brought a sweater. And gloves. The place was arctic cold. No surprise really; they were going to pull out all the stops to make sure the Gray survived. As for me, I guess they figured I was used to the deep freeze by now. Or maybe they just didn't care.

Tan met me in the front offices. "I didn't mean now," he said, genuinely surprised. I suppose that was fair, seeing as I'd been at least an hour late every day since I started there. "And you're filthy."

A woman's scream erupted from the lab, interrupting my fashion review. Not the startled kind of scream, either. Not even the "I'm a mother and my kid's been stolen by a pedophile" kind. More like the kind of scream you imagine coming from someone who's being tortured to death. Ironic, seeing as she was being tortured to life.

Tan and I froze.

He unwound first and admitted, "It's been kinda noisy around here. But nothing new, right?" His eyes revealed something else, though: horror. If I had to place a bet, I'd say Tan had bridged the gap between scientific theory and practice and was now swimming in regret. I understood because I'd lived there now for five months.

But I didn't call him on it, as that would only make him defensive. "Far as I'm concerned it's all new. So what's the deal?"

"Hannah Ross Patten. Twenty-two. Drowning victim out at Lake Norman."

I was instantly suspicious. "Lake Norman's like six feet deep." Usually, drowning victims were unfortunate swimmers who got hit in the head by speedboat enthusiasts.

"A hundred and thirty actually—around where they drowned that town to make the lake. She went scuba diving to see it and got tangled up in the weeds. Stayed cold."

"So, wait. A drowning victim can usually be brought back using—"

"Yeah, I don't know what the EMTs tried before she came here. All I know is what's happened since she's been here. She's alive. And a Gray. And that's all you need to know too."

My eyes bugged at the implication. Classic therapeutic hypothermia had been successfully used on many drowning victims, even hours after they were declared legally dead. Cass had the only Gaymar in the region. She could've allowed the EMTs use of it to treat Hannah Ross, and give a twenty-two-year-old girl her life back. Instead, she'd used her as an experiment in necromancy.

I didn't just need to escape this place. I needed to burn it down.

Tan took my silence for acceptance and continued: "So, Elaine, Belinda, and I are exhausted. You're the only other person who knows what to do, but we won't leave you alone. Too much riding on this. We'll take it in shifts. Cass is of course taking the first one. She'll fill you in. I doubt she'll even nap, but if she does, only wake her if you really need her, okay? I'm going home to get some sleep and I'll be back in around midnight." He started for the door and suddenly turned around. "Shower and treat yourself before you find Cass. She's absolutely paranoid about the Gray getting an infection."

An hour later, scrubbed and in scrubs, I felt the hairs on the back of my neck curl when I saw her, prostrate on the Gaymar. I thought I was accustomed to it now, having lived with my dad this way for three months. But looking at a woman this way was a whole new and unwelcome sensation.

She'd been beautiful. The realization made me gag. Her hair was gone—whatever color it had been—but her eyes were wide and round, even when closed in sleep. She had these huge, dark eyelashes, high cheekbones, a delicate nose, and a tiny, heart-shaped mouth. Her skin was flawless too—other than the somber shade of gray it now wore.

I knew those stunning features would be lost on anybody except me. All they would see was the decaying gray of her skin. So unnatural you'd have thought it would crinkle like tissue paper when she moved. But she wouldn't move, would she? Ever again. Like Dad, she'd be immobile. Like Dad, she'd be an untouchable. She'd scare the hell out of anyone who saw her. And she was twenty-two.

I leaned over and whispered in her ear: "I'm sorry."

"Sorry's not necessary, Hemingway." Cass walked through the door donning a fresh pair of gloves.

Her voice was surprisingly calm and appeasing, but every muscle in me torqued. I reminded myself I needed to be here and see where this was going, so I ought to control my temper. Still. I couldn't help feeling pissed on this girl's behalf. "Yeah, why's that? She gave you a release to do this to her?"

"No," she said simply as she checked the monitors. "Her father did." Her ice-blue eyes met mine, challenging. "She's an A, not a B."

I lifted my eyebrows in doubt, but I thought about it: B's don't go scuba diving, do they? Kinda an expensive sport. Then there was where she died—Lake Norman. She probably lived on the lake too. Dad always called that area his bread and butter. He built McMansions for wealthy Charlotte bankers who paid off their contractors late and their cars early.

Then there was her name: Hannah Ross Patten. B's didn't have fancy family surnames built-in with their first names. Women from old-money Southern families did, to remind everyone of their powerful connections even when they married. I said finally, "Hannah Ross Patten, as in, Patten and Prints?"

Cass nodded. "They sold it years ago. In answer to your question, no, she's a bit young to have a DNR, but her Dad was on the A list. He's friends with Calhoun. He called when she went missing in the lake. I told him chances were extremely slim, and I warned him about the limitations of being a Gray, but he was willing to risk it. Hemingway, she's alive because of you. You should be proud."

"Yeah, well, I'm not gonna hold my breath for a thank-you."

I hated what Cass had done. I hated what I'd done. I could only imagine the pain a twenty-two-year-old girl would suffer when she looked in the mirror. And it was never going to be any better. She'd never get married; she'd never have kids. Hell, who would even kiss her? I hoped her dad would. I hoped he'd kiss her three times a day for the rest of his life, knowing he'd done this to her.

I sucked in a breath and decided to just get on with it. "So, what're we doing?"

"Waiting," Cass admitted. "For her to wake up. Hopefully, it's not as long and painful a transition as it was for your dad. I'm just guessing, but I think we aggravated his situation for days when we kept trying to warm him up. I'm hoping Hannah's passage is much shorter, seeing as we're keeping her cool and giving her the hydrogen sulfide. Let's have a look at how we're coming, shall we?"

She lifted one of those gorgeous eyelids to reveal mucous-filled yellow. I gagged, but Cass just said, "Good." She let go and turned to me. "I've got to check in with her dad and I've got to call Calhoun's office. They've asked for hourly updates. Keep checking the hydrogen levels and ready her for an EEG, will you? I want to start running some tests. If she wakes, come get me." She strode out of the room.

I blew on my hands to keep them warm and deliberated Hannah Ross. Some seriously dark thoughts were going through my head. I was wondering if I could somehow end her new life before it began. I had no idea how, short of warming her up. If I did that, she'd start screaming and Cass would come running. Same if I deprived her of hydrogen sulfide. That said, I had no idea what happened if she had too much hydrogen sulfide.

Does it even qualify as murder, to kill someone who's already legally dead?

I shook my head, absolutely freaked. Who was I kidding? I couldn't go that far. Why did I want to kill her, anyway? Would I be helping her? Simple fact was I didn't know Hannah Ross, so I didn't know what she would want in this situation. So as usual, my ethical concerns were just going to have to be added to my list of personal problems, and that was already a ridiculously long list.

I checked her hydrogen sulfide levels and started readying the machine, plugging tiny little nodules all over her head, wiring her to the EEG.

Cass opened the door just as I finished. "Right, let's get to it, shall we?"

Fifteen minutes later I handed her the results. She scanned them, pursed her lips, and said, "Let's run it again."

We ran it three more times, but only two to completion. Hannah Ross woke up in the middle of the third, her eyes registering fear as she let loose another soul-destroying series of screams. I ran for the hydrogen sulfide while Cass barked, "Hannah! It's okay! Hannah!"

I yelled across the lab at her, "Her name's Hannah Ross. Hannah Ross! Not just Hannah."

Cass wrinkled her nose and shouted back at me over Hannah Ross's screams. "That's a middle name. Hannah! Can you hear me?" Cass gave up and turned to me. "I want 50 cc's, NOW. Anyway, what difference does it make?"

"It does matter." I turned to Hannah Ross. "I'm going to give you this now, Hannah Ross. Make you feel better, okay?" I injected the hydrogen sulfide.

The screams died away and I watched her face relax into catatonia.

For the next few minutes, Cass and I submerged ourselves in our mutual loathing. I chucked the syringe at the trash—missed—and sank onto the floor. Not because I was physically tired—I was just exhausted from dealing with her.

I kept my voice calm. "See, this is the thing. Maybe I don't know medicine, or science, the way you do. I get that. But you don't understand people, and particularly Southerners, and you don't listen. Your *patients*"—I let the sarcasm drip on that word—"are Southerners. Her name's Hannah Ross, the Ross part is probably a family name. If I saw her on the street and just called out Hannah, I wouldn't expect her to turn around."

"FINE. Hannah Ross it is. Whatever."

"What is so hard about—"

"All right, Hemingway!" Cass exploded, and then caught herself. She licked her lips and continued, "Sorry. I see your point, but I'm not sure it matters, because I'm not sure she's sentient," Cass confessed, a heady dose of shame in her voice.

I scrambled to my feet. "What?"

"Sentient. As in, possessing a conscious and functioning human brain."

"I know what *sentient* means. So you're saying you've quite possibly made a Gray that's a vegetable. That's great." Her back arched at the accusation, but sagged again and she nodded slowly.

"How do you know?"

Cass picked up the EEG results. "Her brain activity is minimal. Seems to be running just enough to keep her body functioning. I was hoping that was a glitch, somehow tied to the transformation, but there's no change."

I didn't say anything, I just held my hand up. She seemed surprised, but said nothing as she passed me the EEG. The finer points of an EEG mean nothing to me, but even I understand a flat line. I finally asked, "Aren't these how my dad's read? At the hospital, I mean?"

"No," she admitted. "They're not."

"Is it possible that's because he was further along in the process? He was here at the lab all night before he got to the hospital."

"Possible but unlikely. Your dad's condition didn't visibly modify to a Gray until he was at the hospital, remember?"

I did. Every painful moment of my dad's time in the hospital runs in a technicolor loop in my memory. "So, what happens to Hannah Ross, if that's the case?"

Cass sucked in a breath. "I don't know. I'll have to see what her family wants to do." She opened the door to the lab, but she didn't look at me as she continued: "She's an A, not a B, so they have the final say. If they don't want her, I'm hoping they'll let us keep her here. In any case, you shouldn't have to stay for this. I'll call Tan too, see if I can get him in here earlier." She turned all the way around to face me. "While there's definitely some truth to my not understanding Southerners, or even most people, I do understand how you feel, Hemingway. More than you think. And believe it or not, I do care. You're just a kid. I don't want to ruin that for you any more than I already have."

I was dumbstruck and it was hard to say what startled me more—the humanity she was showing me, or the possibility of her inhumanity toward Hannah Ross. I stumbled, "You can't—I mean, we—can't put her down like a dog."

"This might take a few minutes. She should be awake soon, so just try to keep her calm." Cass walked out and shut the door.

I plucked the rest of the EEG nodules off Hannah Ross's face while I resisted the urge to scream.

Hours went by without a word. Desperate for some proof she was sentient, I stroked her smooth, cold hand. I did this sometimes when Dad disappeared into the coma-like sleep of a Gray. If I were light enough in my touch, the warmth would be just enough to bring him back. If I forgot and left my hand on his too long, he'd roar like someone had taken a lighter to his skin.

Hannah Ross's yellow eyes popped open in minutes. I turned away, not wanting to alarm or challenge her, and whispered, "Hey, Hannah Ross. How're you feeling?"

I glanced out of the corner of my eye to see her response. She blinked at the sound of my voice, but her eyes didn't register recognition—or even confusion. I suppressed my disappointment and whispered again, "You're at the research center. You had an accident and they brought you here. Blink two times if you can understand me. Can you do that? Blink two times."

Her eyes shifted to the beeping monitors.

I tried again. "Hannah Ross," I said firmly but softly. "Can you blink?"

Her eyes shifted again, this time to the door. No blink.

"Hannah Ross, can you smile?"

Nothing. My heart beat faster. I was trying so hard to think of something that would bring her brain back that I didn't even register what I was seeing at first—a gray hand, floating out toward the beeping EKG. Her hand.

Hannah Ross was ambulatory.

My mouth dropped open as she sat up. The cooling blanket fell away to the floor. She seemed utterly unaware she was naked underneath, as she struggled to bring her legs awkwardly over the side of the inflatable Gaymar. She pushed with her hands, and her jellied legs landed unsteadily on the cold tiles. She reminded me of a newborn fawn—silent and stumbling—and I reacted to her like one, staying as still as I could for fear of scaring her off. I was so stunned I'm not even sure I could've moved if I wanted to.

Hannah Ross headed again toward the beeping monitor, curious. Her chest was still wired to the EKG, so when she ran out of line, the nodules tugged. The sensation startled her. She didn't know what they were or why they were there.

I lifted a flat palm as I rose slowly from my chair, eyes down. If she was an animal, I needed to treat her like a wild one. I approached the EKG, one step at a time, and pulled the wires out of the machine, rather than her. She watched them fall loose on the floor, the nodules still in her naked gray chest, and then she looked at me as if she was registering my presence for the first time.

I heard Cass's footsteps nearing the door. Hannah Ross heard them too; her head lifted and lowered again, as her back curled into a slight crouch. I wanted to call out and warn Cass, but I figured Hannah Ross would probably freak.

The door swung wide, and Cass barged in with her usual brusque manner, her mouth open to say something to me. But before she could speak, Hannah Ross let loose a wild scream and broke for the door.

"HOLY SHIT!" Cass startled as Hannah Ross shoved past her. Cass grabbed at the EKG monitor to catch herself, but the monitor rolled with the force of her weight. She went down, while Hannah Ross darted away, crashing through the lab and offices, the EKG wires trailing after her.

"HANNAH ROSS!" I screamed and ran after her.

"HEMINGWAY, GO AFTER HER!" Cass yelled as she tried to pick herself up.

I ran straight up the hall, utterly convinced this was the direction she'd taken. I found her, scrambling around the front offices, searching for a way out. She went right past the main door, not even registering that it was a door. She turned at the sound of my footsteps, her yellowed eyes wild with panic.

I could catch her. Easily. Bring her back to Cass, and quite possibly a second death. Maybe that was the right thing to do. She was little more than an animal, and her options weren't any better than an animal's. She could be put down; she could live in her father's house like it was a terrarium, or live here, as Cass's lab rat.

I didn't want to be a party to any of those options.

That's when I realized there was one more. And I was going to take it.

I darted toward the door, deliberately moving fast to scare her. It worked. Hannah Ross darted around the room, knocking over computers and phones, screaming, and scuffling to get away from me. I let her go, knowing the more she messed up the room, the more proof I'd have that I'd fought to catch her.

I meanwhile opened the door to the hallway wide. She hesitated, and I made a sweeping gesture, encouraging her to go as I backed away. She pumped her arms once, took one last look at me and ran out.

I called after her, "HANNAH ROSS!" And smiled, knowing she was gone. She banked left. A few seconds later, I barreled out, banking right as hard as I could, like I was chasing her. I could only hope enough time had passed between our exits to convince the security guards that I'd simply gone the wrong way.

We searched all night, first in the building, then the research park, and finally the city itself, working on a grid in the first thunderstorm of the summer. We didn't find her. The victory I felt when she ran out the door was short-lived. I'd let her go, so she wouldn't be put down. But I was still killing her, wasn't I? She couldn't survive outside in the summer heat and she didn't know it. And I let her go anyway. Why had I bothered? So I could own more of this? Hannah Ross was on my conscience, and she was heavy.

Tan dropped me off at home around midday the next day. Dad's yellow eyes lit up momentarily when I walked through the door, then furrowed with concern.

I met them and said, "I'm thinking." Letting him scrounge around my brain was far easier than repeating out loud what I'd done.

I expected him to say something comforting. Like I did the right thing. Or he'd have done the same. I was not prepared for the response I got.

"Well, this is one holy hell of a mess."

"Thanks," I responded scathingly. "I'm actually thinking about opening a business in fucked-up shit." I flopped down in the Barca lounger and stared at him incredulously. "That's all you can say? What was I supposed to do? They were debating killing her!"

Dad was surprisingly angry. "You were supposed to wait! No one handed the fate of the universe over to you, son. Sometimes you just gotta let things play out a little before you decide. I would've thought you'd learned that by now."

I reeled at the implication and shot back, "Actually, I'm reminded of it every day."

We stared each other down like we had back in the days before Dad became a Gray.

He broke first. "I didn't mean . . ."

"Yes, you did. You know what? Fuck this. No more letting you in my head, no more falling for this 'we're a team' bullshit. Fact is, I've been the only team player here. I've told you everything, but you like to have your secrets: like trying to commit suicide. And meeting with detectives who are trying to put me in jail. So, you'll have to excuse me if I decide I'd like to try some of the individual events." I headed for the door.

"Where are you going?"

"Where do you think I'm going? I'm going back out to look for Hannah Ross." I opened the door, but it forcibly shut again like it was on a spring. I turned toward him and folded my arms. "Nice."

He responded flatly, "You can't go looking for Hannah Ross on your own."

"Why not?

"Because there's a chance she's still alive. And if she is, it's way too dangerous." I snorted at that one and Dad snapped, "I'm serious!"

I raised my eyebrows, daring him to tell me why. His lips pursed multiple times. He was mentally trying to paraphrase some watered-down version of a truth and obviously couldn't come up with anything.

I walked over and leaned on the arms of the velociraptor. "You're still treating me like a kid. All of this," I gestured at him, at the chair, and at the room. "And you're still treating me like a kid. Just stop. And tell me."

His voice boomed inside my head. "*Remember the reporter? Lisa?*"

"Yeah?"

"*I think I killed her.*"

Near the end of his life, Albert Einstein told a friend he'd made "one great mistake in his life," and that was to sign a letter to President Roosevelt discussing the possibility of the atomic bomb. He said he did it out of fear the Germans would make one first. In any case, the Manhattan Project was born because of that letter. It was his brainchild, even though Einstein didn't work on the project.

Turning Dad into a Gray suddenly seemed akin to discovering nuclear fission: even if the idea works and you've saved the world, you've written its ending at the same time. Einstein felt that way on the day of the Hiroshima bombing. His ideas, his endorsement, and most notably his science, made Oppenheimer's psycho invention possible.

I was Einstein. Lifebank was my Manhattan Project.

PART III

CHAPTER NINETEEN

I thought Dad had to be delirious. How could he kill someone, when he couldn't even move? I was frankly a little worried about him. "She had a stroke, remember?"

"Please don't say it out loud."

I ignored him and carried on. "I talked to Burkhardt. He told me."

All the cabinets in the kitchen suddenly flew open.

The dishes and glasses started marching out, smashing first on the counter, only to bounce and smash into smaller bits on the floor.

The lower cabinets opened too, pots and pans slamming against the cabinets and walls. Dad's face was pure steel as he conducted his little symphony.

Moments later, it was silent again.

I exploded: "What the hell was that?!"

"A reminder of what I can do. I was on the phone with her, all right? When she fell."

"That doesn't mean—"

"*I said I'd talk to her, but she started pissing me off. I told her over and over to back off, but she wouldn't. And for a moment, it felt like my head was going to explode. Then I heard her scream and fall.*"

My mouth opened and shut again, remembering his instructions. "*And?*"

"*You know what happened. She died.*"

"*That's it? Dad, that's not exactly—*"

"*I saw the medical report. She'd just gotten a checkup. No history of early strokes in her family, no tumors, clotting, nothing. She was a normal, healthy woman.*"

"*Yeah, but that happens—*"

"*I know. Look, there's only one way to find out for sure, and that's to try it on someone else, which is never, ever going to happen. But I know it, all right? I just know. I killed that girl, and I've got to live with that.*"

"*You've been pissed at me plenty of times. Like now. And I'm still here.*"

"*I've thought about that. It's just different. I love you. I might get angry, but I'd never want to hurt you.*"

"*You met Calhoun. You didn't hurt him.*"

"*I never lost control like I did on the phone.*"

"*And this is why you don't want to talk to anybody? See anybody?*"

I took his silence for a yes.

"*You talk to Lila.*"

"*Do I really have to answer that one?*"

No, he didn't. Getting angry at Lila was basically impossible. "*You tell Burkhardt all this? About Lisa, I mean? That why you met with him?*"

"*Yes.*"

Floored. "*What did he say?*"

"*Pretty much the same as you. No way to prove it, case closed anyway, nothing he can do. Said his boss would think he was insane if he tried to arrest me.*"

"*So you don't want me to look for Hannah Ross because—*"

"*You said she was like a wild animal. You know what happens when you corner a wild animal. They fight back.*"

I searched for something to say and for once, came up with nothing. It was pointless trying to argue with him about his culpability. He had no proof, he knew that, and he'd still managed to convince himself. Hell, he'd even tried to turn himself in.

The next morning, my phone rang—Tan. Hoping news of Hannah Ross would bring my dad down from whatever tree he'd climbed, I immediately asked, "You guys find her?"

"No," he answered. "Hem, I'm calling to tell you that Cass is suspending you. For now. Hopefully, it's just temporary."

I was out. I wanted out and I got out. And suddenly that didn't seem like such a good idea. How was I going to stop this thing, if I didn't even know what's going on?

"This over Hannah Ross?"

"Yeah."

"I gotta talk to Cass. Is she still there?"

"Nah, she went home a couple of hours ago."

"Can you give me her address?" Tan didn't say anything, so I begged. "Please?"

He gave me her address in Kannapolis. I hung up and hunted for my helmet as I informed Dad, "I've been benched by the freak squad."

"What're you planning to do?"

"I gotta ride out and talk to Cass. See if she'll let me back on. I have to stop Lifebank from making any more Grays and I can't do that from here."

"That's what we're doing now? Stopping them?"

Now I felt like the parent, scrounging for patience. "Say you're right and I'm wrong about what you just told me. I don't think so, but just say. They made a Gray. They're going to make more. What happens when Calhoun gets tired of his new pets and just lets them go? What happens when he becomes a Gray? How about when he makes an entire population of them?" Dad said nothing, so I continued: "You said this is a holy hell of a mess. Well, it's my holy hell of a mess. So, I guess that puts me on cleanup detail." I slammed the door on my way out, thought of something and headed back in.

"What did she say to piss you off?"

Dad was momentarily confused, until he realized I was talking about Lisa. He scowled. "Forget it."

"You're doing it again," I accused. "It was about me, wasn't it? She was trying to get you to talk, so she riled you up with claims I'd tried to kill you on purpose."

He opened his mouth to protest but just closed it again in surrender.

"Thank you."

I took my frustrations out on the bike, pedaling like mad for Lake Howell.

I genuinely refused to believe that what Dad said was true: that he could actually kill someone with some kind of Doctor Who mind-meld. That said, I was worried about the fact that he believed it. His ethics were his religion, and he now thought he'd killed someone. By accident, mind you, but he'd done it because he was the creature I'd turned him into. Which meant I'd taken his ethics from him. Along with everything else.

And he was still working hard on leaving me. First, he'd tried to kill himself and now he'd tried to turn himself in. I was angry and tired of being angry. I focused on the road.

I wasn't exactly sure where I was going. Lake Howell's pretty big, although it's not really a lake. It's the county reservoir. Before I was born, people could take their kids swimming there. But after 9/11, the county commissioners closed it, under the theory someone would *obviously* want to poison it, right after they got done with New York. Annoying at the time, but the lake is positively pastoral as a result. The banks are lush with pecans and elms, their branches bowing toward the water, heavy with limbs that skim the surface like a hesitant foot testing the temperature. And it's so clean it reflects the sky's mood—a mournful, silvery sheen on a cloudy day and a vibrant, happy blue in the sun. Even the air's fragrant, thanks to the wild honeysuckle that grows knotty and thick on the banks.

A gator took up residence there a few years ago. Seriously. Nobody knew how he got there, let alone how he survived the winters, but people occasionally spotted him from the bridge. He was so elusive the *Tribune* nicknamed him Elvis. They should've called him Lennon, because last summer, a couple of yahoos hunted him down and killed him. Can't have any monsters in Cabarrus County.

When I turned, the smooth new blacktop of Kannapolis Highway gave way to a single-lane gravel road. I got off and walked the bike, afraid I'd pop a tire.

Set deep in a copse halfway up the lake, Cass's house was situated on two acres of overgrown grounds. The house itself was a crumbling three-story Greek Revival from the 1920s. The white paint was blistering, and the ancient beams were exposed in naked glory in too many places. But the house was teeming with life—a playpen was open on the wide front porch, next to a couple of white rockers. Giant plastic toys were scattered everywhere—on the porch and the grounds—as if to say this family was having so much fun they'd forgotten to clean up. A brand-new swing set was perfectly situated in full view of the lake a hundred yards away.

A guy with a ponytail and a Rasta cap was playing hide-and-seek with a toddler in the yard. His movement was awkward and delicate—he seemed to have some kind of a limp. I called out, "Hey!"

Ponytail squinted at me. "Hello, can I help you?"

"Yeah, I'm looking for Dr. Cass. Does she live here?"

"Ellie? Yeah, she's inside, I'll get her for you." He started for the house only to turn back and offer a hand. "Hi, I'm Ellie's husband, Will Cass."

My mind boggled, incredulous that this friendly, aging hippy guy could possibly be married to Dr. Ass.

But as I offered my hand, I saw the military tattoos on his arms. Ponytail hippy had been a soldier. Given the volume of tats, he'd been one for a long time too. "Hemingway Jones."

"Hemingway." He seemed surprised and pleased. "Hemingway? You're Hemingway Jones? It's so good to meet you finally. Ellie talks about you all the time. I'll just run in and get her. She's making lunch. You want some water or something? Kind of a hot day for a ride. Hey, do you mind watching Ian while I'm gone?" The toddler headed for the sandbox.

I shrugged. "Sure." I was light-headed, trying to envision Lucretia Borgia in an apron.

Cass came out of the house a minute later, her arms folded defensively at the sight of me. While I was obviously causing her some discomfort with my presence, I was struck by how different she looked in this setting. Not just the new do—her curly red hair had been smoothed into a sleek bob— but the creases on her permanently furrowed brow were relaxed. She looked, well, normal. But her tone was curt. "Hemingway, what're you doing here?"

I held up a hand. "I just came to talk. Heard I got suspended."

"You shouldn't have come here. But for the record, I didn't ban you." Cass's focus shifted as the toddler waddled over, his arms full of muddy sand. She beamed at him. I'd never even seen her smile. "Did you make a sandcastle, Ian? Wow, it's beautiful!" The toddler smiled and gave her a goopy handful. "Thank you. There's pizza inside! Let's go see Daddy!" She carried her son up the steps, opened the screen door, and murmured something inside as she handed him off before turning her attention back to me.

I tried to lighten the mood, gesturing to her hair. "Your hair looks awesome, by the way."

"What? Oh, thanks. Just got a Keratin treatment."

Now I felt guilty. "Was that because of what I said?"

"Yes. And fuck you, by the way." After a long pause she started laughing. "God, it's so good to finally say that."

I nodded. "I deserve that." This time we both laughed. She had a rich, snorty laugh that was contagious. I'd never heard her laugh before. I honestly thought she was incapable.

She regrouped and admitted, "But for the record, I didn't fight Calhoun on banning you either."

"There's a surprise."

She looked out over the water and said plainly, "Hemingway, everyone knows you let that girl out."

I'd been all set to lie. I'd rehearsed exactly the right words, but they just didn't come. I'd had enough of lying, even though the truth wasn't exactly working out for me these days. Why break a roll, right? I shoved my hands in my pockets. "Yeah."

I expected her to explode, but she started laughing again. This time bitterly.

"What did I say that was so funny?"

"You're finally honest with me. At a point when I don't want you to be honest anymore."

I didn't understand what was funny. I concentrated on the glistening lake and asked, "Why not?"

Cass smiled at me wanly. "You have to ask?" She sank into the swing like she'd been carrying a hundred pounds of dead weight. "Because I don't want to make any more Grays. I admit I was curious about your dad at first. Very curious. That's the doctor in me. But I didn't become a doctor to do that. I had my own work, reviving humans as humans. Then you turned your dad into a Gray, and suddenly, I've got a new directive. Then we had the B's. I tried to quit after the ischemic subject."

My eyebrows lifted in surprise. "Why didn't you?"

"Did you know Calhoun bought all the patents on my hypothermic work?" I shook my head. "Neither did I. So when I tried to quit, I got a call from that roach of a lawyer. He assured me I'd be walking away from everything I've spent twenty-five years building. He threatened to shut it all down too. Didn't care how many lives it cost. The people who need my work don't deserve that. I don't deserve that. Or maybe I do, after Hannah Ross," she admitted.

Floored. Cass was as much of a prisoner as I was. More, in fact. Which totally sucked, because that meant I had to care about her, and I didn't want to. I was already an epic fail at caring for other people, so adopting more of them didn't seem like a particularly good idea.

I finally asked, "What did Hannah Ross's dad want to do? Before I let her go?"

"He wanted her put down. I told Calhoun I wouldn't do it."

"But someone would've."

"Yes. And technically, it wouldn't have been illegal. She was already dead. That's what Mueller told me." She got up and dusted herself off. "I'm sorry you're involved in this, Hemingway. You're too young to be. I knew you wanted out, so I didn't defend you. I just let you go."

"You know he's dying, right? Calhoun, I mean. He wants to become a Gray." She nodded and I continued: "And you made one that's insentient. I'm just guessing here, but I somehow doubt that's going to cut it with Calhoun. He'll want his mind, and I'm the only one who knows how he retains it."

"That's exactly why you and your dad need to leave, as soon as possible. He's getting pretty irrational."

"I can't leave."

"Yes, you can. If it's money you need, I'll—"

My mind boggled that she'd even offer, but I waved a hand and bypassed that for the bigger issue. "Look, please just let me talk, for once? Okay?" And for the first time, in the entire time I'd known her, Cass stopped ordering me around and listened.

I was so sure she'd stomp on me that I hadn't really thought about what I would say. So I took a risk myself, and told her what Dad thought he'd done, and what he thought any Gray could do. Her eyes widened and then furrowed, worry and improbability wrestling each other in her mind, much as they had in my own.

"So Grays aren't just unnatural, they're potentially incompatible with humans," she mused. "How's your dad handling it? About the reporter?"

My stomach twisted with the knowledge that was the logical, humane, mature question to ask Dad. And I hadn't thought to ask it. I'd simply refuted the possibility.

"At a guess, not too well." I shifted gears. "You think there's any chance Calhoun would stop if he knew?" I asked.

"You say your Dad told Burkhardt. At the house, right?" I nodded and she continued: "Then Calhoun already knows, and no, he's not quitting." She grimaced at me. "He can see you, and hear you. He knows everything you're doing."

"Why wouldn't that make him stop?" I knew I sounded petulant, but the frustration I felt was overwhelming.

Cass shrugged. "Dying and becoming a Gray is the only chance he has at living. He has no time to wrestle with ethics. Once he's a Gray, he'll turn his attention to the product. He'll view that as simply another tweak that needs adjusting."

I thought over what she'd said and attacked something else. "And no way we're bugged. The guys that worked on our house are my dad's best friends—"

"The whole 'I'm thinking' thing was good. Kept your dad out of your head regarding your girlfriend. Use it to talk about where you're going."

My eyes grew wide. I'd never told anyone about "I'm thinking." Not even Melissa.

Cass added, "Those guys might be your dad's friends, but their bread is buttered at the research center." She climbed out of the swing as she said, "Mine's bugged too. Will and I talk out here. That's also why I taped the articles to your door."

"You taped the articles? Why?"

"Because I wanted to make sure you stayed safe." She smirked. "You have a tendency to do the opposite of anything I say, so I thought I'd try another way."

"That's uh, fair." I spitballed: "What if we went public? With everything?"

"You mean aside from the fact that I'm ruined, Calhoun puts you in jail, your Dad dies, and therapeutic hypothermia is taken off the market?"

"To Calhoun. What happens to Calhoun?"

She shrugged. "Public pressure might force him to shut down here, but he'll just move. He hasn't committed any crimes—everything he's done to you and me is legal."

"You know how Stephens is procuring the B's for him?" Cass's face changed. A realization swept over me. "You knew."

"Of course. But I don't know the details, so I'm not much use as a source. That was the deal I struck with him—I'd ask no questions, and he'd offer no answers. In any case, that won't affect him, just all of us at Lifebank."

"I suppose if this all comes out, it will affect your medical license, won't it?"

Cass's lips tightened. "Hemingway, you've just told me exactly why this has to be stopped, permanently. I served in the Navy, the first rule of which I'm sure you already know—the captain goes down with the ship. That's me. If you can find a way to stop Calhoun, do it. Stopping him is a hell of a lot more important than my medical license. That said, I can't get you reinstated, and you have another objective to focus on anyway, and that's getting your dad out of here. That's going to take some serious planning."

I asked quietly, "What about the hydrogen sulfide?"

"Your dad gets what he needs. That was the promise I exacted out of Calhoun when he suspended you." She shrugged. "I'd have stolen it if he hadn't agreed. Stock up on what you can. But you need to find another source for the long run. Calhoun's already toying with a two-week deadline. His body is giving out. If he can't get us to figure out what you did, he'll go after you. So, you and your dad need to go soon, whether you've destroyed Lifebank or not. I might be doing my own disappearing act. My family comes first."

I tried again. "There's gotta be a way we can work together on this."

She was firm. "You can't even call me. And stop asking questions about the B's. Calhoun knows why you want that, and that just moves up his deadline. He wouldn't get arrested for it even if you proved it; he'd simply deny all knowledge. You need to figure out where you can get hydrogen sulfide, and how to get your dad out of here." She thought for a moment more. "And keep looking for Elks."

"You know about that? Do you know what happened to him?"

She shook her head. "No one does. Just that something went terribly wrong. I tried to find him myself when your dad became a Gray. Calhoun's looking for him too, so be careful."

"What are you going to do? I mean, if any more B's come in?"

"I doubt I'll even be involved. He knows we're not on the same team anymore." She walked toward her house without another glance in my direction.

Riding the twelve miles home from Lake Howell, my legs felt like they were rotating a cement mixer.

The Towering Inferno was in full blaze on the plasma screen. McQueen and Newman were at the water tanks.

"Did you get anywhere?" Dad asked.

Newly aware of our studio audience, I scowled and said, "No." I sank into the Barca and just started thinking, hoping he'd barge in without the invitation. "*Cass thinks we have about two weeks.*" Out loud, I echoed Newman's line. "How much you gonna set it for?"

Dad picked up on what I was doing—covering. He took Mac's line. "Five, *Shorter than I thought.*"

Parents.

They can't help but be invasive, can they? Onscreen, Newman took off with the C4.

The movie cut to the ballroom, where everyone was roping themselves off. We both focused on the screen like we couldn't be torn away from it. Mac and Newman stood in the stairwell, the flames licking at their feet. Dad picked up Mac's line. "I'm burning up!" "*We have to think about Charlie and Melissa too.*"

Mac and Newman bolted into the ballroom, joining Borgnine, Holden, and Astaire. They all stared at the ceiling, waiting for the bombs to go off, as I answered him.

"*I got an idea about Charlie while I was riding home. But only if he'll cooperate.*"

"*When the time is right, take it to Burkhardt.*"

"*You've got to be kidding me.*"

"*What, the tox screen? He was dead on. Guy's got instincts. And he's not afraid to break a few rules.*"

The water tanks detonated, and the ceiling of the ballroom started to collapse.

"*You ever get the feeling the ceiling's gonna cave in on us too?*"

"*Sometimes.*"

CHAPTER TWENTY

I got up early and knocked on Charlie's door. He took about ten minutes to answer, and was still in his underwear when he did.

He flagged me inside and asked, "You want some coffee?" as he walked to the kitchen.

I followed him. "Sure."

Charlie shuffled around his kitchenette, emptying a coffeepot so old and crusty that the leftovers had turned into sludge.

He checked the cabinets for mugs—empty—and turned to the dirty dishes in the sink.

"Yeah, uh, I changed my mind. In fact, I think I just gave up coffee. Jesus, Charlie, your house barfed. You ever think of hiring a maid, maybe?"

"Can't afford one."

"Yeah, well, you never know, I might be looking for a job. I've been suspended."

Charlie shut off the water and bent his head over the sink. "What does that mean for your case?"

"Huh? Oh. I've no idea. I'm still on payroll, and Dad's still getting what he needs. Speaking of which, I have to be out all day. I'd appreciate it if you stopped over."

"Today is tough. What happened?"

I shrugged. "Long story. But that's not why I'm here. I'm here to ask you to find a lawyer."

"This is about Smythe? Hem, we've covered this. It's none of your business."

"It is my business, and Dad and I may have to get out of town. Soon. Once we do, I'm telling Burkhardt everything about Lifebank, because there can't be any more Grays. That includes Smythe, and you have some culpability that could get you jail time. The only way out is to turn them in yourself. Get a lawyer, let him negotiate with Burkhardt. That way, you don't end up in jail. And maybe find yourself a bartending job."

Charlie suddenly flung the coffeepot at the wall, where it smashed, dribbling black stains down his otherwise white walls. "You have no idea what you're asking. None. I'll lose my license. Hell, I'll be lucky if that's all I lose."

I cut him off. "You're scared shitless of those guys. You want to keep living this way? Until when?"

Charlie ignored the question. "Hem, I'm sure they'll take you back at Lifebank. You don't have to—"

"You don't get it. Calhoun's crazy. He's also dying. He wants to be what Dad is, and he'll do just about anything to get it out of me—"

"SO JUST TELL HIM WHAT HE WANTS TO KNOW! WHO CARES?"

I could've told him about Dad, but I didn't, because I still didn't believe it.

His voice turned whiny. "Look, I kept your secret, Hem. You know I did. You're gonna pay me back by ratting me out?"

"It's bigger than just you, me, and Dad," I said quietly. "Look, maybe we've all just got to own our mistakes, you know?"

Charlie's mouth puckered in frustration. "And how exactly are you owning your mistake?" He sneered. Thinking better of his tack, he ran his hands through his thinning hair and drew in a long breath, trying to calm down. "Okay, you need to leave, Hem. This friendship has gotten way too complicated."

"I'm going to Burkhardt with or without you. Within weeks. That means you need to get to a lawyer's office. Today."

He started shooing me with his hands toward the door. I'm serious— shooing. Like I was a chicken. I planted my feet and begged: "Just think about it, all right?"

"Out!"

He slammed the door on me once I was on the stoop. Like that would hurt my feelings. Please. These days a slammed door felt like a kiss on the cheek.

Melissa texted an hour later. I grabbed my bike and stuffed the Amazon box I'd ordered for Lila in my backpack and rode hard for the hospital.

The sickly, deodorized smell of the hospital wafted a stink of bad memories my way as soon as I hit the parking lot. The door to Lila's room was open. She looked like she'd shrunk since I last saw her. Mary was fussing over her as the kidney dialysis machine churned. She smiled at me tightly, but her eyes were liquid with grief.

"Lila, look who's here to see you!" Mary pulled me inside the room. "Melissa's just gone to find the doctor. She said you'd be stopping by. If you can entertain Lila, I'll see if I can find her."

"Sure, I'm happy to hang out with Lila. That's why I'm here. But you don't have to find Melissa. She'll be back. Why don't you take a break? You look like you could use one." Mary smiled softly, but the dam broke. She practically ran out of the room.

I called out loudly: "You faking AGAIN?"

Lila didn't take the bait. Her voice was limp as she said, "Hey Hemingway." Her face was scrunched in pain, while her eyelids drooped with exhaustion.

I ignored the twist I felt in my gut at her obvious pain, opened the backpack, and ripped open the box. The butterfly cage slid out and sprung open. "I got this for you. Hope you don't mind roommates. I figured you could use some company . . . so I got these guys too." I pulled out the two monarch caterpillars. "These guys just love sleeping all day! Their names are Mac and Newman, by the way."

She giggled softly. "Those are silly names."

"Well, sometimes parents give their kids stupid names. Like Hemingway, for example. But seeing as you're their mom, you can rename them whatever you want. BUT. Pretty soon they're gonna go into the chrysalis phase, and then they'll hatch into butterflies. You're gonna have to be well for that, so we can set them free and watch them fly. Okay? You want to help me put this together?"

She smiled weakly and nodded.

Lila dozed off within minutes. I was finishing putting the cage together when Melissa walked in. Like her mom, her eyes were ringed with exhaustion. I signaled for us to step out into the hallway.

When she turned to talk, I just gathered her into my arms and held her tight. A few quick sobs escaped from her, but I just held her tighter. Nurses bustled and flowed around us, while extended family members of other sick kids stood in the neighboring doorways, their voices a little too bright and loud to be convincing as positive reinforcement. But at least they were there. I'd always wondered what it was like to have a hospital room so crowded that even the love had to be squeezed in.

Now I knew.

She mumbled into my chest, "The butterfly cage was a beautiful idea, thank you."

"Happy to do it. I figured since she can't go outside, I'd bring the outside to her. I'm going to have to find some milkweed, though."

When she finally broke off the hug, I gestured to Lila's door. "What happened?"

Melissa shrugged. "We knew her kidneys were starting to fail. The dialysis was scheduled, but she collapsed this morning. They think it was some kind of a stroke." Her words became strangled. "They always said it would come to this. The docs here think she's got weeks at best. They pretty much just want to shoot her full of painkillers until she dies."

"Yeah? What does she want?"

"She wants to be awake. So she can be here with us." Melissa wiped away a few tears. "She's worried about us. She told me. Isn't that a joke?"

"I don't think so. I'm worried about you too." I kissed her softly and held her again.

"I found something about that professor, by the way."

My stomach lurched with unexpected hope. "Yeah? You found him?"

Melissa broke away from me again and wiped her eyes. "No. You were right. He's completely off the radar, so I finally switched gears and checked back with the hospital where he did his research to see if anyone there had anything to say. They said he had six test subjects, and they don't know what happened to him or the test subjects, but something went wrong. Everyone assumes they all died, and no one knows where he went. So, I started looking at the papers the days before and after he disappeared. And then I found—wait, I printed it out for you."

Melissa ducked back into Lila's room and returned with her open purse, extracting a wadded-up printout of an article in a local Pittsburgh paper dated a couple of years back. The article was very brief: SUPPLIES MISSING FROM LOCAL LAB.

"I called them back to see if they could tell me what supplies had gone missing, seeing as it was a couple of years ago. Hemingway, it was a substantial supply of hydrogen sulfide. They discovered it was missing the day after he left."

My mouth was still hanging open as Mary and a bevy of doctors and nurses headed down the hallway.

"I have to go," Melissa said apologetically.

"Yeah, okay." She turned toward the room. "Hey wait."

She looked at me quizzically and I planted a long hard kiss on her mouth, which she returned.

"I really have to go," she whispered as the doctors made their way into Lila's room.

"I love you," I whispered back, and hustled away without waiting for a reply I didn't deserve.

Papillion was midway through when I got home. Steve McQueen and Dustin Hoffman were plotting their escape from prison. I plonked myself down on the Barca lounger and watched, eliminating the need for further conversation.

Dad didn't rotate around to look at me. "How's my girl?"

"None too good." I waited for him to ask questions, but he didn't. "*I need you to see if you can get in touch with Cass.*"

"Why?"

I showed him the article.

"*So it's possible you weren't the first to make a Gray.*"

"Exactly. Elks was researching hibernation and suspended animation—just like Cass. She was looking for him too, by the way. Maybe if she knew this, it might give her some more ideas. Because if we can find him—"

"*We might have somewhere to go.*"

"Exactly."

"*You need to tell Melissa.*"

"I know. I couldn't do it today. Everything was too hard."

As the credits rolled, Dad invaded my head. "*There's something I want you to check out. Been bothering me ever since I came home. I've been sensing something. It's faint—*"

"*Sound, smell, or touch?*"

"Smell. I thought it was me at first, but I don't think it is. Bothered me so often I started checking the wind patterns on the computer to see if they're consistent. They are. It's coming from directly east of here."

"And this fits in with the do-or-die schedule we're on . . . how?"

"I have no idea. But I'm guessing it's related because I haven't noticed any other smell since I became a Gray. That's why I keep checking the weather. I'll let you know the next time I pick it up."

"I'll check it out. Hey, how come all Steve McQueen movies are about escaping?"

"Why do you think I watch them?"

CHAPTER TWENTY-ONE

Dad reached Cass in the morning. She didn't have any new ideas on where Elks might have gone; she'd never met Elks. But she suggested I contact one Dr. Boyd, who had. They'd been rivals in the field of hibernation and suspended animation.

I looked up Dr. Boyd, excited to find he lived here in North Carolina —in Durham, a mere two hours away. He ran something called the Duke Lemur Center. I had zero idea how a mini lemur zoo made Boyd a rival in the field, but it was the only lead I had.

I tried calling Dr. Boyd at the Duke Lemur Center, but the receptionist who answered asked me if I realized he was ninety-six years old and rarely came to the center. And no, she wasn't about to give me his number. After she took a message that I somehow doubted would reach the top of his pile in the next two weeks, I searched online and found his home address in Durham.

I stopped several times on my way to the hospital to yank up some milkweed for the caterpillars. In the summertime, it's plentiful and easy to spot. It grows wild even in the sewage trenches along country roads; tiny bouquets of incandescent orange flowers that look color-coded specifically for the monarch as food.

Milkweed is vital to butterflies if you're going to let them go: the leaves and nectar are poisonous to birds and mammals. The monarch's would-be predators think twice about just how hungry they are before chowing down on a milkweed-fed butterfly.

With all that was going on, you wouldn't think I'd worry too much about a pair of butterflies that only live eight months at best. But Mac and Newman were Lila's butterflies. And sometimes I just need the little guys to win out, you know?

Even if I have to tip the scale in their favor.

Weeds in hand, I returned to Lila's room. She was sleeping, and Melissa was in the corner, tapping away on her laptop. I went to the sink, grabbed a Dixie cup, filled it with water and stuck the milkweed inside. I went over to the butterfly cage and stuck the mess inside, silently apologizing to Mac and Newman that dinner was so late, but promising them it was worth the wait.

"You carried that here on your bike?" Melissa whispered.

I shrugged. She shook her head, put down the laptop, stood up, and threw her arms around me. "I love you too, Hemingway Jones."

My stomach was doing happy oscillations at those words, even as I knew what I had to tell her. I choked.

"Oops, excuse me!" rang out. Mary made her way through the door and checked Lila's vitals. "Melissa, why don't you take a break and spend some time with Hemingway? I've got things here, and your dad is supposed to be here in an hour or so."

Melissa rolled her eyes at Mary's optimism about Kevin but nodded. I mouthed a thank-you to Mary. She smiled at me tightly and took a seat by Lila's bed. I grabbed Melissa's hand, and we walked out.

Melissa drove us around for a while, saying nothing, lost in thought and pain. I did my best to fill the void, telling her everything I could—the things that wouldn't incriminate her. I told her about Charlie and the B's, the story of Hannah Ross, and what Cass had said about us, as well as Boyd and the plan I was formulating to go to Durham and find the guy. I also told her about the cameras, the spying, the risk she was taking, just by hanging around me. I did this as a lead-up to what I needed to tell her: that for my dad's sake, we had to leave.

She said nothing, didn't even ask so much as a question. I was about to broach escaping when she screeched to a halt out on St. Stephen's Church Road and rolled down the windows on her Element. It was midday, the sun was bearing down, and the only sound was the dragonflies buzzing across the fields.

I looked at her, unsure why she was stopping.

"I come out here for the silence sometimes. There's rarely a car here in the middle of the day."

"And I'm totally ruining it jabbering on," I responded.

"No. That's not it." She looked out the window, away from me, but her hand snaked across the handbrake and took mine as she asked, "We're going to time out, aren't we? Soon. That's what you're telling me. I mean, you guys don't have any choice but to leave."

"I don't want to go anywhere."

"But you do have to go. You can't be responsible for more of them. And for the record, I don't want you to be responsible for creating more of them either. And that's why you need to find this guy—Dr. Elks. So you and your dad have someplace to go." She thought for a moment and said flatly, "I'm going to lose Lila and I'm going to lose you at the same time."

This was one I could answer. "You aren't going to lose me. Ever. Hey, look at me." She turned and those little hazel flecks in her eyes caught the sunlight. "I may have to leave, but that doesn't mean I get to stop feeling any of this, or wishing I still had this. I've never felt this way about anyone. That said, I don't deserve you—"

Melissa yanked her hand out of mine and erupted. "Oh my God, just shut UP about how little you deserve. I'm sick of it!"

I balked, stunned by her outburst. She was furious.

"You think I haven't guessed? About your dad and that accident? You were at Todd's place. Todd. The guy with the pot farm. And there was an accident. And then there's the fact that you don't drive—ever—even in one-hundred-degree heat, even though you own a brand-new car. And then there are the people who gave you that car. The same people whose lab you hijacked, which you know, isn't usually what happens to people in that scenario. You know what? It doesn't take a detective to figure out what happened, what they're making you do, or why you're doing it."

Floored. I fumbled for words, but she carried on.

"Hemingway, it's obvious you love your dad, and you would never have hurt him deliberately. You made a terrible mistake. But I really don't feel like being part of your penance, okay? Something you grandly sacrifice because you're not worthy of being loved. How about what I deserve, have you thought of that? I've lived like a nun or something for over a year. And I've been happy to do it. I love my little sister more than anything in the world. But if I'm about to lose everything, yeah, I think I'd like you to ask what I deserve."

I was terrified to open my mouth, but I finally squeaked out, "Okay? What do you want?"

She started the car engine. "I want to go with you to Durham. Right now. Durham is two hours from here, door to door. We can be at that professor's house by three—that should be a good time of day for a ninety-six-year-old."

"Are you sure?" The words seemed stupid, even as I said them.

"I've been with Lila today, and I will be back to her tomorrow. And that's all we're going to say about Lila today, okay? The rest of the day is about me. And another thing. Stop calling Dr. Cass 'Dr. Ass.'"

"I didn't invent that."

She talked right over me. "But you are perpetuating it, aren't you? It's demeaning of all women. I am a woman, and you are offending me."

It was years ago, but I still remember when my mom got like that. Dad taught me there are only two words a man can say when a Southern woman is that righteous. I decided to use those words right now.

"Yes, ma'am."

She turned on the ignition again, and turned onto Old Highway 80.

Melissa argued with her parents briefly, but when they demanded she come back immediately, she said, "No," hung up, and tossed the phone into the backseat. She was taking a powder from being the perfect daughter for the day, and that was just how it was going to be.

She steamed another half hour as she drove but finally flipped on the radio, scrolling endlessly for a station that wasn't country music in the middle of the country. When she found a fuzzy version of "Dancing Queen," she cranked it up as loud as it would go, and started singing even louder. And yes, of course I joined in. In fact, I started dancing in the car, even donning her sunglasses and wrapping a scarf I found in the backseat over my head, feigning feminist de rigueur charm just to get her laughing. After that, the cheesy tunes were just the cheesy tunes, and we sang along to all of them, even when we were finally able to pick up the Durham stations and something from this century. We flew the car, we sang, we gestured wildly at the truckers to blow their horns.

I don't think I've laughed that hard before or since.

We pulled up to Dr. Boyd's sixties brick ranch, but a nurse answered and informed us that Dr. Boyd was in fact at the Lemur Center. She wasn't sure when he'd be leaving there, so we beat it for Duke, hoping we didn't miss him.

We pulled up, staring at what looked a lot like the Carolina Raptor Center in Huntersville, only a bit nicer, because you know, Duke University isn't exactly strapped for cash. There were cages and runs everywhere, and a host of tiny primates. Some stopped to stare at us with their weird goggle eyes, their tails waggling.

Melissa screeched, "Oh my God, they're so cute! I just want to cuddle one!"

"Yeah, me too, but we're not here for a school field trip. We have to find Dr. Boyd before he leaves."

"I bet he's that guy, right over there," Melissa said, nodding in the direction of a very elderly man surrounded by people looking at him in awe. He was holding court for lingering visitors, and even the staff was listening in. White-haired and bearded, as you'd expect a professor to be, he didn't use so much as a cane.

He was holding a tiny lemur in his hand as he knelt down and explained to the small children:

". . . Lemurs are prosimians. That's a fancy way of saying they're pre-monkey. They were around before gorillas and even chimpanzees. And they're distantly related to you and me."

The kids burbled questions, mostly if they could hold the lemur (no), and then the adults started asking questions, and then the staff. The more technical the lecture got, the more the kids and the visitors drifted away.

Melissa whispered to me: "Hemingway." She pointed toward a windowless facility. I was confused until I saw the sign above the door. "The Paul Calhoun Hibernation Lab."

"Shit. I don't care. I'm going for it."

Boyd announced he had to go, and as the crowd started to disperse, I leaped into action.

"Excuse me, Dr. Boyd? Please, just a minute of your time. We drove two hours here to find you. My name is Hemingway Jones."

His brow wrinkled. "Where have I heard that name?" His eyes widened. "Not the kid from the research center?"

"Yeah. I'm trying to track down Dr. David Elks. Dr. Cass said you might know where to find him."

His face softened. "I don't know where he is, I'm sorry. I haven't spoken to him in two years. The phone would've been simpler. Or an email." He turned away.

Melissa intervened this time. "Dr. Boyd, please. It's important."

The pleasant demeanor started to evaporate like a summer rain. "I'm sorry, young lady, but I will not talk to him," pointing at me. "Paul Calhoun is a major contributor to this place. I cannot jeopardize my staff or these animals, for a teenager who could best be described as a—" He fumbled for words.

"Hijacker," I said, finishing his sentence. I scrunched my nose. "Unless you think that's too fancy." Melissa elbowed me in the ribs.

"Mr. Calhoun said you were a wiseass. Look, I don't respect what you did, and while I doubt he knows you're here, I cannot entertain you. Dr. Elks was a very good man. I don't know what went wrong, but he disappeared, and I have no idea where he is. Now if you'll excuse me."

I called after him as he walked away. "But I think I do know what went wrong. Because I think I did the same thing in the research center. And by the way, if it helps my case at all, I'm currently employed by your benefactor. Look." I tapped on my phone and pulled up my pay stub from the previous week and turned it in his direction.

At that he stopped, walked over, and put on his reading glasses, examining my phone. "What's this about? Wait. Not here. Follow me."

He hustled us into the Paul Calhoun Hibernation Lab, a long, low, dark, and cool room full of cages. There was nowhere to sit down, as if to remind us we were not guests. He propped himself against a wall, and said, "Why don't you start from the beginning. And don't leave anything out."

I looked long and hard at him, fully aware this was a major risk. Calhoun was his sponsor; he'd made his loyalties clear, and to be fair, I'd committed every crime he imagined I had. On the other hand, what choice did I have? I had two weeks at most and zero leads on Elks. So I told him the parts

I could without incriminating him or Melissa. Boyd asked a lot of technical questions, but the thing that really blew his mind, weirdly enough, was when I described how Dad looked when he was sleeping.

"So he achieves torpor." He was fascinated.

"What?"

"That's not sleep he's doing. It's torpor. A deregulation of the body's temperature, until it drops to the temperature of the room. Brain activity ceases in torpor—everything ceases but the most minuscule metabolic activities necessary to maintain life. Sleep is active—your temperature remains constant at ninety-eight point seven degrees, and your brain remains active." He peeked into the cages of his subjects. "In short, your dad is hibernating in those moments. I have always believed that humans have the capacity to do so. I thought I was going to die without knowing whether I was right or wrong." He laughed softly to himself, his eyes vacant, lost in thought.

"Why would we want to hibernate?" Melissa asked. Boyd was still staring into space. "Dr. Boyd?"

"What? Oh. Sorry. Bit of an odd moment when a couple of teenagers walk in and tell you the answer to your life's work. I will think on that later. Why do we want to hibernate? Think of how much better surgery could go, if the doctor wasn't so restricted by time. How many people with life-threatening wounds wouldn't bleed out in ambulances. Space travel becomes infinitely more possible too. There are so many applications."

"Oh. And that's what the lemurs are for? And this place?"

"They're the only primates that hibernate, so yes. And they predate us here on the planet by a long shot—lemurs have been around for fifty-five million years."

"Do you run experiments on them?" Melissa asked indignantly, gesturing to the tiny creature peering out at us.

Boyd shook his head. "Nothing invasive or debilitating. We not only can't but we wouldn't—they're some of the most endangered animals in the world. But I like your ferocity on the issue. They're going to need people like you. This place is going to need people like you, once your friend's story breaks. What Calhoun is doing is bad science. And bad science ruins all science. Come with me to my office."

We hesitated to follow him out of the lab, partly because we were suspicious and partly because if he didn't know where Elks had gone, what were we doing here? He read our expressions and explained. "Let's see if we can figure out where Dr. Elks has gone."

Boyd's office was seemingly held up on three sides with books stacked to the ceiling. He started tapping away on a laptop. "David is a brilliant guy, good scientist. But his entire experiment was flawed from the beginning, in my opinion—getting squirrels and mice to hibernate isn't going to tell you whether a human can do so. Our physiology is too different. If you want to know whether a human can hibernate, you at least have to see if someone in the family has the gene."

"Makes sense. Why didn't he listen, then?" I asked.

Boyd smiled at me. "Because he doesn't want to be me. I'm ninety-six and still studying how lemurs hibernate. I'm going to die without ever entering the phase of studying the potential for human torpor. My staff plans and budgets for my memorial every year." He peered at his screen and then gave me the side-eye. "So still no ambulation, hmm?"

I shook my head, irritated. I idly started wondering if he'd brought us here simply to pick me over for information about Dad.

He held up a hand. "I'm sorry—I'm still thrown by your news about your father. I will have to save that for another day. Elks. David doesn't have any family. He lost his wife and son in a car accident. That was the reason he took up this scientific inquiry in the first place, as well as why he was in such a hurry to get to an answer. If he created what you call a Gray, I can assure you of one thing: he is caring for that subject with everything he's got."

A ripple of something that felt dangerously like hope blossomed in me. I tried to put it out like it was a kitchen fire.

Boyd continued. "We need to look at the problem another way. Let's start with what we know: hydrogen sulfide and what temperature again?"

"Fifty-five degrees."

"Fifty-five." He tapped lightly on his laptop. "So, if Elks is still alive, which we don't know, and if he made a Gray, which we also don't know, with limited funds and no help, he's likely to go somewhere it stays as cold as possible, even in the summer. And likely somewhere remote. Now. Alaska is the obvious option, but he can't take a flight to Alaska with a Gray, and crossing into Canada is highly unlikely too. So that leaves the northernmost states in the continental US as the most likely." Boyd tapped away on his computer and turned the screen so we could see the map.

I stared at it and turned to Melissa. "What time of year did Elks disappear?"

Melissa glanced at the article. "This was written November first."

Boyd already saw where I was going and googled. "The average temperature in Pittsburgh that time of year is around fifty degrees. Good point. I think we can rule out anything farther than a long day's drive." He tapped on the computer again, knocking out everything west of Wisconsin. He looked again. "Hmm." He tapped away again.

"What?" I asked.

"Well, you pointed out that David likely stole a supply of hydrogen sulfide. That wouldn't last him very long, based on your description. He'd want to have access to some." He googled again, this time pulling up a list of manufacturers and began checking where they were located. "Most of these are in the South."

"I know." I shrugged. "I've looked at stealing some myself."

"Well, it's no good escaping somewhere warm, and he can't leave a Gray unattended for long, based on what you've told me. So, if I add hydrogen sulfide producers in the North to our map, that narrows our search quite a bit. There are only a handful: Pennsylvania, New York, and Massachusetts. Pennsylvania is least likely—he would want to be farther away from the lab and people who might recognize him. Where are the other two? If any one of them is up near Canada, we have a prospect." More typing. He frowned. "They're all in suburbs of Boston and New York. That doesn't seem very likely. Not enough privacy."

"What if we look for thefts of hydrogen sulfide?" Melissa suggested.

Boyd pointed at her. "Smart girl." He tapped again. "Hmmm. Nothing other than his alleged theft since 2014." Boyd shook his head. "Look, I can make some inquiries about David innocently enough amongst some colleagues, and I will. But if your supposition is true, you must understand it's highly unlikely anyone knows anything."

He grabbed a business card from his desk, scribbled something on it and stood up—our cue to leave.

I fumbled for something to ask, some way to forestall the end of this meeting. I'd had so much hope coming here, and it was only magnified by meeting this guy and hearing about Elks. If a guy as smart as Boyd couldn't solve it, how was I going to do anything? Reluctantly, I got up. Melissa was already thanking Boyd at the door.

He handed me his card. "I've written my cell number on the back."

I tried to hand it back. "You know I can't call you."

"Well, buy one of those grocery-store phones! There's a Food Lion a few blocks from here. Text me one word, and I'll know it's you, and I'll save it. That way, if I find anything, I have a safe way to get in touch with you." He looked at us pitifully. "You two stay safe. And please wish your father well for me. In fact, let him know I hope to have the privilege of meeting him one day."

Thirty minutes later, I had a burner phone and sent him the word *torpor*. (I had to check the spelling.) Melissa, waiting in the car, put down her phone and turned on the ignition. I settled back into the seat, gloomy due to a lack of answers, let alone whatever waited for both of us at home.

But she bypassed the highway and headed north through downtown Durham. "Uh, the way home was back there."

"Today isn't about lemurs and missing professors, remember?" Melissa responded, checking her phone. "Today is about Melissa."

"Uh, okay? We're still doing that? And you do realize you're talking about yourself in the third person? I feel obliged to point that out."

Melissa shrugged. "I don't care. At all."

I looked away to cover my smile, but she saw it and smiled back.

"So where are we going?"

"Here." She turned left onto a long, curving driveway, the gravel crunching beneath the tires. What had to have once been a plantation home appeared: massive and immaculate, with grand white columns resting on a wide front porch equipped with rocking chairs. Melissa's beat-up Element looked like a gremlin next to the multiple BMWs and the 4-wheel-drive Mercedes parked there, but she didn't care.

"I'm, uh, not exactly dressed for this kind of place." I apologized, looking at my sweat-stained T-shirt and shorts that smelled distinctly of lemurs.

"And I am?" she asked, gesturing to her own crop top and shorts before climbing out of the car and shutting the door. "C'mon. If I have to lose you, I want one night. We'll leave first thing in the morning. But no talk of my sister, or your dad."

My eyes bugged. "Oh my God, my dad—"

"I talked to him while you were in the grocery store. He's fine, he's got Tan coming over to help him out." She circled around the car to me and looked up at me, her skin glistening with sweat in the August heat, her hazel eyes burning, and said, "One night."

What am I, made of stone? "Okay, but I'm paying."

She smiled. "You have to. I have no money, remember?" We started walking up the steps as she added, "Oh, and they weren't going to give us a room because of our ages, so I told them you knocked me up and we're getting married tomorrow. So, you have to play along and treat me like a queen."

I stopped. "And here I was, worried they were going to hate me for how I'm dressed, or because they recognized me from the papers. My legend grows."

Remorse crept onto her face. "I didn't think about that. I'm so sorry. I—" She turned to head back down the steps. But her hand was still in mine, and I stayed put and tugged her back. I summoned my best Southern drawl.

"C'mon, Linda May! This here's our honeymoon!" I dragged her up the steps. Melissa started laughing. "Now mind these steps, that's my young'un you got in there!"

A bottle-blonde receptionist with heavy makeup looked at Melissa and said, "Oh here's our blushing bride-to-be! Ain't you the sweetest lil' thing! We've upgraded you for your big day! Put you in the honeymoon cabin. You're gonna love it!" Melissa blushed and thanked her.

The concierge was still smiling when she turned to me, but her eyes were brittle with blame. "Hemingway Jones, is it? May I see your card? I have to put a refundable hold of one hundred dollars for incidentals."

I handed it over silently, as Melissa mouthed, *I'm so sorry.* Just to get even I rubbed her belly affectionately. She swatted at my hand, smothering a grin.

Dusk was creeping across the gardens as we weaved our way through heavily landscaped trellises and pathways to Carolina Cabin, the *House Beautiful* version of a "rustic wood cabin" behind the B and B. I admit the cabin was glorious: equipped with a pillowy loft bedroom, a stone fireplace, and an indoor hot tub. Rugs and pillows softened every wall and seat. Sleek robes were side by side on hooks by the door.

When the door closed, I took Melissa in my arms.

I smiled at her. "You know, there are a lot of hotels in Durham. We could totally repeat this scam."

"We have to go back. I—"

I didn't even let her finish. First, because she'd be breaking her own rule. And second, because I didn't want to waste a moment talking when I could be kissing her with everything I've got. She responded in kind, and we began tearing away the small pieces of fabric that were the last barrier between us and the singular unit we'd become.

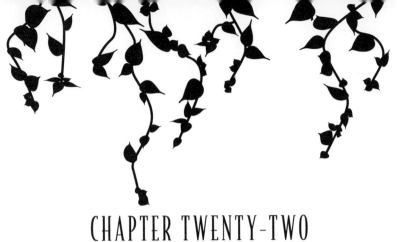

CHAPTER TWENTY-TWO

The morning was gray, gloomy, and insanely humid, with a hot wind on the move as we piled into the car and gassed up. We spoke in monosyllables. The glow of the previous night had turned misty and amorphous, replaced by ominous clouds on the horizon. The radio blared warnings of violent storms and possible tornados on the way. That was nothing compared to the foreboding we felt going home. Our brief respite was over, and possibly never to be repeated, and we were now on countdown. Everything we liked, loved, and knew was about to disappear—Lila, our relationship, and my home.

Melissa reluctantly took intermittent calls from her parents, who hinted at their deep and abiding unhappiness she'd stayed overnight with me in Durham. She endured them to a point, then would cut them off, reminding them she was eighteen and already felt at least a decade older.

I was silently wishing Calhoun would just hurry up and die, because I had no legal way to leave the state, and Dad and I had nowhere to go and no way to get anywhere. I flipped through my phone, silently reviewing our conversation with Boyd—what had we missed? When it came to me, I started googling like crazy.

"Where's that grocery-store phone?" I finally asked.

"Glove compartment, why?" Melissa asked.

I answered her as I reached into the glove box and fumbled with the phone. "Paper mills. I was looking again at buyers of hydrogen sulfide and Google kept giving me articles about environmental risks instead. I must've scrolled past a dozen of them until I finally read one. Did you know paper mills make hydrogen sulfide as a by-product? It's a serious risk for them. They actually pay other companies to come in and clean it up. So, the H_2S is waste there. That totally makes more sense than looking at companies that make it, and—"

"Paper mills are in the North, oh my God."

"Exactly."

"Any prospects yet?"

"A couple of them. One in particular, but I want to run it by Dr. Boyd."

I sent him a text as we heard the first little *dink* on the hood of the car. We both looked up, noticing for the first time how ridiculously dark it had become. Another *dink*—it sounded like a decent-sized rock had hit the roof. Then they started coming in twos and threes, the intervals shorter, the sounds louder, which meant the hail was growing in size.

"There's an underpass just ahead."

Melissa nodded. "I'll pull over."

Underneath the underpass, we spent a few minutes tucking ourselves in as close as we could so more cars could fit in. The hail grew louder, as more and more cars tried to nudge themselves to safety. Eventually, they were forced to park in the lanes. Knowing we'd likely be stuck for a while even if the storm didn't last, Melissa and I finally climbed out and went to the edge of the overhang to watch the storm, along with about fifty other people, some of whom had been forced to abandon their cars to the elements.

We always get a hailstorm or two during the summer, but this one played out like a prophecy. Starting small, the hail grew to a crescendo within minutes, pelting everything in view with grapefruit-sized chunks of ice. Green summer leaves were swirling off trees on either side of the highway, followed by twigs and then whole branches, until the road looked like a giant bird's nest. A tree limb hit the windshield of a Toyota just outside the underpass, cracking it. The guy next to me simply said, "Damn," and grabbed his cell, as we watched hail pucker the body with dents.

Weirdest part was the birds—they shrieked and called out to one another like soldiers pinned in trenches. A bang. Not thunder—a transformer. And we just watched the highway. Fifty people, arms folded, no one saying anything, witnesses to Mother Nature's aerial bombardment.

After twenty or more minutes the clouds rushed north, leaving a trail of deep blue sky and a salad of ice and greenery. Everyone held their breath for about a minute more, as if the slightest sound would give away our hiding place and bring the storm back. They finally relaxed and started calling out to one another, arranging which car would go first and in what order to get out.

I suddenly remembered Dad and called. "Hey. Just wanted to let you know we're going to be a little late. We had the most massive hailstorm . . . no, we're fine, we were right by an underpass. What? I can't hear you, people are honking, trying to get out of here." I plugged my other ear and said, "Dad? Okay, okay, we'll be there as soon as we can." I turned to Melissa. "I'm afraid we don't have time to be polite. We have to get out of here, right now." I said to Melissa. "The storm hit Concord shortly before it hit here: the power is out."

"Shit. Okay, okay, okay!" I'd never heard her swear before. She turned on the ignition and forcefully nudged herself into the queue, obligating the Ford truck behind her to slam on its brakes and honk. "Sorry!" She waved a hand to the rearview.

The highway didn't bend to our will—we picked our way past multiple car crashes, downed limbs, and law-enforcement officers trying to help out. I tried to keep how frantic I was to myself, knowing Melissa would blame herself, but I tapped my foot endlessly and leaned forward in the seat as if that simple act would somehow deliver me home faster. Melissa's parents called too, to make sure we were all right. They insisted they needed her at the hospital right away. By the time we got to my street, there was no time for more than a hurried good-bye and a quick peck for good luck.

The world was so white and bright after the storm that I was instantly blinded by the darkness. I heard the velociraptor zoom toward me, but I couldn't see it.

"Dad? You all right?" I called.

"Warm," was all he grunted.

"I got it!" I started feeling my way toward the generator cautiously, since I couldn't see him. "Why didn't you call the research center?"

"Because it means our little monitoring system is down too. I've been waiting for a moment like this. Can you see yet?" he asked.

"No, not yet. Look, what was the temperature here when the power went off? Do you even know?" I fumbled along the wall, mentally calculating just how long he had until the temperature in here would get intolerable for him. Just as I felt the switch, it exploded and flamed out.

I whipped around in the dark. "Cool trick, but what the hell are you doing?"

He cackled, "Like that? Loads of static electricity in the air. Easy to manipulate." He zoomed to the far end of the room. "Anyway, I need the power out. Getting ready to show you something. God, it's nice to be able to talk out loud in my own house."

"Don't change the subject."

"Right. Ambulation. All along we've hypothesized that being a Gray means I'm either a stationary creature, or something went wrong in my transformation, right?

I threw my back against the wall and folded my arms. I already didn't appreciate the chances he took with the hydrogen sulfide—now he was messing with the temperature too? But he was absolutely frantic with excitement about something—something good—and I wanted to give him his moment. I answered him, still hoping to hurry him along. "Yes. Although I think Hannah Ross proved it's a glitch in the transformation."

"Actually, there's another alternative we hadn't considered. Thought of it while I was watching this show on bears. It was about their hibernation patterns. How their metabolism drops dramatically with the colder temperatures, how their breathing slows."

"Yeah it's called torpor. Boyd talked about it."

I heard the velociraptor rattle. "Dad? You all right?"

He grunted heavily before saying, "I'm fine. You know, it takes bears a couple of months before their bodies adjust after hibernation. So, I started thinking, what if my body's been in some hibernation mode? And I'm slowly coming out of it?"

The velociraptor zoomed past me in the dark to the other end of the room. "Now where are you going?" I demanded.

His voice startled me from behind. "I'm right here."

I turned to find him at eye-level less than a foot away, his yellow eyes glowing with excitement. He grinned. "I moved the chair so you wouldn't hear my footsteps. Thought I'd make it a surprise." He shuffled forward, his movements stiff and awkward, but he was moving.

"Holy crap. You can walk again?"

My stomach fluttered like a parent watching their baby take first steps. I flipped on the flashlight on my phone to watch. Dad's movements were halting, but they promised improvement, and ultimately, freedom. I gaped at him. "How long have you known?"

"I suspected I was regaining some movement a couple of weeks ago—I could wiggle my fingers—but I didn't want to try walking in front of you, because I suspected we were bugged. And because if I failed, I knew you'd take it hard. The first time I tried was during the last thunderstorm, the night Hannah Ross escaped. We lost power for a few minutes. Wasn't pretty, but I did it."

"I don't understand. What's wrong with them knowing you can walk? Tan would be thrilled."

"So would Paul Calhoun. That's the problem. Right now, his only option is to be a walking vegetable like Hannah Ross. If he finds out the quadriplegia is just temporary, he'll squeeze. It's life or death for him." I nodded, seeing his point. He turned toward the velociraptor. The chair switched into gear, motored to him. He sat.

There was something satisfying in watching that empty chair maneuver the room. I asked lightly, "Can we turn the generator on now?"

He looked at me quizzically. "I fried it."

My eyes grew wide. "You did, didn't you? What if we're out of power for hours?" I started fumbling again.

Dad could move. The thought thrilled and relieved me, but worried me too. "What if you move in your sleep?" I asked anxiously.

"I boosted some muscle relaxants off the nurses. Been taking them and I guess they're working, but they'll show up next time Tan runs my bloodwork."

"You're stealing drugs?"

"Don't judge. I can't exactly ask for a prescription, without giving it away, can I? Am I sitting the way I normally sit in this chair? Look at me."

I eyeballed him. "No, your feet are crossed." He uncrossed them hurriedly as I asked, "Why do you want to know?"

"Because the power's about to come back on," he responded.

And with that, I heard the hum of energy returning. I marveled again at his talents as I ran to the fridge and readied a dose of hydrogen sulfide.

CHAPTER TWENTY-THREE

I wandered downstairs in the morning, to find Dad staring off into space, his face exhibiting no small measure of irritation. "Morning. What's going on? I forget to take out the trash or something?"

His voice boomed in my head just as I heard sounds in the kitchen.

"We have a visitor."

I wandered around the corner to find Stephens kneeling in front of the fridge, a medical cooler by her side.

"Uh, hi? Don't recall seeing you here before," I said.

Stephens looked up and smiled at me. "Not my usual detail, I know. But Tan called in sick to work, so you've got me." She grabbed doses of hydrogen sulfide and tucked them into her cooler.

"Uh, Tan usually brings hydrogen sulfide, he doesn't take it away," hoping I wasn't giving away the nervousness I felt.

Stephens continued filling up her cooler.

"There's reason to believe that some of these are tainted, so I've been instructed to collect them."

It was clear from her casual delivery that she didn't care if I believed her pathetic lie or not. I did my best to keep calm. "Surely you've brought replacements."

"Only a few, I'm afraid. We're waiting on a shipment. You'll be the first to know when it arrives." She finished confiscating Dad's lifeline, tucking a couple of vials back into the fridge, shut the cooler, and stood up. "Who knows? Maybe it will arrive on your birthday. Then I can bring you a present."

She waited for me to respond, but seeing as we were dropping pretenses, I simply walked to the front door and opened it.

Unperturbed, she grabbed the cooler and followed. "Bye, Hemingway! Bill."

"Guess they know why I went to Durham."

"Yup."

To make sure we didn't try to run, Lifebank was now going to ration doses. We were going to have to leave, hydrogen sulfide or no, within days. I grabbed Dad's bike and rode to the hospital.

Melissa's eyes had lost their flinty hazel flecks when I met her in the hall. Wearing the same clothes she'd worn when she dropped me off, her hair was knotted messily on her head. It was clear she hadn't slept since we'd returned.

I opened my arms and she folded herself in. "She's in so much pain," she said, her voice dull and muffled in my chest. "You can see it. Mom and Dad are fighting. Mom wants to give her the painkillers, but Dad keeps insisting we should honor Lila's wishes. But it's not like Lila got some pain sampler kit when she was still lucid and decided she could handle it. And she isn't saying anything, so they're both looking at me for support, and I don't know what to do. She wakes in these fits, just groaning. It's awful."

I just held on and said, "There's no right solution."

"I've reminded myself this was coming. Every day. For months. And in my worst moments, I've even thought, 'Just get it over with.' Now all I pray for is just hearing her voice one more time. I can't let it go, I keep hearing her in my head, and I think that's why I've resisted giving her the painkillers. That's so selfish and awful to say. I'm a horrible person."

"No, you love her more than anything in the world, and it's an insanely hard call."

She pulled away, mumbling, "I have to use the bathroom." She started stumbling down the hall.

"Okay." I struggled to ask, but finally choked out, my voice breaking, "Can I see her? Just one last time?"

Melissa turned and wandered back to the door and leaned in, murmuring to her parents. She straightened and nodded toward the door, holding up her index finger. I nodded that I understood—I would have one minute. Melissa then headed down the hall.

I walked in slowly, uncertain of my welcome by Mary and Kevin. But they were in their own worlds of pain, their eyes dull and unfocused. Kevin was staring out the window, while Mary was holding Lila's hand, whispering to her cramped little body.

Lila writhed momentarily, startling all of us. That slight, painful movement broke the delicate silence: Kevin choked out a sob and ran out of the room.

I had to look away from Lila for a moment myself, because I was about to start crying like a toddler, and that wouldn't be fair to Mary or Lila.

You know, even if you agreed to take the rest of the suffering in the world into your arms and hold it above your head for the rest of your life, looking at a lone, dying kid would still be the heavier lift. Their death is a black hole. When you love a dying child, you're on the event horizon. You're not going to survive this: you won't be the person you were while that child was alive. There will always be something tight and dense inside you, crushing you from within, because you're still alive, when you'd have happily traded places with that kid if there was a way to strike that bargain.

I walked over to the butterfly cage to collect myself, sucking in deep breaths until I thought I could keep it together. "Hey, Captain Lila. It's Hemingway," I finally said. "You don't have to wake up. Mac and Newman are sleeping too. They've gone into a chrysalis. Their pupas are all green with just a ring of gold here, see?" I pushed the butterfly cage closer to her bed, hoping her eyes would at least flutter open for a moment. I waited, but she didn't move.

I heard a rustle outside the room. People were gathering. Something was happening. I just looked at Lila, hoping for some sign of my fearless little navigator. "Well, I guess it's a good thing you're getting a nap, because you're not going to want to miss when they emerge, right? We'll let them go together. You and me." I could feel my voice getting desperate. Tears started flowing. My voice broke. "I have to go, and I'm not ready to say good-bye to you, Lila."

I felt a familiar hand on my shoulder. Melissa said softly, "Hemingway. The orderlies are here. It's time to move her to another room."

"Okay," I mumbled, and I stumbled up, bumping into the tray table, rattling a litter of dishes and silverware. "Sorry. I'll go."

"It's okay," Melissa assured me.

The orderlies started filing in, pitching orders at one another as they moved to either side of the bed. I turned for the door.

Melissa suddenly shouted, "Wait, EVERYBODY SHUT UP!"

The orderlies balked. I turned.

"Can you say it again, honey, so he can hear?" Melissa asked.

"Bye, Hemingway," Lila whispered, and she closed her eyes again. In sleep or in pain, I didn't know. I just ran out of the room to find a quiet stairwell I knew all too well in that hospital. It was rarely used by anyone, and therefore the perfect place to go when the sobs and snot and fury finally exploded.

I didn't say anything when I got home. I didn't have to. By the look on Dad's face, he'd been at the hospital with me. I'd gone back to find Melissa, once

I'd recovered enough to be of any use. Not that I was. Visiting was officially over. They were on vigil, family only. She'd kissed me quickly and returned to Lila's room, where she and her mother intended to pray until it was over.

I went to my room for a while, trying to let sleep take me away, but the day belonged to Lila. When I finally gave up and trudged downstairs, Dad was waiting.

"There a breeze out there earlier?" Dad asked out loud.

"I guess so, why?"

The velociraptor sparked to life and whizzed over to the computer screen. Dad started checking the weather.

"You up for a ride? *Remember I said something about the weather?*"

"Not really. Where am I going? *I'm seriously not in the mood.*"

"Doug Allwood's place. Remember him? The cabinetmaker?"

"Doesn't he live like in, I dunno, Hell and Gone? *Please tell me this is just for show. You don't seriously expect me to ride all the way out there, do you?*"

"Not quite, but it's out that way. *He lives in Gold Hill. The wind's coming from the east, like I told you about! I can smell it already! And who knows if we'll get another chance?*" Out loud: "Look, you know he's old. He's got a book he's been saving for me. I need you to swing by there and pick it up. *Follow the smell of burned eggs. You'll pick it up along the way. See where it's coming from.*"

"Don't you have anything else to read? I mean, can it wait?"

"Look, how much do I ask for, really? If riding's such a problem, take that damn car they gave you. Thing's gathering rust in the driveway."

He knew perfectly well I wouldn't touch the car. I was planning on giving it to Melissa when we left.

There's only one road safe for cycling if you're going to the hillbilly east— Gold Hill Road. Even once you've gone all the way down Gold Hill Road, you still have to bank left and climb Mt. Olive for miles more before you get to Doug Allwood's home and shop. He's just outside the tiny one-street tourist-trap town of Gold Hill and the mine. I momentarily wondered whether it was coincidence or the cosmos that kept sending me back there.

The sun sagged in the west by the time I rolled out. Dad called before I even got as far as Todd's, positively bursting with energy as he asked, "You close to Doug's yet?"

"What? Yeah, sure. It's only like, another twenty miles or so."

He ignored my sarcasm. "Is it windy?"

"Sometimes."

"Weather report said there'll be gusts up to fifteen, twenty miles per hour. Just worried about you is all."

"You're worried about me? Aww, that's sweet, Dad. Nothing says love like a forty-mile ride on a fifty-five-mile-per-hour road in the dark. *Hey, if I do pick up the scent, do you really need me to stop by this guy's house?*"

"You've done more on a camping trip. *Yes, I do—that's important. I just called Doug; he's expecting you. Makes a good cover too. If anyone's checking up on you, they'll probably wait at Doug's. I figure once they see you, they'll be satisfied and go. So, when you do pick up the smell, save the investigating until you're on the way back.*" Out loud he said, "You're on my bike, right? You can always use the trails instead of the road." And hung up.

Love you too, Dad.

At least the air was cooler.

The eastern winds show up at least once a summer, bringing the Atlantic to the foothills. It's pretty cool when it happens; the sheer excitement and relief are visible—everyone wiggles around like they've just traded a sweat-soaked three-piece suit for a pair of shorts and a T-shirt.

I took in a few big drags of salty air. Nothing.

I rode, hitting the fields as soon as I could. Trails my ass. There weren't any trails, and he knew it. There are just farms and fields plenty wide enough to handle a mountain bike, but they're slow and bumpy as hell. I hit rock after rock, and at times I skirted back onto Gold Hill just to get a little relief.

The emptiness made me nervous. The houses got fewer and farther between as the sun got lower in the sky. Usually, I did this ride in the morning, in the company of at least one other person. Right now, no one would know where I was or what happened to me if I got hit.

A mile or so after Todd's place, the houses pretty much disappeared. I was the lone human out here, in fields and trees loaded with shadows that lifted and moved with every slicing shift of the wind.

And I still didn't smell anything funky. Except me. I reeked like a sweaty foot.

Most of the wildlife out this way is crepuscular, which is a fancy way of saying they eat and move about at dawn and dusk. Right now, they were busy reclaiming the road. A whole herd of white-tailed deer crossed about five hundred feet in front of me. They were all right—I enjoyed listening to them clog across the pavement and leap off into the field—then they were a memory. But when that gray fox fell right out of the tree, I started rethinking the off-roading. It's pretty freaky-looking, but gray foxes can climb trees— they're the only fox that can—and they move and hunt like big cats. They have serious claws too, so I wasn't crazy about the idea of a big, fat, stupid one launching for me. Wouldn't kill me or anything, but it would definitely require a good plastic surgeon.

The road was just as bad. The snakes were out, loads of 'em, intent on absorbing the left-over heat of the day. I picked my way around them, guessing if I ran over one, the wide mountain bike wheels probably wouldn't kill it. Just piss it off.

The climb on Mt. Olive eliminated most of the wildlife factor because the grade is so steep. I arrived at Doug Allwood's farmhouse in the dark, but the porch lights were still on. I rode up, noting an old Chevy in the grass. I was seriously thinking about giving up the ghost on not driving, and just asking Doug if I could borrow it to get home. Dad would have to be satisfied with his stupid book and live without the source of the stink.

Doug opened the door, his white hair nappy and matted, like he'd fallen asleep in a chair. His face was cross with impatience. "'Bout time you showed up. I been waiting to go to bed."

"Hi, Mr. Allwood. What can I say? I'm a slacker."

He handed me a tiny blue journal. "Well, here you go. Tell your dad I said hey. Been awhile since he hired me on a project." He shut the door and I heard the lock turn.

I stared at the door and finally said, "No thanks on that water. Don't go to any trouble, I'm good. Yes sir, I'll be sure and send Dad your best. I'll also be getting you a newspaper subscription. No seriously, it's on me, just maybe look at it once in a while."

I flipped through the book, curious—what the heck was this? Someone's scrunched handwriting, by the looks of it. But Doug switched off the lights around his house, abruptly ending my reading break. I tucked the book in the back of my pants with a sigh and climbed back on the bike, gingerly placing my now aching ass on the seat.

I was still supposed to follow the smell. But I looked down the lonely road and my body voted—instantly—to head for home.

The bats at the edge of the road sold it. You know, there are plenty of them in Concord. Pull back the shutter on any house during the day, and you're likely to find one or two, snoring away. They're no big deal, they're just tiny little fruit bats. They're kinda cute with their brown fur and rounded mouse-like ears, and they're handy too—they eat their own weight in mosquitoes every day. But get out to Gold Hill in the evening and they're a little overwhelming, thanks to their sheer numbers. Scores of them swarmed over my head, their famously hideous wingspans filling the sky. Their flying skills aren't up to much either. One of them dropped right in front of me, its bald, webbed wings clapping my face and around my ears. I swatted and swore as I turned the bike for home.

Two things happened in quick succession: first, the lights of a car swung out from the field by Doug's and took off, which meant someone had been checking up on me. Then the breeze wafted again. And this time, an unmistakable smell. Rotten eggs.

How the hell could Dad pick up that scent? He was twenty miles away, living inside a vacuum-sealed fridge. But he was right. I spun around again, this time following the scent in earnest.

A sliver of moon rose as I rode, and two dozen bats suddenly vaulted into flight from a copse—something had startled them. I braked and glanced around, looking for the source. A cacophony of cicadas, grasshoppers, and crickets chirped. But there was something else too, occasionally planting a rustling foot in the grass. Something bigger.

A shape loomed in the moonlight at the edge of the copse and froze. Yellow eyes met mine, blinking in wonder and fear at the sight of me. We stared at each other, me fully visible on the road, while only her eyes glowed, the rest of her camouflaged by her skin, which blended organically with the dark.

I finally managed to croak out, "Hannah Ross? Is that you?"

She turned and darted back into the woods. I dropped the bike and ran after her. She moved incredibly fast—more like a gazelle than a zombie. But unlike a gazelle, she made a hell of a lot of noise. Branches snapped; dry leaves crunched. I tracked the sounds, and they kept me within striking distance of her.

I kept thinking, *She's alive, she's alive, and how the hell is she alive?* I had no idea what to do if I caught up with her. Not because I was worried that what Dad said was true, but because I didn't have any way to bring her back to my house, or the research center, or anywhere. I wasn't even sure I *wanted* to bring her anywhere. I was simply responding to an impulse.

I stomped through the creek and the odor grew stronger. My nose and throat burned. Got so bad I doubled over momentarily, propping myself up against a tree, exhausted from running and light-headed from lack of air. I figured she'd lost me when I heard her screech like an owl, as she either skid or fell downhill. I wasn't sure which, but I took off again.

"Hannah Ross!" My voice was dry and raspy. I wasn't looking at my footing. I didn't see that little ridge any more than she had.

I fell about six or eight feet, landing hard in a long, narrow trench that was probably impossible to see even in the daytime, since greenery grew up right from the floor and beyond, giving the illusion of even terrain above. I felt around for a foothold to climb out, but found nothing. I fumbled along in the dark. I kept calling her name, I don't know why. She didn't know Hannah Ross, didn't remember her. But what else was I supposed to do?

I found several footholds, but curiosity got the better of me. I was pretty sure she hadn't climbed out—I hadn't heard a thing since she fell. But finding her was suddenly at odds with another, more immediate agenda: I had to get out of there.

The thought permeated my dulled brain at the same time I found a door in the trench. A frigging door. I felt around—doorjamb, door, and hinges—too firm and proper to be some kids' makeshift bunker for a game of commando.

Whole thing was sealed with rotting boards, but a hole had been punched at the base. A hole that was just big enough that someone as small as Hannah Ross could crawl through.

I knelt down—the space was tight and riddled with weeds—but I stuck my head through. The cold, damp air of a cave stuck to my sweaty face, waking me up momentarily. I tried to call, "Hannah Ross!" But no sound came out, because my lungs abruptly filled—first with fire and then with bile. I yanked myself back out, barfed in the trench, and everything started spinning. I tried to stand up, suddenly in a panic to climb out. I made it about five more seconds.

I don't even remember going down.

The first filtered light of day was peeking through the trees when I woke up. Took me a while to register that I wasn't in the trench anymore—I was about thirty feet away. How had I gotten out? On my delirious own, or Hannah Ross? I didn't know and I'm not really sure I cared, because I probably looked—and definitely felt—awful: pounding headache, scorched throat, shaky arms and legs, mud and leaves caked on my skin, everything infused with the fresh scent of rotten eggs and vomit. My cell phone was ringing. I answered, noting the missed calls—Dad had called about thirty times.

"Hem? You there?"

Todd.

I tried to lick the dirt off my teeth, but found no juice. I finally croaked, "Yeah, I'm here."

"Praise Jesus and Holy Effen Ef, where are you, man? Your dad's like freaking out. He's called me like twenty times."

"I'm out your way. Few miles farther almost to Gold Hill. Hey, do you think you can you come pick me up in the truck? I've got the bike. I'll make my way back to the road, you'll see me."

"What in the Sam Hill are you doing out here? No, wait. Save that. Rather hear the ugly details in person." I could just picture him waggling his eyebrows, thinking I'd brought some girl out there. But before I could protest, he said, "Get to the road. I'll be with you in like ten minutes."

Which meant at least thirty. Just as well. Was probably going to take me that long to find the road and crawl back there.

Before trudging my way out, I called around a few times for Hannah Ross, but I couldn't summon more than a rattle. My throat and eyes still burned like a forest fire. The heat was in midday bloom, the eastern beach breezes history, replaced by the stagnant heat of August, which acted like a microwave on the rotten-egg stink. I knew I should be putting together what the smell was, but what little was left of my cerebrum I dedicated to finding the road and that wasn't easy, because my eyes still burned like the face of the sun.

The bike, amazingly enough, was still there and still intact, despite the fact I'd abandoned it on the shoulder. I sank down beside it in the tall grass, uncaring about snakes or gray foxes or anything. I just wanted to get the hell out of there. I suddenly remembered Dad's book—I tapped at my back, amazed to discover it was still there.

A school bus made its laborious way toward me, the driver beeping the horn, while kids waved out the window. I squinted, tried to smile, and waved back; judging from their reactions, I looked like the star of a creature feature. Bored and brain hurting, I watched them go, surprised when the bus slowed down and turned about five hundred yards past me. Where the heck were they going? I hadn't even realized there was a turn. Thinking I could give Todd a more specific location where to pick me up, I staggered to my feet.

A tiny sign planted at the corner read, "Reed Gold Mine, buses and commercial vehicles only."

A sentient thought finally took root in the sandy soil of my brain. If I was at Reed, the door I'd seen led to the mine. Not the main entrance, just some ancient side exit. Mines are cold. They're also full of deadly gasses, so they have to be sealed and treated regularly. What I was experiencing were symptoms—headache, burning throat, burning eyes, nausea, shaking limbs—symptoms of exposure. Then there was the smell itself—rotten eggs. You know what smells like rotten eggs? Sulfur. Or a compound containing sulfur. Like hydrogen sulfide, for example.

Hydrogen sulfide isn't strictly made by humans. It occurs in nature—often inside caves. Mines too? I didn't know, but it made sense. It's a natural by-product of bacterial breakdown. It's also explosive and deadly stuff, so that would explain why they seal mines when they're done with them. The museum probably hadn't found Hannah Ross's little rabbit hole yet.

I felt like kicking myself. All this time, I'd been trying to figure out how I could hijack hydrogen sulfide from a source, when it was occurring naturally in my own backyard.

Dad had sensed the smell all the way from our house. Grays must sense it like animals detect water. Hannah Ross wasn't sentient, but she'd gone straight to it.

I was so lost in thought that I didn't even hear Todd pull up.

"DUUUDE!!!" he called out the passenger's-side window of the truck. "You rode all the way out here?"

He balked when I turned. I must've looked like I'd been jumped.

"Don't ask," I told him as I loaded the bike into the bed. "And don't tell anyone you found me out here. Seriously. No one. Just let me borrow that iPhone of yours. I need to check something out and I don't want to do it on my home computer."

I climbed into the truck as he tossed me the iPhone and gunned the motor. "We're still on for Tuesday, right?"

My confused, blank look was met with exasperation. "Dude! Um, your birthday? My house? Party? I got grain alcohol just for the occasion. We're making hurricanes!"

"Oh right. Hey, I don't know if I can make it—"

"You have to! Because you owe me. I never get up this early in the summertime." He shifted again and we took off.

My eyes still hurt, but I kept them glued to the glowing screen. The Carolina gold mine trail starts at Reed and dips below the South Carolina border. Most of the mines haven't been active since the 1960s, which means they're cold and empty. At least a few of them probably had issues with hydrogen sulfide. I started branching out—plenty more copper mines in the Blue Ridge too. A lot of those were still active, and therefore inhabited, but I had to admit, I liked the distance and physical barriers the mountains offered.

I finally had at least a temporary solution to the biggest stumbling block in our plans—getting out with enough hydrogen sulfide to keep Dad alive. It wasn't great, as I had no intention of leaving my dad in a cave. But it was something.

CHAPTER TWENTY-FOUR

I stumbled through the door of my house, and cold rushed up to greet me. My eyes took a moment to adjust to the room, as Dad emitted a loud, "Thank God. Todd called and all, but I had to see you to believe it."

His yellow eyes grew wide as he focused on me. I probably looked like a feral cat that had been eating out of the wrong dumpster for months.

"Jesus."

I knew he was reading the fact I'd found Hannah Ross alive. But for our studio audience, I managed, "Sorry. Wrecked on the bike. Must've passed out. I'm showering and going to bed."

"You should call Todd back. Have him take you to the hospital. Get checked out. *We need to talk.*"

I opened the door and started to head up the stairs. "I'll be fine. *Later. Must—*"

"Son, sorry, but do you still have the book?"

As there were no polite words that would cover my exasperation, and seeing as coherency was impossible, I simply pulled his precious book from the back of my jeans and plopped it on his lap and returned to the stairs. I swallowed a few Tylenols to contend with the headache and showered for about a decade. I had to use a toothbrush just to get all the grime out of my fingernails. Animated dreams in primary reds and yellows dogged my sleep, like frames in the climax of a graphic novel. I woke up gasping several times, blindly running to the bathroom and slurping water straight from the faucet to rinse the burn from my throat before I passed out again.

It was morning again before it was over.

I raised the blinds and squinted to see Burkhardt walking into Charlie's house. Still shaky from hydrogen-sulfide poisoning, I gingerly pulled on a pair of jeans, donned a pair of sunglasses, and headed over.

The front door was open. Two uniforms from Concord Police were picking their way through Charlie's mail. They turned to stare at me. Burkhardt was still focused on something in his hand as he said, "Just the guy I wanted to talk to," his tone indicating not so much.

"What's going on? Why are you in Charlie's house?"

He didn't bat an eye. "Got a call from your dad yesterday, actually. Said Charlie hasn't been home for a few days, and he was worried. I started poking around, knocked on the door, no one answered, so I asked at his work. Blackwelder said they'd let Charlie go about a week ago."

"Let go? As in, fired?"

"Yep. Something about some after-hours work, conflict of interest."

A chill of panic ran through me. I'd asked Charlie to go see a lawyer and confess. Now he was missing—fired from his job and, um, missing. I tried to think logically: just because I'd asked Charlie to go doesn't mean he went. Blackwelder could have easily found out about his part-time job and let him go, without any input from me or anyone at Lifebank. And maybe he'd taken off for a few days. "You check with his ex-wife?"

Burkhardt nodded. "She hasn't heard from him and as he's three days late with his alimony check, she's a little pissed. Maybe a little worried. She's how I finally got permission to open this place up. When was the last time you saw him?"

My hands were fluttering uselessly, so I shrugged and shoved them in my pockets. "Few days? Maybe more than a few?"

"Bunch of stubs here from bookies. Looks like he owed them about fifteen grand. You know anything about that?"

Jesus, Charlie.

Should I admit I knew he gambled? I was pretty sure if I did, they'd focus on the bookie. And I just knew that was wrong.

So what was right? I mentally deliberated. I had no reason to believe Calhoun would take and/or harm Charlie. He hadn't harmed Lisa, the reporter, like I'd originally thought. He hadn't harmed me or Cass. In fact, Calhoun tiptoed a very narrow legal tightrope in everything he did.

I glanced around the house. The place was as filthy as it had been the other day. A sweatshirt was draped over a chair, the coffee stain still on the kitchen wall. But that was all Charlie's mess. No sign he'd been attacked.

The two uniforms shifted impatiently, while Burkhardt just stared me down. "Hemingway? You got something you want to tell me?"

I needed to talk to Dad. "Yeah, I knew he gambled. He'd just told me about it. Didn't say how much, but he didn't sound too worried about it. But have you checked at Lifebank? Charlie sometimes makes drops there. Maybe they've heard from him."

"That's not everything," Burkhardt insisted.

I held up my palms. "Well, that's all I've got. Look, Charlie's my friend. I don't know where he is, but I would encourage you to ask at Lifebank. Talk to Dr. Cass." My voice turned pleading. "Seriously. Please. Just ask her."

"Why are you wearing sunglasses indoors?"

"What? Oh. Eye exam yesterday. Still bugging me."

Even I didn't believe that, and judging by Burkhardt's expression, neither did he.

I headed for the door, glancing at the mail and papers on the front hall table. They'd been reviewing them when I walked in. I wondered if there was anything there, something I might recognize, something they might not realize was significant.

Burkhardt called after me. "You still got my card?" I nodded. "You change your mind, or you're in trouble, call me. Even if you just think you're in trouble, call. Okay?"

Surprised by his concern, I couldn't help but say, "I'll be in touch. Seriously. I will. Very soon."

That's when I spotted it—a business card.

I palmed it on the way out the door and waited until I was back in front of my own house before taking a look.

The card read, "Cleatwood Hayes, Attorney at Law," with a Church Street address.

Charlie had gone to a lawyer.

"When did Charlie go missing?" I demanded of Dad.

Dad's eyes drifted to the walls, reminding me they had ears. Out loud he said, "I don't know. I just called Burkhardt because I hadn't seen him in a few days, and I was a little worried."

My fists knotted with worry and cold, and right now, that felt like one and the same thing. I was tired of our studio audience, and if I'd been who I was a few days ago, I'd have started ripping out every last monitoring device in the house on impulse. I was pretty sure that Dad could guide me to exactly where they were. Hell, he could probably short them all out without me lifting a finger. But I was over my impulses, and Dad didn't have any. As much as I found their presence annoying, we had a way of talking around them, and conversely, if we ripped them out, we'd be setting off alarm bells at Lifebank.

Dad silently agreed with me. *"Some guy came to his house last night. I was wondering if it was one of those guys you met in the Bottoms."*

"Did you read his thoughts? Someone named John Charles in them?"

"Yes."

"Then I know who it was."

"*Last I knew, Charlie was off to see a lawyer. He was pissed, but he was going to take your advice. He never came back. He wasn't taken from his house. I'd have picked that up.*"

"*Why didn't you say anything sooner?*"

"*Because I didn't know Charlie had gone missing! You know Charlie—guy works three days in a row without coming home. He hates that house. Hates being alone.*"

Our mental discussion was interrupted by the sound of a phone. I pulled mine out of my pocket, but there was nothing. "That the research center?" I asked Dad.

"It's not me."

My eyes bugged when I remembered—the burner phone. Boyd was calling me. I was about to bolt upstairs to my room when Dad telekinetically interrupted.

"*Eyes. Ignore it.*" Out loud he said, "You leave the TV on in your room?"

"Maybe. *They're going to know there's a phone in the house they can't intercept, no matter what.*"

"*They don't have to know it's important.*"

"*Dad, they're gonna know it's important.*"

"Go get some lunch. Clear your head for a while. *Buy another phone while you're out. Give Boyd a new number when you call him. And son . . .*"

"What?"

"*You're going to have to take that car.*"

I shook my head, grabbed my backpack, tucked the phone inside, and basically ran out of the house with Dad booming in my head.

"*TAKE THE CAR.*"

"*WE DON'T EVEN KNOW IF IT WILL START!*"

I was suddenly grateful I was on Dad's mountain bike. I rode through the backyard, and the neighbor's yard, and cut across the street that ran parallel to my own, heading for my Greenway shortcut. I heard a car wheeling around the corner and dipped behind the houses to watch. The car idled in the street for a few minutes, then peeled out.

I headed back to my shortcut, a dirt path I'd personally carved over many years, and careened right onto the Greenway. Down the path, I dipped off and into a retirement community, guessing they'd be waiting at the end of Branchview, where the Greenway ended. Throwing the bike on my back, I hiked back up the incline and collapsed at the ridge, huffing and puffing and desperate for water I didn't have as I pulled out the phone.

The call wasn't from Boyd. Where the hell was area code 603? I momentarily reflected on the risk I'd just taken for what was likely a robocall. But I dialed.

"Hello, is this Hemingway?"

"Yeah. Who's this?"

"Hemingway, this is Dr. David Elks."

Floored. I started laughing. "Are you freaking kidding me? Where are you?"

"I'm in New Hampshire. A little town called Bennington. Dr. Boyd said to tell you that your suspicion about paper mills paid off."

"So, you're there because—" The words caught in my throat. "Are you caring for someone like my dad?"

"I am."

Tears welled up in my eyes. I wasn't alone in this problem anymore. "And that person is still with you?"

"They are. There's more than one. Look, this is going to have to be a short call and you can't tell anyone where I am or that we've spoken, outside of your dad. Boyd told me a bit about your trouble. It sounds complicated, and I can't have any trouble here, you understand? I have others to think about."

My stomach flip-flopped. Was he leaving me to my own problems? After all the work I'd put into finding him?

I could barely choke out an argument. "But my dad—"

"I'm sorry, that came out wrong. What I meant is you can bring your dad, he's welcome, but unfortunately, you can't stay. In fact, you will need to go in an entirely different direction after you drop him off and not visit until your troubles are over. Can you do that? I'm sorry, I appreciate that's awful, and I'm not accustomed to turning away a kid in trouble. But I understand the police will be looking for you, and I can't have that here. I'm sure you can appreciate why."

I sucked in a breath. "Yeah, I get it. Honestly, don't worry about me. I don't care what happens to me once my dad is safe." Not strictly true—okay, not even close. I had absolutely no idea where I would go. I'd never even considered the possibility of splitting up from Dad, and just being a fugitive. But beggars, choosers, and all that? Elks was waiting. "I just have to figure out how to get him there. That's a long way—"

"There are old meat trucks you can buy quite cheaply. That's what I did."

"Actually, I think I've got that part covered," I answered, thinking of Charlie's hearse, still sitting in his driveway. I was amazed Blackwelder hadn't collected it yet and made a mental note to go over once it was dark and get the keys. "The big problem is the hydrogen sulfide. They've tightened the supply chain from the research center."

He sighed and thought, and finally said, "I can send some. At least a couple of doses, just for the trip; shouldn't raise any eyebrows. But it shouldn't go to your house because they will know you're leaving. Is there anywhere I can send it that isn't your home?"

I paused and thought, and could only come up with one place Calhoun wouldn't think to look. I gave him the address. "You sure you have enough of the stuff to keep him there?"

"Oh, that's not a problem. A paper mill always has hydrogen sulfide, that's why I bought it. I, uh, had some life-insurance money."

Remembering Boyd's story about Elk's wife and son, I decided not to touch that one.

"When will you be on the road?"

"Assuming the H_2S arrives tomorrow, we'll leave tomorrow night."

"Okay. Look. Go through Boyd for everything—don't call here again. And Hemingway?"

"Yeah."

"Your problems with Lifebank will end, I can promise you that much. I can't do anything about your situation with the police, but there are rigid rules of engagement in human trials. Boyd is furious and he's starting the process of reporting Calhoun. Quietly. It's critical you don't engage with anyone from the research center, beyond taking whatever hydrogen sulfide they allocate to your dad. Do you understand? This is important. Your sole job is to get your dad here, safely."

"Got it."

And he hung up.

I did a scan for Bennington, New Hampshire, Dad's soon-to-be home. Population fifteen hundred. Temperatures there range in the fifties by early October and stay well below that until May. Perfect. There might even be a chance for him to get outside, once it was cold enough. See the sky again. The tiny mill Elks had bought had been running since the 1800s, and the plot of land was massive.

Elks hadn't robbed a paper mill of hydrogen sulfide—he'd bought it, so he'd have an unending supply and somewhere safe for his patients to be. Smart dude.

When I got home, Dad read my mind. He was not exactly excited about a plan that was (a) essentially a day-care situation, and (b) didn't include me. But he was equally aware we didn't have a lot of choices. He satisfied himself with the idea that once he was out of the picture, I could go back to Melissa somehow. Because you know, of *course* she was just going to take off into the sunset with a fugitive after her sister died, and leave her parents childless.

I didn't dissuade him of his delusion. There was no point, and frankly, I liked the dream too. Even if it was pointless.

I snuck over to Charlie's house once it was dark, cutting all the way to the far back end of the yard and through the trees, just so anyone watching wouldn't know I'd been there. The keys to the hearse were still in the dish where he kept them, so I grabbed them and took a last glance around. There was no sign he'd returned, and that was my responsibility too.

I closed the back door, careful to lock it in the forlorn hope Charlie came home. I sat in the backyard for a long time. The golds of August had just the slightest crust of brown, and the heat had an edge of damp. Summer was overcooked and starting to rot. The cicadas were still doing their washboard percussion chorus, and that's always worth listening to, especially when they're singing good-bye. My mind wandered over the possibilities once I dropped Dad off. Where would I go? And then it dawned on me that I was going to prison. There was no other way.

I couldn't just disappear after dropping Dad off. It was easy enough for Elks to say, but he didn't know about Charlie, Todd, Melissa, Lila, or Mary and Kevin. I was responsible for all of them, and there was no guarantee that Lifebank would be shut down, or Calhoun arrested, at the exact moment Dad and I chose to leave town. If I disappeared, an irrational, dying billionaire would be searching for me on borrowed time. It wasn't hard to guess what he'd be willing to do and who he'd be willing to hurt to get me back. I'd have to come back, even if that meant I was going to prison. And besides, I deserved it. I'd finally be paying for what I'd done.

I texted Melissa. *I HAVE TO SEE YOU TOMORROW. EVEN IF IT'S ONLY FOR A FEW MINUTES.*

She wrote back instantly: *OK. LET ME KNOW WHEN YOU'RE HERE. I'LL DASH OUT, BUT I CAN ONLY STAY A MINUTE.*

I KNOW.

She knew this was it. I silently said good-bye to the only home I'd ever known, wondering what would happen to it once we were gone. Maybe Dad could rent it, keep Mom's roses alive a while longer, earn some income. Maybe I'd turn state's witness against Calhoun and Stephens, and after a short stint, be free and back home. Maybe I'd find Melissa then, and we'd both be in a place where we could talk about the future, and mean more than tomorrow.

Something nagged at me, told me it wasn't that easy, but it sounded good.

CHAPTER TWENTY-FIVE

"Happy birthday," Dad said as I walked downstairs.

I was officially eighteen. I'd forgotten. Break out the birthday hat.

Dad was waiting with something in his lap. "I have something for you."

"Can we do it later? I'm not exactly feeling like the birthday boy."

He didn't argue, but disappointment was etched on his face.

"All right then, what is it?" I said.

I finally realized the weathered book I'd retrieved from Doug Allwood's house was in his lap. His eyes drifted to it tenderly. "It's your mother's diary. Bet you didn't know she kept one, did you? She started it when they diagnosed her. She made me promise not to give it to you until you were eighteen. That's why I asked Doug to hang on to it after she died. I knew you'd find it if I kept it here. Happy birthday."

The journal lifted and floated toward me, and I took it, my hands shaking. Now I understood why he'd been so obsessed with the book—it wasn't for him; it was for me. He knew I really missed my mother. Desperately. I didn't admit that too often, because I knew my dad hurt enough for both of us. So even if the story in her journal would make me hurt, I was awed at the prospect of having new experiences with her.

"This is singularly the greatest gift you've ever given me. You sure you're okay with me reading this?" I was probably gonna scream if he said no, but I had to offer.

"I'm not only sure, but I'll also be checking on your progress."

I bent down and hugged him. He switched to telepathy. "*Look on page sixty-two later. Your mother scrawled an address. Place I was working at the time when I couldn't find any work locally. Doug checked on it, and it's empty. If something doesn't work out, that's where you go.*"

"*Dad, I'm going to prison. I know you read my thoughts. I'm good with this.*"

"Todd called," he said out loud. "Said something about a party?"

"Not in the mood!" I answered him.

"So of course, I told him you're going," he continued. "It's a party for you. Would be rude not to turn up. Go. Try enjoying yourself, hanging out with people your own age. Be eighteen. *The party's a good cover. And besides, you have to pick up the hydrogen sulfide. Hopefully, they'll give up on watching us for the night once you're there. We'll leave when you get back.*"

I'd forgotten that's where I'd sent the H$_2$S. I had no choice but to go. Out loud I said, "You just never get tired of being a pain in the ass, do you?"

"It has its moments."

I was headed to the hospital but decided to stop by the sheriff's office first. I appreciated this might set off some alarm bells if I was being followed, but I wanted to talk to Burkhardt, just in case there was any update on Charlie.

Burkhardt was at his desk, surrounded by reams of paper and files. He didn't even bother to look up from his laptop.

"You here for me? Or to visit your boyfriend downstairs?"

LOL. He thought I'd be offended if he suggested I was gay. Typical Southern cop.

"We broke up," I responded lightly. "He said I'm a drama queen," I sniffed indignantly.

"You *are* a drama queen." He shut the laptop, clearly not wanting me to see whatever was there.

"Wanted to see if you had any update on Charlie?"

"Nope. Just a constant nagging thought that people around you either disappear or wake up dead."

"Or something in between," I added.

"Or something in between," he echoed. He pinched his brow and sighed. "Why are you here? You could've called to ask about Charlie."

"Yeah, well, I have a listening studio audience at home, so I don't really make personal calls anymore."

His eyebrows rose slightly at this piece of news. He continued to stare at me, trying to assess whether this claim was true or just more bullshit from the bullshit factory. He decided to leave it alone.

I handed him the card from the attorney. "Charlie talked to this guy. Pretty sure he could give you some ideas about where to look for him."

Burkhardt took the card, but shook his head. "He's an attorney. Already talked to him. He's Charlie's lawyer, but he can't tell me anything else without Charlie's permission. Here's a thought. How about you tell me what *you* know about Charlie's disappearance?"

"I already told you what I know. I saw Charlie, I told him to get a lawyer, because he had a side hustle with Lifebank. He was mad, but it looks like he did. Have you talked to Lifebank?"

"I chatted with them. They have no record of any side hustle, not so much as a payment going to Charlie."

"Well, then they're lying!" My voice rose, even as I remembered Elks cautioning me to leave the research center alone. "Look, I saw him there. He'll be on the surveillance cameras."

Burkhardt shook his head. "Already tried. They said I couldn't have those due to their NDAs with big corporations doing top-secret government research. If I had direct proof they've lied, I could try."

"I'm a witness? Charlie told me himself they were paying him."

"Yeah, but you're also a disgruntled ex-employee who already attacked the research center. Do you have anything in writing to prove your claim is true?"

My shoulders sagged. "No."

He nodded. "Why did you ask him to get a lawyer in the first place?"

I had no good answer to that poorly-timed overshare, so I said nothing.

Burkhardt finally nodded. "Look. I'm perfectly aware there's something really off at the research center, and that you and your dad are right at the center of it. I've known that since they hired you to work there. Just start talking to me."

"Oh, I'm going to tell you everything. In a couple of days. Look, there's gonna be some doctors and scientists calling with a rather wild story too. I'd appreciate it if you take that call when it comes in. You're gonna finally be able to lock me up, so there's that incentive. I just have to take care of my dad first." I headed for the door. "Find Charlie."

Burkhardt called after me. "If it's any consolation, I think you're wrong on this one. I think Charlie's laying low."

I turned. "Really? Why?"

"Chatting works two ways or it doesn't work at all." He lifted his eyebrows as a challenge.

I nodded and walked out the door.

I rode to the hospital and texted Melissa. She didn't respond, so I waited in the lobby of the Children's ICU and watched out the window as the sun lowered on the horizon. She finally texted.

YOU'LL HAVE TO MEET ME RIGHT OUTSIDE HER DOOR. THEY'RE GOING TO LET YOU THROUGH. JUST GIVE ME A FEW MINUTES.

I waited until a nurse finally appeared in scrubs. "Hemingway?"

I nodded and followed her. Melissa was at the end of the hall. The butterfly cage was in her hand. Her eyes were dry and colorless, her body limp when I hugged her.

"This is it. She's going," she whispered.

My eyes squeezed shut at the news.

For all the knowledge that someone you love is going to die, no matter how long you've known, it's remarkable how little pain that knowledge deducts from the final tab.

"You have to take this. They hatched." I took Mac and Newman from her without even looking. She continued dully, "You're going too, aren't you? That's why you're here."

"I have to. But as it turns out, I'll be right back. I have to take Dad somewhere safe, and then I'll come right back. But listen to me." I pulled away and looked at her. "This is going to sound weird, but you guys have to leave, at least until I get back, okay? You, and your parents. After Lila is gone, just leave town for a couple of days."

She pushed me away. "What?! I can't do that."

"You have to. Charlie is missing, and I think they took him because he went to a lawyer. When I leave with Dad, they're going to do whatever they have to do to find me. That means they could come after you. I sent you some money for the trip. Please tell your parents I'm sorry, but it's just a couple of days. Don't even pack. Just arrange for someone to take care of Dobro and go straight from here. And when you come back, I will be here. I'll be in jail, but I'll be here, so there's no reason for them to come after you. Promise me you'll do that."

"I can't make any promises right now. I have to get back in there."

"I know. I love you. Please tell your parents I'm sorry. I wish I could be here."

"Just be safe." She turned for the door. "Hem? Please come back."

"I will. I swear it."

I strapped Mac and Newman's cage to the handlebars and rode out to Gold Hill. I passed where I'd had the accident, and my pace slowed, contemplating the normal life I'd found so inadequate until the day I wrecked the truck.

I heard the ping of a text and glanced down.

SHE'S GONE.

My legs went wobbly. I pulled onto the shoulder, gasping for breath. I took Mac and Newman's cage off the handlebars, threw down the bike, and wandered into the field. I was only about a hundred yards from the road, but the hay was as tall as I was and absorbed the sound of passing cars. I listened to the grasshoppers whizzing around me, as I used my free hand to chop my way through the stalks, squinting in the momentary golden glow to find just the right place to set them free.

When I couldn't see anything but high stalks, I opened the cage and tapped on the screens, telling the boys it was time to go. Mac took off first, fluttering high above me before disappearing. Newman took longer, exiting only to rest on a stalk of hay, his fiery orange wings pulsing like a question of whether I was sure he could leave.

I snapped picture after picture of him as he lifted into flight and texted the pics to Melissa, knowing she'd understand. Mac and Newman would only live a few months at best, and before this summer, that would have been reason enough not to trouble myself with a butterfly cage. But losing Lila had taught me that no one would choose a world without butterflies.

I left the cage in the field, apologizing to the farmer, but I didn't know where else to leave it, and I couldn't take it with me. I heard something rustling in the grass and looked around. Nothing. I started moving again to the road and heard it again.

Had Calhoun's goon followed me into the field?

I deliberated calling out, in hopes it was the farmer and I was just paranoid. Instead, I decided on a test: I took two steps and stopped suddenly.

The movement was behind me by only a fraction of a second, but it stopped as well. I was definitely being followed.

I suddenly took off for the bike as hard as I could. The thundering in the grass made no bones about following me now, it was charging, and it was gaining too. A car whizzed by, and I felt a surge of relief, confident that whoever it was wouldn't hurt me in full view of the road. I grabbed the bike, pushed off as fast as I could, and started cycling like mad for Todd's.

A party was the last place I wanted to be, but it was the only place I could think to tell Elks to send the hydrogen sulfide, so I had to go.

The party was already in full gear. I picked my way through half my high school class, their faces stuck to red Solo cups. Todd was tending bar off the back of Mr. Martini's tractor. "Duuude! You made it! How about this, huh?" He gestured to the chaos with pride.

"Yeah. You got the package? I really need to go."

Todd protested. "Dude, you just got here!"

A splash in the pond drew our attention. Todd shouted, "HEY! NO USING THE ROPE SWING!"

The rope swing in Mr. Martini's yard was always the main attraction at our parties. (We had to have a main attraction because there was no other way to keep our friends out of Todd's greenhouses.) The terrain slopes upward on Mr. Martini's side, and a giant hundred-year-old pin oak stands just at the crest, the branches arcing right over the pond. We were eight when Mr. Martini managed to truss a rope swing to it, and we used it for years with his blessing. Two years ago, I came up with the bright idea of leaping off his barn instead of the hill, which added a good fifty feet and a major rush to the ride. Martini caught us and banned us, so then we only got to use the swing when he was away.

"How did you think you were going to have a party without someone using the rope swing? You should've cut it down," I said.

Todd turned to argue with me, but a few of the guys were already on the roof, gesturing for the rope, ready to go. His face was a little wild, considering the infraction was so minor. He shouted again. "C'MON GUYS!

POND'S TOO SHALLOW. WE GOT US A DROUGHT, REMEMBER? I'M SERIOUS! GET THE FUCK OFFA THERE!"

When they started reluctantly making their way back down, Todd turned to me with a petulant look. "The package is in the fridge in the barn. You really gonna take off now?"

"I have to. I can't explain it, man, but I gotta." Knowing this was probably the last time I'd get to see my best friend, I started, "Hey, look, thanks for the—"

I never got a chance to finish. Dubby Barnes, ignoring Todd's warning, grabbed the rope and leaped with a rebel yell, jackknifing for the water.

Impact was a crunch rather than a splash. Dubby writhed momentarily, and then lay flat, seemingly, and impossibly . . . floating.

Some girl started screaming. That kicked things off.

Todd screamed, "Holy motherfucking shit!" as he dialed 9-1-1.

I was ripping off my shoes and socks as I bolted for the water. A couple of guys on the far side swam out to Dubby as well.

One of them shouted across the pond, "HOLY SHIT THERE'S A TRUCK IN HERE! HE LANDED ON A MUTHERFUCKIN' TRUCK!"

I turned to see Todd's face drain of color. And I knew.

Dubby had landed on my dad's truck. The one I'd crashed and killed him with on Gold Hill Road. Todd had ditched it in his own pond, not really thinking about the fact that a drought happens like once every five years here. Now I knew why Todd had been so pent up about rain. And the rope swing.

Just as I'd found a way to get Dad and Melissa to safety, the earth itself was belching up resistance to my carefully laid plans.

"HE'S STILL BREATHING!" one of them shouted, "BUT I THINK HIS LEG IS BROKEN. GET A FLOAT!"

Todd was still slack-jawed at the edge, holding a phone. He ran toward me. His face was creased, and his voice was hoarse with fear. "Ambulance is going to be here in like five or ten minutes. Cops too. Take off. I'm really sorry, man—" He choked up.

I patted his shoulder. "S'all on me, okay? Tell 'em I did that," pointing to the water. I started walking around the pond to where they were going to pull Dubby out. I was going the wrong way in traffic—half the party was throwing down cups and shoving past me to leap into departing pickups.

Todd shouted after me. "Dude, where you going?"

It would've been nice, I thought, to drive to New Hampshire, even if it was only for a day. No Lifebank, no revivals, no bodies, no ghosts, no Burkhardt, no cameras or mics, nothing but me and Dad, and a proper good-bye.

But you can't run from what you've done, can you? I'd already made that mistake once, and now I'd caused another casualty in the process. Dubby was just the latest in a long list. If I hadn't wrecked Dad's truck, Todd wouldn't have stashed it in the pond. He wouldn't be facing major felony charges right now. And Dubby wouldn't be in pieces.

I was the only person there with any medical knowledge, however small. I owed it to Dubby to stay.

I searched for and found a big enough stick to brace his leg, and barked at the crew crowding around Dubby as they dragged the raft onto the ground. I heard the rasp in his voice. "Call 9-1-1 again. Tell them he's possibly got a punctured left lung, so they bring the right equipment, right off the truck. Now who's got a belt? If you do, give it to me, so I can brace his leg before we turn him on his side, get the water out. Hurry up."

I heard the sirens in the distance. They were almost here.

"Hang on, man. Cavalry's coming for ya," I told him.

The EMTs were first on the scene, but Burkhardt wasn't far behind. I found out later he'd been working late when the call came in. We were outside city limits, so this was his domain. He'd heard "truck" and Todd's address, and guessed what he was going to find. He'd ordered divers. I found out later he'd put out an APB on me immediately.

While I talked to the EMTs, he talked to Todd and the other partygoers. The divers made their way into the pond, using underwater lights to examine the truck. One of them rose within minutes, signaling Burkhardt with a thumbs-up. Our eyes met across the pond. He waved at me to come back, like I was just being called to dinner. I nodded and started walking toward him.

The path was well outside the emergency lights. I was halfway around when I felt a gun press into my back. I froze. John Charles's dad patted my pockets, retrieving my cell phone. He pushed me east into the woods with the end of the gun. "Walk."

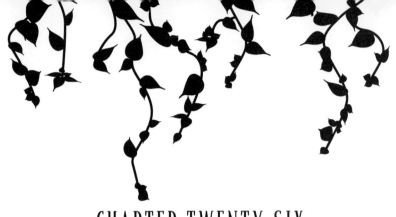

CHAPTER TWENTY-SIX

"You drive," Russell ordered as we arrived at his low-slung Chevy. He spoke in a low voice into his AirPods while he kept the gun on me from the rear driver's side.

My hands were shaking as I climbed in the car. Despite growing up in the South, I'd never had someone point a gun at me before. I gripped the steering wheel to cover my tension. "Where are we going?"

"Where you think? Research center. You look straight ahead, and you drive. You try anything—brakes, signaling—and I'll knock you out with this gun and drive until I can find somewhere to shoot you."

"Okay. Where's my dad?"

"How the hell should I know? Just drive." One hand on the gun, the other on his cell, he called and said, "We got a serious problem. They're going to be looking for him."

We passed through downtown, just blocks from my house. I drove slowly, trying to hit every light that I could, my brain screaming out for Dad. Nothing. I abandoned any ideas of escaping and drove to the research center.

I asked him, "Two? Or the Core Lab?"

"Two. In the depot."

The guard waved us through like he was expecting us. No ID, no pass, no questions about the guy in the backseat.

The elevator doors opened on Lifebank's floor. The first thing I saw was Mueller and Belinda, standing in the hallway waiting for us in scrubs. Seriously, Mueller was in scrubs! What was he going to do? Acupuncture? He smiled at me grimly and turned to Belinda. "They're arriving at the Core Lab in the next couple of minutes. Perhaps you would like to go wait for them?" Phrased as a question, Mueller's words had the distinct impression of an order.

But Belinda merely nodded, walked past me, and hit the elevator button again. Mueller turned to me. "Hello, Hemingway. This way please." He gestured toward Lifebank.

"Who're we waiting on?" I asked, glad of the stall. More time for Burkhardt to find me.

Or reach Dad. Or something.

Mueller ignored me and knocked lightly before opening the door I'd once barricaded with a body in a dewar.

Inside Lifebank, Calhoun was tapping away on his phone. Dad wasn't the only one in a velociraptor these days—Calhoun looked like he'd lost twenty pounds. His skin sagged like an empty flour sack around his skeletal frame, his mouth was slack, breath heavy and wet, but his green eyes were still piercingly sharp. He looked at me like I was a turkey and he'd suddenly developed an appetite.

"You didn't keep our bargain," he said calmly. I opened my mouth to retort, but he cut me off. "And I don't have time to waste on your idiotic retorts. You know what I want, and you know why I want it. I want to be a Gray. A thinking one. Not like that zombie Belinda made."

"And why do you think I'd do that for you?"

"Oh, you'll do it."

"You going to force me? You already tried that. Didn't go over too well."

"You are one arrogant little prick, but so am I. You've no idea."

"Actually, I do. Hannah Ross? You're definitely the bigger prick. Congratulations."

"I can't believe you're still thinking so small!" His hands clenched into claws, just to illustrate how puny my angry little thoughts were. "This is why people like you need people like me. So the world can actually benefit from what you've discovered. You . . . you've unlocked the secret to extending life, and what do you want to do with it? Throw it away because it offends your precious fucking morals. You're just as bad as those Flat Earthers you despise. You just call it ethics instead of religion."

I nodded. "So, you think I should find a church, maybe?"

He shouted at me. "What's possible is what's meant to be. Grays are possible and therefore they should exist. There's nothing else. These subjects you're so worried about, did what, exactly? Watched college sports? Ate Big Macs? The world hasn't exactly missed them, has it?"

"And Hannah Ross?" I asked.

"I've extended her life! Who knows how long she'll live? And I did it with your science."

The words *your science* stung, I admit. My science. My zombie. I folded my arms. "You know what? Go ahead and put yourself on a table in front of me and see what happens. Oh, and seriously, don't worry about the prick comment. I get that a LOT."

Impatient, he turned to Mueller. "Is that woman ready yet?"

Mueller picked up his phone.

"What's the big hurry?" I was still trying to buy time.

"Your friend's stupidity with that truck has caused all kinds of trouble. For both of us. Kannapolis police called me the minute that deputy put out an APB on you. I don't have the same influence over the sheriff's department that I do over the city police. I couldn't stop them, but I could get a warning. That's why you're here instead of in jail. We only have so much time until that deputy realizes where you are."

I nodded. "Don't do the crime if you can't do the time."

"I'm tired of arguing with you. Religion, ethics, they're all the same crap, Hemingway. You'll learn this if you live as long as I have. There's nothing out there. In any case, you're going to tell Belinda how to turn me into a Gray right now. I don't like bullying but I'm not averse to it, either. I'll fight just like any animal in the kingdom to survive."

"I wonder if anyone's told you they all still die?"

Calhoun was about to explode when Mueller hung up. "They're ready. We should go down."

"I'll head down. Tell Stephens we'll be doing this in the Core Lab, not here. Prefer my equipment." Calhoun squinted at me again and said loudly, "Get what we need from him and then he stays here until it's over." Calhoun hit the switch on his velociraptor and headed off.

Muller gestured toward the conference room. I walked as slowly as I could. Everything right now was about stalling. He said nothing, but bypassed me and opened the conference-room door.

I didn't move. "Where is my dad?"

Mueller smirked. "At home, having a nice rest. That wasn't hydrogen sulfide you gave him this morning, Hemingway. We knew we would need you here tonight. We had Dr. Stephens swap out the dose for saline."

My stomach twisted into knots knowing Dad didn't have what he needed and there was no one there to help. But I refused to show Mueller any fear. I was about to respond with more snark when something else occurred to me. "Wait. How did you know you would need me here tonight?"

Mueller tsked at me like I was a toddler. "You should realize by now that Mr. Calhoun knows more than you think. Including what your dad thinks he did to that reporter. Dr. Stephens says no, but since Mr. Jones was not needed here, there was no reason to take the risk. Now. Your father has been without hydrogen sulfide for some time. Are you prepared to tell us what you know?"

And there it was again. I'd spent the last six months doing everything I could to keep my dad alive. The idea of giving up on him came hard. But when I took him to Lifebank I did so because I didn't know what he would want in that situation. Now I did. His need to ensure Calhoun never became a Gray superseded his desire to live as one himself. I sucked in a breath and finally answered, "No, and he wouldn't want me to."

Mueller shook his head and sighed. He typed in a pass code to access the surveillance system.

Melissa popped up on the screen. In a small conference room. With John Charles's dad apparently holding her arms behind her back. She was screaming, but the sound was off. My legs felt wobbly underneath me and my breath shortened. After she screamed more, he shoved her face into the camera. She seemed to understand that someone was watching and mouthed something at the camera over and over. I realized she was talking to me—she guessed if she was on camera it was likely to prove something to me. Her message was three unmistakable words, over and over. "Let me die."

I looked at Mueller in cold fury. "What's to stop me from kicking your ass right now? You don't even have a gun." I moved toward him to show I was serious.

Mueller held up a hand and said coldly, "Physical force is not my way of doing things. Once Mr. Calhoun is temporarily incapacitated, I am in charge. That means I can personally ensure your safety—you and the girl. If you harm me, you will get no such assurances from anyone else."

I exploded. "This is INSANE! How can you even see any of this working? Calhoun will be wanted for kidnapping and who knows what else!"

Mueller shrugged. "I've worked for Mr. Calhoun for thirty years, and I can assure you he's not subject to the same laws as we are. Frankly, the threat to his mortality is the most humbling experience he's ever had." He checked his watch. "You're running out of time. After ten minutes, he instructed Russell to hurt the girl. Just write it down. Let him become a Gray. I will get you out of here once we know it's successful." He pulled out a chair at the table where paper and a pen were waiting.

There was no weighing what to do when Melissa was a hostage. I didn't care if I died, Dad didn't care if he died. Melissa had to survive. I sank into the chair, grabbed the piece of paper, and scribbled a page full of instructions and handed it to him.

He looked at it suspiciously. "That's it?"

I nodded. "They were close. It was mostly the timing, rather than dosages that made the difference."

"You realize if you're lying you and the girl both die."

"I get it. And I'm sure you can appreciate I don't care about myself. I've told you what I know."

He grabbed his phone and started dialing as he shut the door. I heard the lock go immediately after that.

I sat in the dark for a long while, trying Dad over and over, knowing it was probably pointless. If we were going to get out of here, everything was down to me.

If I could get out, there was no question that Melissa was my first objective. But the campus was huge, I had no idea which building to look in first, let alone second, third, or fourth, and I'd have limited time before they noticed I was gone and hunted me down. So, there was no point in trying to escape until I'd formulated a plan.

When I got out, should I just call Burkhardt immediately? Let him deal with it? A dozen scenarios ran through my head, and most posed too many risks to Melissa. First and foremost, Russell. He would do anything to make sure he got away, including holding her hostage from the cops. And what about Dad? Everyone that knew how to help him was either here, committing crimes against humanity, or missing.

And then there was the big picture: Calhoun would almost irrefutably become a Gray. Even if Mueller kept his word, his power to set me free would only be temporary at best. Calhoun would be a Gray like Dad, with the same superpowers. He'd still be petty enough to want to find me and exact revenge for my stalling, let alone, what I could tell the world about him.

Then there was the stewardship for what I'd done. As Dad had seen from the very beginning, I couldn't give that immortality to a man with limited morality. At his core, Calhoun confused nature with science. He didn't *love* scientific discovery. Science is about advancing humanity. Calhoun couldn't give a shit about humanity.

He reveled in nature, where cruelty is a necessary and accepted practice. One lion kills another, and even its offspring, to take control of the pride, and that's all there is to it. Nature is indifferent to emotional and physical pain, and survival is the reason for every evil. Nature was justification enough for Calhoun to exact whatever he wanted, however he could get it. He was a menace, and I'd just jotted down a how-to that would make him an even more powerful shithead.

Still. Could I seriously kill him? I'd killed someone once by accident. What little was left of me wouldn't survive taking another life, no matter how deserving. But who else did I expect to do it? And who had the right to decide? Definitely not me.

I was finally asking the right question. And the answer was obvious, even if a ridiculous long shot.

So, I began. I started talking in my head, saying everything I've written in this confession. I forced myself to describe Dad's death, the lab, the meeting with Mueller, and my work in the lab with Cass and Stephens. The grisly stories of the two subjects that died again on the table, and then Hannah Ross. To be fair, I included stories of love too—putting Dad in the bath, killing mosquitos with Melissa, and planning flights of fancy with Lila. Admittedly, these memories were tiny and frail next to the atrocities, but as Dad had taught me, while a grown man's heart weighs less than a pound, it is the lone pound he can't afford to ever lose. I wanted her to know I hadn't entirely lost mine.

Once I was done, I stacked a chair on the conference table and stood on it, lifting the ceiling tile to peek. The HVAC access was close: the other end of the conference table. I climbed down, slid the chair across the table, climbed up and started crawling. I was in the hallway within minutes.

They'd gotten sloppy in their race against the cops. Or maybe I'd muddied the waters with all the crimes I'd committed in the last six months so much that they'd forgotten the inciting one—that I'd hijacked this lab. No locked door in this place was ever going to keep me in. They'd nearly stopped me by coming in through the ceiling, so I just stole their idea.

It was time to find Melissa. And thanks to my musings, I had a pretty solid bet as to where she was. I hit the stairs.

CHAPTER TWENTY-SEVEN

The lobby of the Core Lab was empty. Not surprising. Somewhere in this building, Calhoun was likely being transformed into a Gray, and he didn't want any fifteen-dollar-an-hour guard to oversee that process on surveillance cameras. He'd likely made them all go away and shut the surveillance system off, which made this the safest place to be in the entire complex.

I went right to the guard station and started messing around on the computer to enable the access control system. There was only one elevator that went where I was going, and it required security approval. I used Stephens's user ID and started guessing at her password. *Fiftymillion!* worked like a charm.

I started rifling around the guard station for anything I could use as a weapon when I went up. I found a crowbar in the bottom cabinet. Had that always been there to jimmy a door, or had it been supplied after I hijacked the lab? At a guess the latter. Who said crime doesn't pay?

I got on the elevator and wedged myself into the corner before hitting the button. I didn't know whether Russell would come to the elevator when it arrived or not, but it was better to be ready for him. The bell pinged and the elevator opened—I heard a TV blaring. Russell stepped into the elevator a moment later, his gun pointed out in front of him, shoulder height. Which was handy because it left him no way to protect himself when I cratered his nuts with the crowbar. He went down in a heap, dropping the gun. I grabbed it and rapped his head with it, knocking him out.

New to assault, I had no idea what to do with him now. He could be out five minutes or two hours, but I wasn't taking any chances. I dragged him out of the elevator and into Calhoun's office, figuring there had to be a lockable closet in there. There was, and a key ring with a number of conveniently labeled old-fashioned keys inside the top drawer of Calhoun's desk. Guess he didn't trust his own access control with his personal crap.

Russell was already starting to groan by the time I unlocked the closet and stuffed him inside. After locking it up, I suddenly remembered his phone. Despite all my villainy, I'd still forgotten to confiscate the goddamn cell phone. I couldn't leave him to call anyone, and besides, I needed that phone. I swore under my breath that once this was over, I was giving up all criminal activity because I was a really shitty criminal.

I unlocked the closet, and he grabbed at my ankle. I had to rap him again with the crowbar before I could search for his phone. I'd only be able to call 9-1-1 with it, but that was the only number I would need, once I had Melissa safely out of here. I started running down the hall, turning knobs, glancing inside.

I finally found her at the end of the hall, in a small conference room on the floor.

I checked her pulse and breath. Slow, but still alive. "Oh my God, oh my God, please be okay! Mel! Wake up! We gotta get out of here!" I tapped at her cheeks, pinched her ear lobes—nothing. I glanced around the room—a vial of ketamine was still on the table. They'd drugged her.

As I'd have my arms full carrying her, I hid the crowbar under the table—no reason to give Russell a weapon when he woke up and got out. I struggled to lift Melissa to a sitting position—she was absolutely limp. I finally managed to get her over my shoulder, firefighter style, rose, and head-ed for the elevator. I could hear Russell kicking at the closet door all the way from the lobby.

The first pinks of morning were appearing on the horizon as I managed to barge through a side door and into the parking lot. Running in the open was definitely a risk, but I didn't know what else to do—I didn't have a car. So I opted for the door nearest the dumpster, relying on what little cover it provided.

I could see the flashing lights of Kannapolis Police in the distance, at the end of the massive parking lot and shrubbery that surrounded the research center.

It appeared Calhoun was using them to keep the employees at bay. If I wasn't so desperate to find an escape, and horrified by the idea the cops might prevent me from getting Melissa to a hospital, I'd have laughed—we'd come full circle: Calhoun was now hijacking his own lab.

Instead, I started frantically using my free hand to check the handles on the few cars nearby.

I heard the car behind me before I saw it. I assumed it was a cop. There was nothing I could do. Melissa was still over my shoulder, and I wasn't leav-ing her behind.

A voice called out to me. "You WERE here. I knew it."

I rotated around, stunned to see Charlie in the driver's seat.

"Get in, let's go!"

"When the hell did you get here?"

"I've been here all night. Only way I could be here—they're not letting anyone else in. I heard about the APB. When you didn't answer the door at home, I figured you were here. HURRY UP. We've got to get out of here."

"I'm gonna need help getting her in the backseat."

Charlie sighed, and kept the car idling, as he climbed out and awkward-ly tugged at the seat, pushing it back as far as it would go. "You're gonna need to protect her head when we put her in. I'll get her legs."

Gently I set her down on the backseat. "You got a phone?"

"Yeah." We ran around either side of the car and he handed over a pink iPhone. "It's Barbara's. Lawyer said to wait it out until something moved, so I've been hiding at her place."

Burkhardt had been right. Again. But I didn't have time for Charlie's explanations. I started dialing 9-1-1.

Two things happened as I was doing this. First, as I was glancing up to see if we'd been spotted, I saw a man in the window—Kevin. Kevin was in the window of Building Two, either looking for his hostage daughter or a prisoner himself. I was so fixated on him being there—out of place and a major problem—that I didn't see the approach until a pair of knuckles rapped hard on the driver's-side window. Charlie and I jumped.

A familiar uniform and badge shaded the window and a deep voice said, "Get out."

I didn't move. I was so close, I couldn't believe I was about to be upended now. I simply said, "Can we do this later? The arrest, I mean? We've gotta get Melissa to the hospital." I gestured and Burkhardt glanced at the backseat. Realizing she was unconscious, he opened the door and checked her pulse. "What's she had?"

I started rambling, pleading. "They kidnapped us. They drugged her."

We all started talking at once—me, Burkhardt, and Charlie, who was protesting his ignorance. "He just called me for a ride, I swear it."

I ignored Charlie and continued rambling. "Calhoun had us kidnapped. He wants to know what I did to my dad. His goon gave her ketamine—we really gotta get her to a hospital. But I just saw her dad in the window, I think he's a hostage. And my dad—"

Burkhardt rose from Melissa, his voice heavy with resolve. "Your dad is fine. I saw to him myself."

"Really? Okay, well then, let's go get Kevin." I gestured to Building Two.

"Can't. I don't have any jurisdiction to go in there, no matter what you say. You're a wanted felon, with an unconscious girl in the back of a car, and you're claiming you didn't do it, but the wealthiest, most respected billionaire in the state did. And no one has reported her dad missing. There's no evidence of foul play at the research center, it's just closed. Calhoun can close it anytime he likes—he owns it. So, until your girl wakes up and tells me she was kidnapped, there's nothing I can do."

"You gotta be shitting me."

"I know my job . . ." Burkhardt kept going but another voice boomed inside my head.

"SON."

"Dad? Oh my God. Are you okay? Where are you?"

"I'M FINE. DO AS BURKHARDT SAYS."

"But Kevin—"

"Burkhardt's not going to let you go back in. You're wasting time. I'll handle it."

Burkhardt was still yelling at me. He'd reached a crescendo, his face was red with fury. "AND THE WORST PART IS, I ACTUALLY FUCKING BELIEVE YOU!"

I was stunned by how much that admission mattered to me. "Wait. Really?"

"YES. Now, get in the car!" He pointed at Charlie. "You in the passenger seat." He pointed at me. "You ride in the trunk. I don't want to waste any time arguing over custody of you, and there's no room for you in the back."

"LET ME KNOW WHEN HE'S OVER THE TRUNK."

Charlie fumbled over to the passenger side without a word. I went to the trunk, but waited for Burkhardt to open it. All business, he went to the handle, but it wouldn't budge. He leaned over the trunk to shout to Charlie, "Pop the trunk!"

"Now, Dad."

"Sorry about this, deputy."

The trunk suddenly flew open, hard, clocking Burkhardt on the chin. He fell backward.

"RUN."

I did, straight back through the side door of Building Two, not caring who saw me. Now Burkhardt had jurisdiction to come in. I just had to find Kevin before he caught me.

The lobby was as eerily empty as the Core Lab. I took the stairs two at a time to the second floor—no need to give Russell the ding of an elevator as a warning. I opened the door slowly and looked around. Empty halls. I hustled for the atrium, but no one was there. There was no need to look in all the labs—if Kevin and Russell were anywhere on the second floor of this building, they were in Lifebank. I listened at the door before going in, but heard nothing.

I entered to find Kevin, pacing the floor, his hair disheveled, his eyes alarmed, his voice soft and petulant. "She has to live," was all he said to me.

"It's okay, I got—" was as far as I got before someone hit me over the head from behind.

CHAPTER TWENTY-EIGHT

"WAKE UP SON, PLEASE."

And I did. I woke on the floor of a surgical room, judging by the sound of medical equipment and the noxious Lysol smell that was doing a spectacular number on my concussion. I had no idea how I'd gotten to the Core Lab, but that's where I was. The floor was frigid, and that helped to restore my brain to some measure of consciousness. I tried to open my eyes, but discovered I could only open one—two just blurred everything.

Stephens looked over. "Oh look, he's awake."

A male voice responded. "Is he? Good." The next thing that happened was a sharp kick to my nuts. Seeing stars didn't cover it—whole constellations of pain rippled through me. I struggled to focus on the argument between Stephens and Russell.

Stephens barked, "STOP IT. We don't have time for your bullshit. Why did you bring him here? Especially after you knocked out a sheriff's deputy? Now you have prisoners in two separate buildings. You're not very bright, are you?"

A dim thought penetrated my brain: Burkhardt hadn't gotten past Russell. There was no cavalry coming.

Russell and Stephens were still arguing. "And you're a bitch. What was I supposed to do? This one's already escaped once. And all those cops outside?"

"THIS IS NOT THE TIME! Now there's a missing deputy. Mueller can only hold off the police so long!"

The sound of Calhoun's voice forced open my lone, blurry eye again. He wasn't a Gray, not yet. There was still time.

I tried to crane my neck around to the sound of his voice, but only caught sight of his feet and the wheelchair.

"Son. Whatever you do, don't move."

Dad was with me. I wasn't entirely alone.

Calhoun barked, "Russell, you've waited too long. There's no leaving here with him now. Take him downstairs. You know what to do, and you'll need to hurry. Belinda, prep. NOW. The transition has to have started before they are allowed in. They won't dare touch me once I'm in surgery."

Russell grabbed the back of my shirt and dragged me to the door. When he opened the door, all I could hear was, "What the fuck?" before he fell to the ground beside me.

But I saw two bare, gray feet pass by me. She'd come.

Hannah Ross crossed to the center of the surgery, her yellow eyes fixated on Stephens, who knocked over an entire rolling table of instruments in her efforts to back away. They fell to the floor with a crash, but Hannah Ross didn't even flinch. Fury held every muscle in her body rigid with accusation. She was taller than I remembered, and her naked form was proud and beautiful and otherworldly in her righteousness.

I'd guessed that Hannah Ross had been following me for some time. She'd been the rustle in the grass on Gold Hill Road before Todd's party, and likely, she'd been following me ever since the mine. I figured something in her knew I was in some way responsible for what she'd become. Dad's ambulation had confirmed it in my head—she would regain sentience in time. That said, I'd known it was a long shot she'd be close to the biotech, or able to get there if she wasn't, and it was an even higher improbability that she'd regained enough consciousness to understand everything I said. But I'd confessed to her, told her who did this to her and why, in the hope she understood.

Because when I asked myself the question who had the right to decide whether Calhoun, Stephens, or even I faced justice, she was the only—and rightful—answer.

All that said, I doubted she'd thank me for it, let alone save me now. And that seemed about right. Why should I be saved? Burkhardt was right: I'd started this, and I'd invited her here. Whatever she was going to do—to me, to Calhoun, to Stephens—was her right. We'd stolen her death from her.

Finding my feet was an impossibility. I swooned at even raising my head. I settled for rotating on the floor to an angle where I could see Hannah Ross have her due.

She remained fixated on Dr. Stephens for a matter of minutes in which no one spoke or moved, everyone taut and unsure what she would do. Calhoun finally said quietly and weakly, "Belinda," as though to remind her of her obligation to help him. I peered at him through my lone eye and saw he was shaking.

Hannah Ross turned at the sound of his voice too and moved toward him. Her hand reached out, and Calhoun jerked his neck backward to avoid her touch.

New loathing for Calhoun regurgitated in my throat. She was everything he wanted to be, and he couldn't even bear her touch. He'd condemned her to that life as an experiment, an acceptable loss. Hannah Ross dropped her hand to her side, comprehending his rejection as well. She simply continued to watch him quiver.

"Belinda! Get me out of here!" Calhoun finally hissed.

And that was enough. Hannah Ross shuddered at the dissonance in his voice. Calhoun made a small sound, and his head lolled onto his chest.

My mouth gaped open. Dad had been right.

Hannah Ross regarded Calhoun's immobile body with seeming indifference.

"Oh my God. Paul?" Stephens called out.

Belinda stepped closer to Calhoun's body and her eyes went wide. She turned to Hannah Ross in disbelief, clearly never having believed Dad was right about losing his temper. Her fluttery motions drew Hannah Ross's attention.

I struggled for breath and voice, and coughed out, "Don't run, it won't do any good."

Belinda bolted for the door. And amazingly, Hannah Ross let her go.

Now her yellow eyes were on me, and I wasn't confused by the wrath in them. Nor did I doubt what she intended to do next. I struggled to sit up. If this was it for me, she at least deserved to think she hadn't killed someone when they were down.

"No, son, you don't deserve that. Just stay still. Let her see you care."

She knelt down to meet me there, her eyes a cold and incandescent fire.

I admit, I realized in that moment I didn't want to die, and this was news to me. I'd imagined myself indifferent to that outcome for six months, and now that it was here, all the reasons to live flashed to mind—Dad, Melissa, Charlie, Lila, the roses in the front yard. Even Mac and Newman made a guest appearance in my memories of why living was great.

I didn't need Dad's coaching—I did care, and I wanted her to know that. She reached for me, and I was scared, but I held myself steady. Unlike Belinda or Calhoun, I was familiar with the chilly touch of a Gray. Her touch was curious, rather than affectionate. I let her do what she wished. She touched my face and my shoulder hesitantly, then let her fingers hunt for the things she no longer had—the hair on my head, the blush of my skin, the warmth of my pulse. Each seemed to grow her incomprehension of her own fate, and caused her no small measure of pain. And her pain was contagious.

"I'm sorry, Hannah Ross," was all I could finally choke out.

She looked at me for an eternity, and I held her gaze as best I could with my blurry vision and wobbly self. Even if she killed me, she had a right to believe that whatever she was, there were people who would love her, that what was still human in her could contact other humans, and be welcomed, at least somewhere.

I sent her all the love I could, along with my regret. We stayed this way for I don't know how long, and then she suddenly rose.

"*Go.*"

The words came unbidden into my head, weak and awkward and in a voice that wasn't Dad's. I was certain I'd imagined it, because it was all that I wanted, and I had no reasonable expectation that it was real.

And then I heard it again, more forcefully this time.

"*Go.*"

"*DO AS SHE SAYS, SON.*"

She turned her back on me, drifting past the body of Paul Calhoun, still collapsed in the chair, and went to the medical equipment. She started ripping it all apart as if to prove her point. She was enraged, and if I wanted to fuck around, I was going to find out. I staggered first to my knees and grabbed a chair to help me stand. My vision blurred with every inch of elevation and I swooned repeatedly.

I heard the hiss of an oxygen tank as she continued to destroy the lab. That got me moving. When I got to the door, I noticed Russell was gone— when had he regained consciousness and escaped? I didn't know, and it didn't bear thinking about.

I crashed through the hallways of the research center, stumbling and falling multiple times, which only added to the lack of coordination I was already experiencing. I'd been concussed and kicked in the nuts, and narrowly escaped with my life. When I got to the lobby, I could see the flashing lights of all the police cars. Mueller was outside, arguing with them, but at the sight of me the cops started moving in.

I stumbled forward, out into the sun, realizing we'd made it. We were through. Melissa was at a hospital by now, Calhoun was dead, my father and Charlie were okay too. Dad had somewhere to go, no one would be chasing him, and I was totally going to prison but that sounded just great.

"GET DOWN."

But my reflexes were slow, and my brain was full of cobwebs. I didn't hear the boom so much as I felt it. A sudden burst of air, throwing me forward, smashing me into the ground as hard and fast as a bug on the windshield of a moving car.

In the smoke and chaos that followed, I fumbled around, my brain vaguely grasping the enormity of what Hannah Ross had done. A flow of EMTs surged around me as police stormed past me on their way into the building. Everyone was stumbling into the smoke. The screams and shouts were just a dull, dissonant roar.

"Whoa there, you need to sit down," an EMT told me, throwing a blanket over me despite the heat. Did you get all those injuries in the blast?" he asked as he took my pulse.

"What?" I shouted.

"Your injuries! Did you—"

I cut him off because I wasn't interested in my injuries. "I gotta find someone—"

"Let them find YOU. We gotta get you to the hospital."

The only word I heard was *hospital.* Melissa was at the hospital. I'd just scrounged a ride exactly where I was going.

"Yeah, okay." And I passed out again.

The ER was overflowing with people from the blast. Leaving the rolling bed and disappearing into the fray was easy. Finding Melissa was harder. I peered in exam room after exam room, Dad talking softly in my head, saying he had something to tell me, but I was searching, not listening. People turned to stare at me. That was no mystery—I'm sure I looked like a refugee from the front.

I heard her before I saw her. My hearing was still dulled but I could detect her voice anywhere. She was screaming through tears that she had to get back to the research center. I hurried into the room, and knelt beside her bed, taking her hand.

"Shhh. It's okay. I'm okay, you're okay."

"GET OFF OF ME!" she screamed as she jolted upright and yanked at my hand, throwing it off. She swooned with the effort—the ketamine was still affecting her.

I got in front of her, assuming she was delirious. "Mel, it's me. Hemingway. I'm here. It's okay, we got through it."

But her eyes, while reddened, weren't confused. She pointed a finger at me, her voice loud and accusatory. "You should have let me DIE. I told you to LET ME DIE. You were never supposed to tell! You swore to me you wouldn't!"

"They had you! I couldn't do that. And it's okay, Calhoun is dead."

"JUST GET AWAY FROM ME!" she spat at me. I just stared at her in disbelief, so she shouted again, "GET AWAY FROM ME!"

A male nurse boomed, "Is there a problem here?" He took one look at me. "Young man, you need to leave my patient alone. Please return to the waiting room."

"Son, let her be. I have to tell you this—"

I wanted her to tell me. "Mel, I don't understand." Then my eyes went wide. I'd forgotten about Kevin. Had Russell taken him to the Core Lab? Or was he in Building Two when the blast went off? "Oh my God. I was so confused after the blast. I'll find your dad—"

"OUT. Do I need to get security?" The nurse squinted at me as he put himself between me and Mel. "You look familiar . . ."

I ignored him and he started tugging at me to leave. I raised my voice. "I tried to rescue your dad! He was looking for you! But I got knocked out!"

Mel's eyes were suddenly swimming with tears. "Just get out of here. Get out of my life." She was sobbing uncontrollably as she started fumbling in an attempt to climb out of the bed.

"Uh-uh, young lady. You stay right there," the nurse said, firmly. He turned to me. "YOU. OUT! NOW! WAITING ROOM."

A voice rang out. "MO! They need you in the Depot! They got one coming in!"

Mo the nurse turned. "I'll be right there—"

A person hustled toward Mo and said in a low voice, "It's one of them—"

"One of what? I've got a situation here."

"Like that guy a few months ago. And they say it's a kid."

A gargled sound came from Melissa. She was suddenly up again and struggling for the hall.

"Shit." He turned to me. "You. Waiting room. NOW." And he headed after her.

But my knees buckled beneath me and I sank to the floor. I didn't really hear what they were saying, I didn't have to. I already knew.

"There was nothing you could do."

Images flashed across my confused brain, paired with questions I'd asked myself but not answered in the moment: why Calhoun had planned to take me that day, why Melissa had said to let her die, why Kevin had been in the building, how I'd misunderstood his statement, "She has to live." Why Calhoun wasn't already a Gray.

Because they hadn't believed me. Not enough to proceed with transforming Calhoun right away. They'd tested what I said.

On Lila.

And that's it, all of it. "Accessory After the Fact" is the legal reason I couldn't tell Burkhardt, or Melissa, or even Boyd everything at the time.

Dad and I didn't say too much on the ride to New Hampshire, other than for him to explain how Burkhardt rescued him. Once I'd disappeared from the lake, Burkhardt got a search warrant for the house within a couple of hours. He had every intention of going straight to the research center, but after finding Dad, he knew he couldn't just call an ambulance and leave. EMTs wouldn't have known what to do, and getting the H$_2$S Dad needed authorized, delivered, and administered meant he was stuck there until morning. So once again, my fault.

I couldn't say anything to Dad, other than to mumble I loved him as I said good-bye in New Hampshire.

I've gone over and over it in my head. In the altitude of intense moments, the air gets thin, you know, Mel? You use every meager breath to push for the peak and the lack of oxygen gets you confused about everything but your primary objective. Getting you and Dad safe was that peak. I couldn't lose you. I just couldn't. And that thought dominated every corner of my brain while you were at risk. Sure I'd idly wondered about all the things that were off as they were happening, but there were too many moving parts and there was too little time to focus on anything but getting you out.

I'll be honest, I don't think I ever contemplated where your dad went on his drives. I just assumed he drank and hid it from you. He was just this guy I mildly resented because he was failing you so badly. But even if I'd dedicated a full month to your dad's disappearances, I still don't think I'd have ever guessed he was negotiating with Lifebank.

I get why he did it, and I don't blame him, and I hope you don't either. This all started with me, and in the end, I made the choice to tell what I knew. I couldn't let you die. I just couldn't. I have to live with that. I also need to do my penance.

I came back home right after I got Dad to New Hampshire, like I said I would. But you know that—you still wouldn't talk to me.

And for the record, I told Burkhardt everything too, but he dropped the charges. Dad wouldn't testify against me for the accident, and when it came to hijacking the lab, he said there wasn't sufficient evidence, given that Calhoun was dead, and Mueller and Stephens were gone. But that wasn't the real reason.

I did argue with him. I wanted jail. If I couldn't be with you, I figured the least I could do was my time. But I found out Calhoun's heirs put a lot of pressure on the mayor to shut the whole thing up. Apparently, they're willing to renovate the entire county so long as they never hear my name or Lifebank in the same sentence ever, ever again. And everyone bought their bullshit press release about "a tragic accident at the lab that took the life of Paul Calhoun."

In the end, Burkhardt suggested it would probably be best for all involved if I left town and didn't return.

I wasn't entirely willing to go with that. I did write to Brother Frank about Smythe Funeral Home—remember him and his protest? While technically Smythe Funeral Home was related to the research center, it wasn't "on the grounds"—I appreciate that's a slippery slope. But at least Brother Frank delivered—he dominated the local papers for weeks. Which meant Burkhardt was free to prosecute Russell and you are safe from him. I heard he got five years, and the B families got some justice. At least someone did.

After that, I thought about going public with the whole thing. The only reason I didn't was because of you and Lila. Please know if you ever do want to expose the truth, I will follow your lead. You won't even have to see me. I'll just provide whatever evidence and statements are needed.

I didn't know where to go when I walked out of Burkhardt's office. I wanted to do something that would help you. And if I can't go to prison, and I can't expose the truth, that only leaves finding Stephens for you. I have no idea how, but I'm on it. Daily. If I can find her, and you give permission, I will go public with everything, until the same town that's been collectively bribed by the Calhouns is screaming for prosecution. In fact, I'm up here right now freezing my ass off because I got a nibble she might be here. In any case, I just hope I find her before she finds another billionaire. She knows what to do now, and that makes me responsible for whatever happens.

I did find something online in the Concord paper this morning that might be related: a personal ad. Who puts out personal ads anymore? In any case, it read, "Seeking teenage boy with infuriating intellect and obnoxious attitude for project. Contact Curly." And a number. I'm pretty sure that's Cass, and that she wants to help. Or who knows, maybe I'll just have an interesting chat with a pedophile. But I'm calling, either way.

When I'm not working the problem, I have to live with myself, and that's the hardest part. At night, I stand outside in a T-shirt and watch the northern lights until I'm verging on frostbite. There's something deeply clarifying and authentic about the cold.

Please take up Dr. Elks on his offer. He said you refused initially. Just so you know, he's very kind, he's been great to Dad, and Dad actually likes it there. He says it's a bit like an early retirement—he's got friends, and now that the weather's turned cold, he's even going ice fishing on the grounds sometimes.

I appreciate that's an entirely different situation than the one Lila's in, but it's the best I've got. I worry you refused because you didn't want to run into me. You don't need to worry, because I won't be there. I can't have my own family together after my role in what happened to yours. So, I won't be going to New Hampshire or Concord. Those spaces belong to you, as I know you won't be in them if I'm there. In fact, the whole world is yours. Just tell me where not to be.

Please tell Lila I'm sorry. I know that doesn't begin to cover it. I'm sorry for involving you. I did and do love you, as I said at the start. I *know you want me to stop, but I can't shut it off, I've tried. I think it's permanent. I will do everything I can to help you too. Just send word through Elks.*

Yours forever,
Hemingway Jones

"You should forgive him," Lila insists. "He didn't do this to me."

"I know," I answer sullenly, but my eyes are on Lila's tiny gray hands, as they flutter a little in the bed. The sight gives me hope and simultaneously infuriates me. Lila's movement will come back, we both just need to be patient. Will those fingers ever grow, I wonder for the thousandth time, or is Lila trapped in a child's body? And for how long?

"You remember I can hear you thinking, right?" Lila asks.

Damn. No. I'm still not used to that.

"I'll be back in a minute, okay?" My voice cracks, giving me away.

Outside, the weather is bitter, but the running soon warms me, as I knew it would. This is my new personal time. It takes the edge off the fury that still grips me and makes me choke. Every. Single. Day. I started running to get outside the radius of Lila's new talents. But now I've done it so often I run for physical release too.

I feel the ice only a split second before my ankle rotates and I fall on the sidewalk. It hurts, but after a brief check doesn't appear to be broken. Good. We don't need any more invalids.

Still, I'm not going to try and get up right away. Snow is starting to fall. I watch as it lands on my hands and legs. I let the damp seep inside me and cool the boiling, toxic mix of outrage and longing I still feel for Hem. His words still have a palpable effect on me, and I want those feelings frozen.

Lila is far more at peace about the situation than I am. And she is right; it isn't Hem's fault, it's mine. I asked to be involved. Hell, I'd demanded it.

And my Dad solicited Lila's involvement with Lifebank, not Hemingway. But Hem was the catalyst, and I brought Hemingway into our lives.

I broke my family. Dad is gone—he finally realized that none of us could think of a single word to say to him. Lila is here in a form she never asked for or wanted to be, with zero expectations of ever living a normal life, growing up, having friends, or even being safe in her own bed. Even our home is gone—we could never renovate a 1904 Southern colonial to accommodate her. We now live at Hemingway's, not just because he begged us to do so, but because it's the only place that can accommodate her. And that only adds indignation to my fury.

My faith is gone too. The one thing that has given me strength and a sense of order and comfort throughout my life. But faith demands forgiveness, and that's where we had to part ways. Because my anger still demands a nightly venue.

I need to get back. My ankle is still a little wobbly. It's going to be a slow walk rather than a run. And that is fine, more time outside. Hemingway is wrong about a lot of things in his letter, but he is right about one: there's something deeply clarifying and authentic about the cold.

ABOUT THE AUTHOR

Kathleen Hannon is a senior communications director for an artificial intelligence company, the mother of two grown daughters, a philomath, lover of all pets, and a hopeless romantic.

She worked as a Hollywood development executive for many years, on such films as *Terminator 3* and *U-571*. Left with nothing to edit during the writers' strike of 2007, she drafted her middle grade novel *Bye for Now* (Egmont, 2011) for her daughters as she reinvented her career. After a couple of screenplays for Hollywood, she has returned to books. *The Confession of Hemingway Jones* is her first YA novel.

Hannon lives in Davidson, North Carolina, with her daughter and their two cats, Alfie and Bingley, whom she affectionately refers to as "the interns."

ACKNOWLEDGMENTS

It seems fitting that a book about the resuscitation of the dead is a narrative of its own on the topic. Hemingway first showed up in my head more than a decade ago, frantically telling me his horrific narrative, and wouldn't stop talking until I'd written a draft exactly as he'd told it to me.

But I failed him, caving to commercial pressures, and the manuscript faltered. Humiliated, I put Hemingway on the shelf and didn't write for years. So the first people I have to thank are the ones who have believed in Hemingway from the very beginning and ultimately coaxed me into bringing him back to life: my manager, Jeff Field, and my best friend in the world, Rachel Lipman.

I also have to thank CamCat editor in chief and dear friend, Helga Schier, for asking to read the first 100 pages. The three of you have given me back my love of writing, and a spirit I thought I'd lost.

I'm no scientist, doctor, or legal mind, so I also must thank all those who helped my research: Dr. Jon Hobbs, Dr. Martha Summer, Dr. Kim Cass, Dr. Juan Restrepo, nurse practitioner Jennie Sass, former sheriff Brad Riley, and most notably, Dr. David Casarett, whose non-fiction book *Shocked* is an extraordinary resource regarding clinical care of the dead.

Another round of thanks to my readers: Dominique Beaudry, Chris Bradley, Anissa Arbes-Thaddeus, Sophie Davis, Lauren O'Brien, as well as my extraordinary daughters Emma and Rowan for their input.

Finally thanks to everyone at CamCat: Sue, Elana, Audrey, Ellen, and Maryann!

If you like

Kathleen Hannon's *The Confession of Hemingway Jones,*

we hope you will consider leaving a review

to help our authors.

Also check out another great read from CamCat Books:

Jeff Wooten's *Kill Call.*

CHAPTER ONE

ON AUGUST 9 AT 1:32 IN THE MORNING, HANNA SMITH IS GOING TO DIE.

Thirteen days. That's all she has.

She stands less than a hundred yards from me, texting in front of Markle's, a designer jeans store. Two bags stuffed with clothes hang from the crook of her left arm, a huge purse on her right.

She's in workout clothes, and her long blonde hair is pulled back in a ponytail. She's seventeen and goes to Miller's Chapel. I go to Bedford with the rest of the public-school kids. It's Saturday afternoon and the mall is packed. People swarm around me as I sit on a bench in the middle of the promenade. Somewhere a baby is crying.

I feel ya, kid.

I don't want to be here. It feels way too stalker-ish. That's not what I am. This whole thing feels wrong, but Dad says it's important, so here I am, trying to be cool. I don't feel cool. I feel like there is a huge spotlight on my head and everyone is staring. Only no one is actually staring at me. I'm not antisocial, but I hate crowds. It's probably because of what I am.

I lean back, trying and failing to be nonchalant. I'm bad at this. Hanna's in her own world, hammering away at her phone with her thumbs.

In thirteen short days, Hanna Smith is going to die.

But only if I'm not there to save her.

A life for a life.

It's the only way.

My phone vibrates in my hand, and I jump, almost dropping it. I check the text, trying to be chill. Nothing to see here, just a dude sitting in the mall on his phone.

PARTY NXT SAT—B thurrrr!!!

It's a huge group text from Jacoby Cole. My phone buzzes with replies before I manage to mute it. How do people type so fast?

"Hey, Jude."

I flinch at the sound of my name and look up.

Molly Goldman smiles down at me, her hazel eyes bright. "Did you get Jacoby's text?"

I glance over at Hanna, but she's gone. She was standing there for ten minutes, and I take my eyes off her for a second—

"Jude? You okay?"

I look up at Molly. "Sorry. I was just—yeah, Jacoby's text. Just got it. Guess you did too?"

"Yep. Bet you're dying to go, huh?"

Molly and I have been friends since elementary. She knows I'm not the party type, or—in general—the social type. The short bark of laugher that escapes me is a little much. "You bet, can't wait."

Molly sits beside me, pushing a lock of curly red hair out of her face. "You waiting for someone? Not sure I've ever seen you here."

I glance one more time to where Hanna was. Still gone. I should go, but . . . Molly. I've always had a thing for Molly, but I've been in the friend zone, well, since forever. "Football starts next week," I say. "I need new cleats. Coach thinks we can win state."

"I've heard," Molly says.

"Yeah, right. Lucas." Lucas is Molly's boyfriend, my teammate, and a grade A dick. Next year he'll be playing college football somewhere big. I don't even know if college is a possibility for me.

We sit in silence for longer than is comfortable. I clear my throat. "Lucas decided where he's going to college?"

Molly hesitates. "No, but, well—just so you know, Lucas and I aren't seeing each other anymore."

I clear my throat again, for real this time. "What happened?"

"Not sure I want to talk about it."

"Yeah, sure," I say.

"So what have you been up to this summer?" she asks.

"Eh. Working with Dad, roofing, off-season football . . ." *Planning my first kill,* I add to myself. "You know, the usual." I can't help but laugh at the absurdity of my words.

Molly elbows me. "What's so funny?"

"It's nothing."

"It's something. And now you have to tell me."

For a fleeting few moments, I consider throwing it all away. Letting it all out, telling her everything. The dreams, what they mean, what Dad is, what I am. It's ridiculous. Molly would think I was crazy. Sometimes I think I might be.

All this goes through my head in seconds, but it's long enough to be odd. I shake my head and shrug, trying and failing to think of something to say.

"Awkward silences are fun," Molly says, "but I want you to use your words, Jude."

"Well, awkward silences are kind of my thing, and I hear you're single now." I hesitate, not sure where that came from. Since the dreams started six months ago, life has been stressful.

Molly's smiling though, obviously not offended. "Honestly, I appreciate you not giving me a pep talk about Lucas."

"Not a chance of that, "I say, surprising myself again.

Molly laughs for real, and I smile. It feels good to talk and laugh, and I do have a question now. I take the leap. "Can I ask you something?"

"Oh, this sounds interesting. Asking permission. Go on."

"Ah, never mind."

"Too late, now you have to ask."

I hesitate for just a second and go for it. "Why Lucas Munson? I never understood."

I'm expecting the standard. *He's nice, he's cool, he's interesting,* but Molly surprises me. "You know your problem, Jude?"

"*My* problem? I thought we were talking about Lucas."

"He asked, Jude." Molly's eyes measure me.

He asked.

"Uh," I say. "That's it? He asked? It has to be more than that."

Molly shrugs. "Sure, but it has to start somewhere."

Life is strange. Never thought I'd come to the mall, a place I hate, to definitely not stalk a girl, to be hit on by another girl. And not just any girl. Molly Goldman is flirting. *With me.* It doesn't seem possible, but she *is* flirting.

I swallow and force the next sentence out of my mouth. "You want to come . . . help me pick out some cleats? We can go to the food court after. Mall pizza is, surprisingly, not horrible. I mean if you don't want to, it's cool. I thought, you know, why not?" I clamp my mouth shut, not trusting myself to speak anymore.

Molly searches my face for a second, her eyes narrowing, as if trying to read my thoughts. I meet her eyes, but it isn't easy. After a lifetime, she smiles. "Okay, sure. I've already eaten, but yeah, why not? I can hang for a while."

"Cool." I laugh, standing up as nonchalantly as I can. It's not easy. I'm so self-conscious of every movement now. It's like some evil scientist has control of my body, making my palms sweat.

I take two steps, smiling back at Molly . . . and run straight into Hanna *Freaking* Smith.

CamCat
Books

VISIT US ONLINE FOR MORE BOOKS TO LIVE IN:
CAMCATBOOKS.COM

SIGN UP FOR CAMCAT'S FICTION NEWSLETTER FOR
COVER REVEALS, EBOOK DEALS, AND MORE EXCLUSIVE CONTENT.

CamCatBooks   @CamCatBooks   @CamCat_Books   @CamCatBooks